"You're done ‖‖‖‖‖‖‖‖‖‖‖‖‖‖‖‖"

Robbie took hold of her chin and leaned close. "You'll take your stand here, with me."

"You're doing it again. You're seeing something that's not there. I'm not the brave woman you keep saying I am. I have all I can do to get up every morning and face another uncertain day."

"But ya still get up, lass."

"I don't want you to want me," she whispered. "It will only hurt us both."

"Too late," he murmured, cupping her face. "When you found me on the mountain and chose to save my life rather than run, it was too late for the both of us."

As she looked into his compelling gray eyes, Catherine thought about how secure she felt in his arms when he hugged her. How brave. And yeah, how strong.

So strong, in fact, she could finally quit wondering what it would feel like to be kissed by Robbie MacBain, and simply kiss him herself.

Mimicking his hold on her, Catherine cupped the sides of his face and pulled his mouth down to hers. He tasted like very fine scotch, a perfect blend of heat and masculine appeal that set her mind spinning. Catherine opened her mouth, yearning for more, and melted against him, tasting, teasing his advancing tongue, welcoming the tremors racing through her.

Robbie broke the kiss, his lips forging a trail of quivering pleasure along her jaw, up her cheek, and across her temple. "I'm thinking we should stop now," he whispered. "Before I forget my noble intentions."

A Featured Alternate of the Doubleday Book Club
A Featured Alternate of the Rhapsody Book Club

BOOKS BY JANET CHAPMAN

Charming the Highlander
Loving the Highlander
Wedding the Highlander
The Seductive Impostor

Published by Pocket Books

JANET CHAPMAN

TEMPTING THE HIGHLANDER

POCKET STAR BOOKS
New York   London   Toronto   Sydney

An *Original* Publication of POCKET BOOKS

A Pocket Star Book published by
POCKET BOOKS, a division of Simon & Schuster, Inc.
1230 Avenue of the Americas, New York, NY 10020

ISBN: 0-7434-8630-7

First Pocket Books printing September 2004

10   9   8   7   6   5   4   3   2   1

POCKET STAR BOOKS and colophon are registered trademarks of Simon & Schuster, Inc.

Front cover photo illustration and design by Min Choi
Front cover photo © Koji Yamashita/PanStock/PictureQuest
Back cover art by Robert Papp

Manufactured in the United States of America

For information regarding special discounts for bulk purchases, please contact Simon & Schuster Special Sales at 1-800-456-6798 or business@simonandschuster.com

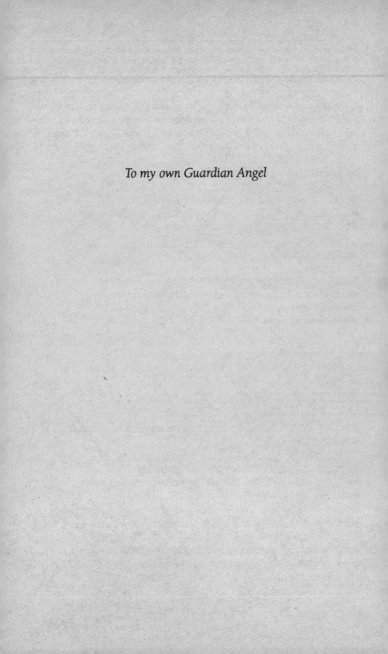

To my own Guardian Angel

Acknowledgments

Thank you, Grace Nugent, for standing with me from the beginning. Your unwavering support and encouragement has always been, and still is, a most cherished gift.

TEMPTING
THE
HIGHLANDER

Chapter One

"Come on, baby. Give it to me, you sweet thing."

Robbie MacBain came awake totally alert and battle-ready, with absolutely no idea what was going on.

"That's it. Move for me, baby."

What the hell? He had *not* gone to bed with a woman, so he shouldn't be hearing a husky, seductive voice in his ear. He knew he was in his bedroom at the farm, but, more important, he knew he was alone.

"Just a little bit more, sweetie."

Robbie sat bolt upright in bed and tried to see through the darkness. Nothing. No woman. Yet her voice had been quite distinct—and soft and sexy and close.

"Come on," she whispered with fading patience. "I've got to get going. Oh, for God's sakes, just move!"

At the squawking of several disgruntled hens, Robbie snapped his head toward the baby monitor on his night-stand. And he cursed, throwing back the covers and jumping out of bed.

The henhouse.

He was supposed to be guarding the henhouse.

He scrambled into his pants and grabbed his shirt, stopping only long enough to glance at the clock by his bed. Five-thirty, he saw, breaking into a grin as he slipped on his shirt and found his socks.

Deciding earlier that he didn't need to be sleeping outside on this cold March night, he had put the baby monitor in with the hens and let the electronic device do his job. And it had worked, he decided as he hopped first on one foot and then the other, pulling on his boots and tying them.

This was the third henhouse raid this week. Only half a dozen eggs were taken each time, and there was always a dollar bill left in their place. But it was the principle of the thing. Someone was *buying* his eggs. He didn't much care for mysteries, and that sexy-voiced woman on the monitor was one mystery he was suddenly eager to solve.

Robbie ran down the stairs and skidded to a halt in the kitchen. Quietly, he opened the farmhouse door and crept onto the moon-shadowed porch just as the woman came sneaking out of the henhouse.

He blinked into the night. If he hadn't just heard her voice on the monitor, he would swear his thief was a kid. She looked like a child, squatting beside a backpack as she carefully placed her stolen breakfast in it.

She spotted him when he stepped off the porch.

She dropped two of the eggs when she stood with a startled squeak, swung the pack onto her back, and bolted for the pasture.

"Hey! Hold it!"

She scaled the paddock fence with the agility of a cat.

With an utterly male grin Robbie broke into a run. His thief certainly had a nice rear end. And he also happened to notice, as he vaulted over the fence himself, that what height she did have came from a pair of long legs that swiftly carried her into the night.

But he was six-foot-seven in his socks, and Robbie didn't doubt for a minute he would quickly run her to ground. Then he'd find out who she was and what she was doing stealing his eggs.

Robbie's smile was gone a little over a mile later. She was getting away! Rasping for breath through gritted teeth, Robbie forced his legs to move faster. He'd arrogantly told his boys that he could catch a simple egg thief, and "No, thank you," he didn't need their adolescent help. He was not about to let last night's bragging to them turn into hoots of laughter this morning.

Robbie chased the woman for nearly two miles before he finally realized he wasn't going to catch her. The long-legged little cat had left the pasture, sprinted down the gully and over the knoll, and disappeared into the thick forest of TarStone Mountain.

Dammit! It was a cold walk back in the stingy morning light. Robbie used up most of his litany of curses during the first mile of his return and was down to swearing in Gaelic by the time he reached his yard.

He stopped in the middle of two dozen foraging chickens that had escaped out the open henhouse door, and looked back at TarStone to see the rising sun pecking over its summit.

"It looks like scrambled money for breakfast again," Cody said as he stepped out of the henhouse, snapping a wrinkled dollar bill between his hands. "We got any cheese to go with this?" he continued despite Robbie's warning glare. "Ain't nothing like burnt toast and dollar-bill omelets to start the day right."

Robbie took a threatening step forward.

The sixteen-year-old juvenile delinquent pocketed the

dollar bill, crossed his arms over his chest, and smiled. "Is that egg I see on your face, boss?" he asked.

Robbie also folded his arms over his chest. "No, you're seeing my decision that you're cooking breakfast."

Cody's smile disappeared. "I cooked yesterday."

"You did such a fine job and you can do it again today."

Muttering what Robbie guessed was a nasty curse, Cody stomped off toward the house. The screen door opened and Gunter stepped onto the porch, moving aside to let Cody go slamming past him.

Robbie sighed. Gunter wasn't dressed for school, but for work. With his arms still crossed over his chest, Robbie turned to face his next challenge.

"Harley called. Two of the loggers are sick," Gunter said as he approached. "So I'm going to work today."

Robbie wasn't surprised that the eighteen-year-old would rather spend a day of hard labor in the woods than go to school. Hell, Gunter would rather muck out stalls than go to school.

"Harley said two loads of saw logs are leaving today," Gunter continued, stopping in front of Robbie, his nearly black eyes more eager than defensive for a change. "You need me to run the loader."

"I can run the loader."

"You have a meeting with Judge Judy this morning."

Damn. He did. And those saw logs needed to go out today.

"Her name is Judge Bailey, and she's all that's standing between you and an eight-by-ten cell."

"I only have metal shop and one regular class today," Gunter continued. "I'll make it up tomorrow."

Robbie returned Gunter's direct stare and weighed the boy's need for an education against his desire to escape the structure of the classroom.

Hell, everyone needed a safety valve occasionally, and a long day working in the woods just might serve to remind Gunter that an education would make him an easier living.

Besides, the kid deserved a reward for going two whole months without starting a fight at school.

Robbie nodded agreement. "Tell Harley I'll come out to the site after my meeting with Bailey. And Gunter?" he said as the boy turned to leave. "You only have ten weeks left to get your diploma. Anyone can endure anything for ten weeks."

A faint grin appeared on Gunter's usually stoic face. "I've endured your cooking for a month," he said softly.

Bolstered by that grin, Robbie smiled. "Gram Katie is bringing over a lasagna for us tonight," he offered in concession. "With salad and homemade rolls."

Gunter turned fully to face Robbie, his expression serious. "When are you going to look for another housekeeper?"

Robbie shook his head. "Word's out about you hoodlums. I couldn't offer enough money to bring another woman here."

"We've learned our lesson," Gunter said. "If it will save us from your cooking and doing our own laundry, we'll treat her like the queen herself."

"I'll be sure to put that in the ad," Robbie said, turning at the sound of a cane tapping a hurried rhythm on gravel.

Gunter turned, too. And seeing Father Daar walking down the driveway from the woods, the boy spun on his heel and sprinted for the house.

It took all of Robbie's willpower not to do the same.

"I'm wanting a word with you, Robbie," Daar said, using his cane to scatter the chickens. "I need your help on a matter."

"If this is about your well pump, I've already ordered a

new one," Robbie said, hoping to forestall the old priest who lived in a cabin halfway up TarStone Mountain. "It'll be in tomorrow, and the boys and I will install it after school."

Daar was shaking his head. "I'm not here about the pump." He stepped closer and lowered his voice when Rick came rushing out of the house. "It's a bit more important than that."

"Peter overstuffed the dryer again and started a fire!" Rick shouted from the porch. "Where's the extinguisher?"

Robbie bolted for the house, leaving the priest in a flurry of flapping hens. This was all he needed, for his mother's old homestead—which had survived four generations of Sutters—to be burned to the ground by a fifteen-year-old delinquent who thought household appliances were really demons trying to suck him into the nether-world.

This was the second fire Peter had started this month. Three weeks ago, it had been the toaster, along with the curtains, and part of one cupboard that had gone up in flames. They still hadn't gotten the smell out of the house.

Robbie grabbed the fire extinguisher hanging on a peg not two feet behind Rick, ran into the laundry room, and doused the flames already spreading up the wall.

Stepping back into the kitchen, wiping powder off his face, Robbie scanned the group of wide-eyed young men staring at him as if he held their fates in his hand. Which he did.

Four boys, all wards of the state, all in his care for the last eight months. Well, except for Gunter. Gunter had been liberated on his eighteenth birthday six weeks ago, but the boy seemed in no hurry to leave.

That was fine with Robbie. For as long as it took Gunter to get a toehold on life, he would have a home here.

Much to Judge Bailey's dismay.

Bailey did not care to see the other three boys, especially fifteen-year-old Peter, living under the same roof with a known brawler who was nefarious in three county courtrooms and assorted detention centers. Hence today's meeting.

"You moron!" Rick said, punching Peter in the arm. "Are you *trying* to get us sent back to foster care?"

"What in hell is *this* place?" Peter growled, rubbing his arm and glaring at his older brother.

"This ain't no foster home," Rick snapped. "And it's a hell of a lot better than the detention center. Dammit, I'm not leaving here because of you," he said, moving to punch him again.

Robbie caught Rick's fist in his own. "Nobody is going anywhere but to school," he said softly. "If the house burns down, we'll live in the barn. You're all staying here until you decide you'd rather be someplace else."

"It would be easier if you'd just hire a new housekeeper," Cody said, pulling his burning toast from the shiny new toaster.

"We'd have a housekeeper if you hadn't run off the last three," Robbie reminded him.

"None of them had a sense of humor," Cody said with a snort, scraping the black off his toast into the sink.

"I'll be sure to put that in the ad," Robbie said, setting the empty fire extinguisher by the door to take to town and refill again. He headed into the downstairs bathroom to wash his face and hands. "You boys have to take the school bus today," he said through the open door. "Gunter, take the pickup to work." He stepped back out of the bathroom, wiping his hands on his shirttail because he couldn't find a towel. "And don't go anywhere but to work and back," he warned, giving the youth a level stare. "And don't make me sorry for letting you miss school," he added quietly.

"How come Gunter isn't going to school?" Peter asked.

"Because I already learned how to run a dryer and a toaster without starting a fire," Gunter told him.

"Where? In home ec?"

It took only a threatening step forward from Robbie to stop Gunter's advance on Peter and a warning growl to get all four boys moving toward the door.

" 'Morning, Father," Cody said around a mouthful of toast as he stepped aside to let the priest in the house.

" 'Morning, Father," Gunter mumbled as he squeezed by.

" 'Morning, Father," both Rick and Peter said as they rushed out to the safety of the yard.

Daar gave each of them a silent glare as they strode past.

Robbie couldn't help but smile. For the last eight months, the old priest had used sheer terror to bully the boys into respecting him. Daar had given them a piercing glare upon their arrival, pointed his cherrywood cane at them, explained he was really a wizard, and warned that if they didn't act civil around him, he'd turn them all into dung beetles with his powerful staff.

They'd nodded respectfully, only to roll their eyes at each other once they turned away, apparently deciding to humor the obviously crazy old man.

Robbie wondered what their reaction would be if they knew Daar really *was* a wizard?

His full name was Pendaär, and besides turning delinquents into dung beetles, the ancient *drùidh* was also capable of bringing ten Highland warriors eight hundred years forward through time. Robbie knew this because his father, Michael MacBain, had been born in twelfth-century Scotland. So had Robbie's uncle Greylen MacKeage, along with Morgan, Ian, and Callum MacKeage.

And since providence had seen fit to gift Robbie with the powers of guardianship over his two clans, the warriors had happily dropped Daar's care onto his capable shoulders about five years ago, after many lectures that Robbie not believe *anything* the old priest told him. It had been a long five years, with innumerable escapades that could have turned into disasters but for Robbie's vigilance.

"About my little matter," Daar said, waving a hand through the lingering smoke as he made his way to the kitchen table.

"I'm afraid it will have to wait," Robbie said, going over to the counter and pouring them both a cup of coffee. "My day just filled up. I now have to buy a clothes dryer on my way to see Judge Bailey."

Daar snorted and thumped his cane on the floor. "I could take care of that old hag if you'd let me."

"Martha Bailey is not old and she's not a hag," Robbie told him, setting a cup of coffee in front of him. "She's only doing her job." He took a seat at the table. "And our deal is you don't mess with the magic if you want to stay living on TarStone Mountain."

Daar harrumphed, took a sip of his coffee, and shuddered in disgust before taking another sip.

Robbie took a sip of his own coffee, stood up, dumped it down the sink, and went to the fridge to look for some juice.

"My matter can't wait," Daar said. "The vernal equinox is tomorrow."

Robbie stilled, the fine hairs on the back of his neck rising in alarm. He slowly straightened from peering into the fridge and looked at the priest. "What's so important about the vernal equinox?"

"All the planets will be lined up just right."

"Right for what?"

"To fix this little problem we have."

It was the "we" that most alarmed Robbie. Daar's little problems had a way of becoming huge headaches for Robbie, and when "we" was attached, it usually meant a full-blown migraine.

Robbie closed the fridge door, set his fists on his hips, and glared at the priest. "And what exactly is *our* problem?"

Daar turned away to face the table and spoke to his coffee cup. "Your papa and the others are going back to their old time come June," he whispered.

Robbie could only stare at Daar's back.

"I have only three months to extend the spell that brought them here," the *drùidh* continued to his coffee. He finally turned to look at Robbie. "They will have been here thirty-five years on this summer's solstice, and that's when the spell runs out."

It wasn't a headache Robbie felt but a painful pounding in his chest that made it difficult to breathe. He was going to lose his father in three months? And Grey and the others? Dammit. They had wives. And children. And a supposedly stable life here.

"Say something," Daar whispered.

"Make it stop!"

"I've tried!" the priest snapped back, thumping his cane on the floor again. "I nearly blew up the summit house trying, and I started a landslide down TarStone!"

"That landslide was you?" Robbie whispered, his head filling with images of the destruction. "And the summit house fire last month? You started that?"

Daar looked down at his cane, rubbing one of the weathered cherrywood burls with an age-bent hand. "I also caused the flood that took out the town bridge last week." He lifted his chin. "I was trying to figure out a new spell to extend the old one."

Robbie ran an unsteady hand over his face. "Let me get this straight. You've known about this . . . this thirty-five-year time limit all along, and you're just telling us now?"

"Not *us*," Daar said, his eyes widening in alarm. "Just you. Laird Greylen and the others can't know about this."

"Why not? It's their lives about to be destroyed."

"But we can stop it," Daar said with an eager nod. "You'll go back in time and get me a new book of spells, and then I'll be able to extend the old spell to keep them here."

Still standing by the fridge, still reeling in shock, Robbie slowly shook his head. "Oh, no. I know all about your attempts to replace the book you blew up twenty years ago. As long as you don't have those spells, we are all safe—fires and landslides and floods notwithstanding."

"But that's what I'm trying to tell you. The five remaining Highlanders are *not* safe. Come the summer solstice, they're headed back home."

"They are home!"

"To their old home!" Daar shouted. He heaved a huge sigh. "Robbie," he said softly, getting up and coming to stand in front of him. "I brought Greylen MacKeage here to father my heir. Ya know that already. But what nobody knows is that I only needed him here long enough to sire seven daughters and protect his youngest girl, Winter, until she's old enough to begin training as my successor. For me to have cast a permanent spell, I would have had to make concessions."

"What kind of concessions?"

Daar took a step back. "I would have had to live out the rest of my unnatural life in modern time."

Robbie stepped forward. "So, for your own selfishness, you chose to rip apart the lives of five men. Twice!"

Daar raised his cane as a puny defense. "I wasn't thinking that far ahead. And it was only supposed to be Greylen, not the others. They were an accident."

"Which makes me what? Another accident?"

Daar frantically shook his head. "Nay. You are their salvation. You were born their guardian and have become a fine warrior, Robbie. And now it's time to fulfill your destiny."

"By getting you a book of spells and restoring you to full power," Robbie said, crossing his arms over his chest and settling his weight back on his hips. "How very convenient that my destiny perfectly matches your need."

Daar gasped, stepping back and bumping into the table. "Ya think I'm lying?" He pointed his cane at Robbie. "A pox on ya, MacBain! I'm a priest!"

Robbie sprang from his negligent pose and advanced on the priest until that cane was touching his chest. He towered over the *drùidh* and gave him a look so threatening that Daar stumbled backward into his chair and sat down with a thud. "Don't even attempt to curse me, old man," Robbie whispered. "My guardianship over my two clans is protected by divine right." He leaned even closer, glaring into Daar's widened blue eyes. "You've been allowed to live here only because Winter MacKeage will need your help in the future. And until then, you will stay quietly up at your cabin and consider yourself lucky to be under the protection of a benevolent laird. Because," he continued, pulling the cane from between them and tossing it onto the table, "I would not be as forgiving as Laird Greylen if you had interfered in my life the way you did his."

"It . . . everything worked out for him. He loves his wife and daughters and his new life here. All the Highlanders are happy."

Robbie grunted, straightening away from him. "Only because you can't further interfere in their lives."

"I'm not completely powerless," the *drùidh* said, defiantly lifting his chin now that there was some distance between them.

"Aye. You can still start fires and floods and landslides."

"I can still travel through time," Daar added, once again leaning forward. "And the planets will be lined up just right tomorrow eve."

Robbie closed his eyes and scrubbed his face with both hands before looking back at the tenacious old priest. He heaved a weary sigh. "There will be no time travel, *drùidh*. No spells and no book."

"Then in three months, there will be five fewer men living in Pine Creek," Daar returned. "It's going to happen, Robbie, whether ya like it or not. Unless," he quickly added, "ya travel to thirteenth-century Scotland and get me a new book."

Robbie stared at him in silence. How many times had he been warned not to believe Daar? And how many tales had the old priest spun over the last five years, attempting to gain Robbie's help in replacing his book of spells? But this was by far the most devious story to date. Daar knew Robbie would do *anything* to protect his family.

"No," Robbie growled.

"Meet me on the summit of TarStone at sunset tomorrow," Daar said, grabbing his cane and standing. "And bring yar sword."

"No."

"Ya might want to find the MacBain plaid your papa was wearing when he came here," the priest continued, walking to the door. "Ya can't wear clothes made of modern materials or take anything else with you that hadn't been invented back then."

"No."

Daar stopped, his gaze lifted to the ceiling but focused

inwardly in thought. "I should probably send ya back about ten years after the Highlanders disappeared."

"I'm not getting your book, old man."

Daar leveled his crystal-clear blue eyes on Robbie. "Ya have no choice," he softly told him. "Not if ya want your family to stay intact. Tomorrow at sunset on the summit," he said, turning and walking out the door.

Robbie stood rooted in place for several seconds, then rushed out onto the porch. "Why me?" he asked the retreating priest. "Why not Greylen or my father or Morgan? They know that time, the ways of the people, and the terrain."

Daar stopped in the middle of the driveway and turned to face him. "Though still vital men, they're too old, Robbie," he said. "I'm needing a powerful warrior in his prime. Someone strong and cunning and capable, who can be lethal if need be."

"What about Callum's son? Or one of Morgan's boys?"

Daar shook his head. "Their strengths run to business, not warring. MacBain raised you as a guardian. He understood your calling and prepared you well." Daar shot him a crooked grin. "I'm thinking your short career as a modern soldier may also prove helpful, though you won't be able to take any modern weapons with you."

"It's a moot point, because I am *not* going."

"Then I suggest ya enjoy what little time ya have left with your papa and uncles," Daar said, turning away and walking into the woods.

Chapter Two

Robbie loosened his tie the moment he slid behind the steering wheel of his truck and finally released the breath he'd been holding for what seemed like the entire meeting with Judge Bailey. He started the engine, pulled out of the courthouse parking lot, and headed toward Pine Creek.

The meeting had gone well, for the most part. Martha Bailey had agreed to let Gunter stay with Robbie, as long as the young man didn't get into any trouble more serious than detention at school. But one brawl, one incident that required the sheriff to be called, and Gunter was headed to jail—only this time, it would be the adult county lock-up for the eighteen-year-old.

That had been the better part of their meeting.

On the flip side, if Gunter involved any of the other boys in his indiscretion, then Rick and Peter and Cody might also be placed back into the system—which for them could well be the youth detention center, since all three boys had a history of running away from foster homes.

Robbie put on his sunglasses and sighed. At the urging of his father, he'd left a career in military special ops five years ago and come home to Pine Creek determined to make a difference on a more local level. It had taken him two years to buy up enough land to build a profitable logging operation and another two years to convince Maine's juvenile courts that he could help hard-case kids.

Judge Bailey had been his greatest obstacle at first, only to become an even greater ally once she realized that Robbie had a gift for working with delinquents. Martha was good at her job because she liked kids, and she was determined that Robbie succeed where the system had failed.

She was also a self-admitted sucker for tall, handsome men in suits who weren't afraid to stand up to her. She was happily married and nearly old enough to be his mother, but she flirted like a schoolgirl.

Robbie was not above flirting back if it helped achieve his goal. Which was why he had brought lunch from the local diner for their meeting, that they'd shared across Martha's massive desk in her tiny office. Hell, he'd even buttered her roll for her in an attempt to butter her up, hoping she'd turn a blind eye to the fact that Gunter was still living under his roof.

So far, so good. Gunter could stay, and Robbie could continue to ease the young man into adulthood.

The two brothers, Rick and Peter, were slowly settling in, and Rick's comment this morning that he didn't want to leave was encouraging. Eventually Peter would get over his fear of all things mechanical and with the help of a tutor make it through high school.

Cody, however, required a firm nudge toward the sober side of life. Robbie just had to figure out how to make the kid care enough about himself to stop getting into trouble.

Four juvenile delinquents was his limit. There was room for more boys in his mother's old home, but if he couldn't keep a housekeeper more than a month, he was in danger of losing the ones he did have to food poisoning.

Libby, his stepmother since he was eight, and Gram Katie and his MacKeage aunts helped out by bringing over evening meals occasionally, which was about the only time he could count on all four boys to be on their best behavior. Food seemed important to the teenagers.

Well, second only to sex.

Robbie had dealt with more than a few giggling teenage girls since the boys had come to live with him, and he had quickly learned that keeping the two sexes apart was an exercise in futility.

He smiled as his truck crested the knoll above the sleepy town of Pine Creek. Snowmobile season was just about over, and the ice was beginning to rot on Pine Lake, effectively shedding itself of ice fishermen.

Spring was the do-nothing time of year in the northern Maine woods. Mud season was fast approaching and would bring the logging industry to an abrupt halt in a few weeks. His crew of twelve men—and a fortune in machinery—would sit idle until the forest thawed and then dried enough to be worked again. Most of his men already had vacations planned, and Robbie wanted to take his boys to Boston over the April school break.

Or he had hoped to, until Daar's visit this morning.

Robbie passed Dolan's Outfitter Store and turned onto the road leading to his parents' Christmas tree farm. He scowled, thinking that of all the outrageous schemes Daar had come up with, this was the scariest. The priest was playing on Robbie's only real fear—which Robbie had grown up knowing was his father's greatest fear, as well as that of his Uncle Grey and the other MacKeage men.

The *drùidh* had brought ten Highland warriors forward in time thirty-five years ago, but only five of them remained. The other five, all MacBains, had perished in the first two years. Most had died chasing lightning storms in an attempt to get back to their original time.

Robbie was named after his great-uncle Robert MacBain, and it was the old warrior's sword that he had learned to wield once he'd grown big enough to lift it. His father had taught Robbie the skills of a warrior from the time Robbie could sit a pony, while himself attempting to straddle the chasm between two very different worlds.

Robbie worshiped his father and was awed by his ability not only to survive such an unimaginable journey but to thrive and eventually find happiness. And Robbie adored his stepmother, Libby. She'd married his papa just before Robbie's ninth birthday and had thoughtfully given him two sisters and a brother to torment.

His younger sister, Maggie MacBain—now Maggie Dyer—had just given birth to a baby girl, making Robbie an uncle and giving him one more soul to worry about. Not that he minded. Protecting his rapidly expanding family of MacBains and MacKeages, and now wayward boys, seemed to be a calling Robbie could neither dismiss nor resist.

Keeping Daar in line, however, was proving a challenge.

Robbie pulled into the driveway of his father's farm, stopped the truck between the machine shed and the Christmas shop, and shut off the engine. He stared through the windshield at the endless rows of Christmas trees marching through patches of melting snow, then let his gaze travel across the gravel yard to the large, white clapboard house where he'd grown up.

What was he going to do about Daar? He could not, in

good conscience, dismiss the old *drùidh's* claim. Not at the risk of his family. But could he confide in his father? Ask his advice? Maybe even take him back in time to help get the book?

Nay. He could not put his father through such an ordeal again. And Libby would die from worry. And Greylen MacKeage would likely unleash his own fury on Daar, and just where would that leave Winter MacKeage?

The five Highland warriors ranged in age from fifty-eight to eighty-five years old. They deserved, and had earned, the right to a peaceful old age. It was up to him to keep them safe from Daar's magic.

The passenger door opened, and his father slid into the seat beside him, filling the remaining space in the cab of the truck. "Ya're wearing a suit and look like ya're carrying the weight of the world on your shoulders," he said softly. "Does this mean Gunter has to move out?"

Robbie smiled and shook his head. "No. He can stay as long as he behaves." He turned to face his father more fully and stared into the mirror image of his own gray eyes. "Have you seen a strange woman around town, about five-six or five-seven, with shoulder-length brown hair and a soft white complexion?"

"You lose another housekeeper?" Michael asked, raising an inquiring brow.

Robbie's smile widened. "No. Only some eggs. I found her raiding my henhouse this morning and chased her halfway up TarStone before I lost her."

Michael's other brow rose. "Ya lost her? In a foot race?"

"She was all legs," Robbie defended. "Have you seen anyone new in town?"

"Nay," Michael said, looking toward TarStone Mountain. "Ya say she was stealing eggs?" He looked back at Robbie, a frown creasing his weather-tanned brow. "It's still below freezing at night. Surely she's not camping out?"

Robbie shrugged. "She might be. This was the third raid this week." He also let his gaze travel up the densely forested mountain and blew out a tired sigh. "I'll have to go find her, I suppose."

"I can help."

"No, you can't," Robbie said with a chuckle. "Maggie wants that nursery finished before the kid outgrows her cradle."

Michael scowled. "It would have been done *before* the babe was born if Libby and Kate and Maggie would only stop changing their minds. What does a wee bairn care about crown molding or the color of window trim?"

"What's today's color?"

"Either mauve or lilac." He shrugged. "Not that I can tell the difference between them. But apparently my grand-daughter will be scarred for life if she has to sleep in a room painted the wrong color."

"You still can't bring yourself to call the babe by name, can you?" Robbie said. "Aubrey is a lovely name."

"It's a man's name," Michael shot back. "And it's English."

"Russell Dyer is English."

"Don't remind me."

Robbie patted his father on the shoulder. "Russell's a good man, Papa," he said as he opened his door and got out.

Michael also got out and gave Robbie a crooked smile over the hood of the truck. "I know," he softly conceded. "Maggie chose well."

Robbie snorted and turned toward the house. "No thanks to you. You're damn lucky they didn't elope."

"I wasn't against the marriage," Michael defended as they walked to the house. "I was just trying to make them slow down. Maggie's not even twenty-two yet, and she's already married and has a bairn."

Robbie stopped to look at his father. "And at what age did women marry in your old time?" he asked.

"Society has gained eight hundred years of wisdom since then. And twenty-year-olds are too young to map out the rest of their lives."

Robbie scaled the porch stairs two at a time and opened the door for his father. "I seem to remember a story about an even younger man trying to run off with a lass from another clan," he said gently. "Were you not so deeply in love with Maura MacKeage eight hundred years ago that nothing else mattered?"

Michael stopped in the doorway and looked Robbie square in the eye. "I was young and foolish and so full of myself that I started a war, blaming the MacKeages for Maura's death instead of myself. And that," he whispered, "is the arrogance and ignorance of youth."

"Do you ever miss the old times, Papa? Have you ever wanted to return, if only for a little while?"

Michael stared at him in silence for several seconds. "I have had such thoughts," he finally admitted, his voice thick. He slowly shook his head. "After your mother died, and before I met Libby, I started up the mountain more than once, with you in my arms, intending to make the old *drùidh* send us both back."

Robbie went perfectly still. "What stopped you?"

"You," Michael said, placing a steady, strong hand on Robbie's shoulder. "I'd get halfway to Daar's cottage, and you'd do something as simple as wave at a chipmunk, and I'd stare at you and think . . . I'd think . . ."

"What?" Robbie asked. "What stopped you?"

"Your mama," Michael whispered, looking toward TarStone Mountain. "Mary would fill my head with memories of her. Of us together. And I knew I couldn't do it," he said, looking back at Robbie. "I could not take you away from your future."

"Daar said your coming here was an accident."

"Aye. If ya don't believe in destiny, then an accident is as good an answer as any."

"So you truly feel that your ending up here and falling in love with my mother was destiny?"

"Aye," Michael said, nodding as he finally entered the house. He tossed his jacket over a chair at the table and led Robbie through the kitchen and into the library. "I have never kept anything from you," he said as he went to the hearth and stirred the coals of the dying fire. He looked over his shoulder. "Ya know my history and that of the MacKeages and Father Daar. Ya understand the magic that brought us here even better than we do. You're mindful of Winter MacKeage's destiny as Daar's heir, and ya proved yourself a true guardian at the tender age of eight."

"When I carried Rose Dolan through the snowstorm."

"Aye," Michael said, turning to face him. "Ya knew even then, even before we did, that ya had a special calling." He smiled. "Have ya forgiven me for asking ya to come home five years ago?"

"There's nothing to forgive," Robbie said, grinning as he prepared to throw his father's words back at him. "It was the arrogance and ignorance of a twenty-year-old that made me run off and join the army."

Michael's eyes danced. "Are ya sure it wasn't Vicky Jones that sent ya running?"

Robbie shuddered. "That girl was downright scary," he muttered. "She actually told me she'd been planning her wedding since she was ten."

Michael turned serious. "Just as I think twenty is too young to get married, I'm thinking thirty is too old to still be single. Dammit, son, when was the last time you even went on a date?"

"I had a date a few weeks ago."

Michael snorted. "Ya took *Cody* with ya."

"And Peter nearly burned down the house while I was gone," Robbie said with a chuckle. "Honest, Papa, I don't enjoy living like a monk. It's just that I don't have time to date."

"Because you're too busy being a guardian to *everyone*."

"But I'm so good at it."

"Aye. Too good." Michael turned and placed a log on the glowing coals before facing Robbie again. "But at what price, son? Ya cannot take care of others at the expense of yourself. It's time ya married and had bairns of your own."

Robbie walked to the hearth and took down Robert MacBain's sword, grasping its familiar weight in his fist as he turned to his father. "Would you mind much if I took this home with me?"

Michael glared at him. "Ya might ignore my petitions for grandbabies, but ya cannot ignore your man's needs. You're afraid, son," he said softly. "But your fear is misguided."

Robbie rested the flat of the sword on his shoulder and raised a brow. "And what exactly am I afraid of?"

"Of letting a woman distract ya from your calling."

Robbie chuckled and started out of the library. He stopped at the door and turned back to his father. "Didn't we have this conversation twenty-two years ago, only wasn't I the one trying to talk *you* into getting married? If I remember correctly, you said a man can't suddenly decide to get married and simply pick the first available female; that he must find a woman to love first."

"Isn't it amazing how our words come back and bite us on the ass?" Michael whispered with a smile.

Robbie nodded. "Aye, Papa. Both our asses are sore." He

lifted the sword from his shoulder and touched it to his forehead in salute. "If such a woman even exists, who can love me despite my calling, I can only hope our paths cross while I'm still man enough to enjoy her."

Michael waved him away with a snort. "Go find your egg thief before she has to spend another night on the mountain. And don't let Peter anywhere near that sword," he added, following Robbie through the kitchen. "The boy will likely skewer your new clothes dryer."

Robbie descended the porch stairs and stopped in the driveway to look back at his father. "How did you know I had to buy a new dryer?"

"Daar was here this morning, looking for breakfast."

"What else did he say?"

Michael gestured at the ancient weapon in Robbie's left hand. "Only that ya might be by to pick up Robert's sword."

"And did he give you a reason for my wanting it?"

"Nay," Michael said. "Is there a reason?"

Robbie shrugged. "Only that my palm itched to hold it again. Maybe later this week we can have a match?"

Michael nodded. "I'll give ya a few days to practice first, before I wipe the ground with your arrogance."

Robbie gave him a final salute and turned and walked to his truck, waving good-bye over his head as he quietly let out a frustrated sigh. If Daar didn't quit his meddling, he was about to feel the business end of a dangerously sharp sword.

It was nearly five o'clock and just starting to get dark by the time Robbie pulled out of the logging yard behind the last load of saw logs, his stomach growling in anticipation of Gram Katie's lasagna. He headed toward Pine Creek, then turned onto a less traveled shortcut home that would take him around the north side of TarStone Mountain.

Gunter had left nearly an hour ago, after putting in an impressively hard day of work, according to Harley, who'd been grateful for the young man's help.

Robbie glanced out the truck window and decided he'd head up the mountain tonight to look for signs of his egg thief, rather than wait for her to come to him, figuring she wouldn't be raiding his henhouse again after this morning's chase.

Who the hell was she? The woman had no business camping out this time of year, if that's what she was doing. And she certainly didn't have to steal food. She only had to walk up to any house in town and knock on the door, and anyone would be more than willing to help her. Yes, she was quite a disturbing mystery.

"Well, speak of the devil," Robbie whispered as he slammed on the brakes, bringing his truck to a halt in the middle of the narrow tote road.

The woman had just stepped out of the ditch not a hundred yards away. She stopped and stared at him for the merest of seconds, then bolted back into the woods.

"Oh, no you don't." Robbie scrambled out of the truck. "You're not getting away this time."

He ran up the road and jumped the ditch, pushing through the tangle of alders before breaking into the forest. He stopped only long enough to let his eyes adjust to the dimness and listened to the snapping of limbs off to his right.

"Hey, wait up! I just want to talk to you!" he shouted, moving through the old-growth forest in her direction.

He heard a loud crash, a muffled grunt, then more limbs snapping as she scrambled away. He quickened his pace, weaving around large trees, ducking under branches, while still trying to listen, being careful not to make any noise himself.

The sound of his idling truck came to him then, quickly followed by the realization that the lady was headed back through the alders to the road. He turned and pushed his way through the bushes, stepping into the ditch just in time to see her climbing into his truck.

"Dammit, no!" he shouted, running toward her. "Stop!"

The rear tires chittered on the loose gravel, spewing up rocks as his truck sped toward him. Robbie jumped back into the ditch with a curse and stood ankle deep in rotting snow and freezing mud, staring at the taillights of his truck. "You little witch," he growled as she disappeared around a curve.

The silence of the forest settled around him, and Robbie stood rooted in place, amazed if not awed that she'd stolen his truck. He looked over at the broken alders she'd come through and saw a dark lump hanging in them. He sloshed out of the ditch, pulled the lump free, and realized that she must have gotten tangled in the bushes and been forced to sacrifice her backpack in order to escape.

"Well, my quick little cat," he whispered, unzipping it and peering inside. "Maybe now I'll find out who you are."

He reached inside and pulled out a loaf of bread, a jar of peanut butter, a pint of jam, and a fistful of mittens.

Mittens?

Child-sized mittens. With the price tags still on them.

The lady has kids?

One pair of the mittens was barely the size of his palm.

She has little kids.

"Well, hell." He dropped the food back into the pack, stuffed the mittens in his jacket pocket, and reached deeper into the pack. This time his fingers closed around a wallet. "Bingo," he said, pulling it out. He tucked the pack under one arm and opened the wallet, but it was too dark to read the name on the license. He closed it back up and reached inside the pack again, this time pulling out three knit caps.

He stared at the caps and heaved a weary sigh. Damn. His mystery woman had just become a really big problem—times three. He shoved everything back into the pack, hooked it over his shoulder, jumped the ditch again, and started walking the two miles home.

And just what was he going to tell the boys when he showed up without his truck? Certainly not that he'd been outmaneuvered by a pint-sized thief twice in one day!

Twenty minutes later and less than half a mile from home, Robbie stopped at the sight of his truck sitting in the middle of the road ahead, the lights still on, the engine still running, and his little thief nowhere in sight.

So, the lady had a conscience. She hadn't stolen his truck, only borrowed it long enough to put some distance between them. Just as she hadn't really stolen his eggs but had bought them.

Robbie scanned both sides of the road as he approached the truck. He opened the driver's door and set the backpack inside. He reached behind the seat, moved his sword out of the way, and grabbed the flashlight. He turned and aimed the light at the ditch, trailing the beam along the alders until he spotted where she'd continued her flight toward the mountain.

Who the hell is she?

Robbie tossed the flashlight onto the seat and climbed in, flicked on the overhead light, picked up the backpack, and pulled out the wallet.

"Catherine Daniels," he read from the Arkansas license.

Arkansas? She was a long way from home. She was also five-seven, one hundred thirty pounds, with brown eyes and brown hair. She was twenty-nine years old, as of January fifth of this year, and an organ donor.

Robbie studied the picture on her license and couldn't help but smile. Catherine Daniels was a pretty little thing, with huge doe eyes, a turned-up button nose, and a shy smile. Her hair was shorter in the photo than it was now, falling in wisps around her porcelain-skinned, china-doll face.

"Well, Catherine, what else can you tell me about yourself?" he asked, flipping through the wallet.

He found a somewhat battered photo of an obviously younger Catherine and two children. The boy standing beside her looked about three or four years old, and the baby on her lap couldn't be much more than one. He turned the photo over and found a five-year-old date scrawled on the back, along with the names Nathan, age three, and Nora, age one.

Which made them eight and six now.

Robbie lifted his gaze to the dark mountain beside him. Dammit. Were all three of them out there? Defenseless? Cold? Hungry? They were definitely scared. At least Catherine Daniels was scared, considering how desperate she'd been to get away. But scared of what? Or was it of *whom?*

Robbie looked back at the photo. It was a studio setting, but someone had been carefully cut out of the family portrait. All that remained of the fourth person was a large, beefy hand sitting on Catherine Daniels's right shoulder.

Robbie tucked the photo back behind the license, opened the money section, and counted two hundred and sixty-eight dollars. Not much money for being three thousand miles from home.

"Come on, Catherine, tell me more," he whispered, picking up the backpack and pulling out the food and the caps.

He held the pack to the light and spotted a bundle of papers in the bottom. He took them out, removed the rubber band holding them together, and shuffled through them.

He found Arkansas birth certificates for Nathan and Nora, divorce papers ending a six-year marriage to Ronald Daniels three years ago, and court papers giving Catherine full custody of her children. But it was the last paper that caught Robbie's attention. It was a letter from the Arkansas Penitentiary System informing Catherine Daniels that her ex-husband was being paroled on January fourteenth, after serving three years of his five-year sentence.

The letter was dated January fifth. Quite a birthday present Catherine had received this year. It didn't say what crime Ronald Daniels had been incarcerated for, only that it was the parole board's opinion he was ready to reenter society.

Robbie let his gaze travel toward TarStone. Did Catherine not agree with the board's findings? Was that why she was here, hiding on his mountain, avoiding contact with people? But why Maine? And why his mountain, of all places? The weather alone was enough to cope with, especially with two young children. Children without mittens and caps—and supper.

Maybe they were only passing through. Or maybe Catherine had family up this way or was trying to get to Canada.

Dammit. The more he learned about her, the more of a mystery she became.

Robbie folded the papers and placed them back in the pack, along with the food and mittens and wallet, then put the truck in gear and started for home with a new sense of urgency.

He hadn't traveled a hundred yards when his truck phone rang. "MacBain," he said.

"Robbie, this is Kate. Where are you?"

"About two minutes away. Did the hoodlums leave me any lasagna?"

"There's plenty. Ah . . . you need to go to town and pick up Cody at the health clinic. He's okay," she rushed to add. "He just needs a ride home."

Robbie sighed. "What happened?"

"Sheriff Beal called half an hour ago. It seems one of the boys Cody was with got hurt. But he's going to be okay, too."

"Hurt doing what?" Robbie asked, accelerating past the turn to his house and continuing on to town.

Kate made a frustrated sound. "I don't know exactly. The sheriff said something about a potato gun, John Mead's skidder, and a chase through the woods. The boy who got hurt ran into a tree and broke his nose."

Robbie let up on the accelerator, letting the truck ease back to the speed limit. This wasn't a crisis, only a bunch of bored high-school brats shooting potatoes at logging machinery.

"Are Gunter and Peter and Rick home?" he asked.

"I've got them doing dishes as we speak," Kate said, a smile in her voice. "Robbie, what's a potato gun?"

"It's a homemade cannon fashioned from a length of plastic pipe that you shoot potatoes out of."

"A cannon?" Kate repeated. "But what makes it . . . were the boys playing with *gunpowder*?" she asked in outrage.

"No. Hair spray is usually the propellent of choice."

"Hair spray!"

"It's a neat invention, Kate," Robbie assured her, "that's relatively harmless and not at all accurate. I doubt the boys did much damage to Mead's equipment, other than make a mess."

"Sheriff Beal didn't sound so amused," she shot back.

"And he's not releasing them until their parents come get them. Robbie, don't you dare let him take Cody away from us!"

Robbie smiled, picturing Kate with her hackles up. Libby's eighty-one-year-old mom was more protective of the boys than he was. Maybe he should let *her* go rescue Cody from Beal.

"I won't let anyone take Cody, I promise. You just make sure to save me some lasagna."

"I've saved enough for both of you," she told him. "Ah . . . Robbie? I called your truck phone earlier, and a woman answered."

Catherine Daniels had answered his phone? "What did she say?"

"She told me you were unavailable at the moment and to try calling back in half an hour. Who is she?"

"Er . . . just someone I'm doing business with. I'm at the clinic, Kate. Thanks for bringing over supper. You don't have to wait for us. This might take a while."

"I'll wait."

"Don't you dare do any cleaning," he warned, knowing Kate only too well. "That's the boys' responsibility."

"Too late," she said with a laugh. "I did the bathrooms while the lasagna was reheating."

"Kate," Robbie growled.

"And if shooting a potato cannon is so harmless," she said, cutting him off, "you go easy on Cody. Try to remember that you were sixteen once."

"Ah, Kate," Robbie said with a laugh. "I was never sixteen. Good-bye. And thanks," he softly added, hitting the end button on the phone and snapping it back in its cradle. He got out and stood beside the truck, looking first at the lighted windows of the clinic and then over at the looming shadow of TarStone Mountain.

He blew out a tired sigh.

There were days when he felt he was being pulled in a dozen different directions, when he thought the whole world might fall apart if he blinked. And days when he feared he couldn't live up to his calling.

And then there were days—like today—when he didn't even come close.

Chapter Three

There were no meetings scheduled, his logging operation was back to full manpower, and the boys had fed
themselves and gotten off to school without starting any
fires. Robbie led his horse into the strengthening March
sun, determined finally to get down to the business of finding Catherine Daniels.

He was just closing the barn door when he spotted the
snowy owl perched on one of the paddock fence posts.

"Well, hello, little one," he said, walking over and gently
stroking her feathers. "I was hoping you'd show up today. I
could use your help."

The snowy leaned into his touch, closing her eyes with
a soft sound of pleasure.

"Where have you been?" he whispered, cupping her
broad white head. "I've missed you."

The owl stretched tall, turning in his palm and lightly
nipping his thumb. Robbie laughed and went to mount his
horse but then stopped and turned back. "My sword?" he
asked, bending over to look her in the eye. "I'm hunting a

woman and two children, and I intend to offer them shelter, not scare them to death."

His old friend merely blinked at him.

Robbie tied his horse to the fence rail and set his hands on his hips. "I don't care what that crazy *drùidh* is concocting. I can't leave the lady out there another night. Daar's matter will just have to wait."

The snowy opened her wings and bristled in agitation.

"I am not bringing my sword!" he snapped, thinking nothing of speaking out loud to the bird. He'd been talking to the owl for twenty-two years now, though their conversations usually tended toward the snowy lecturing and Robbie arguing. "And besides, you can't just disappear for six months, then suddenly show up and start giving me orders."

The snowy let out a rattle that sounded suspiciously like laughter. Robbie crossed his arms over his chest. "Can you honestly tell me this isn't another one of Daar's schemes?"

She silently stared back.

Robbie leaned down until the owl's face was mere inches from his. "Then help me," he whispered. "Buy me some time to find Catherine Daniels and her children. Convince the *drùidh* to wait a few more days."

The owl sidestepped away, emitting a loud shrill.

"I realize Papa and the others are in danger." Robbie set his hands back on his hips. "But dammit, what if I *can't* get the book? What if I fail?" He held up his hand. "There's a difference between being cautious and being afraid! You can't expect me to go hurtling blindly through time. I need to think about this."

The snowy turned on the rail until she faced away from him.

Robbie dropped his head with a sigh, and pivoted on his heel and headed to the house. He took the porch stairs two at a time, trotted through the kitchen, and ran up the inside stairs to his bedroom. He lifted the mattress on his bed, pulled out his sword, and stomped back downstairs and back outside to his horse.

"I hope to God you know what you're doing," he muttered as he slid the sword into the sheath on his pack and then settled it over his shoulders. "Because I sure as hell don't."

The owl spread her wings and flew over the paddock toward TarStone. Robbie mounted and urged his horse forward, following his pet into the forest.

He remembered their first meeting. It had been his eighth birthday, and he'd been up on the mountain, bawling like a baby. There had been an incident at school that day, some silly thing he couldn't even remember now, where his lack of a mother had been sorely evident. So he'd run up TarStone, sat crying on a log, and wished with all his might for a mama.

Providence had sent him a snowy owl instead. The beautiful, mysterious bird had appeared from nowhere, announcing her arrival with a high-pitched whistle as she glided down to the log beside him. She'd folded her wings and sat silently, her large golden eyes unblinking as she stared at him.

Being somewhat prone to fanciful notions back then, Robbie had named his pet after the mother he'd never known. And, being eight, he'd never questioned the fact that not only did he talk to the owl, but she answered him. He couldn't explain it, even now, but he always knew what Mary was thinking, what she wanted or needed from him, and that he could count on her in a crisis.

She'd saved his life more than once over the last twenty-two years, the first time when he'd carried four-month-old Rose Dolan through a snowstorm one Christmas Eve. After settling a blue light of warmth around him, freeing him to use his own life energies to keep Rose alive, the owl had led his father and Libby to where he'd collapsed in a snow-drift. When he was eleven, Mary had driven off a disgruntled bear he'd surprised while hiking one day. When he could drive at sixteen, she'd flown in front of his truck, bringing him to a screeching halt mere inches from a washed-out culvert.

Mary had always been there for him, for both Gram Ellen's and John Bigelow's deaths, in his room after a nightmare, and in his thoughts when he'd been overseas as a soldier.

So if she insisted he bring his sword on today's little adventure, he had no call to argue with her.

Well, maybe a little. He needed time to prepare for the journey Daar had planned—time and a lot more faith in the *drùidh's* abilities to make it happen. He knew only too well how the magic could backfire, having seen many examples of Daar's incompetence over the years. Hell, he could be sent anywhere, or to any time for that matter, with just one wrongly spoken word.

Or he could be turned into a dung beetle.

Robbie looked at his watch, then up at the sun. He had about six hours, at best, before sunset. He looked at the vast forest blanketing TarStone. Six hours to find Catherine Daniels and bring her to shelter.

Then he would go to the summit—and meet with either his destiny or disaster.

Where the hell was MacBain? It was less than an hour to the vernal equinox, and he needed to give the boy instructions before he sent him off.

Daar paced the path he'd worn between a boulder and a stunted pine tree, his hands clasped behind his back and his head bowed, as he repeatedly whispered his incantation. But he was having a hard time focusing on the words, what with his mind being so cluttered with worry.

Of all the mistakes he'd made in the last eighteen hundred years, this might well be the one that did him in. What had he been thinking thirty-five years ago, to have cast such a foolish spell? Letting the Highlanders get sent back to their original time would be suicide. Every one of the MacKeage and MacBain offspring—including, if not especially, Robbie—would turn their backs on him when they lost their loved ones on this summer's solstice.

It was all up to Robbie, though Daar did worry about placing such a delicate matter in such a young warrior's hands. Not that he didn't think Robbie could succeed; it was the ramifications that truly scared him.

Cùram de Gairn was a young, dark, powerful *drùidh* known for his trickery more than his mercy. He would not care to have his book of spells *borrowed,* any more than he would care that Pendaär was the one doing the borrowing.

They had crossed paths a time or two over the cen turies, and not once had the experience been pleasant for either of them. The last incident, nearly a hundred years ago, had been a dispute about a woman. In fact, it had been Greylen MacKeage's mother they had battled over, both of them hoping to match her up with just the right lineage to produce an heir. Pendaär had come away victorious but badly weakened. Judy MacKinnon had married Duncan MacKeage, and nine months and two weeks later, she'd given birth to Greylen, the promised sire of Pendaär's heir.

Cùram had mysteriously disappeared after his defeat and had resurfaced only six years ago. The blackheart was living with the MacKeage clan in thirteenth-century Scotland, probably hoping to set up another suitable match. After all, begetting heirs was the sole focus of a *drùidh's* last few centuries of life.

That Cùram was only five centuries old—quite young in wizard years—and already thinking about such matters made Pendaär uneasy. The tricky bastard was up to something. But what?

"If you think any harder, your head's going to explode."

"Ya're late!" Daar snapped, twisting to glare at Robbie.

"Nay, priest, I'm not. So let's get on with this madness," he said, dismounting from his horse. "I have pressing matters to see to."

"Ya needn't growl at me, boy. It's not my fault a wee woman has bested ya."

Robbie turned toward him. "You know I'm hunting a woman?"

Daar nodded, giving him a smug smile. "If ya wasn't so stubborn about asking for help, I could have told ya three days ago that she's living in that old cabin on West Shoulder Ridge."

Robbie climbed back onto his horse. "I'll be back in four hours."

"Nay!" Daar said, grabbing the horse's reins. "Ya'll be back at sunrise. Then ya can go after your woman."

"She can't spend another night on this mountain. There's a storm moving in."

"She and her bairns are as snug as bugs and will be fine for tonight. But *our* problem can't wait. The planets will be in position in less than twenty minutes."

"Then tell me what your damn book looks like," Robbie said, dismounting again. "And where to find it."

Daar took a cautious step back. "It's not a matter of simply walking in and taking it, then walking back out."

"Then what sort of matter is it?" Robbie asked, crossing his arms over his chest. "Where is this book?"

"It's on MacKeage land, but it belongs to another *drùidh.*" Daar shifted nervously. "And it's not exactly a book but a tree."

"A tree."

"Aye," he confirmed, nodding. "A large oak growing deep in the forest about three or four miles from the MacKeage village."

"You expect me to bring back a tree?"

Daar held up his hands about ten inches apart. "Just a wee section of it," he quickly assured him. "From the tap root."

"What does a tree have to do with a book of spells?"

Daar gestured impatiently. "It's a tree of life, MacBain. They're scattered throughout the world and can only be propagated from their tap roots, not their seed. But each tree is nurtured by a *drùidh* and its knowledge carefully guarded so that life's continuum won't be disturbed."

"And if I bring you back a piece of this root, you'll have the knowledge to rework your spell?"

"Aye. I'll grow a new tree, and then I'll be able to keep the Highlanders here."

Robbie eyed him suspiciously. "It takes a long time to grow a tree."

"It will be large enough by this summer's solstice."

"That's cutting it close."

"Aye," Daar agreed. "But I have little choice. Which is why you have only two weeks to get the root."

"Two weeks?"

Daar nodded. "This won't be resolved in one trip. Tonight you'll look over the situation, then decide the best way to proceed. Take off those modern clothes," he instructed, going over to the boulder and picking up a length of cloth and a wide leather belt.

"This is my MacKeage plaid," Daar continued, holding it out to Robbie. "From when I lived with them in the old days. It should help ya move around inconspicuously. Ya do remember your Gaelic, don't you?"

Robbie stiffened. "You're not coming with me?"

"Nay. My presence would be known immediately."

Robbie hesitated, then finally slid his pack and sword off his shoulders, shrugged out of his coat, and started unbuttoning his shirt. "How will I recognize this tree?" he asked, unbuckling his belt.

"Ya can't miss it," Daar assured him. "It's larger than all the other trees, gnarled with eons of wisdom, and carries the mark of its *drùidh*, Cùram."

Robbie went utterly still. "The *drùidh* is a guardian?" he whispered, obviously recognizing the Gaelic title.

Daar snorted. "He's a lot of things, including a black-heart and a tricky bastard. That's why ya must look the situation over carefully and not rush into anything."

"How old is this Cùram?"

"He's a young man like yourself," Daar told him as Robbie pulled off his boots and stepped out of his pants. Daar sucked in his breath at the sight of the imposingly naked warrior. "This just might work," he whispered, handing him the plaid.

Robbie stopped wrapping the cloth around himself and raised an eyebrow. "You have doubts?"

"Nay," Daar said quickly, holding out the belt. "Only worries. I know you're well trained, Robbie, and highly motivated." He stepped closer and lowered his voice. "Ya can take Mary with ya, if ya want."

The young warrior looked off to his right at the snowy owl sitting on one of the boulders not a hundred yards away.

"She doesn't much care for you," Robbie said, looking back at Daar. He shook his head. "I'll not put Mary in danger."

Daar snorted. "That blasted bird can take care of her-self." He canted his head skyward. "In fact, she might enjoy a chance to see your papa's homeland."

Robbie wasn't paying him any mind but had walked over to the snowy and was holding out his hand. Mary opened her wings and hopped onto his arm.

Robbie returned and pulled his sword from its sheath. "How do I get back here?" he asked. "And when? You mentioned sunrise. Does that mean I have only twelve hours in the past?"

"Nay. Ya might be days in the old time. But," Daar said, cutting him off before he could argue, "it will only be the length of one night in this time. No matter how long you're gone, you'll always be back by sunrise."

Robbie nodded and turned to the setting sun. "How are your planets looking now, priest?" he asked.

"They're ready for us to begin. Here," he added, holding out his hand. "Take this cherrywood burl from my staff. When ya're ready to come back, grasp it in your fist and merely will yourself home."

Robbie took the knot of wood, looked down at himself, and laughed. "No pockets," he said, looking back at Daar.

"Tuck it in your belt. Are ya ready?"

"Not quite," Robbie whispered, turning to face him. "If something should go wrong . . . if I don't come back, I want your promise you'll tell my father and Greylen what's happened. And promise you'll give them the chance to stop your spell from sending them back." He stepped closer. "They have the right to fight for their lives, even if it means they die trying."

Daar clutched his staff to his chest and nodded.

"And tell my father about the woman on West Shoulder Ridge."

Daar nodded again.

Robbie stepped away, tucking Mary against his chest and covering her with the hilt of his sword. "Then do it now, priest!"

Daar raised his staff, closed his eyes, and began chanting his spell to move matter through time. He implored the elements to gather into a collective charge, coaxing the churning energy into the tip of his glowing staff.

A rolling darkness swept over the mountain, sparked with flashes of blinding light and thunderous heat. The wind rose, howling in protest of the unnatural happening.

Daar pointed his staff at Robbie. Fingers of energy arced toward the warrior, sending tendrils of pulsing colors around him, the air screaming at the disruption of time.

"Godspeed, MacBain!" Pendaär shouted, bracing himself for the final jolt as the storm tightened smaller and smaller.

The blow came in an angry boom, shaking the mountain, cascading pebbles and displacing boulders in a deafening growl.

And as suddenly as it had begun, it was over. A peaceful silence returned, and dusk softly blanketed the mountain. The sun was set, winter abandoned to the first night of spring. And Daar could only stare, clutching his spent staff to his chest, at where Robbie had stood.

"Aye. Godspeed," he whispered.

Chapter Four

Robbie spotted the low-hanging branch just in time to avoid getting his head knocked off. He ducked without breaking stride and scrambled down the bank to the stream, catching himself from falling by using his sword like a cane.

Mary called from somewhere upstream, her piercing whistle carrying through the dark forest in urgent echoes. Robbie splashed into the frigid water, slipping on the loose rocks, falling once and stubbing his bare toe on a piece of ledge.

The breaking limbs behind him sounded like gunshots as the four warriors closed in, their battle cries filling the night air with menace.

Robbie wiped the sweat from his eyes with the back of his sword hand, pressed his right hand more firmly against his throbbing side, and sloshed out of the stream and up the opposite bank, breaking back into a run.

He'd quietly been going about his nightly business of searching for Cùram's tree when the attack had come, unprovoked and completely unexpected. The chase had been going on for over three miles now, and Robbie didn't know if the ambushing bastards were merely out for a night's sport or if they truly were as inept as they appeared. Either way, he was reaching the end of his strength, and if he didn't turn and fight, the chase itself would likely kill him.

He stopped on a clearing of ledge and turned, planting his feet and lifting his sword, preparing to skewer the first man who broke through the trees.

He heard them floundering in the stream, heard them curse, then heard two separate shouts and a loud splash.

Robbie pulled his right hand from his side and rubbed his fingers together to see if the blood was congealing, then looked down at the deep gash on his hip, squinting to see it in the stingy moonlight.

Dammit, one of the ambushing bastards had tried to slice him in half and might have succeeded if Robbie hadn't knocked his sword away just in time. He took a deep breath, tightened his belt to add more pressure to the wound, wiped the blood off his palm on his plaid, and used both hands to steady his sword.

Mary called again. Robbie looked up and saw the snowy flying through the trees toward the stream.

"Nay!" he shouted in Gaelic, automatically speaking the language he'd been using for the last three days. "You will not be part of this game, little one," he said quietly, knowing she could hear him.

He stepped back into the forest, just off to the side of the path he'd made, and hid behind a large oak. Hell, if it had worked for the ambushing bastards, it could work for him.

The first warrior broke into the clearing, and Robbie let him pass unchallenged. The second and third men, both dripping wet, also ran by. Robbie stuck out his foot, tripping the fourth bastard, then used the flat of his sword to propel him into his comrades. And with a battle cry of his own, he sprang toward them, his sword aimed at the downed warrior. He checked his movement at just the last second, piercing soft skin and slicing upward until the man screamed in pain.

The other three appeared so surprised by the attack that they actually backed away. Robbie advanced, arcing his sword in an upward motion, then carefully slicing it across the chests of the two closest men.

The fourth bastard finally gathered his wits and brought his own sword up in defense, thrusting forward just as Robbie stepped to the side, slid his sword between the man's thighs, and lifted. The shocked warrior sucked in his breath and went utterly still. Robbie raised his sword a little bit higher, just to make sure the man understood the gravity of his situation.

"Now, gentlemen," he said in Gaelic, passing a warning glance at the other three men. "I've had enough sport for one night. What say we call it a draw?" He lifted his sword even higher, causing the warrior to whimper. "Or will you let your friend's bed be cold and lonely from now on?"

It seemed none of them wished to address his challenge.

"Okay, then. Set down your weapons, while this gentleman," he said, nodding toward his captive, "takes off his plaid."

All four sets of eyes rounded in the stingy moonlight.

"Now!" Robbie snapped.

The warrior whose manhood was being threatened immediately dropped his sword and started undoing his belt. The bastard with the bleeding backside rolled away from his own sword and awkwardly scrambled to his feet with a groan. The other two, each clutching his chest with one hand, bent down and gently set their swords on the ground.

Robbie nodded. "That's better." He reached out and took the man's plaid. "And now I suggest you start running back the way you came, just as fast as your sorry-ass legs can take you. And I want to hear your war cry, and it had better be moving away. Go!" he growled, dropping the tip of his sword and stepping back.

The two warriors with bleeding chests grabbed their buddy with the bleeding ass and quickly staggered back down the path toward the stream. The naked warrior, however, seemed unable to move.

"If I ever catch ya on MacKeage land again, I'll have your balls hanging from our keep."

Still the man didn't move.

"Or would you rather I do it now?"

The bastard didn't need to be told a third time and shot after the others, his naked white butt flashing through the trees and disappearing into the dense forest.

"I'm not hearing ya!" Robbie shouted.

Muted cries rose from the forest, along with snapping limbs and groaned curses as the four of them scrambled away. Robbie turned and kicked their swords into the trees, tossed the stolen plaid over his shoulder, and headed in the opposite direction.

He ran until the wound in his side made him stop. He stood bent over, his hands braced on his knees, panting against the throbbing pain. Mary silently glided in, landing on the ground in front of him. She folded her wings and stared.

"I know this isn't where we arrived three days ago," he said in a winded whisper, gingerly lowering himself to the ground. "But it's as far as I'm going tonight."

Mary sidled closer and nipped his shoulder.

"We didn't ask the priest if I have to stand in the exact place I landed when I want to return," he continued. "But what's the worst that could happen? We'll probably get back only a mile or two from the summit of TarStone."

He lay back on the moss, spread his arms wide, closed his eyes, and sighed. "I just need to rest awhile," he whispered. "The last three days here have been rather . . . eventful."

Mary hopped up onto his chest, turned her back to him, and used her beak to tug on his belt.

Robbie let out a pained chuckle. "I do believe the bastards wanted to kill me." He lifted the stolen MacBain plaid and laid it over the MacKeage plaid he was wearing, groaning when his wound twitched in protest. "There's some irony in that."

Mary finally tugged the cherrywood burl free.

"Soon, little one, once I get my strength back," Robbie whispered. "If my own ancestors didn't kill me, that godless storm likely will."

Mary paid him no mind, holding the burl in her beak as she spread her wings to encompass his body. It began as a whisper of breath first, slowly building to a loud, roaring wind. The air thickened and churned above him as lightning filled the sky with gathering energy.

Robbie gripped the hilt of his sword, gritted his teeth, and closed his eyes against the blinding tempest. The weight of the snowy suddenly lifted from his chest and was replaced by the plop of the humming cherrywood burl.

"Nay!" Robbie shouted, trying to catch her.

The bird beat her wings, powering herself out of his reach, and let out a loud, shrilling whistle as she disappeared into the night forest.

The storm tightened around Robbie with a deafening roar, drowning out his own howl of anger. He collapsed back onto the ground, clutching his sword and the MacBain plaid to his chest. He gritted his teeth against the pain he knew was coming. He hoped like hell that Daar was right, that although he'd been here three hellish days, he'd been gone from modern time only one night.

Robbie's last conscious thought, though, as the vortex consumed him, was of the Highlanders back home. The six MacBain and four MacKeage warriors who had disappeared ten years ago were now legends, and the war his papa had started was still going strong.

And Cùram de Gairn's tree of spells did not exist.

Chapter Five

Catherine Daniels sat upright in bed when the lightning strike cracked so loud the cabin shook. She turned to check on her children and was both amazed and relieved to see they were still asleep. She climbed out of bed, felt her way across the cold floor of the rustic cabin, and quietly wrestled open the half-rotten wood door.

What in heck was going on around here? This was the second thunderstorm since last night, but the sky was filled with stars that faintly shone in the gentle light of dawn. Maine had the weirdest weather. One day it was snowing, the next day raining, and the next day it was warm enough that they didn't even need their jackets. And now thunderstorms but no rain and lightning without clouds.

She couldn't wait to leave this desolate place, though for the life of her she didn't know which direction to travel. She'd gone as far north as she could without bumping into Canada, and the thought of actually traveling to another country was simply too scary.

She'd been on the run two and a half months, since she'd received the letter from the parole board, and she still didn't feel she'd run far enough. Ron had nearly caught up with them in Iowa, and it was then that Catherine realized she couldn't go to her childhood home; she had to find the last place he would think to look for her. And Ron knew she despised cold weather and that she'd had enough of rural settings growing up on a ranch in Idaho. In fact, she was counting on him expecting her to find a crowded city, and she hoped he was hunting for them in Chicago.

She'd made the right decision to change course abruptly and come to Maine, though having her car die had certainly put an end to her options. And then she'd gone and lost her backpack and a good chunk of her money to that huge, frightening man who kept chasing her.

"It's cold, Mommy. Close the door."

Catherine turned and wrestled the door shut, careful not to tear it off its rusted hinges. "Sorry, sweetie," she said, lighting the candle on the table. The old one-room hunting cabin they'd stumbled onto six days ago filled with dim light, and she walked back to the sagging bed. "Did you sleep well?" She brushed the hair off her daughter's face, feeling her forehead for a fever. "Your breathing sounded a lot better last night. I think your cold is gone."

"Does that mean we can leave today? I don't like it here, especially when you leave us alone."

Catherine leaned over and kissed her forehead, then ruffled her hair. "Maybe tomorrow, sweetie. I still have to find us some new transportation."

"They don't have buses or taxis this far out," Nathan interjected, rubbing his sleepy eyes. "We'll have to hitchhike."

"Hitchhiking is not an option," Catherine told him, reaching over and feeling his forehead.

He pulled away. "I ain't sick."

"I'm *not* sick," she corrected, going over to the rusty old woodstove and opening the door to prod the dying embers. "*Ain't* is not a word."

"Is too," Nathan countered, climbing over his sister and out of bed. "Johnny showed it to me in the dictionary."

"Johnny Peters is one of your friends I don't miss. And *ain't* is not a *proper* word."

Nathan walked up and handed her the last piece of wood in the box. "Then how come they put it in the dictionary?" he asked. "The F-word's in there, too. And so ain't *damn.*"

Catherine sighed, closed the stove door, and absently wiped the rust on her hands onto her pants. "People are judged by their language, Nathan. And using words like *ain't* and *damn* and the F-word gives the impression they're ignorant."

"I don't say *damn*, Mommy," Nora piped in, climbing out of bed, only to suck in her breath when her socked feet touched the cold floor. "I wanna go home," she whispered, jumping back into bed. "It's too cold here. And dark. It's dark all the time."

"The days are lengthening," Catherine assured her, finding Nora's shoes and putting them on her feet. "It's almost spring. It'll warm up."

"Can we come with you this morning?" Nathan asked, slipping into his sneakers and grabbing his jacket from the peg. "Nora cries the whole time you're gone."

"Here, I'll walk you both to the outhouse," she said, grabbing Nora's jacket and putting it on her. "And check for raccoons before you go inside. Remember what happened last time."

"Can we go with you, Mommy?" Nora asked, echoing her brother with pleading eyes. "We'll be real good. We promise."

"Oh, sweetie," Catherine whispered, squatting down to her level. "I don't leave you here because I think you'll be bad but because your daddy is looking for a woman and two children. If I go into town alone, no one will remember me once I'm gone. But they will remember a strange woman with two children, and if your dad comes through here asking questions, they'll tell him they saw us."

"We could hide in the bushes close to town," Nathan said. "Just don't leave us way up here."

Catherine straightened, opened the door, and urged them outside. "Okay," she agreed. "You can come with me today, but you can't go in the store."

"Can we go steal eggs with you?" Nathan asked, walking backward to look up at her as they walked toward the out-house.

"I did not steal those eggs. I bought them."

"You were pretty winded when you got back the other day. And the eggs were broken," he said as he turned and slowly opened the outhouse door. "And then you lost your backpack."

Nora stood far out of the way while both Catherine and Nathan peered inside. "It's clear," he said, quickly forget-ting their conversation. "Me first."

But Nora beat him to it and slammed the half-rotten door shut behind her. Nathan turned to Catherine. "Are you going to steal a car too, Mom?" he whispered.

"Of course not. Now that your sister's feeling better, I'm going to find a job."

"A job?" he squeaked, his eyes rounding. "We're gonna stay here?"

Catherine looked at her eight-year-old son and shrugged. "It's the end of the line for us, Nathan," she said softly, pulling him away from the outhouse so Nora wouldn't hear them. "There's nowhere else to run. And we're almost out of money. I have just enough left to either buy us a cheap car or rent a place to stay. But if I spend the money on a car, then we won't have any money left to buy gas. And we can't keep running forever, honey."

"But then Dad will find us," he whispered. "You said we gotta be careful about things like credit cards and your social number. That he can use them to find us."

"It's a social security number," she told him, squatting down to eye level and tugging on his coat with a smile. "But maybe I could be a seamstress and work out of our apartment. That way, I won't have to give any numbers to anyone."

Catherine nodded at hearing her own thoughts of the last few days. She'd been mulling over the possibility of stopping long enough to earn some money, and voicing it out loud actually made it sound plausible.

"We can really get a place? With our own bathroom and a kitchen?" Nathan asked, his eyes lighting with excitement. "And you can bake us cookies again?"

Catherine reached out and hugged her young son to her chest, pushing his head down on her shoulder so he couldn't see her misting eyes. For two and a half months, she'd been riddled with guilt and fear. What she was putting her precious children through was unconscionable, but letting Ron Daniels anywhere near them again was even more unthinkable. She had risked her life in the hopes of getting seven or eight years of freedom—enough to get her babies grown and safe—but the state of Arkansas had given her only three.

"I can work, too," Nathan told her, clinging tightly. "I'm big now."

"You are big," she said, squeezing him just as tightly. "You take care of your sister, find us firewood, and help me out a lot." She patted his back and stood up, took his hand, and walked to the outhouse. "Did you fall in?" she called to Nora.

A tiny giggle came through the door. "I'm done," the little girl shouted, bursting out the door. "The only reason I don't mind the cold is no spiders," she said with a shiver, moving so Nathan could go in next. "We really can go with you today?"

"Yes," Catherine told her, leading her back to the cabin. "Your cold is much better, so you can make the hike. And I'll even buy you treats for being such wonderful children."

Nora skipped on ahead but couldn't get the heavy cabin door open. Catherine picked up two pieces of wood from the dwindling pile outside and opened the door. She put the wood in the stove and started rummaging through the small assortment of cans for something she could heat up for breakfast.

Not two minutes later, Nathan came bursting through the door, his eyes wild and his face as white as snow. "There's a dead man in the woods!" he shouted, running up and grabbing her arm. "Come on, Mom. We have to get out of here!"

Nora let out a scream and threw herself at Catherine.

Catherine leaned down and stopped Nathan from tugging on her, taking him by the shoulders to look him in the eye. "Are you sure you saw a man?" she asked softly. "And not a funny-looking log?"

His eyes huge with fright, Nathan nodded. "I almost stepped on him." He took a deep breath. "I was looking for firewood up on the hill," he said with another gulp, pointing at the back cabin wall. "He's . . . he's only half dressed. And he's dead."

Nora whimpered, burying her face in Catherine's sweater.

Catherine took a steadying breath of her own. "Nathan," she said calmly. "How do you know he's dead?"

"I . . . I poked him with a stick, and he didn't move."

Catherine gently pried her daughter off her. "You sit on the bed and wait for us, sweetie," she told her. "Nathan, show me where this man is, then come back and sit with your sister."

She urged him toward the door, only to have Nora grab her sweater again and stop her. "I'm not staying here!" the girl cried. "Don't leave me!"

"Okay," Catherine said softly. "We'll all go."

She opened the door and took hold of their hands, letting Nathan lead them around the side of the cabin. They walked up the hill a little over two hundred yards, then Nathan stopped and pointed.

"There," he whispered. "On the other side of that tree."

Catherine turned both of her children to face her. "I want you to stay right here," she told them. "Right by this stump. Nathan, hold your sister's hand," she instructed, putting Nora's hand in his. "And don't either of you follow me."

"Mom!" Nathan hissed. "We have to leave! Whoever killed him might still be here!"

Catherine forced herself not to look around but kept her eyes on her children. "We don't know that someone killed him. He could have had an accident. I have to go see," she gently told them. "And if he is dead, then we'll leave. We'll go tell the authorities."

She hesitated only long enough to make sure they stayed put, then turned and walked toward the tree Nathan had pointed to. It took all of Catherine's willpower to make her legs move. She'd never seen a dead body other than in a casket, and those had looked rather tranquil, as if they were sleeping.

Was the dead man bloody? Gruesome? Ravaged by wild animals? No. Nathan had poked him. He wouldn't have stayed around long enough to do that if the man had been mutilated.

Catherine stopped just before the tree and looked to make sure her children hadn't followed. Nora was clinging to Nathan, who was hugging her back, both of them staring at Catherine with wide, terrified eyes. She smiled assurance, turned back to the tree, took a deep breath, and stepped around it.

Well, she definitely wasn't looking at a log. It was a man, all right, and he certainly did appear dead.

Catherine leaned around the tree to see her children in the strengthening sunrise. "I'm just going to check if he's alive," she told them, so they wouldn't panic when she moved out of sight.

"Mommy!" Nora wailed. "Come back!"

"It's okay, sweetie. Nothing bad is going to happen. You and Nathan just wait one more minute."

Catherine turned back to the half-naked man and stepped closer, picked up the stick Nathan must have used to poke him, and held it like a club. She took another step closer, studying him.

He was a huge man, well over six feet tall, with dark auburn hair and several days' growth of beard shadowing the harsh planes of his face. He was wrapped in a length of plaid cloth, cinched around his waist with a wide leather belt. There was another, different-colored plaid lying beside him.

Catherine took a quick step back when she noticed the long sword clutched in his left hand, half covered with leaves and the edge of the plaid blanket he was wearing.

A sword?

The man looked like Mel Gibson in *Braveheart,* only scarier.

She crept closer and slowly bent down, keeping her stick poised to strike. She reached out and touched his shoulder, only to gasp at the realization that he was warm.

Not dead. Unconscious.

Catherine scanned his body and saw the blood seeping through the cloth on his right side. She also noticed several scratches on both his arms and legs, some of them deep. Only half of his broad chest was covered by the cloth, and she could see a large gash on his right shoulder. There was a bruise on his left cheek and another one on his temple. He'd been in some sort of fight. She leaned forward, still careful not to touch him, and saw a good deal of blood covering the ground.

"Mommy!" Nora shouted.

Catherine stood up and leaned past the tree. "I'm okay, sweetie. And he's not dead, he's unconscious. He's bleeding quite badly, though."

"Then come back, Mom," Nathan hissed. "We gotta leave before he wakes up."

Catherine looked back at the man. If she didn't stop that bleeding, he never was going to wake up. She looked back at her children.

"Nathan, I want you to go get that old wheelbarrow from behind the outhouse and bring it here. Nora, walk over to me and stand next to this tree."

"No!" Nora cried, shrinking back.

"It's okay," Catherine assured her, holding out her hand for her to come. "He can't hurt us. He's just a poor wounded man who needs our help. Go, Nathan," she said more firmly. "He's bleeding to death."

Nathan urged his sister forward, then turned and ran back down the hill to the outhouse. Nora walked over slowly, her eyes rounded in apprehension.

"There's nothing to be afraid of, sweetie," Catherine

said softly. "Come see for yourself. He's just a man."

Nora finally reached the tree and sidled up to it, hugging it for protection, and peered at the ground behind Catherine.

"See?" Catherine said. "He can't hurt you."

"He . . . he's big," Nora whispered.

"Yes, he is. And he's hurt real bad, baby, and we have to help him."

Nora looked up at her mother. "Can't we call an ambulance?"

"I'd have to run down the mountain to call one, and he could die before an ambulance can get here. We have to take care of him ourselves," Catherine explained, turning back to the man. She set down her stick and started loosening his belt enough to slide it out of the way. "Now that you see there's nothing to be afraid of, can you do me a favor, Nora?"

"Wh-what?"

"Can you run back to the cabin and get me a towel?"

"The blue one?" the little girl asked.

"The blue one would be just fine," Catherine assured her, carefully peeling back the sticky cloth. "And grab a couple pairs of my wool socks and bring them also," she called to the retreating girl.

She looked back at the man. He was covered head-to-toe with dirt and leaves, and his skin, even his tanned face, was ashen.

Catherine slowly lifted the cloth away from his right side, sucking in her breath at the sight of the ugly gash just above his hip bone. It was about six inches long, and deep, the skin pulled wide as blood slowly oozed from it.

"Well, mister, we may have found you just in time," she whispered, gently prodding the cut to see if anything more than blood was involved. No organs or intestines popped out, and Catherine blew a small sigh of relief. She wasn't up to performing internal surgery, but her many years assisting her dad in his veterinary practice had left her capable of stitching closed a wound like this one.

"What's the wheelbarrow for?" Nathan asked, pushing it over the bumpy roots of the large pine tree.

"To get him to the cabin," Catherine explained, moving to shield Nathan's view as she lifted the plaid to see if he had any other wounds. She dropped the cloth as if she'd been burned, bowing her head to keep Nathan from seeing her blush. Her daddy's animal practice hadn't prepared her for anything like this. The guy was a brute of a man and looked as if he had more testosterone than blood in his veins. In fact, that was probably all that was keeping him alive right now; his powerfully fit physical condition was compensating for losing so much blood.

"How are we going to get him in it?" Nathan asked, walking over and staring down at him. His eyes suddenly widened. "That's a sword!" he said, reaching down to grasp it.

Catherine caught his hand. "Don't touch it."

Nathan stepped back and blinked at her. "What's he doing with a sword? And he's dressed funny."

"I have no idea," Catherine admitted. "Maybe there's some sort of gathering in Pine Creek, where people dress in period clothes. You know, like when I took you and Nora to that Civil War reenactment last summer. This guy is dressed like an ancient warrior. Maybe there's a Scottish festival going on."

"Here's the towel, Mommy. What's the socks for?"

Catherine took the towel from Nora, placed it under the plaid, and slid his belt down to hold it over the wound.

"He's in shock, sweetie, and his body temperature is dropping. Here," she said, handing one pair of socks to Nathan. "Put these on his feet."

She carefully pried the sword from the man's left hand, slipped one of the socks over his fist, then slipped the other one over his right hand.

"He's got six toes!" Nathan blurted, stepping back. "On *both* feet!"

Catherine snapped her gaze to the man's feet. His toes did look rather crowded. She looked up and gave Nathan a reassuring smile. "I've heard of people having six toes."

"Is he a monster?" Nora whispered, hugging the pine tree again. "He's awful hairy, and he's real big and scary-looking."

"He's not a monster," Catherine said firmly. She took the socks away from her gawking son and put them on the man's feet herself. "Come on, help me get him into the wheelbarrow," she said, standing up. "The sooner we get him back to the cabin and I stop that bleeding, the better we'll all be."

"We ain't gonna be able to lift him," Nathan said, grabbing the wheelbarrow.

Catherine didn't bother correcting his speech but squatted beside the man's head and grasped him by the shoulders. "When I lift him up, try to wedge the nose of it under his back," she instructed. "Okay, now."

She lifted him only a few inches, then had to ease him down and get a better grip. Good God. The man was solid dead weight.

"Again," she said as she lifted, grunting against the strain. "Push it under him, Nathan."

Nathan wedged the nose of the wheelbarrow under his back. Catherine pulled the man more upright, carefully eased him back against the wheelbarrow, then moved to between the handles and took hold of him again, this time under his arms.

"Okay, Nathan," she said, panting from the exertion. "I'm going to give him a final tug while you push on his legs."

"I don't want to touch him," Nathan whispered.

Catherine didn't much care to be touching him herself. The guy was solid muscle, with not an ounce of fat on him anywhere. He was so warm to the touch, and so frighteningly male, she wasn't sure if she was trembling from being this close to such an imposing man or if her muscles were quivering from moving his dead weight.

"Then get on the side and try to pull the wheelbarrow under him," she suggested. "You can help, too, Nora. Get on this side, opposite Nathan, and pull when I lift him up."

Neither child moved. "Come on, you two," Catherine pleaded. "Don't wimp out on me now. It's going to take the three of us to save his life. This is our chance to be heroes."

Just as she thought it would, the words *wimp* and *heroes* galvanized Nathan. He bent down and grabbed the side of the wheelbarrow and looked over at Nora.

"Come on, sis," he urged. "You can be a hero, too."

Not looking all that convinced, the six-year-old hesitantly took hold of the rusty metal and looked at Catherine.

Catherine nodded. "Okay. On the count of three. One. Two. Three!" she growled, pulling on the man with all her might.

He rose only about six inches, but it was enough for Nathan and Nora to slide the wheelbarrow under his backside.

"We did it!" Catherine cried, grabbing the handles and pulling them down.

The wheelbarrow dropped level with a jarring thud, and both Catherine and Nathan scrambled to stop it from tipping sideways. Nora scrambled back to her pine tree.

"You're both my heroes," Catherine whispered. "Now we just have to get him to the cabin without bypassing it and rolling him all the way down the mountain."

Her plan was easier said than done. They nearly lost him out of the wheelbarrow more than once and almost ran him into the side of the cabin. Getting him through the narrow door was even more of a challenge, but they finally wheeled him up to the bed and rolled him into it. All three of them were panting by the time they finished.

"Are we a great team or what?" Catherine said, tightly hugging her two kids. "Good job, guys. Nathan, take the bucket and the large pot, and get some water from the spring. Nora, you carry in what's left of the wood from the pile outside." She patted both of them on the backside to get them moving. "We have to hurry," she said, going over to her suitcase and rummaging through it, looking for her sewing kit. "I have to get him cleaned up, warmed up, and sewn up."

Nathan stopped by the door. "And then what?" he asked.

Catherine looked up from her suitcase. "And then . . . I don't know," she admitted. "I guess the three of us head down the mountain and tell someone he's up here."

Both children appeared to like that plan and hurried to do their chores. Catherine set her sewing kit by the bed, lit the last of their candles, and turned and stared down at the man.

He looked vaguely familiar.

She might have seen him in Dolan's Outfitter Store when she'd been buying the hats and mittens, or they might have passed on the street.

She suddenly stepped back. No, it couldn't be him. But the more she studied the giant, taking in his size and build and auburn hair, the more she realized who he was.

Well, darn it to hell. Of all the blasted bad luck she'd had lately, this was the prize. The man she'd stolen from—and had outrun twice—was bleeding all over her bed.

Chapter Six

Robbie came awake with enough presence of mind to keep his eyes closed. He held himself perfectly still and listened to the hushed conversation of at least three people while he considered his situation.

He was warm, stiff with pain, and apparently alive. Those were the pluses. He didn't know which time period he was in, couldn't decide how badly he was hurt, and for some reason, he couldn't move his hands.

The good seemed to outweigh the bad, but the conversation was proving a bit hard to grasp—something about a pretty sword, a Sasquatch, a dead car, a job, sewing, and cookies.

It was the mention of the Sasquatch and car that made Robbie think he was back in the twenty-first century.

But a *pretty* sword?

That remark had come from a young girl.

He could make out the soft voice of a woman, her tone sometimes coddling, sometimes instructing, and oftentimes trying to restrain laughter. He also heard a young boy whispering—he was the one who had called the man in the bed a Sasquatch.

Catherine Daniels, and Nathan and Nora.

Robbie stifled the urge to shout with joy.

He didn't have to find his little thief—she'd found him!

None of which explained why he couldn't move his hands.

Robbie cracked open his eyes and looked through his lashes, squinting at the candlelit scene. Catherine Daniels was sitting beside the woodstove, facing her two children sitting at the table. The boy was dividing his attention between his mother and the sword standing in the corner by the door. The girl was watching Catherine sew his MacKeage plaid as if that needle and thread were the most exciting thing since sliced bread.

"Where will we sleep tonight?" Nathan asked softly, darting a frown at the bed Robbie was in, then back at his mother.

"We'll pile our jackets and some blankets on the floor by the stove," Catherine told him, not taking her eyes off her work.

"I thought we was going to tell somebody he was here," Nora whispered, scooting off her chair and moving closer to inspect her mother's sewing.

Catherine finally looked up. "We'll have to wait until morning." She glanced at Robbie, then back at her children. "I don't dare leave him alone. Not until he wakes up."

"What if he don't wake up?" Nora asked.

"If he's not awake by morning, I'll stash you guys someplace safe and run down the mountain."

This time, Robbie had to stifle a snort. That should take the lady only half an hour, the way she ran.

The lure of Robbie's sword finally defeated Nathan, and

the boy slid off his chair and sidled over to the corner.

"Stay away from that," Catherine said. "It's quite heavy and the edges are sharp."

And bloody, Robbie wanted to add. He assumed she'd noticed that fact when she brought it in and hoped she thought it was his blood on the blade. It wouldn't do to have Catherine Daniels thinking he was in the habit of maiming people. Not with what he had planned for her.

"Could I have something to drink?" he asked.

Three pairs of startled eyes rounded on him. Nora squeaked and moved to the other side of her mother. Nathan stepped forward as if to defend them but changed his mind at the last minute and grasped Nora by the shoulders.

Catherine Daniels, once she got over her surprise, broke into a beautiful smile. "You're awake," she said, standing up and setting her sewing on the table.

She picked up a cup and brought it over to him. Robbie went to reach for it—and finally realized why he couldn't move his hands. Both wrists were bound to the side rails of the bed. He shot his gaze to Catherine.

Her smile disappeared. "I . . . ah . . . we don't know you," she explained, canting her chin defensively.

Robbie relaxed into the pillow and gave her a crooked grin. "You not only run like the wind, Catherine, but you're smart as well."

Her face paled. "You know who I am?"

"You left your backpack hanging on a bush along the road near my house," he told her, his smile widening when her eyes rounded. "That drink?" he asked, nodding at the cup in her hand.

"Oh." She leaned down, lifted the back of his head, and held the cup to his lips.

An ice-cold beer couldn't have tasted better. Robbie

drank every drop of water but for the ones that ran down his chin. "Thank you," he said with a sigh as she lowered his head. "What time is it?"

"Almost five in the evening."

"What day?"

"Ah . . ." She shrugged one shoulder. "I don't really know. I haven't kept track of the days."

"How long have I been out, then?"

"We found you this morning, up behind the cabin."

"So this is Thursday?"

"I really don't know."

Robbie decided to ask her something she did know. "What condition am I in?" he asked, lifting his head to look down his body. All he saw was an old blanket covering him, but the pain in his right side told him that eight-hundred-year-old wounds still hurt like hell the next day.

"You have a deep gash just above your right hip," Catherine said, setting the empty cup on the stool beside the bed. She waved her hand at his torso. "And another cut on your shoulder And you've lost a lot of blood."

"But the bleeding has stopped?"

She nodded. "I've sewn up both wounds. And I washed your smaller cuts." She hesitantly leaned over and set her delicate hand on his forehead, then quickly pulled back. "You don't have a fever," she said, her face tinged pink. "But you need to see a doctor as soon as possible."

Robbie was still trying to get over the fact that she'd taken a needle to him. "Sewing flesh is messy work," he said, lifting one brow. "And should involve at least a passing knowledge of human anatomy."

Catherine Daniels's smile returned. "People aren't so different from horses and cattle."

Robbie lifted his other brow.

"My dad was a veterinarian," she told him. "And I did

rounds with him every summer through high school. I had some silk thread in my sewing kit, but the doctor will probably redo the sutures. I just wanted to stop the bleeding and close you up to lessen the chance of infection."

"And I thank you for that, Catherine," Robbie said with a slight nod. He looked toward her children standing beside the woodstove, their eyes huge and apprehensive, then back at her. "How did I get from behind the cabin to here?"

"In a wheelbarrow," she told him. "These are my children, Nathan and Nora," she added, turning and waving them forward. "Nathan is eight, and Nora is six." She took hold of their shoulders once they approached and faced him again. "They helped get you in here."

Robbie nodded to them. "Thank you," he said.

"Do you have a name?" Catherine asked.

"Robbie MacBain. I live at the bottom of this ridge, in the white farmhouse with the chicken coop that sits next to the large barn. I believe you're familiar with the place?"

Catherine's face colored with another beautiful blush.

Robbie thought about how he was going to get down off this mountain and how he could persuade Catherine Daniels to come with him.

"There's probably people out looking for me, including four teenage boys who are likely starving to death by now," he said, hoping to ease her into the fact that he had four boys at home. "Any suggestions on how I let them know I'm okay?"

"Mom can run really fast," Nathan interjected. "She can tell them you're here."

"But it's dark out," Catherine said quickly, squeezing her son's shoulder. "And I won't leave my children. I'll go get help in the morning."

"Or you could help me walk down tonight," Robbie offered.

She shook her head. "You wouldn't make it a mile. And you'll probably start bleeding again."

"I'll make it. Just find me a stick to lean on."

"That still doesn't change the fact that it's pitch black outside. And the wind's come up, and heavy clouds moved in this afternoon. There must be a storm coming."

Robbie went silent and stared at her, thinking that he already knew quite a lot about Catherine Daniels. Such as the fact that she was a bit stubborn and a mite bossy. He also knew she could outrun him, was bold enough to steal his truck, and smart enough to tie him to the bed for her own protection. She was willing to save the life of a complete stranger, resourceful enough to work with what she had, and desperate enough to drag her children thousands of miles across the country. She was perfect.

"Then how about you untie me and at least help me get to the outhouse?" he asked.

Nora scrambled from under her mother's arm, ran to the opposite corner of the cabin, and pressed her little body against the wall.

"That's not going to happen, Mr. MacBain," Catherine said, urging her son over to the woodstove and waving at Nora to join him. "We'll have to devise another means."

Robbie chuckled. "It's not like I'm a threat to you or your children, Catherine. You say I can barely walk, so I can't hurt anyone but myself. So let's avoid both of us being embarrassed."

Her blush kicked up three notches. She folded her arms under her breasts and stared at him, obviously trying to decide what to do. She suddenly turned to Nathan.

"Go out and find two big sticks," she told him.

"Mom, no!" Nathan hissed. "He's too big."

"But he's in no shape to cause trouble," she assured him. "Now go," she repeated, nudging him toward the door. "Nora, you stand outside by the woodpile. I'll leave the door cracked so you won't be scared."

Apparently deciding outside was less scary than inside, Nora ran after her brother. Catherine walked over to Robbie.

"You aren't wearing anything, Mr. MacBain," she whispered. "I need to wrap the blanket around you."

"Where's my plaid?"

"Your plaid? It . . . it's right here," she said, going to the table and picking up his MacBain plaid. "The one you were wearing is bloody and torn. You can use this other one."

"Here's the sticks, Mom," Nathan said, walking inside with two large sticks almost as tall as he was.

"Set one of them by the bed," she told him. "And keep the other one with you." She turned the boy to face her. "I want you to walk beside us to the outhouse, and if Mr. MacBain tries anything, you smack him as hard as you can on his right side," she instructed, turning to give Robbie a warning glare.

"You want me to hit him?" Nathan whispered, stepping back. "But that will make him mad."

Catherine shook her head. "He'll drop like a stone, Nathan. But only hit him if I say so, understand?" She waited until he nodded. "Go stand with your sister, and leave the door cracked."

She watched him leave and turned back to Robbie.

Robbie grinned. "You don't pull any punches, do you?"

"I don't care to be defenseless, Mr. MacBain," she said, working free the knot on his right wrist.

"Since you're about to help me get dressed, do you think you can start calling me Robbie?" he asked, keeping his arm at his side once she freed his wrist.

She walked around the bed and undid the other knot, saying nothing. Once she freed him completely, Robbie slowly lifted his arms and flexed his shoulders.

"Ahhhh," he rumbled. "I was beginning to stiffen up."

"You're a lucky man," she said, staring at him with large doe eyes. "If that gash on your side had been a little deeper or three inches higher, we wouldn't be having this conversation. How did you get hurt?"

Robbie slowly sat up, clutching his throbbing side with his hand. "I tripped and fell on my sword," he said, shaking his head in disgust.

"What were you doing up here, dressed like that and carrying a sword?"

"I was practicing for the festival this summer," he told her, breathing tightly against the pain. He glanced up and caught her staring at his bare chest. "The competition can get fierce, and I usually start training months ahead. I . . . ah . . . I must have rolled quite a ways, to be banged up like I am."

Her face nearly crimson, she finally lifted her gaze from his chest. "You're lucky you didn't slice your head off."

"Aye, I suppose I am. What are you doing here, Catherine?"

She looked away and picked up the MacBain plaid. "My car broke down on the other side of the mountain."

Robbie took hold of the cloth to stop her from wrapping it over his shoulders. "There's nothing but wilderness on the other side of this mountain. Why were you over there?"

"I was lost. I thought the dirt road was a shortcut to Caribou." She shrugged and tried covering his chest with the plaid again, but this time Robbie stopped her by grabbing her wrist.

Catherine Daniels exploded. She jerked free and punched him on the shoulder, putting all of her weight behind it. Robbie let himself fall back with a gasp of pain, and lay perfectly still, watching her. She was backed up against the wall.

"I'm sorry," he said, not moving. "I wasn't thinking."

Nathan burst into the cabin, his stick raised to strike. Catherine rushed around the bed to stop him. "It's okay, honey," she said calmly. "Mr. MacBain just hurt himself trying to get up."

Nora ran into the cabin with a blood-curdling scream. "Something's out there!" she shouted. "Coming up the hill!"

Catherine took the stick from Nathan and headed outside, only to stop when she realized she was leaving her children with a stranger who was no longer tied up.

"Come stand by the door," she told them, pulling them outside behind her.

Gritting his teeth against the pain, Robbie rolled off the bed and stood up. He quickly wrapped the plaid around himself, found his belt hanging over a chair, and cinched it around his waist. He headed out the door behind them, grabbing his sword on the way.

Four mounted shadows moved into the clearing and stopped just inside the circle of light coming from the cabin. Robbie immediately relaxed, set his sword against the log wall, and leaned on the door casing to ease the throbbing in his side.

"Is that you, boss?" Cody asked, grinning at Robbie. "I almost didn't recognize you in that skirt."

"It's okay, Catherine," Robbie assured her. "These fine young gentlemen are here to rescue us."

Catherine slowly lowered her stick but raised it again when Gunter moved his horse closer. She backed up, herding her children behind her until they were nearly around the corner of the cabin.

Gunter stopped and looked from Robbie to the three frightened Danielses, then back at Robbie. "Do you need rescuing?"

"How did you know where to look for me?" Robbie asked.

"That crazy old priest was sitting on the porch when we got home from school," Gunter explained, dismounting and walking forward. "Your horse was tied to the rail. He said we should try looking for you on West Shoulder Ridge, since he'd already searched the entire summit."

Gunter stepped closer and lowered his voice. "He wouldn't let us tell anyone you were missing. Not even your father. But he wouldn't say why."

Robbie nodded. "It's just as well you didn't. There's no need to worry them. I—ah—I had a little accident."

Gunter let his gaze scan down Robbie's body, then looked back up at him. "Nice duds," he drawled. "Who's the lady with the kids? Our egg thief?"

Robbie nodded. "And if we play our cards right," he said quietly, so Catherine wouldn't hear him, "she could be our new housekeeper."

Gunter turned to Catherine, and Robbie watched in amazement as the young man shot her a smile warm enough to toast bread. "Ma'am?" he said, stepping toward her, his hands tucked behind his back in an unthreatening gesture. "It's mighty cold outside. Why don't you bring your children out of this wind while we decide what to do?"

Robbie couldn't quit gawking. Was that really Gunter? Hell, the kid was all but oozing charm. Robbie looked at the other boys. They were as dumbfounded as he was.

"We have about three hours before the storm hits," Gunter continued, stepping aside for her to pass. "Just long enough to get you and your children off this mountain."

Robbie hobbled out of the way so she could enter the cabin, and made his way to one of the chairs and gingerly sat down.

The other three boys quickly dismounted and crowded into the doorway. Catherine took her two children to the woodstove, placing it and herself between them and the men. Robbie noticed she was still holding her stick.

"Catherine," he said, drawing her attention. "You can't stay up here. They were predicting over a foot of snow when I left yesterday."

Her large, worried brown eyes scanned the five of them, then returned to his. "Can . . . can you take us to town?" she asked. "To a motel or something?"

"We can do better than that," Gunter interjected. "We have a ton of room at home, a well-stocked pantry, and a fireplace to curl up in front of."

She shook her head. "I think we should go to a motel."

"Will you trust your children with the boys so I can talk to you alone?" Robbie asked. "They'll take them outside, and we'll leave the door open so you can see them."

She tightened her grip on her stick.

"I found the papers in your backpack," Robbie quietly said.

Stiffly, her face pale with trepidation, Catherine slowly led her children outside. Cody and Peter and Rick moved out of her way.

"Try to make friends with the kids," Robbie whispered to Gunter as he walked by. "They're a big part of the solution to our problem."

Gunter nodded, smiled at Catherine as she came back in, and immediately squatted down to Nora's level once he was outside.

"Are you running from your ex-husband?" Robbie asked.

She stood by the woodstove, facing him, and nodded.

"What was he in jail for?"

"Domestic abuse," she said succinctly.

But it was enough for Robbie to get a much clearer picture. And it also explained why she'd exploded when he had gripped her wrist. "Are you sure he's after you, or did you run when you got the letter because you only thought he might be?"

"He nearly caught us in Iowa," she said softly.

Robbie nodded. "Okay," he said just as softly. "What if I can help you? You have no transportation, not much money, and no place to live. I have a large house, four hungry boys, and a pressing need for a housekeeper."

Her eyes widened. "You're offering me a job?"

"I am. That is, if you can cook."

She nodded, then fell silent, watching her children out the door. Robbie followed her gaze and saw Gunter, now sitting on the ground, showing Nora the small, shiny rock he always carried in his pocket. Rick was showing his jackknife to Nathan.

"It's an all-male household, Catherine," Robbie continued. "Will that be a problem for you?"

"They're too old to be your sons," she said, still watching out the door. She turned her gaze to his. "Who are they?"

"The state of Maine considers them foster kids," he told her, shrugging. "But I prefer to think of them as young men who only need a nudge in the right direction. Where were you headed when your car broke down? Do you have family in Maine?"

"No. I was headed to the last place I thought Ron would look for me."

"Would he look for you in Pine Creek?"

"No. He'd think I'd go to a large city. I'm hoping he's looking in Chicago right now."

Robbie nodded. "Would you be comfortable living and working in an all-male household?" he asked again. "The boys can be a handful sometimes, but they're basically good kids."

"You have room for the three of us?" she asked, still not answering his question. "Nathan and Nora and I could have our own bedroom?"

"There's two spare bedrooms," he told her. "Ah . . . I feel it's only right to warn you that we've lost three housekeepers in the last eight months. Do you have a sense of humor, Catherine?"

She finally gave him a small, hesitant smile. "Teenagers don't scare me."

"But I do."

"Yes."

"I'm the oldest of four siblings," he told her. "My parents own a Christmas tree farm about two miles away. My sister just had a baby and lives in Greenville, and my brother and little sister are away at college. I have four aunts and uncles nearby and a slew of cousins. I don't smoke or have more than the occasional drink, and I don't need to bully a woman to feel like a man."

Her smile widened the tiniest bit. "It's usually the employer who asks for references."

"These are unusual circumstances. I really am desperate for a housekeeper, Catherine." Robbie decided it was time to close the deal. "I'll pay you six hundred dollars a week, plus room and board for the three of you."

Her smile disappeared and was replaced with disbelief. Catherine looked back outside at the four boys talking to her children. "They're hellions, aren't they?" she whispered.

"On their best days," he admitted with a chuckle. "But they only want direction. That's my job," he said when she looked at him again. "Your job is to keep them fed and my house relatively clean. Catherine," he said, slowly standing up but making sure he kept his distance from her. "My MacBain word of honor, you need not fear me. How about we give you a week to test the waters? If you're uncomfortable, or if you simply decide you don't want the job for whatever reason, you can move on. But anything's got to be better than what you have now."

She looked at her children and was silent for some time, then took a deep breath and looked back at him. "Okay, Mr. MacBain," she said. "I accept your offer."

Robbie made sure she didn't see his relief—or his triumph.

"For a one-week trial," she clarified before he could finish rejoicing. "And you pay me in cash."

"Gunter," Robbie called out the door, deciding it was time to get this show on the road before she changed her mind. "Bring the kids inside so they can pack their things." He looked at Catherine. "Anything that can't be tied to a horse can be gotten later."

"I only have two suitcases. But there's more stuff still in my car on the other side of the mountain."

"We'll get your car once the storm is over."

Nathan and Nora rushed in with Gunter and ran up to their mother. She squatted down and pulled both of them to face her. "We're going to go stay with Mr. MacBain and the boys," she told them. "They need a housekeeper."

"We're going to live with them?" Nathan asked, darting an uncertain look at Robbie. "Mom," he whispered. "I don't think we should do that."

She gave both children a hug. "It'll be okay," she assured them. "If we don't like it, we can move on after a week."

Robbie picked up his MacKeage plaid from the table and started to wrap it over his MacBain plaid.

"Your clothes were tied to your saddle," Gunter said, heading back outside. "We brought your horse with us."

With only a whisper, Catherine set her kids to gathering up their things. She placed her sewing kit into the larger of the two suitcases, and Rick came over and carried it out to the horses the minute she'd snapped it shut. In no time, the boys had everything tied to the saddles, the four of them obviously eager to get their new housekeeper home and installed in the kitchen.

Gunter handed Robbie his clothes and boots, then left Robbie alone to get dressed while he got everyone settled on horseback.

In less than half an hour after the boys' arrival, the eight of them were headed down the mountain. Catherine was mounted behind Cody, Nathan behind Rick, and Nora, bless her brave little heart, was quietly riding in front of Gunter.

It had taken Robbie a full minute—and the help of an old stump—to climb onto his own horse. His side felt as if it were on fire, and he was weak as a babe from the loss of blood. But he'd taken the time to slide his sword under the cabin floor when no one was looking, deciding he could pick it up later, before his next exciting adventure for Daar.

The old priest would probably consider his journey back to thirteenth-century Scotland a complete disaster, but Robbie preferred to look on the bright side—he was going home with a new housekeeper. And he was alive and able to fight another day.

He did have to be careful, though. The last person he could face right now was his stepmother, Libby. She was a doctor, but, more than that, she was a healer. If she so much as touched Robbie in the condition he was in now, she would know immediately what had happened. Five seconds later, so would his papa. And within the hour, all five of the Highland warriors would be knocking on Robbie's door, demanding to help.

And that, Robbie vowed to himself, would not happen.

He was their guardian. It was his responsibility to keep them safe and happy and living here with their families for the rest of their natural lives. Failure had never been part of his vocabulary, and he wasn't about to become acquainted with it now.

Chapter Seven

$\mathcal{F}$or the first time in what seemed like forever, Robbie woke up to the smell of breakfast and the sound of a woman in the kitchen downstairs. He lay in bed, smelling and listening and smiling. Catherine Daniels was up early this morning, not that he should be surprised. She appeared to be a determined little thing—determined to protect her children and now obviously determined to do her job in exchange for shelter.

Heavenly, strong-smelling coffee. Bacon. Toast. And he would bet his farm the little cat had raided his henhouse again.

Robbie threw back the covers to jump out of bed, only to be stopped by the sharp pain in his side. He finished rising more slowly, uttering curses, and leaned over to examine his wound.

Catherine had done a neat job of stitching him up, though she had used bright pink thread. He looked in the bureau mirror at his chest, running his finger lightly over the cut on his shoulder. It would barely leave a scar once it healed. He carefully stretched his arms over his head, slowly working the kinks out. He would ride back up the mountain to Daar's cabin today, before the priest showed up here and scared off Catherine and her children.

That brought his thoughts to Mary. Why had that contrary owl stayed behind? What could she possibly hope to accomplish? He had to go back and get her, just as soon as he was healed enough to survive another journey through the storm. Only this time, he was taking both plaids.

Robbie pulled some clean but wrinkled jeans out of his bureau and struggled into them. Then he found an equally wrinkled shirt and slipped it on, whistling through his teeth at his protesting side. Bending down to put on his boots wasn't even worth contemplating, so he carried them down the stairs in his hands.

He found the table already set. And obviously clairvoyant, Catherine had poured his coffee. It was sitting— steaming, smelling divine—at the head of the table. His new housekeeper was nowhere in sight.

Someone came treading down the stairs, also obviously awakened by the smell of coffee and perfectly cooked bacon. Gunter peeked around the corner, only to scowl. "You haven't been cooking. This must be the lady's doing."

Robbie nodded and sat down at the table while Gunter poured himself a cup of coffee. The boy stopped, lifted the lid of the frying pan on the stove, and sniffed.

"We can't lose this one," he said, coming to sit down across from Robbie. "I had a talk with the others while we unsaddled the horses last night. They'll do whatever it takes to keep her here."

"Then no running girdles up the flagpole," Robbie suggested. "And no live fishing bait stored in the fridge."

Gunter snorted. "I doubt the lady wears a girdle," he said before taking a sip of his coffee.

Robbie took a sip of his own coffee, that Catherine had poured for him, realizing it was more than any of the other housekeepers had done. Hell, none of them had ever been up early enough to make a pot!

Catherine walked out of the downstairs bedroom, where she and her kids had slept last night, stopped in the middle of the kitchen, and hesitantly smiled. "Good morning," she whispered, her face turning a warm pink. "I bet you're both starved," she said, going over to the stove and filling two plates with bacon and eggs and toast.

"Good morning," Gunter said when she set one of the plates in front of him. "And thank you."

"Thank you," Robbie echoed. "And good morning."

She murmured something in reply, and hearing the pounding of feet on the stairs, poured three more cups of coffee and filled three more plates, setting them on the table as each one of the boys came down, their eyes blinking and their mouths watering.

"Oh, Lord," Cody groaned. "I've died and gone to heaven. Will you marry me?" he asked Catherine, his hand over his heart as he eyed his breakfast.

"Are you asking me or the eggs?"

"Both," Cody affirmed, his morning grin rusty but visible. Then he spotted Robbie. "Hell, man, you look like you ran into a train." He turned incredulous eyes on Catherine. "I retract my proposal," he whispered. "I don't want to mess with anyone who can do that to him."

"I did it to myself," Robbie said, fingering the bruise on his cheek. "When I fell."

"Hey, lady. I hate scrambled eggs," Peter growled, pushing his plate away and glaring at Catherine.

Robbie went to rise from his chair, ostensibly to kick the boy in the butt, but at the sight of Catherine's returning scowl, he sat back down. Maybe he shouldn't be too quick to intervene but should simply sit back and watch. After all, this could prove to be interesting . . . or the worst idea of his life.

"My name's Catherine, to those of you who are interested. But I will respond to 'lady' or 'ma'am' or 'hey, you,' so long as the tone is civil. Now, boy, if you tell me how you like your eggs, I'll fix you some new ones."

Well, damn. If that didn't beat all. Peter actually looked contrite. The rest of the guys looked startled.

"My—uh—my name's Peter. And I prefer my eggs over easy, with catsup," he quietly informed her.

She rewarded Peter with a smile and then looked at the others. "I know you introduced yourselves last night, but I can't put faces to names this morning. I was . . . it was a bit confusing last night."

"I'm Rick, and I'll take my eggs any way you want to cook them. And he's Gunter," he said before Gunter could open his mouth. "But don't pay him no mind. He only looks scary."

"My name's Cody, and I'll eat anything." Cody darted an accusing look at Robbie. "Well, almost anything. So long as it ain't burnt or covered with grit."

"And you can call me Catherine," she offered, darting a shy look at Robbie before she turned back to the boys. "And my son's name is Nathan—he's eight. And my daughter's name is Nora—she's six." She took a steadying breath. "If they act shy with you, please try to be patient. They haven't been around many strangers, and never around so many men."

The *men* label scored the woman several points, Robbie noticed. So, Catherine wasn't going to talk down or tread lightly around them. That was good. And she definitely could cook. All the plates were cleaned in record time and chairs scraped back and school things quickly hunted up. Until Peter suddenly groaned.

"Damn!" he cursed, slapping his head with his hand as he tossed down his school bag. "I had an assignment for Mrs. Blake. She's going to have my ass if it's not in today."

"Oh! I'll write you a note," Catherine said, rushing over to the counter and grabbing a pen. "I'll explain how you spent the night rescuing us."

Robbie quietly sipped his coffee. Hot damn, he was a smart man. Already Catherine was acting more like a mother than a housekeeper. The three younger boys were giving her incredulous looks, and Gunter was smiling again. And damn if the woman didn't scribble the note, send them off, and disappear into her bedroom before Robbie could finish patting himself on the back.

Aye. He was seriously thinking of proposing to her himself.

Quietly, careful not to wake her exhausted children, Catherine unpacked her suitcase and put their meager belongings in the large bureau and closet.

Breakfast had gone well, she decided. She'd managed to serve five males without having one panic attack and gotten four of them out of the house without incident. The fifth one, her new boss, would head into town soon, she hoped, to see a doctor.

Then she'd be able to start breathing again.

Had she lost her mind last night, agreeing to come here and be their housekeeper? No, she had been desperate. She knew she couldn't keep running. She'd dropped ten pounds in the last two and a half months, and her children had lost the sparkle in their eyes. Pine Creek was the end of the road for them, and six hundred dollars a week, plus room and board, was nothing to spit at.

Robbie MacBain, apparently, was as desperate as she was.

But Lord, did he have to be so handsome? Not only was he tall, but when she'd cleaned him up and sutured his wounds, Catherine had had plenty of time to notice how ruggedly male he was. And he had the most compelling gray eyes she'd ever seen. But more than his looks, the man emitted an aura that screamed testosterone. It was the way he comported himself. The way he *looked* at a person. He was staring straight into their souls when he turned those beautiful gray eyes on people. She could see it when he looked at one of his boys and could feel it when he looked at her.

Robbie MacBain was ten times the man Ronald Daniels was—ten times bigger and stronger and handsomer. And ten times more potentially dangerous.

Last night, he had offered her sanctuary. And he'd given his word that she would be safe in his house. Oh, she dearly wanted to believe him.

Catherine sighed, walked back out to the kitchen, and stared down at the empty plates, the spilled catsup, and the drying egg yolk on the tablecloth. Then she looked around.

Then she shuddered.

She had only peeked in the living room this morning, before anyone had gotten up, but that room had looked no better.

Robbie walked into the kitchen from outside, kicking the snow off his boots, and stopped when he saw her.

"Did we get much snow?" she asked, reminding herself to breathe, forcing herself to relax.

"Only about five inches." He pointed to the living room. "Your backpack is sitting beside the hearth, and everything's still in it. Nathan and Nora might want to take advantage of the caps and mittens and play in the snow today. It will probably be gone by tomorrow."

"Thank you. Are you headed to town to see a doctor?"

"No. I'm riding back up the mountain to see Father Daar."

"But you can't." Catherine advanced on him without thought. "You need to be checked out. Twenty-four hours ago, you were nearly dead."

He held up his hands, stopping her. "I'm fine, Cat. Still weak and a bit sore, but I'm mending just fine." He gave her a crooked grin. "You do good work."

Catherine realized that she had just scolded the man and immediately stepped back.

Robbie stepped closer. "About my little accident," he said. "I'd rather no one knows I got hurt. If anyone calls today, especially my father, introduce yourself as my new housekeeper, but let's keep how we met between you and me, okay? I don't want to worry my family."

Not knowing what to say, she simply nodded.

"The phone's likely to ring off the wall," he continued. "I run a large logging operation, and people are always calling here for something. You can either answer and take a message or let the machine do it."

"Okay," she said, turning and picking up several of the empty plates off the table.

"About Father Daar," Robbie said, drawing her attention again. "He's an old priest who lives halfway up the mountain. You'll probably be meeting him soon, since he likes to invite himself over for meals. Don't be surprised when he shows up."

"Okay."

He turned toward the door but stopped and looked back at her. "You did good this morning, Cat. With both the breakfast and with Peter. The boys need to know you can give as good as you get. They'll quickly come to respect you, and then you're home free."

"My—my name is Catherine."

He stared at her, the corner of his mouth kicked up in another grin, and slowly shook his head. "You're not even close to being a Catherine," he whispered. "You're a beautiful and fierce and agile mountain cat, so you might as well get used to the name."

Catherine had no clue how to respond to that, so she turned away, hiding her hotly blushing face, and started running water in the sink over the dishes.

"Catherine," he said, making her look at him again. "I meant every word last night. You have nothing to fear from me."

She didn't know how to respond to that, either.

He must have decided her cheeks were about to combust from embarrassment, because he finally walked out the door, closing it softly behind himself.

Catherine stared at the spot where he'd stood.

A mountain cat? Cat, not Catherine. Beautiful, he'd said. Fierce. Agile. She suddenly smiled. Being compared to a cat was a compliment, she decided. And she would give him agile, and she certainly wanted to be fierce. But beautiful?

Catherine snorted. She was about as pretty as a rag doll left in the weather for a month. He'd just added that part to score a few points.

He must really, really be desperate for a housekeeper.

Robbie stopped his horse in front of Daar's cabin and sat staring at the old priest standing on the porch, obviously waiting for him.

"What happened to our agreement that you'd go to my father if I didn't come back by sunrise?"

"But ya did come back," Daar said. "I heard the storm. And I looked everywhere for ya, until I went to your boys for help."

"I couldn't make it back to the place where I had landed."

Daar nodded. "I suspected as much. Ya needn't worry about that," he told him. "Even if you're a thousand miles away, you'll always return to TarStone. It's the mountain that pulls ya. So, are ya gonna sit there all day and scowl at me, or will ya come sit down and tell me what happened?"

Robbie stayed right where he was. "Mary's still there."

"Ya left her?" Daar asked, straightening away from the rail.

"She left me. She willed the storm to come, then flew off before I could catch her."

"But why?"

Robbie shook his head. "I couldn't tell what she was thinking. The energy must have interfered."

"Then ya must go back. Tonight."

"Nay," Robbie said, shaking his head again. "I'm too weak to survive the journey. I need a few days to heal."

"Heal from what?"

"Four MacBain warriors ambushed me on the third night."

Daar's eyes widened, and he suddenly cackled with laughter. "Old habits die hard for those bastards," he said, only to sober quickly. "So, the war your papa started is still going on?"

"It would seem so. There's no tree, priest. And no Cùram de Gairn, either."

Daar thumped his cane on the porch. "It's there! Ya just didn't look hard enough. I told ya Cùram was a tricky bastard."

"I scoured the forest for three days, and there's no large oak with any marks on it."

Daar scratched his beard with the butt of his cane. "He's disguised it," he whispered. "He knows I'm wanting a piece of the root, and he's cloaked it in a spell."

"He *knew* I was coming? And you couldn't have bothered to warn me?"

Daar held up his hand. "He knows nothing about ya, MacBain. He probably thinks I'd send back one of the old warriors and was most likely expecting Greylen." He stepped back up to the rail. "But if he discovers that you're my knight and that you're also a guardian, the game changes. He can't actually harm ya. It's forbidden."

"Apparently, my ancestors don't know that," Robbie drawled. "They had no qualms about trying to kill me."

"*Pfhaa,*" Daar sputtered, waving his hand in dismissal. "Those lawless MacBains couldn't kill a wounded pig if their lives depended on it."

Robbie canted his head. "Will you explain that to me?" he asked. "My father is a great warrior—and he's a MacBain."

Daar stared at him for several seconds, and Robbie could almost feel the *drùidh* trying to decide what to say. The old priest finally let out a sigh, folded his hands over the top of his cane, and leaned forward.

"I suppose ya need to know what you're up against. But ya must promise not to breathe a word of what I'm about to tell ya, Robbie," he said quietly. "It could cause a terrible upset."

He leaned closer and lowered his voice even more. "Greylen's mother, Judy MacKinnon, had an identical twin named Blair."

"That's my grandmother's name. Blair MacKinnon married my grandfather, Angus MacBain, and their first son was Michael."

"Aye," Daar said, nodding. "Blair is your grandmama, but ya have no blood ties to Angus. Blair came to their marriage already carrying Michael in her womb and passed him off as belonging to Angus."

Robbie shook his head. "Angus would have known he wasn't the first man Blair had been with and would have rejected her on their marriage night."

"Aye," Daar agreed, nodding. "But women have been fooling men about such things since the beginning of time." He shrugged. "It's survival that compels them, Robbie. Ya must remember that it was a time when such things mattered."

"Who is my real grandfather, then?"

"Duncan MacKeage."

"What? But he was married to Judy MacKinnon. Are you saying he fathered babes on both women? On sisters?"

Daar leaned over his crossed arms on the rail. "Judy died when Greylen was less than a year old, and Blair came to the MacKeage keep to tend her dead sister's child for Duncan. But she had already been promised to Angus MacBain by contract and stayed with the MacKeages for only a year before she finally did her duty and married Angus."

"But you say she went to Angus pregnant?"

"Aye. Judy and Blair were identical twins, and Duncan felt he was losing his young, beautiful wife all over again. The night before Blair was to leave, Duncan drank too much and ended up seducing her. It was a terrible thing to witness the next morning," Daar continued, gazing off into the forest. "Duncan was in a fine rage, either from guilt or want, I don't know which. He even threatened to go to Blair's father and claim her for himself."

"Then why didn't he?"

Daar straightened and focused back on Robbie. "If

Duncan had kept her, he would have started a war among all three clans. And so I persuaded him to let Blair go."

Robbie canted his head. "You had another reason for stopping the match. What was it?"

The old priest's face darkened. "Aye," he whispered. "I did. Identical twins were not welcome in that time, Robbie, and usually one or both of them was killed out of fear of the black magic. But Judy and Blair's mother refused to let that happen."

"Mothers had no say back then," Robbie pointed out. "Not when a husband thought otherwise."

"Aye, but even though they truly were identical, there was one tiny difference. Blair MacKinnon had six toes on each foot."

Robbie went perfectly still.

Daar nodded. "That's why you and Michael both have twelve toes. They're a gift from your grandmama and the only reason you were even born. Cara MacKinnon persuaded her husband to spare her daughters by claiming they weren't truly identical."

"And our gray eyes?"

Daar shrugged. "The twins had gray eyes."

"So what are you saying, priest? That my father and Greylen are brothers?"

"Aye. Half brothers, both fathered by Duncan from twin sisters."

Robbie shifted in his saddle. "So Greylen MacKeage really is my uncle," he whispered, staring at Daar. "It still doesn't change anything, though. Who slept with whom eight hundred years ago has nothing to do with Grey and my father now. Where's the danger in knowing they're brothers?"

"Cùram," Daar said succinctly. "If he ever learns Judy MacKinnon had an identical twin sister, he would be here before the thunder could finish shaking the ground."

"But why?"

"Think, Robbie. Two offspring from identical sisters and fathered by Duncan: Greylen and Michael. And *their* offspring—your seven cousins and your brother and two sisters. Winter MacKeage has already been promised as my successor, and only one *drùidh* can come from Judy MacKinnon. But that still leaves Michael's children."

"But my father didn't have seven daughters," Robbie pointed out. "He only had two."

"Aye. But the seven sequence is my continuum. Cùram's continuum is not so constrained."

Robbie ran both his hands over his face, scrubbing hard and thinking even harder. He suddenly stopped and looked up. "You're saying one of Michael MacBain's daughters, one of my sisters, could be Cùram's heir?"

Daar was shaking his head before Robbie could finish. "Not only your sisters," he said quietly. "It could be your brother. Or you."

"Then pray it's me, priest, so I will stop this madness!"

"Nay, Robbie," Daar whispered. "Pray that Cùram never finds out the truth about your papa. Going up against a *drùidh* as powerful as Cùram could destroy ya."

"Better than becoming one!"

"I beg your pardon," Daar said, straightening his shoulders and puffing out his chest. "Being a wizard is a noble profession. Your cousin Winter is blessed, not cursed."

"I want nothing from the magic, priest. I only want to protect my family."

"Aye, I know that, Robbie. And the best way you can do that is to keep our secret and get me the root of Cùram's oak tree."

"I couldn't find it," Robbie repeated. "Nor Cùram. None

of the MacKeage clan I spoke with had any knowledge of either a special tree or the *drùidh*."

"Ya didn't actually *ask* them, did ya?"

"Of course not!"

Daar nodded. "Good, then." He scratched his beard again, his gaze focused off in the distance. "Maybe Mary can find out something," he speculated. He looked at Robbie. "Maybe that's why she stayed behind. Meet me back on the summit at sunset in three days, and ya can give it another try. Oh, and one more thing," Daar said when Robbie started to turn his horse to leave. "Ya stay away from your stepmama. If Libby so much as touches ya, she'll know exactly how ya got hurt."

"I've already thought of that," Robbie told him. "And now I have a warning for you. We have a new housekeeper. So mind yourself around her, and don't scare her off."

Daar perked up. "The woman from West Shoulder Ridge?"

"Aye," Robbie said with a nod. "But for her I'd be dead now, and you'd be telling your sorry tale to the Highlanders."

"I will be most gracious when I come visit," Daar assured him. "Can she cook?"

"I imagine Cat can do anything she puts her mind to."

"Cat?" Daar repeated. "What kind of name is that?"

"It's my name for her," Robbie said, turning his horse away.

"MacBain!" Daar snapped, stopping him yet again.

"What?"

"Ya cannot be tempted by this woman," he warned. "I don't care if she did save your life, *our* problem comes first."

"I have my priorities straight," Robbie said. "Just make sure yours are." He walked his horse back up to the porch, causing the wizard to step back. "Because if I find out you're playing me in order to get your book of spells, or if I ever learn that you've lied about any of this, there won't be a place, or a time, where you'll be safe."

Daar gasped and took another step back until he was pressed up against the cabin wall. "When did ya find out?" he whispered. He shook his head. "It was the storm, wasn't it? Ya became aware of all your guardian powers while in the storm."

"Aye," Robbie growled, nodding. "Fully aware."

That said, Robbie pointed his horse down the mountain and decided to turn his thoughts to more pleasant things.

He wondered what Cat was cooking for supper.

The first thing Robbie did upon returning to the house was stop and take off his boots on the rug by the door. The second thing he did was tiptoe through the spotless kitchen to the downstairs bedroom and see his new house-keeper sound asleep, her arms thrown protectively over her children. The third thing he did was open the oven door and spend a full minute breathing in the smell of the pair of stuffed roasting chickens.

Then he ladled himself a steaming mug of the hot cocoa he found on the stove and went into the spotless living room.

And then he got mad.

The lady and her kids *should* be sleeping the sleep of the dead. They'd cleaned the downstairs of his house, every last nook and cranny of it, not a speck of dirt left unrouted. The damned woman must have worked herself and her kids to death. And that made him mad.

So Robbie sat in the living room, quietly simmering with anger, and listened to truck doors slam and four pair of boots bang onto the porch.

"Oh, shit, man! Hey, don't push."

"Then get out of the way. What are you doing standing in the door? Move!"

"It's blue."

"You're face is gonna be black and blue if you don't get out of the way."

"Don't go in there! Can't you see, you moron? The kitchen floor's clean. Take off your boots."

"Oh, shit! It *is* blue."

There was a sudden silence. Despite his anger, Robbie had to smile. He could almost picture the unbelieving faces standing in the kitchen door. Hell, even he had forgotten the damned floor was blue.

"Wow, look at this place. What's that smell?"

"Oh, God. It's roasted chicken. I know it is."

"It's awfully quiet in here. Do you suppose the little girl still takes a nap?"

"She's little and a girl, ain't she? So everybody keep quiet. Little girls need their sleep."

Somebody snorted. Four pair of boots dropped onto the rug.

"Ssshhhh!"

"Hell. Get a grip, you guys. You're gonna wake the women."

"Women? What makes you think Catherine is sleeping?"

"Wouldn't you be, dip-shit, if you had cleaned this place?"

And on and on it went, in whispers, until the four boys had come to grips with what they were seeing. They finally tiptoed into the living room, all sipping cups of hot cocoa, only to smile at Robbie.

"Wow, man. Did you see this place?" Rick asked.

"I saw," Robbie returned quietly, his anger reemerging. "And I am not pleased."

"Why the hell not? The house has never looked so good," Peter said.

"It shouldn't have gotten so dirty to begin with," Robbie pointed out. "Catherine Daniels is not our slave. I want all of us to pitch in from now on. Everybody picks up after himself, and everybody helps with the dishes, the vacuuming, and the laundry."

Everybody groaned.

"And if you guys are anywhere near intelligent, you won't run this one off. You will be nice and polite and helpful to her and her kids, and maybe we can all go on eating well. Or do you like bachelor life?" he asked.

Everybody heard the growl in his voice and nodded.

"We'll treat the lady like a queen. And we'll be nice to her kids, won't we?" Rick promised, giving each of the boys a warning glare.

"She doesn't seem so bad," Cody conceded. "Not like the other ones. Hell, the second lady couldn't even take a joke."

"It's hard to laugh when your girdle is flying from the flagpole," Rick accused, glaring at both Peter and Cody.

"I bet Catherine's underwear would be a sight prettier."

"Leave the lady alone," Gunter said softly.

Peter quickly nodded, his hands going up defensively.

"Catherine and her kids need to be here," Gunter continued, looking at each of the boys. "They were living in that old cabin, for chrissakes, and probably need this place more than we do. And be careful with the girl, Nora. Do any of you realize that she's barely spoken to any of us? And she only whispers to her mom and brother? Be nice to her."

Everybody nodded again. Robbie hid his smile. Well, hell. This was the first time he'd seen these guys agree on *anything* all at the same time. Had a miracle fallen into his lap or what?

"Oh, hi. You're back," Catherine mumbled as she walked into the living room, her eyes blinking with sleep.

Robbie sucked in his breath. She looked like an angel. Her hair was disheveled, and her cheeks were flushed. Her eyes were . . . well, sexy-looking. Robbie felt his insides clench, his anger turning to desire with the suddenness of an explosion.

Hell. If Catherine Daniels even caught a hint of what he was thinking, she'd run screaming back up the mountain to her hidey-hole—and he wouldn't be able to catch her this time, either.

"I—ah—dinner will be ready in two hours," she whispered, her cheeks flushing at the boys' undisguised gawking.

"I've changed my mind," Cody whispered. "I'll marry you."

Her blush deepened.

Robbie thought to intervene, but Gunter beat him to it.

"Ignore the moron, Catherine. The boy thinks with his taste buds, and chicken is his favorite," Gunter said. "And the house looks great. We really didn't know the kitchen floor was blue," he added, lightening the mood.

She gave him a thankful smile. "I was as surprised as you." But then she sobered and gave them each a tentative look. "I didn't get to the upstairs today," she confessed, not seeing Robbie's glare at that admission, since she was looking at the boys. "I didn't want to go into your bedrooms without permission, so I didn't get any laundry or make the beds. I wanted to speak with each of you first."

"You were respecting our privacy?" Rick asked.

Catherine nodded. "If you have clothes that need washing, just leave them in the hall if you don't want me going into your rooms. But if you want me to change your beds, put away your clean clothes, and vacuum and dust, then all you have to do is show me what's off limits and what's not."

"It's all off limits," Robbie said.

Catherine spun around, her eyes wide and confused. "What do you mean? I'm just trying to do my job."

Robbie stood up.

She took a step back.

"The boys will help with the housework. They will wash their own clothes, make their own beds, and do the vacuuming. They'll be responsible for keeping their bedrooms clean, and they'll help with the supper dishes."

Her chin rose throughout his speech, and she was scowling at him by the end of it. But as soon as she realized what she was doing and just how defiant she appeared, Robbie watched her instantly deflate. Then he saw her realize what she was doing again, and her shoulders squared and her chin rose—but just a little.

"Then what am I supposed to do?"

"Cook. Take care of your kids. Go for walks." He smiled. "And you can shop. You can be responsible for buying the food and anything else we need." Yeah. That was a good idea. He hated shopping. "You can handle that. Women love to shop."

If she hadn't been so wary of him, Robbie would swear that Cat was near to stomping her foot in frustration.

"But we can't figure out the washing machine," Peter said. "It's possessed by demons."

"I can show you," Cat quickly offered, turning away from Robbie, probably before she said something she'd be sorry for. She turned back to Robbie. "But the bathrooms," she said with a shudder. "I want to be in charge of the bathrooms."

"Why would anyone volunteer for that?" Cody asked.

"Because I have this thing about clean bathrooms. And

keeping them sanitary is sort of an art." That said, she turned back to Robbie, folded her arms under her breasts, raised her chin as high as she dared, and waited.

Robbie curtly nodded agreement, then left her standing in the living room with four incredulous boys staring at her.

If the lady had a thing for bathrooms, who was he to argue?

Chapter Eight

It was *Saturday morning,* day two of her new house-keeping job, and Catherine was in the chicken coop with her children. The four boys were in the house, cleaning their bedrooms and trying to master the art of vacuuming.

Her boss was in the huge garage with several men from his logging crew, examining the tree harvester they'd trucked in late last night. The gigantic machine was broken, and Catherine had learned it was one of three that Robbie owned and would leave several of his men idle until it was fixed.

She had also learned that all four boys worked in the logging operation at least ten hours a week, doing various jobs. Peter, being only fifteen, was responsible for keeping track of the maintenance records for all the machinery. Cody and Rick did some of the maintenance, changing oil and air filters and keeping the equipment clean. Gunter actually ran some of the equipment, often working right beside the loggers.

Robbie had told her he wanted to nudge the boys in the

right direction, and it seemed his logging operation was his means to that end. Catherine decided she had to admire anyone who took on the task of guiding four wayward boys into manhood.

Actually, there were a lot of things she was coming to admire about Robbie MacBain. The man seemed to have the patience and disposition of a saint. At the supper table last night, and without accusation or condescension, Robbie had told Cody he had to spend this Sunday cleaning John Mead's skidder, which Catherine had learned was a large machine that dragged trees out of the forest. Apparently, Cody and a few of his friends had shot something called a potato gun at the skidder, smearing it with potato pulp. Catherine guessed it would be an unpleasant job, considering the potatoes had had four days to dry.

Cody had taken his punishment rather well. Nathan had certainly been impressed, with both the potato gun and Cody's promise to show him how to shoot it. Catherine's first instinct had been to forbid Nathan to go anywhere near anything called a gun. Robbie had read her reaction and spoken up before she could, promising her a potato gun was just the thing for an eight-year-old boy to experience. And for some reason that she couldn't quite understand, Catherine found herself trusting Robbie's judgment when it came to dealing with young males.

Catherine brought her thoughts back to the task at hand and urged Nathan and Nora further into the henhouse. "Don't make any sudden moves, and talk softly when you're working in here," she told her round-eyed children as she peeled Nora off her leg.

"You have to make sure they always have clean water and plenty of food." She smiled encouragement. "And for a reward, these little ladies will give us plenty of eggs."

"Do they bite?" Nathan whispered.

"No. But they may try to peck you. Just ignore them, and they'll leave you alone."

"Will they be mad at us for stealing their eggs?" Nora asked, clinging to Catherine's leg again. "Aren't eggs their babies?"

"No, sweetie. There's no rooster here, so the eggs can't turn into chicks. And the hens won't mind us taking them."

"Do we have to do this?" Nathan asked with a groan.

"Yes. You need chores of your own. We live here now, so we all have to do our part. Everybody works."

"I made our bed this morning," Nora boasted.

And a sorrier bed she'd never seen, Catherine thought. "And you did a wonderful job. But you have to let go of my leg, sweetie," she said, peeling her off her again. "And come see the nests. This is where you'll find the eggs. Your job will be to bring the basket down every evening and gather them up."

She turned to her son, only to have to pull him back into the henhouse, as he'd slowly been inching his way outside. "Nathan, you keep their water bucket and grain feeder filled. And when the grain gets low, tell Mr. MacBain, and he'll buy some more."

Nathan's eyes rounded. "Can't I tell *you,* then you can tell Mr. MacBain?"

"No," Catherine said firmly, her heart breaking at the sight of his pale face. "That's part of your job. Mr. MacBain is the boss, and everyone goes to him when they need something."

"But he's big," Nathan whispered.

"Yes, he is," she agreed. "Most men are. Gunter's big. Cody and Peter and Rick are big. And Nathan, when you grow up, you'll be big, too." Catherine hunched down and looked her son square in the eye, then pulled Nora closer.

"You know I wouldn't stay here if it wasn't right for us. Try to look at Mr. MacBain and the boys as protectors, like guardian angels."

"I like Gunter," Nora confessed shyly. "He was nice to me when I was scared of the horse the other night."

"I like Gunter, too," Catherine said, giving her a squeeze.

Yes, the softly spoken Gunter had taken Nora onto his lap and wrapped his coat around her for the ride down the mountain two nights ago.

"Mommy, look! There's some eggs already!" Nora squealed, which caused several panicked hens to flap wildly.

Which finally caused Nathan to bolt out the door. He ran into the legs of a tall, masculine body. "M-Mr. MacBain."

"Good morning, Nathan. Getting henhouse-raiding lessons from your mom?"

"I—we—I was just going to get the hens some water, sir."

"Maybe you should take the bucket with you."

His face flushed scarlet, Nathan bravely ventured back into the henhouse and picked up the water bucket. Keeping his head down, he quickly moved around Robbie and ran to the house.

"I'm collecting eggs," Nora piped up, feeling proud of herself and her two oval prizes. She was also feeling safe behind her mother's legs. "It's my new job."

With an indulgent smile, Robbie nodded to the girl and then turned his questioning, smiling eyes on Catherine.

"I want my kids to have their own chores," she told him, her own face reddening. "And chickens are a good place to begin. I thought you wouldn't mind."

Robbie nodded, looking as if he couldn't decide if he dared to laugh or not. Which brought the heat up another notch in Catherine's cheeks. "Is it okay?"

"You're their mother. If you want to give them chores,

then by all means do." He canted his head. "You up to a trip into town?"

"To shop?" she asked. "As in what women do best?"

Robbie MacBain at least had the grace to wince. "I guess that was a pretty sexist remark, wasn't it? But I truly do hate to shop," he confessed by way of apology. He straightened from the door and let her out, along with Nora, who was clutching her two eggs to her chest. "I have to go pick up a well pump," he continued, walking beside them. "I can drop you off at the market and then pick you up when I'm done. How would that be?"

"Just let me get Nathan and Nora ready," she agreed, moving swiftly away from him, hoping it would help her breathe normally again. Good God, the man really was big.

"Ah . . . about the kids. Would you be willing to leave them here?" he asked.

Catherine spun around and stared up at him. She bit her lip and pondered. She didn't want to, but she and her children *had* been living in one another's pockets for the last two and a half months. Nathan and Nora were fast becoming clinging vines. Finally, she nodded.

"They'll be fine here, Cat. Gunter and Rick will keep an eye on them. They'll be safe."

She nodded again, having nothing else to say. Holding on to Nora's shoulder, Catherine led the silent girl back to the house to put her eggs away. Then she would start to snip some of those vines tying her family together. Her kids weren't going to like it any more than she did, but they were safer here than they had been on the mountain when she'd gone to get food. They would survive.

And, she hoped, so would she.

Condoms?

Somebody had put condoms on the list, just below a

request for a three-bladed razor. Condoms. That was all. Nothing was written beside it—not what kind or how many.

Catherine's face burned beneath the fluorescent lights of the supermarket. Already her cart was full of shaving cream, razors, deodorant, and athlete's foot medicine. Now it appeared she was also expected to buy rubbers.

There were several different handwritings on the list, obviously put there by several different boys in need. So who needed condoms? She had seen Robbie adding to the list. Did the man expect his housekeeper to buy his sexual aids? And how many? Three? A dozen? *A gross?*

Catherine kept her eyes on her cart, willing her face to cool, and made her way over to the aisle of personal stuff. She found what she was looking for right next to the feminine douche and panty shields. Well, darn it. She was a mature, twenty-nine-year-old woman. She could do this. She only wished she knew who she was buying them for. Did Robbie have a girlfriend? She snorted. Of course he did. He was handsome, wasn't he? All handsome men had girlfriends.

Did he think she was going to be one of them? Not in this lifetime. She'd sworn off men three years ago. She'd been lying in the hospital at the time, but she'd still had enough sense to make a vow against the entire adult male population.

Looking up and down the aisle, then finally back at the display, Catherine began to read. Lord, what a variety. Plain ones, gold ones, and ribbed ones in various sizes. Heck, there were even some that glowed in the dark! Looking up and down the aisle again, she finally grabbed a package of each. Then she smiled, grabbed two packs of the ones that glowed in the dark, and wished she could be a fly on the wall when the person asking for condoms claimed his *necessities.*

She quickly rearranged her cart to conceal her purchases and headed to the front of the store, determined to get through the checkout without blushing herself to a sunburn.

As the many different cans of shaving cream went down the conveyor belt, followed by the many different deodorants, followed by the condoms, the lady running the register widened her eyes with each purchase. The condoms finally caused the woman to look up and raise an eyebrow. "Having a pajama party?"

Cat raised her chin. "Want to be invited?"

The grandmotherly woman sniffed and went back to checking items—until the truck pulled up in front of the store, nose in. That was when the woman looked from Catherine to the truck, then back at Catherine. Her eyebrow rose again.

Catherine looked for a giant hole to crawl into. The bug shield on the truck sported bold lettering that said "FOUR PLAY."

Catherine had seen the moniker when she'd climbed into the truck this morning. Lots of people lettered their bug shields, and the truck *was* a four-wheel drive, so the wording made sense. But it made a different kind of sense when a person considered that the large Suburban belonged to a bachelor.

Robbie walked into the grocery store, his hat pulled low over his eyes against the sun, and found his housekeeper standing at the cash register, her face scorching red. He approached the checkout in time to see the grocery boy toss several familiar-looking packets into a bag as the youth asked Cat, "That your ride, lady?" nodding his head toward the door.

Robbie turned and looked at his truck. And then it

dawned on him. Red face. Small packets. "FOUR PLAY." Catherine Daniels was mortified. He was in trouble.

Pulling his hat lower to hide his own flush and barely able to control an urge to laugh, Robbie grabbed four of the bags and took them out to the truck. He came back through the door just in time to see Cat hand the check he'd given her to the cashier.

"Robert MacBain," the lady read. She looked at Cat. "You staying out there?"

"I'm . . . ah . . . I'm the housekeeper," Cat whispered.

He should have checked the list this morning. Dammit, Catherine Daniels was going to quit just as soon as she got in the truck. First she was going to give him hell for contributing to the delinquency of minors, and then she was going to quit.

But she *had* bought the condoms.

Robbie grabbed the remaining three bags, only to have the contents of one spill out. Good God! Glow-in-the-dark rubbers! His shoulders started to shake.

His blushing housekeeper bent down, picked up the packets, and stuffed them in her pocket. Muttering something that sounded rather nasty, she ran from the store.

Robbie took his time placing the bags in the back of the Suburban, all the while willing his shoulders to quit shaking. Lord, what a picture. Catherine Daniels was sitting in the front seat, facing forward, her hands on her cheeks. He finally found the courage to get in the truck and, without saying a word, backed it away from the curb and headed out of town.

It was a six-mile, silent ride home.

Was she going to quit?

Would he let her?

Her two kids were sitting on the porch when they

returned, and Robbie drove up to the back door, then went in search of the boys to unload the groceries.

And as soon as they were done, he would have a little talk with them about condoms and women and embarrassing situations. And then he was going to turn around and leave without asking which one had added them to the list.

"There's an old man inside," Nathan whispered, taking Catherine's hand as they walked into the house.

"And he's got a really fluffy beard," Nora added. "And he said my eyes was pretty, just like twinkling stars."

"I hope you thanked him for the compliment," Catherine said, stopping inside the doorway and bending down to untie Nora's laces.

"I complimented him back," Nora boasted as she held on to her mother's shoulder and kicked off her boots. "I told him his eyes was all wrinkled at the edges."

Catherine looked up, horrified, but had to move aside without correcting her daughter so that Robbie could come in.

"You have company," she told him. "An elderly gentleman."

"Aye. Gunter told me he was here. It's my uncle, Ian MacKeage," he explained, glancing toward the living room as he shed his own boots. "The boys will unload the groceries in a few minutes. Do you have any of that pie left from last night?"

"One piece." Catherine handed her children the coloring books and crayons she had bought them, urged them toward their bedroom, and walked over to the counter. "I'll make a fresh pot of coffee."

But before she could grab the pot, Robbie took hold of her arm to lead her into the living room. Catherine broke free with a gasp and took several steps back.

"I'm sorry," he said, tucking his hands behind his back. "I would like to introduce you to Ian," he continued, dismissing the incident as if it never happened. As if she hadn't overreacted.

"He lives just over the ridge," he continued, nodding toward the sink window. "My four uncles own the TarStone Mountain Ski Resort. The lights you see at night are the ski trails."

Thoroughly disgusted with herself and hoping her face wasn't flaming red, Catherine ducked her head and scooted past him into the living room. She came to a stop when the elderly, barrel-chested, wild-haired man rose from a chair by the hearth.

"Ian," Robbie said, walking over to him, "this is our new housekeeper, Cat Daniels. Cat," he said, smiling at her frown for not introducing her as Catherine, "this is Ian MacKeage, my uncle. Don't believe anything he tells you about me."

"And I have tales that would curdle your blood, lass," Ian said, holding out his hand to her.

Catherine walked over and watched her hand completely disappear as Ian's large, blunt fingers gently wrapped around hers. "It's nice to meet you, Mr. MacKeage. I believe you've already met my children, Nathan and Nora?" she asked, about to apologize for her daughter's wonderful *compliment*.

Ian beat her to it. "The wee one's a bonny lass," he said with a chuckle, still holding her hand. "Candid, too. And your boy's one to be proud of."

"Th-thank you. Would you like some coffee and a piece of pie? It's cherries from a can, but the crust is homemade."

"Thank you, but no," Ian said, finally releasing her and turning to Robbie. "I'm just out for my daily walk and was hoping I could talk this boy into accompanying me back."

"You needn't be afraid of bears, Uncle," Robbie drawled, his eyes shining with warmth. "They don't much care for tough old hides like yours."

Ian snorted. "They're more worried I'll eat *them*." He turned to Catherine. "Nice to meet you, Cat," he said, heading for the kitchen. "I hope ya know what a mess you've gotten yourself into here," he added over his shoulder as he reached the coat pegs by the door. "I could find ya a big stick if you're wanting one," he offered, shrugging into his coat and turning to face her as he buttoned it up. His smile was quite visible through his bushy beard, and his eyes really did wrinkle at the corners. "Nothing like a good smack with a stout stick to get your point across."

"Ah . . . thank you," Catherine whispered, not knowing how else to respond. "But disciplining the boys is Robbie's department. I'm just the housekeeper."

"It wasn't the boys I was referring to," Ian said over his shoulder as he walked out the door. "Come on, young Robbie. At my pace, it'll be dark before I get home."

Catherine stood at the window of the closed kitchen door and watched the two men slowly make their way across the yard and disappear into the woods. The house was unusually quiet but for the steady, comforting tick of the grandfather clock in the corner and the occasional giggles of her two children coming from the bedroom.

When was the last time she'd heard them giggle?

She liked it here, Catherine suddenly decided. Large males and condoms notwithstanding, this wonderful old house had an almost palpable sense of security—four boys and one determined man, and an apparent extended family, bound by the common goal of living each day with hope.

Catherine wanted to hope. Nathan and Nora could thrive here, and with a bit of encouragement, they could not only learn to trust again but look ahead instead of over their shoulders.

And maybe she could, too. She would start with Robbie MacBain. The next time he touched her, even if it killed her to do so, she would not panic and pull away. She couldn't very well expect her children to be brave if she couldn't even control her own reactions to a simple, innocent touch from a man.

Ronald Daniels would not win.

It was just as she told her kids. They had five guardian angels, and now the offer of a stout stick, to back them up.

Chapter Nine

Robbie held the low-hanging branch out of his uncle's way, thinking he should have the boys trim back the edges of the overgrown tote road running between his home and the ski resort. Ian leaned on the stick he'd left in the forest so no one would see him using a cane to steady his eighty-five-year-old legs. Robbie hid his smile and tucked his hands behind his back, matching his stride to that of the old warrior's.

They walked in companionable silence up the gently rising road for several minutes, until Robbie quietly asked, "What's on your mind, Uncle?"

"Death."

"Death in general or of someone in particular?"

Ian looked at him from the corner of his eye. "My own. Thinking about one's mortality is an everyday event at my age."

"I imagine it is."

"I don't want to die here, Robbie."

"I don't think you have a choice, Uncle. None of us does."

The old man stopped and canted his head. "It's not death I'm thinking to avoid but the place. I've a wish to see my children before I die. And I'm needing to wrap my arms around my wife and bury my face in her bosom. I miss the smell of the village fires, the heather in the fields, and the clanking swords of sparring warriors. I want to go home, Robbie," he whispered. "And I want ya to take me."

"I can't do that, Uncle."

"Aye, ya can," he softly contradicted. "Ya was given the task of watching over Daar for us, not because you're the eldest but because you're our guardian. And I'm thinking ya have the ability to grant my request."

"Have you spoken with Grey about your wanting to go back?" Robbie asked, neither affirming nor denying Ian's claim.

"Nay. Only you."

"What about Kate? The two of you have been companions for over twenty years now. Are you willing to leave her?"

"It was Kate who gave me the courage to finally ask ya," Ian said with a nod. "She's always known my heart belongs to my wife, and she's been after me for some time now to find a way to get back to Gwyneth. We've had a good friendship, and I care a great deal for Kate," he added. "She'll not only understand, she'll be happy for me."

"And the rest of us?"

"You will be happy for me, too. Grey and Morgan and Callum and your papa have wives and children and grandbabies now. Their home is here, and mine is back there. That's why Kate kept encouraging me to go speak with Daar." Ian laid his hand on Robbie's arm. "But I'd rather bring my matter to ya. It's you I trust."

Robbie led Ian to the edge of the road, and they both sat down on a fallen log. "But the journey itself could kill you,

Uncle. Surely you remember how violent it was thirty-five years ago."

Ian's face paled. "You've been," he whispered. "You've already traveled back, haven't ya?"

Robbie said nothing.

"It was three nights ago, wasn't it?" Ian speculated, taking hold of Robbie's arm again. "I heard the thunder and felt the entire mountain shake. And the next morning, I heard it again."

He pointed at Robbie's waist. "That gash on your side. It was made by a sword, I would bet. Ya went back and nearly got yourself killed."

"What makes you say that?"

"The little lass, Nora. She told me they found ya lying in the woods, and that they thought ya was dead. She said her mother used thread from her kit to sew up a cut in your side." He pointed at Robbie's face. "Ya didn't get that bruise on your cheek from bumping into a door, and ya didn't go to Libby so she could heal ya, because she would realize how ya got hurt."

Robbie sighed and stared across the road at nothing. "They mustn't find out," he finally said, looking back at Ian. "Grey and Callum and Morgan and my father—they can't know about this. Did Grey hear the storm?"

"Nay," Ian said, shaking his head. "He and Grace are down visiting Elizabeth at college. And the others live too far away to have heard it."

Robbie nodded. "Then please don't tell them."

"What are you and that crazy priest up to?"

"It's . . . complicated. I went back to try to get a new book of spells for Daar."

"*What?* Ya know how dangerous it will be for us if that old fool gets his hands on the spells."

"But if he doesn't," Robbie quietly explained, "then your

wish will be granted on this summer's solstice. But you won't be going back alone."

Ian went utterly still, his face turning pale again around his widened hazel eyes. "All of us?" he whispered.

"Aye," Robbie gently returned. "In three months, if Daar can't extend the original spell that brought you here, all five of you will go back."

Ian looked away, saying nothing.

"I won't let it happen, Uncle."

Ian looked back at him. "I can help," he said, squaring his age-stooped shoulders. "I'm old, but I ain't dead yet. I can't wield a sword anymore, but I know that time, the people, and the land. I can help," he repeated with a growl, grabbing Robbie's arm again. "Take me back with ya."

Robbie gently pulled Ian's hand free and held it in his. "I saw Gwyneth," he quietly told him. "When I went back, it was ten years after you had left. She never remarried and lives with your daughter, Caitlin." He smiled. "Caitlin is married to a fine warrior, and she has three bairns."

A huge grin spread through Ian's beard, and he squeezed Robbie's hand. "How did my Gwyneth look?"

"Beautiful," Robbie whispered. "And very busy spoiling your grandbabies."

"Did ya actually speak to her?"

"Aye. I told her I was a distant relative, and had been away for several years, when she wondered why she didn't know me. She fed me and spoke of her husband, asking if I remembered Ian MacKeage."

"What did ya say?"

"I said I remembered a giant, ill-tempered, wild-eyed warrior who scared little children when he walked by."

Ian snorted and pulled away, clasped his hands together, and looked up at Robbie with eyes far more shining than wild. "And Niall?" he asked. "Did you see my son?"

"He's Laird Niall now."

"No!" Ian grabbed his chest. "But how can that be?"

Robbie shrugged. "He was elected, I gather, a few months after Greylen disappeared. You're all legends, Uncle. Grey and Morgan and Callum and you, you've all become the talk of the campfire."

"And Megan and James? How are they?"

"Megan married a Maclerie warrior and has five bairns, Gwyneth told me." He took hold of Ian's hand. "And James died three years after you left, in a hunting accident. I'm sorry, Uncle."

"It was hard times back then," Ian said, turning away and swiping at his eyes. "The cost of mistakes was high." He turned back to Robbie, his sad eyes looking worried. "What would happen if I suddenly showed up? How would I explain where I've been?"

"With the boldest lie we can think of," Robbie suggested. He stood up and helped Ian off the log. "Not that I'm saying you *can* go back. I need to think about the ramifications," he explained as they started walking again.

"What ramifications?"

"We would have to come up with a good lie for this time as well. Men can't just disappear. People would investigate."

"You only have to say that I returned to Scotland. Ya don't have to mention what *time* I returned to."

"Aye. That would work. But there's still the storm and your age to consider." He stopped and turned to him. "There's a good chance you might not survive."

"Then I die trying." Ian gathered the front of Robbie's jacket in his fists. "Give me the dignity to go down fighting, Robbie. Give me the gift of seeing my wife again."

Robbie covered Ian's hands with his own. "I understand your want," he told him, pleased by the spark in Ian's eyes. "But it's not really my decision to make. It's ultimately yours." Robbie took a shuddering, painful breath. "And if you truly wish to go home, then I will be honored to help you get there."

He leaned over and kissed Ian on his bearded cheek, then wrapped his arms around him in a gentle hug. "In one week, Uncle, I'll take you back," he whispered near his ear, closing his eyes against the sting of his imminent loss. "Spend these next days making peace with all who love you. But remember, you can't tell them you're going. They mustn't know what I'm doing, for their own sakes."

Ian hugged him back and stepped away with a firm nod of agreement, then turned, brushing at his face as he started for home again.

Robbie silently fell into step beside him.

Aye. Every warrior deserved to die trying. And with a boon from providence, Ian would again bury his face in his wife's bosom before that happened.

It was late Sunday evening, and Catherine was sitting in a chair by the hearth, sewing the ripped pocket of a shirt. She realized now that she should have set out a larger box when she'd asked if anyone had any clothes that needed mending. The cardboard box she'd tossed down on the living-room floor, with Nathan's crayon letters spelling out "MENDING," was overflowing.

She should have known, having an eight-year-old male of her own, how hard boys were on their clothes. Multiply that by four—no, five, as she'd seen Robbie sneak a shirt into the pile—and the task could be daunting.

But it was a task she welcomed. For Catherine, sewing was not only a stress reliever, it was also her greatest joy.

Back in Arkansas, she had taken in sewing to earn extra money. Being a janitor at the local high school had paid well enough, but making wedding dresses and prom gowns of her own creation had paid even better. She'd almost been ready to quit her day job and become a seamstress full-time when the letter about Ron's release had come in the mail.

She had missed sewing these last couple of months, Catherine realized as she carefully made the small invisible stitches on the pocket of Rick's shirt.

Nathan and Nora were already sound asleep. So was Cody. The boy had come dragging in around five, eaten supper without much conversation, and climbed the stairs and fallen into bed without even asking what was for dessert. Catherine would bet he'd think twice about where he aimed his potato gun in the future.

Gunter and Rick were out in the machine shop helping the mechanic dismantle the tree harvester. Peter was sitting at the kitchen table doing homework—sighing, erasing, and occasionally cursing.

Robbie walked into the living room just then, a bowl overflowing with apple cobbler and ice cream in his hand, a spoon in his mouth, and a cup of hot cocoa in his other hand. He sat down on the couch facing the fire, set his cocoa on the side table, pulled the spoon from his mouth, and smiled at her.

Catherine was proud of herself. In only four days, she had learned how to breathe normally around the huge man. Now she only had to learn how to stop staring at him.

"You have to be careful what you wish for around here," he said, using his spoon to point at the box by her feet. "You're liable to be rewarded in spades."

In an attempt to look relaxed and not at all bothered by

his being so close, Catherine shrugged and smiled back. "I don't mind. I'm really a seamstress by trade."

He lifted a brow. "Really? What do you sew?"

"Dresses, mostly. For weddings and proms and other special events."

"That sounds complicated," he said, digging into his ice cream. "I remember Maggie's wedding dress. Or rather," he said with a snort, "I remember the weeks of deciding which pattern was the *right* one and then finding someone to make it."

"Is Maggie your sister?"

"Aye. She just had a baby last month. They named the lass Aubrey," he added, popping the spoonful of ice cream and cobbler into his mouth.

"Aubrey's a beautiful name," Catherine whispered, looking back at her sewing when she realized she was forgetting to breathe again.

Robbie MacBain certainly scared her, though she thought it wasn't because he was a man but because he was such a *handsome* man. She had thought her libido was long dead, but darn if it hadn't been showing signs of stirring lately. It couldn't be because she had cleaned him up and could still picture his hard muscles, long sculpted legs, broad shoulders, powerful chest, and amazingly taut stomach. No, she didn't care one whit about that kind of stuff. It must be the fire in the hearth heating her cheeks.

"I'd like to talk to you about Nathan and Nora," Robbie said, again digging his spoon into his second bowl of tonight's dessert.

Catherine looked up. "What about them?"

"They should be in school."

She immediately shook her head. "No. Ron still has too many connections in law enforcement, and he could trace us if I tried to register them. I've been careful not to leave any paper trails. School is out of the question."

He canted his head at her. "What do you think will happen if he does find you?"

"I—I don't know, exactly," she admitted. "And I don't care to find out."

"He doesn't have custody of Nathan and Nora, and you are legally divorced. What would he want from you, Cat?"

"Revenge," she whispered.

"For?"

"For spending three years in prison."

"Ah," he rumbled, nodding his head. "You mentioned he was in prison for domestic abuse. Against you or against your children?"

"Me."

"So you're saying he beat you up, you pressed charges, and he was imprisoned, and now you feel that for him, revenge is worth the risk of going back to jail?"

"Why else would he be following us?"

"Maybe to see his children?"

Catherine shook her head. "Possibly Nathan but definitely not Nora. Ron only paid attention to his son, and then it was only to teach him how to be a *man.*"

"Will you tell me exactly what put him in prison?"

Catherine ducked her head and started sewing again.

"I've given you my word that you're safe here, Cat. Even if Ron does find you, there's not a damn thing he can do to you. But I need to know what I'm up against. What he's capable of."

She looked up. "It's not your responsibility to protect us."

"Aye, it is," he said, setting his half-eaten dessert on the table and leaning forward to rest his elbows on his knees and clasp his hands together. "I'm sorely tired of going through housekeepers," he said with a crooked grin. "And since you seem more than able to handle the boys and you cook like a five-star chef, I have no intention of losing you. Who is your ex-husband?"

Catherine took a deep, shuddering breath. It had been ten years since she had dared to trust anyone, since her parents had died and Ron had strode into her life and swept her off her young, naive feet with the promise of taking care of her. But didn't her new boss deserve to understand why she was so frightened? And why she was so sure Ron would come after her?

"He's a monster," she quietly told him. "He has a terrible temper, and he expects his children to be perfect, automated robots—quiet, obedient, respectful, disciplined. You've seen them around people; they're scared of their own shadow. Nora was still quite young when Ron went to prison," she continued. "But Nathan," she softly hissed. "In order to win his father's approval, he was beginning to act just like him."

"Why did you stay with him?"

"I tried to leave several times," she said, looking down at her sewing. "But Ron was a well-respected, decorated police officer, and no matter who I went to for help, he always convinced them he was a model husband and father. But the day I saw Nathan slap Nora," she told him, looking back up, "I knew I had to do something drastic, so there wouldn't be any question what kind of man Ron really was."

"What did you do?"

She lifted her chin. "I set him up. I made sure I had witnesses I trusted, I sent my children to a friend's house, and I waited until Ron got home from work."

"And then?"

"I calmly told him I had found a judge willing to give

me a restraining order against him and that he had to move out that night."

Catherine flinched when Robbie suddenly stood up and walked to the hearth, grabbed the poker, and started prodding the fire. She took another deep breath and continued, deciding that he had started this, he could darn well hear the whole of it.

"Ron reacted just as I expected. But the police didn't arrive until he had almost killed me."

"And your witnesses?" he asked in a harsh whisper, staring down at the fire, his arm resting on the mantel and his fist clenched around the poker. "Where were they while you were fighting for your life?"

"They tried to intervene. Ron broke Jeff's nose, and Angela, Jeff's wife, got a concussion." She grinned at Robbie, even though he wasn't looking at her. "They were more than happy to testify at Ron's trial."

"Okay," he said, finally looking at her. "Ron got sentenced to five years in prison, you got a divorce, and he was paroled three years later," he summarized. "And now you're here with your children, looking over your shoulder for your ex-husband."

He started toward her but stopped the moment he saw her stiffen. He walked over to the couch and sat down, his elbows on his knees again and his hands clasped tightly as he leaned toward her. "I admit I had doubts about your revenge theory, but I don't anymore."

"Thank you."

"But you can't keep running, Cat. For how long? Another year? A lifetime? When does it stop?"

"When Nathan and Nora are old enough to take care of themselves."

"That's years away, Catherine. Hiding requires a great deal of energy, and the toll it takes on a person is enormous." He leaned even closer. "The three of you will be insane by then."

"Then what do you suggest I do? Wave a white flag and tell Ron, 'Here we are, come get us'?"

He smiled, leaned back, and picked up his dessert. "Aye," he said, digging his spoon into the ice cream. "That would work. Or you could simply negate the power he holds over you by living your life as if Ron Daniels doesn't exist."

It was anger heating Catherine's cheeks now. "How simple it is for you to give me advice. You have no idea what it's like to be helpless, and no idea what kind of monster Ron is."

He ate his mouthful of ice cream and cobbler, staring at her with unreadable eyes. He swallowed, sat forward again, and smiled. "Aye, but I do, Catherine," he said softly. "I've dealt with more than one Ron Daniels in my lifetime. Bullies can only bully those who let them. When stood up to, they back down more often than fight."

"I tried that already," she snapped, getting so mad she could actually feel the blood rushing to her head. "And it only bought me three years."

"Aye," he agreed with a nod. "So maybe it's time you found another way to defeat your demon."

Catherine tossed her sewing in the box and stood up, her fists clenched at her sides so she wouldn't strangle the man. "*Defeat him!* I don't have one-tenth of Ron's strength."

"But I do," he said calmly.

"We are not your responsibility!"

Robbie also stood up. Catherine was so mad that not only didn't she step away, but she actually stepped closer.

Robbie tucked his hands behind his back. "Anyone living in my house, or anyone working for me, is my responsibility," he said with quiet authority. "Should it be one of the boys, you or Nathan or Nora, or one of my loggers, I have their backs. My parents, siblings, aunts, uncles, cousins, and Father Daar—they are all under my protection."

Catherine snorted. "When were you elected king of the world? Nobody takes on that kind of responsibility. It just isn't done, because no one person can handle it. Besides," she said, stepping even closer, "people need to be responsible for themselves. Otherwise, what's the point?"

"We are all sitting in the same boat, Catherine, rowing toward the same horizon. Without helping each other, none of us would get there."

"Then who helps you?"

"What?"

"Who has your back?"

He looked so confounded that Catherine's anger suddenly disappeared. Robbie MacBain obviously didn't think he needed anyone watching his back.

"That's not how it works. What would I need protection from?"

"From yourself?" she ventured. "From taking on so much responsibility that *you're* the one who will be insane in a few years? Why did you take in the boys?"

That question seemed to startle him even more. "Because they had nowhere else to go, other than a detention center."

"But why you?"

He shook his head as if to clear it. "This conversation is not about me," he whispered. "It's about Nathan and Nora going to school."

"I *want* them to go."

"Then trust me enough to take a stand here, in Pine Creek, on my turf."

"I—I'll think about it," she whispered, turning and

walking around the couch toward the kitchen, her knees shaking from the roller-coaster ride of emotions.

"Catherine?"

"Yes?"

"My cousin Sarah MacKeage teaches at our elementary school. I can arrange for us to take Nathan and Nora in tomorrow, so the three of you can look things over."

He wasn't going to give up, she realized. "Don't think I'm not on to you, Mr. MacBain," she told him, shaking her head. "I know why you're doing this."

"And why is that?"

She pointed at the melting remains of his second helping of dessert on the side table. "None of you has quit eating since I got here. You want my kids enrolled in school so I'll feel committed to stay on as your housekeeper."

He crossed his arms over his chest and narrowed his eyes. "You're a suspicious woman, Cat," he whispered.

"Aye," she said, feeling brave enough to mimic his brogue because of the distance between them. "And smart, too."

He let out a bark of laughter and turned and picked up his dessert. "Good night, little Cat," he said, sitting back down in front of the fire. "Sweet dreams."

Catherine turned and closed the book Peter had left on the table, then sauntered into her bedroom feeling quite proud of herself. She had just stood toe-to-toe with a giant and had managed to come away without a scratch. This taking a stand thing might not be such a bad idea after all.

Chapter Ten

Catherine woke up to the sound of whispering coming from the kitchen. She squinted at the clock by her bed and saw it was only four o'clock, still hours before sunrise.

She heard a soft, feminine giggle and quickly looked over to see that Nora was still in bed, still sound asleep.

So who was in the kitchen? She recognized Robbie's voice, low and even-toned, whispering something about a she-devil, which was quickly followed by another quiet giggle.

Robbie had snuck a woman into the house!

Catherine could smell coffee. He'd made a pot of coffee, and now they were sharing a cup before he snuck her back out.

Of all the nerve. It was one thing to have a girlfriend, but to bring her home with four teenage boys sleeping just down the hall was irresponsible.

So, the condoms were his. The man had a lot of brass to ask his housekeeper to buy his birth control and then use it in the bedroom right above hers. The more she thought about Robbie's indiscretion, the madder Catherine got. She was not living with, or working for, someone who didn't have the decency to keep his love life private.

Catherine slipped out of bed, careful not to disturb her children, and quietly tiptoed to the door. She pulled her robe off the back of it, shrugged it on, and cracked the door open just enough to peek in the kitchen.

The woman was sitting on his lap. And she was smiling up at Robbie MacBain as if he hung the moon.

Catherine frowned. She looked like a teenager, or maybe early twenties at best. She had thick, beautiful red hair that fell in tight waves down to her waist, a sprinkling of freckles across her porcelain button nose, huge baby-blue eyes that shone like sapphires, and a figure that would make a dead man groan.

Robbie had one arm wrapped protectively around her, his other hand resting on her knee as he leaned down to look her in the eyes and whisper something. He gently lifted his hand, cupped her hair, and kissed the top of her head.

The girl buried her face in Robbie's broad chest, snuggling closer as he continued to whisper, his lips moving against her hair. He stroked down the length of her arm, his broad, powerful hand a salacious contrast to her tiny, feminine body.

Catherine closed the door and leaned against the wall beside it, covering her burning cheeks with her hands and shutting her eyes on a sigh.

"FOUR PLAY." How perfect for a cradle-robbing womanizer. And how bold of him to advertise his favorite indoor sport to the public.

Catherine sighed again, loosening the front of her robe and fanning it to cool her body. Was she any better than that babe in the kitchen? Hadn't she gotten all google-eyed when she had spent almost an hour cleaning and stitching him up? And didn't she forget to breathe whenever he got close?

Darn it. This was not decent. There were young children in the house, four impressionable teens, and an outraged mother. No wonder the man had gone through three housekeepers. He was about to lose his fourth!

Catherine straightened away from the door, tightened the belt on her robe, opened the bedroom door, and boldly walked into the kitchen.

The girl didn't even have the decency to get up but turned her smile on Catherine from the security of Robbie's lap. Robbie MacBain didn't move, either. But his eyes did widen when they landed on Catherine's angry face, and he broke into an amused grin.

"You must be Cat," the girl said to Catherine before turning to Robbie. "You're right, she does look like she can handle the hoodlums."

Catherine simply stared at her, nonplussed.

"And I'm thinking she's about to handle us," Robbie said with a chuckle, finally standing up and setting the woman on her feet. His arm still around her, he turned toward Catherine. "Cat, I'd like you to meet Winter MacKeage, my cousin. Winter, this is Catherine Daniels, the answer to my prayers."

Catherine couldn't even work up the sense to respond. His cousin? This tiny jewel of a girl was Robbie's *cousin*?

They didn't look at all related. Winter MacKeage barely came up to his chest, her eyes were a crystalline blue to his pewter gray, her hair was flaming red, and her delicate neck was tinier than Robbie's wrist. For as rugged and intrinsically male as Robbie MacBain was, Winter MacKeage was utterly feminine, right down to her dainty socked feet.

"Winter came here looking for sympathy," Robbie said to Catherine, his eyes still laughing. "Her cat died."

If she didn't gather her wits and say something soon, Winter MacKeage was going to think she was an idiot. "I—I'm sorry," Catherine whispered. "It's hard to lose a pet."

Robbie rolled his eyes. "Hessa was nineteen and should have died years ago." He looked down at Winter. "Pure crankiness kept that ornery she-devil alive this long."

Catherine gasped, and Winter pinched Robbie's forearm and stepped away from him. "Hessa was not a devil," Winter said, crossing her arms under her breasts and glaring up at him. "And you shouldn't speak ill of the dead."

"Ah . . . how come I didn't hear you knock?" Catherine asked, thinking to change the subject before their conversation turned into a fistfight.

Winter turned to her. "I didn't want to wake anyone, so I threw pebbles at Robbie's window."

"More like rocks, you mean," Robbie said with a snort. "I think you cracked the glass."

Things were going from bad to worse. The two cousins were squared off against each other, Winter looking as if she wanted to smack Robbie, and Robbie's eyes narrowed in laughter.

Catherine walked around the table and grabbed the frying pan out of the oven. "I'll make us some breakfast," she said, "while you tell me about Hessa, Winter." She stopped and gave her a warm smile, deciding that if Robbie wouldn't give his cousin any sympathy, then she would.

Winter sat down at the table, wrapped her hands around her cup of coffee, and sighed. "She was a birthday present when I turned three," Winter told her. "From Robbie," she said, lifting her chin and glaring at her cousin again.

Robbie held up his hands. "Hey, I didn't know that

innocent-looking kitten was the spawn of the devil."

"Hessa was a good cat. She only liked biting you to get a reaction." Winter broke into a grin of her own. "She especially liked to hide when you came over and pounce on your toes because she knew you could never catch her."

"I'm still having a hard time catching cats," he said softly, glancing at Catherine, his eyes crinkling at her blush.

"How did she die?" Catherine asked, looking at Winter.

Winter looked from her to Robbie, then back at her, a speculative gleam in her eye. "In her sleep," she said. "I woke up and found her snuggled against me in the middle of the night, appearing peaceful but very, very still. I think her heart simply stopped beating."

Robbie walked over to Winter, lifted her chin with his finger, and smiled down at her. "There's no greater blessing than dying happy, baby girl," he said gently. "Celebrate your nineteen years of friendship."

"Aye," Winter whispered, turning her cheek into his palm. "I am. I just wanted you to be the first to know about Hessa."

Robbie leaned down and kissed her head, then took her hand and pulled her to her feet. "Don't worry about breakfast for us, Cat. I'm going to walk Winter home, get Hessa, and take them up the mountain to bury our old friend."

Catherine had a hard time swallowing the lump in her throat. This powerful, towering giant really did have a heart. And what Robbie had said to her last night, about watching over his entire family—she was seeing the proof that he hadn't been boasting. Winter had come here first, needing his comfort and getting it.

And then it dawned on her what Robbie had said, and she shot a startled look at Winter. "Walk you home?" she repeated. "You *walked* here through the woods in the dark? All by yourself?"

Winter stepped into her boots with a laugh and pulled her coat from the pegs. "Of course," she said. "I'm more at home in the woods than at Gu Bràth."

"Gu Bràth?"

"That's my home," Winter explained, pointing out the porch door window. "At the ski resort. It's a replica of a huge Scottish keep, made with stone from the mountain." She stepped closer and took hold of Catherine's hand. "You must come over for tea, and I'll give you a tour."

Catherine nodded, returning Winter's contagious smile. "I'd like that very much."

Winter nodded back. "And I'll be your first friend in Pine Creek," she announced. She leaned forward. "Do you want me to bring you a stout stick from the forest?" she whispered.

"Thank you, I think I would like to have one," Catherine returned just as softly.

Winter stepped away with a laugh, opened the door, and walked onto the porch. "Good-bye," she said. "I'll be back later this week to show you the way to my house. Come on, Robbie, I want to be on the summit by sunrise," she finished as she ran off the porch and disappeared into the darkness.

"You have a naughty mind, Catherine Daniels," Robbie said, stopping in the doorway.

"For wanting a stout stick?"

"Nay. For that look on your face when you came striding out of the bedroom."

"I . . . it was . . . I—"

He let out a bark of laughter, lightly tapped the tip of her nose with his finger, and quickly turned and disappeared into the darkness behind his cousin.

Catherine closed the door and stared through the window, her hand on her nose where he'd touched her.

Complete and utter chaos ruled the kitchen, and Catherine couldn't do a darn thing about it. First she'd ruined a batch of muffins, then two dozen biscuits. Now she was cooking the old standby of eggs and toast, but even the toast was scorched.

It was all Robbie's fault, of course. Oh, she knew his game. The man was methodically trying to tear down her defenses. Darn it, it had been a simple, fleeting touch on her nose. An unthreatening action, not even sexual in nature but a brotherly thing to do.

But if that wasn't enough to start her day off with a bang, now she was standing in the middle of a kitchen full of hungry young men and two wide-eyed children who had just been told they were going to school today.

"Mommy, what if my teacher's a man?" Nora whispered to Catherine's shirt sleeve—a sleeve the girl had wiped her nose on three times already this morning. Catherine looked at the dry eggs, at the boys waiting for breakfast, then down at Nora. But Gunter, bless his intuitive soul, came to her rescue.

"All the teachers at your school are women," he promised, carrying Nora to the table and setting her down in his lap. "And you'll meet new friends. Some pretty little girls like yourself, who would love to have you for a pal. You went to school in Arkansas, didn't you?"

"Yes."

"And didn't you have fun? It's more fun than hanging around this old farmhouse all day."

"But who will help Mommy?" Nora frowned at Gunter. "She has to make a lot of food for you guys. She told me so. And she needs my help."

Catherine smiled. Her poor daughter had washed potatoes, standing on a chair at the sink, until she had decided that she was going to be a nurse when she grew up and not a housekeeper.

"I want you to do something for me today," Gunter told Nora. "I want you to come home after school and tell me the names of four new friends. And one of those friends has got to be a boy."

"A boy!"

"Uh-huh," Gunter said with a nod. "Boys make good friends. I'm your friend, aren't I?"

"Yes," Nora returned, smiling now. "And I will. I'll tell you the names tonight."

"Good girl. Now, eat your breakfast so you won't be late."

"I can't find my book bag," Peter cried, frantically pawing through the group of them stashed by the door.

"It's under the table," Catherine calmly told him.

"Aw, hell. My favorite shirt's got a tear in it," Rick said with a groan. "And I don't have any clean ones."

"Yes, you do. They're on hangers in the laundry room," Catherine calmly told him.

"Oh. Yeah, that's right. I forgot I left them there."

"Mom, can I wear my boots to school?" Nathan asked, his mouth full of toast and peanut butter.

"No."

"Why not?"

Catherine turned a motherly frown on her son. Those boots were rubber mud boots, and he was not wearing them to school. She told him so with her eyes.

He answered by shoving the rest of his toast in his mouth.

Despite her reservations, Catherine was taking Robbie's advice and becoming committed. She would deal with Ron if he found her, and she would deal with these pesky womanly urges churning inside her. And maybe—just maybe—the next time he got too close, she would tap Robbie MacBain on the tip of *his* nose.

Robbie found two of his fingers being held by a tiny hand that had the grip of a quarterback. He and Nora were walking through the elementary school, just behind Nathan and Catherine, who was having to push the boy the whole way down the hall. Principal Dobbs was leading the procession, pointing out all the interesting artwork on the walls.

"You'll like Mrs. Jones, Nathan. She does a lot of projects and is always taking her class on field trips. Third grade is such an exciting year," Mrs. Dobbs continued, oblivious to the tension following her.

Robbie didn't know who was more nervous, Nathan, Nora, Cat, or himself. He had promised to keep them safe, but could he really do that when they were at school? He'd talked to the principal, told her a little about the situation, and the woman and her staff would be on the lookout for Ron Daniels.

But Catherine's claim that her ex-husband could find them through a paper trail made Robbie curious. He was going to have to use a few of his old military contacts to learn more about Ronald Daniels, so he would know exactly what he was up against if the bastard suddenly showed up in Pine Creek.

They came to Nathan's room, introductions were made, and after a rather lengthy, shaky good-bye, they headed to Nora's classroom.

Nora's grip tightened on Robbie's fingers, and he squeezed her back reassuringly, surprised that the little girl had taken his hand at all. Truth told, this was one situation he felt a little unsure of. He'd never been a frightened little girl, so he was simply letting his gut be his guide—and taking some cues from Cat, who had also been surprised when her daughter had taken his hand.

"Nora, this is Mrs. Peters," Cat said, squatting down in front of her. "And she's going to introduce you to your new classmates. So try to have some fun today, sweetie," she softly crooned. "And remember to learn those names for Gunter. He expects to hear them tonight."

"One boy," Nora reminded her, nodding her head and slowly letting go of Robbie's hand. The young girl finally peeked into her classroom. "Oh, Mommy, look! It's just like back home. And they got a snake!"

Well, that was that, Robbie discovered. Snakes, apparently, were just the thing. Nora forgot all about being scared, and she forgot all about waiting for her teacher to introduce her. She ran into the room and right up to the startled young boy who was watching the snake.

"Hi. My name's Nora. What's yours?'

Robbie would have burst out laughing, except that Catherine was looking so lost, he merely tucked his hands behind his back and rubbed together the two fingers Nora had been holding.

He wanted to take Cat by the arm and lead her away, since it appeared she was going to plant herself here for the day, but he wasn't up to causing a scene in the hall. So, smiling at Mrs. Peters and nodding at the principal, Robbie gently urged his housekeeper out the side door of the school.

"Can you get back in through that door?" Cat asked, eyeing it.

Robbie tried the knob. "No, why?"

"Just checking. Schools are supposed to keep all the doors locked except the one at the office, so strangers can't come in during the day."

"Cat, they'll be safe here. The principal and staff won't let anyone take them from school except you or me."

She looked up, startled. "What did you tell them?"

"You're not the first divorced mother they've seen, Catherine. For a noncustody parent to take any child, they need written permission from the custodial parent. Unfortunately, custody battles are not exactly an uncommon occurrence today."

"Oh. I see. Yes. I know Nora and Nathan will be fine. And—and thank you for coming with me today. I think I'll just go do some shopping before I head home."

Robbie lifted a brow. "And just how are you planning on getting back? We rode in together, remember?"

"I'll run."

"From town?"

"You said it's only six miles."

He looked down at her clothes. "You're not dressed for that kind of running."

"Yes, I am," she told him, moving her jacket aside and peeling back the waist of her pants. "I'm wearing running shorts under my jeans."

"Cat," Robbie said softly. "You can't hang around town just to be near your kids."

She immediately ducked her head, which told Robbie his guess had been right on the mark.

"But I still want to run back." The smile she gave him was rather provoking. "I might even beat you home."

"Do you carry mace?"

"What?"

"Do you usually carry protection when you run?"

"No."

"Are you crazy?"

She widened her smile. "I can outrun just about anyone. If someone bothers me, I'll just head for the woods."

Well, okay. She had a point there. But he was still going to pick her up a canister of mace, one with a clip, so she could clip it to her waistband.

"So you'll run straight home? You won't get lost?"

"Now who's being a worry wart?" she teased, walking over to the truck.

And that was when Robbie's jaw dropped—right along with her pants. She shed her jacket, boldly unfastened her jeans, kicked off her shoes, and stripped down to her bare legs. She tossed the jeans and shoes in the truck, then pulled out her backpack, found her running shoes, and—dammit to hell!—bent over to put them on.

Holy mother of God! Those shorts were barely legal when she bent over! To hell with the mace, Robbie decided, wiping a shaky hand over his face. He was buying the lady a gun.

No, that would pull her shorts down!

Guessing she was only about half a mile from home and feeling that she'd managed to run off most of her anxiety over being separated from her children, Catherine slowed from a steady jog down to a walk. She set her hands on her hips, panting to cool her body, and smiled at the feel of her pounding heart and quivering muscles. It felt good to be running again, not *from* someone but *toward* something.

She had entered two marathons and over a dozen five-mile races in the last three years, even winning four of them. She was quite fast over short distances, but the twenty-six-mile marathons had nearly killed her.

But what hadn't killed her had only made her stronger, she decided, watching her huffing breath puff ahead of her in the crisp spring air as she looked around. She liked this part of the country, she suddenly decided. It was rugged and stunningly beautiful, with its granite cliffs, towering spruce and pine trees, and misty-topped mountains.

It was also a six-mile *uphill* run from town.

Catherine finally caught sight of the driveway to her new home, not because she spotted the mailbox but because Robbie MacBain, mounted on horseback, was waiting at the end of it.

Had he truly been worried about her?

He'd certainly been startled when she had stripped off her jeans. The guy had looked positively dumbstruck, though Catherine wasn't sure if it had been because she was going running or because he'd just discovered she had legs.

"I'm impressed," he said as she approached. "You made good time, especially considering it's all uphill."

Catherine pulled her ponytail free and worked her fingers through her hair to reshape it, tying it back off her heated neck. "I hope there's plenty of hot water, because I'm going to need a thirty-minute shower. I'm out of shape."

"Really?" he hummed, turning his horse to walk beside her up the driveway. "I hadn't noticed. Did you enjoy yourself?"

"For the most part," she told him, looking up with a frown. "All except for those darn logging trucks. They kept blowing their air horns at me. There's no reason they can't share the road."

He muttered something she couldn't make out as he twisted in his saddle, pulled a jacket off the back, and tossed it down to her. "Why don't you put this on?" he suggested. "Before you catch a chill."

Catherine set the heavy wool coat over her shoulders, noticing that it came down to her knees. "Are you going back up the mountain to visit the priest?" she asked, nodding at his horse.

"Aye. That's why I waited for you. To tell you I won't be home tonight."

"All night?"

"Aye. Daar's not feeling well, and I thought I should stay with him. I'll be back shortly after sunrise, though. Do you have a problem dealing with the boys on your own this evening?"

"No," she said as she climbed the porch stairs. She stepped over to the porch rail and turned to him. "How do I get Nathan and Nora from school?"

"Take my truck. The keys are in it." He shook his head. "I'm afraid your car can't be saved, Cat. The engine seized. We could put in a new one, but that would only be throwing good money after bad. You should be able to get two hundred dollars for it, though, from the scrap yard."

Catherine sighed, took off the coat he'd lent her, and held it over the rail to him. "I was afraid of that. Thank you for bringing it back. Ah, can you take the cost of the towing out of my pay?"

He urged his horse up to the rail and took the coat from her. "It didn't cost us anything and was a good exercise for the boys."

"Then I'll thank them tonight by making a special dessert."

"You'll save me some?"

Catherine canted her head. "You have a bad sugar addiction, Mr. MacBain. Have you spoken to a doctor about it?"

He leaned over in his saddle, getting quite close, and Catherine forced herself to stand firm and not back away. And if he tapped her on the nose again, by God, she was going to tap him back.

"There are worse vices, Cat," he said softly.

She was disappointed when he straightened away from

her. Darn it. Just when she'd worked up the nerve, too.

"My father's number is by the phone. His name is Michael. If you have any problems, don't hesitate to call him, okay?"

Catherine nodded.

"My foreman's name is Harley. His number is also posted. But Gunter can deal with him for you."

"He's a smart kid," Catherine said, thinking of how the young man had distracted Nora this morning.

"Aye. If only he'd come to that conclusion himself," Robbie said as his horse fidgeted away. "I'll be back shortly after sunrise," he added, giving the horse its head and breaking into a canter toward the woods. "Sleep well tonight, Cat," he called over his shoulder.

And just like that, he was gone. Catherine stood at the rail, staring at the woods where he'd disappeared, and rubbed her right index finger against her thumb. What would he have done if she'd tapped his nose? Probably fallen off his horse!

But how would he have taken her gesture? As a pass? An invitation for something more? Maybe a kiss?

Oh, what would it be like to be kissed by Robbie MacBain?

She remembered Winter sitting in his lap this morning. The young woman had looked comfortable. Protected. Cherished.

Catherine knew all men were not like Ron Daniels. Some of them were actually nice.

Was Robbie MacBain?

Chapter Eleven

Things had gone rather smoothly this morning, since her two children were eager to go to school. Robbie still wasn't home yet, but everyone else had been fed and rushed out the door, and Catherine was now bringing up the rear of the impromptu parade marching down the driveway.

Her heart was near bursting with joy. All four boys had insisted on waiting for Nathan and Nora's bus before they headed off to school themselves. Her excited daughter was holding Gunter's hand and telling him, for the twentieth time, the names of her four new friends.

Including Chad, the snake boy.

Nathan had attached himself to Cody's side and was asking a million questions about the potato gun and when were they finally going to shoot it.

Rick was carrying Nora's book bag, which he had presented to her last night after a trip to the attic, and Peter was—well, the poor boy had his nose stuck in a history book, trying to find the date of the Boston Tea Party before his first-period test.

"Mom, will you tell Mr. MacBain that the hens need grain?" Nathan asked as they gathered near the mailbox. "We're all out."

Catherine smiled. "You can tell him at supper."

"Chad wants me to go to his house to play," Nora said. "He's got two baby snakes."

"Is that Chad Perkins?" Rick asked, suddenly interested.

"Uh-huh," Nora confirmed, nodding.

"I'll take her over to Chad's," Rick offered, looking at Catherine.

Cody snorted. "You just want to ogle Jenny Perkins."

Catherine became a bit interested herself. "Does Jenny go to your school?" she asked Rick.

His face turning a dull red, he merely nodded.

Peter dug his nose out of his book, eyed Nora speculatively, then looked at Catherine. "There's an ice cream shop in town. We could take Nathan and Nora for an ice cream Friday night," he offered. "Gunter can drive," he quickly added. "So you don't have to worry about anything."

Being a janitor at a high school for three years, Catherine had learned a lot about the hormone-driven minds of adolescents. There was something about seeing a guy—of any age—acting nice to a child that made young women sit up and take notice.

Catherine looked at all four boys, who were all eagerly waiting for her answer, and burst out laughing. "So, you're asking to borrow my kids to attract girls?"

All four faces reddened, but no one denied her claim.

"Can we go, Mom?" Nathan asked.

"Sounds like a plan to me," she said. "I'll even treat."

"You will?" Cody said, clearly surprised. He suddenly frowned. "You're not coming with us, are you?"

She shook her head. "I wouldn't want to cramp your style."

"You'll really trust us with your kids?" Rick asked.

"Of course. As long as you have them home by nine."

Four sets of young, masculine shoulders straightened.

"It's the bus!" Nora cried, darting toward the road.

Gunter barely caught her by the coat. "You don't leave the driveway until the bus has stopped and you see the driver nod to you," he instructed, squatting down and smiling to soften his lesson.

"I forgot," Nora whispered.

"Here's your bag," Rick said, sliding it onto her shoulders and patting her head. "And sit in the back of the bus," he added, turning to Nathan. "The frost heaves are more fun in the back."

"What's a frost heave?" Nathan asked.

"It's a huge bump in the road made by culverts when the ground thaws," Rick explained, taking hold of Nathan's hand and walking him past the front of the bus as Cody and Peter followed.

" 'Bye, Mommy," Nora said with a wave as Gunter led her by the hand to the bus.

Catherine waved wildly. "Good-bye! Be good, you two!"

But only three boys were left standing on the side of the road when the bus pulled away. "Where's Gunter?"

Rick jangled a set of keys. "He asked the driver if he could ride in with them, since it's their first day," he explained as they walked back into the driveway. "It's only a short hike from their school to the high school."

"That was really sweet of him," Catherine whispered, amazed but not really surprised.

Cody snorted. "Sweet? Gunter? What have you been drinking this morning? Gunter is about as sweet as pine pitch."

"You're all sweet," she said with a laugh. "Thank you for being so kind to my kids."

Their faces turning red again, the boys quickened their pace to the four-door pickup they used to get to and from school.

"We're only being nice so you'll keep cooking," Cody said, running now. "But one burnt meal, lady," he called over the bed of the truck as he opened the back door, "and the squirts are toast."

"He's teasing, Catherine," Rick assured her as he slid behind the wheel.

Catherine gave him a smile and waved good-bye as they headed out of the driveway, then stood quietly and admired the beautiful view, in no hurry to face the mess in the kitchen.

Holes, some of them several acres in size, had opened up in the ice of Pine Lake. But in the cove near the tiny town of Pine Creek, she could see one remaining ice shanty and expected that if it didn't soon get pulled off the lake, it would be swimming with the fishes.

A gentle sense of permanency suddenly swept through her. Catherine could almost imagine that her life was normal; she was an everyday woman sending her kids off to school, looking forward to a full day of motherly chores, in a beautiful old house in a wonderful corner of the country.

It was a rather seductive illusion.

Catherine finally turned away from the view and headed to the house and the messy kitchen. But she stopped, her foot on the bottom step of the porch, when she heard a noise coming from the woods.

Robbie emerged out of the forest and rode his horse straight to the barn. Catherine changed direction and followed him, stepping through the barn door just as he pulled the bridle off his horse.

She didn't even try to stifle her gasp. He looked like hell. His eyes were bloodshot, his hair matted and knotted with twigs, and he had a new bruise on his jaw. There was a bloody cloth wrapped around his right hand, and he had a definite limp when he walked over to hang the bridle on a peg.

"What happened?" she asked, rushing to him. "You're hurt. Is it your side again? Did you pull out the stitches?"

"Nay," he said, limping back to his horse. "Only my hand is bleeding." He lifted the stirrup and started tugging on the cinch buckle with his good hand.

Catherine crowded him out of the way. "Let me do that. You go get in your truck. I'll take care of your horse and then drive you to the doctor."

He stepped out of her way but didn't leave. "Can ya handle a horse?" he asked, his voice gruff and his brogue unusually thick.

"I grew up on a ranch in Idaho," she told him, freeing the cinch and pulling the saddle off. She carried it to the side of the aisle and set it down with a thud. "Go on," she repeated, waving him out. "I'll put him in a stall and give him some hay."

"Has everyone left the house?"

"Yes. About five minutes ago."

He slowly turned and limped out, and Catherine led the horse to the first empty stall she found. She grabbed several flakes of hay, tossed them in behind the animal, checked to see that he had water, and ran out of the barn.

Robbie was just climbing the porch stairs.

"Get in the truck!" she shouted.

He continued into the house.

"Stubborn man," she muttered, jogging to the house. She came through the door and found him standing in the middle of the kitchen, already stripped down to just his pants and boots.

"What are you doing? You don't need to clean up to go see the doctor."

"I'm not going anywhere but in the shower," he said, sitting down in a chair. He leaned over to unlace his boots but groaned instead, set his elbows on his knees, hung his head, and stared at the floor. "I just want a hot shower, for you to sew up my hand and find me some aspirin, and then help me upstairs," he told the floor. He looked up. "Can ya do that, Catherine?"

She was gaping at his chest and shoulders. The man was filthy. Scratched. And he had several new bruises. "You didn't babysit the priest last night, did you?" she whispered.

"No."

"And you hadn't just fallen down the day I found you."

"No."

"How did you get hurt?"

He stared at her, his sunken, bloodshot eyes unreadable, then slowly shook his head. "I'd rather not say." He canted his head. "How are ya at telling fibs, Catherine?"

"Fibs? What sort of fibs? And to whom?"

"Everyone. My father and Libby. The boys. And whoever else asks." He gave her a weak smile. "I don't want anyone to know I'm banged up. Especially my father and Libby."

"You're more than banged up," she said, stepping forward and taking hold of one of his boots. "You look like hell."

"Thank ya. But I'm more exhausted than hurt," he said with a sigh, leaning back in the chair as she unlaced and pulled off his boot. "A shower, aspirin, and twenty-four hours of sleep, and I'll be back in fighting form."

"So you can go out and get in another fight?" she asked, pulling off his other boot.

"Ah, Cat," he groaned, scratching his naked chest. "I had them outnumbered."

"Them? You had *them* outnumbered?"

He reached out and lightly tapped the tip of her nose. "I'll be fine, Catherine," he said, slowly standing up.

She scrambled out of his way, scrubbing her nose with the palm of her hand.

"I'll use the shower downstairs, if that's okay with you," he said, limping into the bathroom before she could answer.

Catherine was left standing in the middle of the kitchen, staring at the scattered clothes and drops of blood on her clean floor.

What had happened to him last night? And why didn't he want his family to know? And them? Who in heck was *them?*

Her boss expected her to sew him up again and tell fibs. But what could he possibly be doing on that mountain at night, dressed the way he had been the first time she'd found him, and carrying a sword?

The only answer Catherine could come up with that made even a little bit of sense was that he was crazy. Either that or she was, because she was going to sew him up and then fib to everyone, because . . . because . . . darn it, because he had asked her to.

He trusted her. Yeah, Catherine decided, squaring her shoulders and absently rubbing her nose again. Robbie trusted her to keep his crazy secret.

She let out a sigh, picked up his jacket and boots and set them by the door, gathered up his shirts and socks and tossed them into the laundry room, then headed upstairs to find him some clean clothes.

When was the last time anyone, other than her children, had trusted her? Not since her parents had been alive.

She had forgotten how empowering it felt. And besides, this was her chance to show Robbie MacBain that even self-appointed guardian angels needed help once in a while.

Catherine came back downstairs carrying a clean change of clothes, wondering how tough her boss really was. The last time she'd put a needle to him, he'd been unconscious, but that wasn't going to be the case this time. She snatched up her sewing kit as she passed through the living room and continued into the kitchen, dropping the kit on the table and going to the bathroom.

"I have clean clothes for you," she called over the sound of the shower.

"Set them on the hamper."

Catherine stood at the door, her hand on the knob, and tried to remember if the shower curtain was opaque or transparent.

Darn. It was both. Mostly opaque, but with clear plastic fish swimming through it. Well, shoot. She had seen every imposing inch of the man's body six days ago. Surely she could handle another peek, couldn't she?

Catherine slowly opened the door and, keeping her eyes glued to the floor, walked in and dropped the clothes on the hamper, then spun around to leave just as the shower shut off.

"Could you hand me a towel?"

She stopped in mid-stride, slowly turned back, and looked at the large hand reaching out past the curtain.

Breathe, she reminded herself, pulling the towel from the rack by the vanity. She stepped closer, the curtain moved, she looked up, and Robbie's head emerged through the steam, along with one broad shoulder and half of his now clean, naked chest.

"Are there any leftovers from last night?" he asked, taking the towel and swiping it over his face and then down his chest, using both hands—which caused the curtain to fall away just enough to reveal his right hip and long, muscled right leg.

Catherine turned away. "Y—Yes. I threw together a barley soup with the leftover roast."

He made a sound that was half groan and half anticipation. "Can you heat me up some?" he asked.

She could probably do that by holding it on her cheeks. Catherine headed out of the bathroom, but he stopped her again.

"Cat."

"Yes?"

"Was Daniels your first?"

"M-my first husband?" she whispered.

She heard the shower curtain slide all the way open. "Your first man," he softly clarified, standing directly behind her.

"I don't believe that's any of your business, Mr. MacBain."

"Aye, but I do," he said, touching her shoulder with just enough pressure to turn her around to face him. "It's important for two people entering a conspiracy to know a bit about each other. Have you ever been in a relationship that was good, Catherine?"

"It was good with Ron. At first," she amended, keeping her eyes focused on his so she wouldn't look down. "Things didn't start going bad until after we moved to Arkansas." She suddenly frowned. "What do you mean, a conspiracy?"

"My nighttime adventures on the mountain and your helping me keep them a secret." He slowly reached out and touched her hair, lifting it off her shoulder, and held it between two fingers. "Was Daniels your first?" he repeated.

It was all she could do not to back away, though

Catherine didn't know if she stood her ground because she was determined to be brave or if her knees were just too weak to move.

"I-I had boyfriends in high school."

"I think the operative word here is *man,* Catherine. Was Daniels your first lover?"

What in hell did he want from her? He was dripping water and blood all over the bathroom and . . . and making a pass!

"Yes," she snapped, pulling away and grabbing up his clothes. She shoved them at his chest, which caused him to lift both hands to catch them—which caused the towel he'd been holding around his waist to drop to the floor.

Catherine spun around and ran out of the bathroom.

"Cat," he growled, stopping her just outside the door.

"What?" she growled back, still facing away.

"Just so ya know, it's my intention to see that he isn't your last," he whispered, softly closing the door behind her.

Catherine stood rooted in place.

His intention? Had he just made her a promise or a threat?

Robbie stared up at the ceiling, watching the shifting shadows mark the rise of the sun, and listened to the quiet stirring below as his household prepared itself for another day.

He'd slept nearly twenty-one hours straight.

Every muscle in his body urged him to just lie still, to not demand anything of them quite yet. He ached in places he'd forgotten he had. The small, neatly sutured cut on his right hand throbbed with the rhythm of his pulse, his mouth was dry, and his eyelids felt as if they passed through sand every time he blinked.

Aye. A complaining body and a growing sense of unease was all he had to show for his second attempt to find Cùram's tree. He didn't even have Mary. He'd caught sight of the snowy several times, but his independent-minded pet had remained well out of reach and stubbornly silent.

He'd stayed there seven full days this time, searching both the MacKeage and the MacBain villages for Cùram de Gairn, but he might as well have been hunting a ghost.

At least the MacKeage camp had heard of Cùram, once Robbie had actually dared to mention the man by name. But the last anyone remembered seeing him had been a month ago. To the MacKeages, Cùram was a warrior known mostly for his unusual tactics on the fighting field and for his jeweled sword that he claimed had been a gift from the fairies. He was a young, handsome, rather quiet man, who was said to rise as eagerly to the call of war as he did to the call of the ladies.

As for the tree itself, Robbie was sure it was there; he could *feel* the hum of its powerful energy when he walked the woods north of the MacKeage village. But he had seen no tree with any sort of markings or any oak larger than one he could wrap his arms around.

He was certainly honing his skills with a sword, though. First on the training field with several MacKeage warriors and again with a chase through the forest by five MacBain idiots.

His ancestors were sorely trying his patience. He had hoped to avoid actually killing anyone, but by God, the next MacBain who cut him was getting his soul dispatched to hell.

With a groan pulled from the deepest regions of his body, Robbie finally crawled out of bed. The house had grown quiet with one final bang of the porch door, and he limped over to the window, rested his arms on the sash, and watched Catherine and the four boys walk Nathan and Nora down the driveway.

Robbie found his first smile in eight days. Nora was perched on Gunter's shoulders, her tiny hands waving excitedly as she talked nonstop. Nathan was walking between Cody and Peter, showing off one of his school papers. Rick was carrying two small backpacks as he followed, listening intently to Nora.

And bringing up the rear was his fourth and *final* housekeeper, her hands tucked in her pockets, her face bathed by the early-morning sun, and a contented smile on her sweet little mouth.

He had her, Robbie thought with a smile of his own. Certainly not in his bed yet, but he had the little cat almost eating out of his hand. He snorted. She should damn well be getting used to his body by now—she'd seen him naked enough times.

She was also getting used to his touch, albeit slowly, and seemed to be breathing easier whenever he got close. She had enrolled her kids in school, was amazing with the boys, and apparently didn't mind telling a good fib. And she kept sewing him up without demanding to know how he kept getting hurt.

Robbie guessed his size wasn't helping his cause. Hell, his gender was the biggest barrier he had to break through. But he would. Because he had realized, when he'd opened his eyes in the cabin and found himself tied to the bed, that not only had his egg thief saved his life, but that she was *the one*.

He'd promised his father that if he ever crossed paths with a woman who could handle his calling, he'd snatch her up before she could know what she was getting herself into.

Aye, Catherine's fears were mere illusions masking her

true nature. The woman was strong in an utterly feminine way, brave, compassionate, resourceful, intelligent, and beautiful. She was perfect for him. He need only convince *her* of that truth.

Time was on his side. Proximity, too. She couldn't very well remain guarded against him while living under his roof. Aye, providence had brought Catherine here, but now it was up to him to win her heart.

Robbie watched her wave good-bye to the retreating school bus and then to the boys as they drove out of the driveway. Claiming Catherine might require some gentling, a deep well of patience, and a bit of cunning—but hey, all was fair in love and war, wasn't it?

He rather hoped Ronald Daniels did show up. What better way to impress the lady than to slay her dragon?

Robbie turned from the window, lazily scratching the healed wound on his shoulder, and smiled. He had the little cat to himself for the day, and he might as well give her tail another gentle tug.

He slipped into his pants, wondering just how open-minded Catherine Daniels was, since he was about to ask her to take out the pink silk stitches in his side and shoulder. By Catherine's count, they'd only been in for a week, but including the seven days of his last adventure and the one day he'd slept away, his wounds had been healing for over two weeks.

Aye, he would soon learn if she could live with the magic.

Chapter Twelve

Catherine placed the last breakfast plate in the dishwasher and picked up a cloth and started wiping the table just as the phone rang. She ran to it quickly, not wanting it to wake up Robbie, and caught it on the second ring.

"Hello," she said into the receiver.

"Ah, hello. Is Robbie there?" came the obviously surprised voice on the other end of the line. "Nay, before ya get him, am I speaking to the brave woman who took on the task of babysitting five men?"

She frowned at the wall. "Yes, this is Catherine Daniels."

"I'm Robbie's father, Michael," he said. "And I've been hearing some impressive tales about ya," he continued, now with an obvious smile in his voice. "Are they true?"

"Ah . . . that depends," Catherine whispered, tightening her grip on the phone. "What exactly have you heard?"

"Only that you're wise enough to want a stout stick," he said with a chuckle. "And that you're beautiful as well."

"You've been talking to Winter," Catherine said, carrying the portable phone over to the table and sitting down.

"And Ian," he added. "Have ya needed to use the stick yet?"

"Not yet. The boys have been perfect angels."

"It wasn't the boys I was referring to," he said softly. "Is my son there, or has he left already?"

"He's not here," Catherine said, squaring her shoulders as she planned her fib. "And I'm not sure where he went or when he'll be back. Can I give him a message for you?"

"Aye. Could ya tell him his mum is wishing to see him. It's been over a week since he's even talked with her."

"Oh, sure, I'll tell him. But he's been awful busy. One of his tree harvesters broke down, and the priest up on the mountain—Father Daar, I think he said his name was—hasn't been feeling well, so he's been looking after him. And then he had to rescue me and my children and then tow my car, and I think there was something about a well pump that he had to replace."

A soft chuckle came over the phone. "Ya not only housekeep, I see, but ya're protective as well. That's good, Miss Daniels. Those boys could use some mothering."

Catherine wasn't sure if he was lumping Robbie in with the boys or not. "Please, call me Catherine," she told him.

"Aye, then, Catherine, if ya could just ask my son to squeeze us in between his many chores, I'd appreciate it."

"I-I will," she whispered, realizing she had sounded like a babbling idiot. What a great first impression.

"And Catherine?"

"Yes?"

"If I might make a suggestion, if my son hasn't already? Be mindful when you're running on the roads around here. Our truck drivers can get easily distracted, and I'd hate to see ya in the middle of an accident."

"I always move to the edge when I hear one coming," Catherine said, lifting her chin defensively, wondering if she had become the talk of the town.

"Aye," he said softly. "But lass, ya might want to think about . . . well, maybe ya should wear long pants when ya run."

Long pants? "But nobody runs in long pants," she told him. "They're too hot and restrictive."

Then what he meant dawned on her. Catherine closed her eyes and let out a loud groan, only to gasp and quickly cover the mouthpiece. Great. Two strikes against her, and she hadn't even met the man yet.

It sounded as if he also covered the mouthpiece of his phone, but she was still able to hear his sigh. "I've offended ya, lass, but that wasn't my intention. I'm only wanting to make ya aware how dangerous running the roads can be."

"I understand. And thank you. I'll tell Robbie to call you when he gets home."

Another sigh came over the phone. "Thank ya, Catherine. And we'll be over one day soon, to properly welcome ya to Pine Creek. Until then, good-bye."

"Good-bye," she repeated, pressing the off button before closing her eyes and thumping herself on the head with the phone.

"Dumb, dumb, dumb," she muttered. "Could I be any dumber?" She whipped around at the sound of laughter coming from the living-room doorway. "How long have you been standing there?"

"Long enough to know that you can fib like a Trojan," Robbie said with a lingering chuckle. He shook his head. "I come by my protectiveness honestly, Cat. My father might be blunt, but he means well. He's sincerely worried for you."

"I'm so embarrassed," she muttered. She stood up and

placed the phone in its cradle. "Doesn't anybody in Pine Creek run?"

He walked over to the counter and poured himself a cup of coffee. "Nay. Jogging is more of an urban exercise. Life here involves enough physical labor that few people need to add running to their schedule. Don't worry about it, Catherine," he continued, easing himself into a chair at the table. "If you wish to run, then run. People will eventually get used to seeing you and . . . your legs."

She spun around to the sink. "How are you feeling this morning?" she asked, diving her hands into the dishwater and vigorously scrubbing the frying pan.

He softly chuckled. "Much better. I was only wanting a good nap. Thank you for heading off my father this morning. I appreciate how difficult it is to fib."

"Why have you been avoiding Libby?" she asked, still facing away until her blush calmed down.

"She's a doctor."

Catherine turned in surprise. "I've been sewing you up, risking your getting an infection, and your stepmother is a doctor? Why don't you just go see her?"

"She's a very intuitive doctor," he said. "She'd know how I got hurt."

Unlike good old dumb her, who didn't know a darn thing. She turned back to the sink. "Is there a way you could get hold of some antibiotics, or do you keep any for your horses?" She looked back at him. "I know animal drugs and could figure out a safe dose for you."

He shook his head. "I won't get an infection. You sterilized the needle and thread yesterday, and my side and shoulder healed cleanly. In fact," he said, standing up and pulling his shirttail out of his pants, "I was hoping I could get you to take out these stitches today."

"But it's only been a week."

"Aye. But I'm healed. See?"

Sheer curiosity compelled her to dry her hands on her apron and lean over to lift his shirt. She tugged on the waist of his jeans to see the wound and frowned. Without even thinking, Catherine straightened and unbuttoned his shirt, pulled it to the side, and leaned up to examine the cut on his shoulder.

They were both completely healed! All that remained of the once deep wound was a thin red line with pink thread sticking out every quarter inch.

"You have an amazing constitution," she whispered, lightly running her finger over the scar. She looked up, realized she was a hair's breadth away from his face—and his mouth—and quickly stepped back.

Robbie finished taking off his shirt and started unbuckling his pants. Catherine let out a small squeak and headed toward the living room, his soft laughter propelling her into a run.

Honest to God, the man was driving her crazy. He couldn't say what he had yesterday in the bathroom, standing there all huge and wet and naked, and expect her not to act like an idiot every time she got close to him. It was her darned libido. Not only had Robbie MacBain managed to stir it awake, but yesterday's promise—or, rather, yesterday's threat—had exposed her fear like a raw nerve constantly being poked. Well, she would just poke him back, she decided, taking the scissors out of her sewing kit. She marched into the kitchen, determined to ignore the fact that he smelled nice and warm and sexy and that he *looked* even sexier.

"I need to go to the logging yard today and would like you to drive me," he said, sitting in his chair again, scratching the stitches on his shoulder.

"You can't drive yourself?" she asked, leaning over and

using the sharp point of her scissors to gently loosen one of the stitches—which would be easier if her hand would quit shaking.

"I could," he said, twisting his head to see what she was doing to him. "But I'm still half asleep and prefer to—ow!"

She used her fingers to pull the snipped thread out of his flesh. "That did not hurt."

"You poked me with the scissors."

"Only because you moved. Quit talking."

"Wouldn't you like to see a tree harvester in action?" he asked, ignoring her edict. "Ow!"

She straightened and scowled at him. "You didn't complain this much when I sewed you up yesterday," she said, using the scissors to point at the small bandage on his right hand.

"I was numb with exhaustion yesterday," he said, rubbing his shoulder.

Catherine moved his hand out of the way and went back to work. "Don't watch," she suggested. "It makes you anticipate the pain, and you tense up."

"You know this from personal experience?" he asked softly, his breath wafting warmly over her hair.

"Yes," she absently answered, quickly snipping three threads in a row, then leaning away when he growled.

She moved his hand out of the way again, snipped the last two stitches, quickly rubbed the sting away with her fingers, and started pulling them out. "There. All done," she said as she straightened. "Now, stand up and lean against the table, and I'll take out the ones on your hip."

"I've a worry you're enjoying this," he muttered, standing up and leaning against the table.

Catherine sat in his chair, scooted it around to face him, pulled down the edge of his open jeans to see his scar, and . . . She stopped and looked up, realizing the provocative position she was in.

The door opened, and an old man, dressed in a long black robe and thin white collar, walked into the kitchen. "God's teeth!" he shouted. "If ya're needing privacy, then lock your door!"

Catherine flew out of her chair so quickly she would have fallen if Robbie hadn't caught her by the shoulders and stood her on her feet.

The priest thumped his cane on the floor and glared first at Robbie's naked chest and open pants, then at Catherine.

Robbie stepped between them, facing the priest, and slowly did up his jeans and fastened his belt. Catherine looked behind her, wondering if she was small enough to crawl in the oven.

"Most people knock before entering someone's house," Robbie said, crossing his arms over his chest.

"I haven't knocked in thirty years!"

"But you will from now on," Robbie softly returned. "And you'll apologize to my housekeeper for making assumptions."

Catherine gasped and pinched Robbie's back for speaking so rudely to a man of the cloth.

He didn't even flinch but continued, "And you'll start waiting for an invitation to visit rather than showing up unannounced."

They were both going to fry in hell—she could already feel the flames on her face. Catherine used the point of her scissors this time to shut Robbie up.

He reached around, snatched away her scissors, gave her a good glare, and turned back to the priest. "I'm waiting for that apology."

But Catherine wasn't. She spun on her heel and hightailed it into the living room, tugged open the front door, and rushed onto the porch that spanned the entire front of the house. She immediately scooted between two windows until her back was pressed against the clapboards and stood perfectly still, her hands on her burning cheeks and her heart thumping so hard it hurt.

Her parents were rolling over in their graves. They'd raised her to respect religion, especially anyone doing God's work.

The front door opened, and Catherine eyed the stairs at the end of the porch, wondering if she could reach them before Robbie reached her. The priest stepped through the door, alone, and folded his hands over the top of his beautiful wood cane.

He had wild, long white hair that was a disturbing contrast to his perfectly trimmed beard, shoulders stooped by gravity and time, and age-bent fingers covering the head of a cane that was only slightly more crooked than he was. He looked positively ancient—except for his eyes, which were a sharp, crystal blue.

"I am sincerely contrite, Miss Daniels, for making such a terrible assumption," he said gruffly. "Robbie explained that ya was tending his wound, and I apologize for thinking different." He held out a gnarled hand to her. "I'm Father Daar. I live up on TarStone."

Even though she wanted to run the other way, Catherine's manners compelled her to step forward and shake his hand. "It's nice to meet you, Father," she whispered. "Ah . . . would you like a cup of coffee and some shortbread?"

His eyes sparked with interest. "Shortbread, ya say?" he asked, using her captured hand to lead her inside. "I haven't had shortbread in ages. Did ya flavor it with lemon?"

Catherine tried to get her hand back, but he was using it to lead her through the living room into the kitchen. "With just a few drops of lemon juice," she told him, finally escaping when he sat at the table.

Robbie was nowhere in sight.

She found a clean mug, poured the priest his coffee, then got down on her knees and reached far into the back of a bottom cupboard. Father Daar's laughter and Robbie's snort drew her attention when she straightened.

"So that's where you hide the dessert," Robbie said from the bathroom doorway. He buttoned up his shirt, tucked it inside his belt, and walked over and set her scissors on the table. "I finished taking out the stitches," he told her, lifting one brow. "And managed to do it without once poking myself."

"Then you should probably remove the stitches in your hand when the time comes," she suggested sweetly, getting two plates from the cupboard. She cut the shortbread, set it on the table in front of the men, gave them forks and napkins, refilled Robbie's coffee, and headed to her bedroom.

But she stopped at the door when she heard Father Daar urgently whisper to Robbie, "Ya have to go back *tonight.* We're running out of time."

Go back? Tonight? And do what, get beat up again?

Catherine turned to them, crossed her fingers behind her back, and hoped she didn't fry in hell for fibbing to a priest. "Oh, I forgot to tell you, Robbie. Your father and Libby are coming for supper tonight. I told them we eat at six."

Robbie looked from her to the priest, then back at her, one eyebrow raised speculatively. He finally shook his head at Father Daar. "My family obligations come first."

Father Daar eyed Catherine suspiciously. "Ya're making

commitments for yar boss without checking with him first?"

Crossing a second set of fingers, Catherine nodded. "It seemed important to his father, and I didn't dare refuse."

The priest looked back at Robbie but nodded toward her. "I warned ya a woman would only complicate yar life. They just love interfering in a man's work."

"Oh, I don't know," Robbie drawled, leaning back in his chair and smiling at Catherine. "They come in handy sometimes. I think they add a certain . . . excitement."

Catherine uncrossed her fingers and closed her hands into fists, smiling back at him. "I'm sorry I won't be able to drive you to work this morning, but I have to *run* into town."

That wiped the smirk off his face.

Catherine spun around, walked into her bedroom and softly closed the door, and leaned against it and closed her eyes with a sigh.

Excitement, huh?

Oh, she'd show the man some excitement, all right—and a good deal of leg!

"Your plan isn't working, priest," Robbie growled, knowing it wasn't Daar putting the bite in his voice but Catherine.

She was intending to run all over the countryside again, dressed in *short* shorts and leaving a trail of ditched logging trucks in her wake. He was going to have to do something about that.

"Then come up with a better plan!" Daar snapped, glaring at him. "Just as long as ya make it happen soon. I still need to nurture that root into a sapling."

Robbie took a calming breath and looked away from the bedroom door and tried to focus his attention on Daar.

"How long has that oak been growing on MacKeage land? Would it have existed when the Highlanders lived there? Would they know about it?"

"Nay," Daar said, shaking his head. "Cùram's only been living there six years now."

"But you're saying it *is* there, that I just can't see it?"

"Aye. He's hidden it from ya."

"And you still won't come back with me to unmask his spell? What would happen if he discovered you there?"

Daar hunched over his plate of shortbread, curled his hands around his cup of coffee, and spoke down to it. "Twenty years ago, I might have stood a chance against him," Daar whispered. He looked up at Robbie. "But only a chance. A hundred years ago, I might have beaten him." He straightened his shoulders. "Hell, I did beat him, when I matched Judy MacKinnon to Duncan MacKeage." The old *drùidh* narrowed his eyes. "But if ya take me back there now, Robbie, ya may as well run me through with yar sword," he whispered. "Cùram would finish me."

The door to Catherine's bedroom opened, and she came striding out, dressed in shorts, a sweatshirt, and running shoes. A person could have heard a mouse sneeze as she silently walked across the kitchen, her chin held high and her fists clenched at her sides. She didn't even look at them. She merely opened the porch door, stepped out, and softly closed it behind her.

Robbie slowly bent the fork in his hand until the tines touched the handle, and turned to Daar. "Just tell me how to find the tree. Give me something to work with."

Daar shook his head. "I have nothing. As it is, ya're going to have to use yar own powers to travel back and forth from now on. My staff has grown too weak," he said, fingering the nearly smooth cherry cane lying on the table beside his plate.

"My own powers," Robbie softly repeated.

"Aye. Ya can no longer deny them, MacBain. Ya've learned the full extent of your gift, and ignoring it won't make it go away."

"I don't want that kind of power!"

"Do ya think I *asked* to be a *drùidh*? It's not exactly something ya wish for. Providence decides our destinies. Yar own mother understood this, and it didn't stop her from having you. It's not a curse, boy," Daar snapped, leaning forward. "It's a gift. Yar mama not only gave ya life but the gift of yar calling. Embrace it. Use it! Explore the full extent of yar abilities, and thank God that ya have the means to protect those ya love."

Robbie carefully set the destroyed fork by his plate and stared down at the tiny bandage covering the dagger cut on his right hand. Aye, he had seen his calling in the midst of the violent storm, and it had scared the holy hell out of him. He'd come face to face with his mother, as the beautiful mortal woman she'd once been, and she had shown him his destiny.

"It was Mary who revealed my powers to me," he whispered, still staring down at his hand. "She showed me everything."

"Aye," Daar said softly. "And ya saw that guardians even have power over *drùidhs*, didn't ya? Mary showed ya how she saved her sister's life by using my own staff to protect Grace from the freezing waters of the high mountain pond."

"Aye," Robbie said, still not looking up.

"It's what keeps everything balanced," Daar continued. "For as powerful as *drùidhs* are, providence has given the world an army of knights to protect it as well."

"Then what's your role?" Robbie asked, looking up. "Why do *drùidhs* even exist?"

"To nurture the knowledge. To grow our trees and keep the continuum moving forward."

"And blow things up in the process," Robbie muttered, standing up and carrying his uneaten shortbread to the counter. "Four days from now, I'll be on the summit at sunset, and I'll have Ian MacKeage with me."

"What! Nay! Ya cannot."

"Aye, I can," Robbie told him, glancing toward the porch, then back at the priest. "Ian has asked me to take him back, and I have agreed."

"But the continuum. You're going to upset the energy. He knows too much of the future."

"He'll not mess with the magic," Robbie assured him. "He only wants to go home and be with his wife and children."

Daar also stood, but he snatched up his uneaten shortbread and stuffed it in his pocket. "Then may God have mercy on us," he whispered, walking to the door. "Because if that old goat manages to upset the continuum, we're all doomed."

"That didn't seem to be a worry when you cast your spell to bring them here," Robbie pointed out, walking onto the porch behind him.

Daar stopped at the bottom of the steps and looked back. "They would have woke up back in their original time, not minutes after they'd left," he explained. "And probably finished trying to kill each other. It was already part of the original spell, that they wouldn't remember this time." He pointed his cane at Robbie. "But it only works if they go back by way of my first incantation," he said. "You and Ian are going back ten years after that, to after Cùram arrived."

"Ian will give me his word not to upset your energy," Robbie promised. "He only wishes to die in the arms of his family."

Daar stared at him in silence for several seconds, then finally nodded. "Aye. If Ian gives his word, that's enough," he softly agreed. "Then I'll meet ya on the summit in four days," he confirmed, turning toward the woods, reaching in his pocket and pulling out a piece of shortbread as he walked away.

Robbie looked up at TarStone and blew out his breath. Aye, only four days before Ian MacKeage walked out of their lives.

Catherine ran downhill toward town, setting an easy pace for the first mile to let her muscles warm up. She tried to concentrate on the rhythm of her feet hitting the ground, but thoughts of Robbie and Father Daar kept interfering. What in heck were they up to?

She did know the priest was part of whatever Robbie was doing up on the mountain, though she'd caught only enough of the conversation to realize that whatever it was, time was running out. *Just as long as you make it happen soon*, she'd heard Father Daar say in an angry whisper. But then he'd lowered his voice, and the conversation had been muted by the solid door of her bedroom—even pressing her ear to it hadn't helped.

Make *what* happen?

And darn it, why did she even care! Just because Robbie MacBain appeared to be one of the good guys, and just because she was starting to trust him, wasn't enough reason to get huffy over his refusal to confide in her.

She was his housekeeper. She cooked and cleaned for the man, and when he got beat up, she sewed him back together and fibbed to his father. Robbie was under no obligation to explain his nighttime adventures to his hired help, even if she could work up the nerve to ask him outright.

An air horn suddenly blasted behind her, and Catherine screamed and nearly fell into the ditch. She scrambled off the road and up the bank, turning to see a huge logging truck barreling down the hill. The driver kept his hand on the deafening horn and used his other hand to wave at her. He even shot her a wink before suddenly giving his attention back to the road when his front left tire hit the gravel of the opposite ditch. The ground under her feet actually shook as the man wrestled the overloaded truck back into his lane and disappeared around a curve, once again blasting his horn.

"You idiot!" she shouted after him, waving her fist through the dust billowing around her. "I hope you have six flat tires!"

Her only answer was the fading blast of his horn.

With a sigh to calm her racing heart, Catherine was about to jump the ditch when she spotted a silver pickup truck rounding the curve down the hill. It was traveling through the lingering dust at a much slower speed than the logging rig, and she could see only one occupant.

She spun around and ducked into the bushes, deciding she'd entertained enough idiots for one day. The pickup slowly made its way toward her, and Catherine squatted behind a tree, her eyes glued on the approaching truck as the silhouette of the driver sharpened.

He looked . . . familiar. Catherine scooted back and flattened herself to the ground, her heart beginning to pound in terror as the pickup neared.

No! It couldn't be him. Ron couldn't have found her!

She could finally see his features clearly through the dispersing dust—a man with thick brown hair, a darkly stubbled jaw, and tiny narrowed eyes fixed on the road ahead.

She went utterly still, oblivious to the mud seeping into

her clothes, trying to convince herself that it was nothing more than her imagination running wild. It wasn't Ron.

"You are *not* Ron," she said in a strained whisper.

The driver was too old. And definitely too weather-tanned for someone who had been in prison for three years. And his hair was peppered with gray, and there was a small white dog sitting on his lap, its nose pressed against the window. It wasn't Ron. She could *see* it wasn't Ron.

Now all she had to do was convince her pounding heart.

Catherine lay in the muddy grass for a good ten minutes, getting her breathing under control and trying to fight the terror freezing her in place.

The sound of another light truck came from the direction of home, and Catherine inched forward until she saw the dark Suburban coming down the hill. She scrambled to her feet with a cry of relief and ran into the road.

Robbie braked to a stop beside her, his smile vanishing the moment he saw her muddy clothes. Catherine opened the door and scooted into the seat, folded her hands on her lap, and took a shuddering breath.

"What happened?" he asked, scanning the road through the windshield before looking back at her. "Did you fall? Were you run off the road?"

"I . . . ah, I tripped when a logging truck went by."

Taking hold of her chin and turning her to face him, he moved his dark pewter gaze over her body, then brought it back to settle on hers. "You're as pale as a ghost, and you're still trembling. Are you hurt?"

"No. Just shaken up," she said, pulling away from his grasp and letting out another shuddering breath. "Can you take me home before you go to the logging yard?"

He hesitated, apparently undecided if he believed her or

not. "Cat," he said with a growl. "You've got to run on the tote roads from now on."

She forced a smile. "What about the bears that might eat Ian?"

"I'll get you a bear bell, so they'll hear you coming and be gone long before you see them." He started to reach for her chin again but stopped when she stiffened and simply lock his gaze on her.

A deep, almost electric silence filled the truck. She could see he was in his guardian angel mode, trying to convince himself that she was okay.

She was far from okay, but she wasn't about to tell him why. Her terror was her business, not his. It hadn't been Ron; she knew that with the same certainty that told her Robbie was about to touch her again—with or without her consent.

And she couldn't handle that right now, no matter how sincere his concern. It had been all she could do not to run screaming from the truck when he'd taken her by the chin, and if he so much as tried to brush the mud off her knee, she would likely have a panic attack that rivaled a volcanic eruption.

"Are you going back up the mountain tonight to get beat up again?" she asked, breaking his stare by turning to look out the windshield.

"You're worried about me?"

She looked back at him. "One of these days, you're not going to come back. You were almost dead when I found you. And where would that leave the boys and your family, that you're so determined to look after?"

"I'll always come back, Catherine."

"Are you going up there tonight or not?"

"Nay. I checked my calendar after you left, and your lit-tle fib to Daar wasn't a fib after all. Marcus Saints is coming for a visit this afternoon, and so is Judge Bailey, but she won't be staying for supper. Only Marcus."

"Who are Marcus Saints and Judge Bailey?"

"Saints is a social worker who keeps tabs on the boys. And Martha Bailey is all that's standing between them and the detention center."

Catherine slapped her chest to catch her gasp. "They're coming to the house today?" she squeaked, her previous terror turning to horror. "Darn it, you have to warn me about stuff like that! Turn around. I have to get home!"

"Don't worry," he said with a chuckle, putting the truck in gear, checking for traffic, then making a three-point turn in the road. "They won't arrive until after school."

"But I need to start planning for supper now."

"The way you cook?" he said as he headed back up the hill. "You could make stone soup, and Saints would be drooling all over himself. And the house is fine, Cat." He snorted. "It's a hell of a lot cleaner than the last time they visited. Marcus threatened to call the health department."

Chapter Thirteen

The moment they got home, Catherine told Robbie to go to his logging yard, and she spent the rest of the morning and most of the afternoon in near hysterics. She thawed enough beef to feed an army, scrubbed all three bathrooms until they sparkled, dusted, straightened the boys' bedrooms and remade their beds, vacuumed upstairs and down, washed the kitchen floor, peeled ten pounds of potatoes and carrots, and threw together a double batch of yeast rolls.

In five hours, by the time the kids got home from school and Martha Bailey and Marcus Saints arrived, Catherine felt as if she had run a marathon—and had somehow managed to survive this one as well.

Not knowing what to expect but expecting the worst, Martha Bailey had surprised Catherine. She was a tiny woman, pretty in a haphazard sort of way, and genuinely warm. She had also become quite giddy and had burst into a huge smile when Robbie walked out of the barn to greet her and Marcus.

Now, Catherine was nervously pacing the kitchen porch while they held individual interviews. They were down to the last two boys; Marcus had Gunter in the living room, and Martha was talking to Rick at the kitchen table.

Nora was terrorizing the barn cats with Cody, Nathan was doing his henhouse chores, and Peter was sitting on the front porch, his nose in a book—sighing, erasing, and occasionally cursing.

Robbie was rinsing off the last of the logging-yard mud from his truck, which Catherine had told him to face toward the garage doors so their guests wouldn't see the bug shield. He had chuckled at her command, explaining that the shield had been a gift from the boys, but he *had* turned the truck inward to wash it.

Unable to stand the suspense any longer and deciding she could pretend she needed to check on supper, Catherine finally entered the kitchen, only to run into Martha Bailey on her way out. "Oh! I'm sorry."

"That's okay, Miss Daniels. I was just on my way to find you." Martha smiled sadly. "I can't stay for supper, I'm afraid. I have my own crew to feed. And from what I've been told and from what I've been smelling all afternoon, I'm going to miss a real treat. All the boys could talk about was your cooking."

Catherine could only nod.

"Peter said that you make a tasty barley soup." Martha's smile returned. "Peter said a lot of things. All the boys did. Welcome to Pine Creek, Catherine. I certainly hope you'll be staying." She canted her head. "Although I suspect that if you try to leave, four boys and a handsome giant will hunt you down and drag you back."

"I think they were all starving to death," Catherine said, relaxing for the first time today. She shook her head. "I've been warned the boys might be a little hard to handle, but I haven't seen a sign of that since I came here."

Martha patted Catherine's arm. "It's amazing how good food can tame the beast. Keep it coming, and I doubt you'll have any problems. I'll be back next month, and maybe then I'll get to sample your cooking. Good-bye. And good luck."

Okay, Catherine decided as she watched the woman get into her car and drive away, Robbie was right. Martha Bailey was one of the good guys. But Marcus Saints seemed . . . well, the man looked as if he picked his teeth with hardened criminals.

Nathan came dragging up the porch stairs just then, holding his hand cradled against his chest.

"What happened to you?"

"Those chickens are ferocious, Mom. They pecked me."

Catherine reached down and inspected the boy's wound. One of the old hens had managed to draw blood, but just barely.

"You'll live, Nathan. Come on, I'll clean you up and put on a Band-Aid."

"It's a dangerous job, and I don't want to do it anymore."

"Let me guess," she speculated, pushing him into the house ahead of her so he wouldn't see her smile. "You still haven't told Mr. MacBain that you need grain."

"No."

"Are you going to?"

"No."

"Nathan."

"I hope they starve."

"Nathan."

"Why can't you just tell him for me?"

"Because, young man, that's your job."

"But he's scary," Nathan whispered, looking up at her with huge puppy-dog eyes.

"He's been nothing but kind to us, Nathan. He's not like your father," Catherine whispered, squatting down and taking hold of his shoulders. "You have nothing to fear from Mr. MacBain." She brushed the hair away from his face. "Honey, if you tell him the hens need grain, he'll see what a responsible young man you are and respect you for doing your chore. And Nathan, you'll respect yourself if you approach him bravely and do your job. You'll be one of the boys here. You don't see them being afraid of Mr. MacBain, do you?"

He thought about that, frowning. "No," he finally admitted. "And Mr. MacBain will be proud of me, too."

Catherine sighed. "Nathan, you do your chores for yourself. Not for Mr. MacBain and not for me. I want you to see that you can deal with people, especially men, and not be afraid. You don't have to prove anything to anyone but yourself."

"I understand," he whispered. "I know you're scared I'll grow up to be like Daddy. And I'm trying not to."

Catherine felt a sharp stab to her heart. When had her beautiful little boy realized her greatest fear? "Come on, let's tend that vicious old hen wound."

Peeking toward Gunter and Marcus in the living room, Catherine lifted Nathan onto the counter, got the first aid kit from the cupboard, and started cleaning his wound. Robbie came in from the yard, walked past her and Nathan to the stove, lifted the lid on the huge steaming pot, and started stirring the stew.

Catherine took the spoon away from him and shooed him upstairs to change his wet shirt. She headed back to Nathan, replacing the lid on the stew as she walked by, but turned when Nora came running into the kitchen, screaming bloody murder.

She ran to her daughter. "Nora, what is it?"

"A monster!" Nora wailed. "Daddy's in the barn!"

Just then, Cody slammed through the door, looking frantic and hysterical himself, and Nora whimpered and tried to run away.

Catherine froze in shock, clinging to her daughter. Ron was here! He was here!

"Daddy's in the hayloft!" Nora cried again, burying her face in Catherine's stomach.

"It was me," Cody said, drawing her attention. "I was just playing. I forgot. I'm sorry!"

Gunter tore past her with a deadly, feral growl and dove toward Cody before anyone had time to grasp the situation.

"You bastard!" Gunter shouted, his fist aimed at Cody's shocked, bloodless face.

Catherine finally came out of her stupor, realizing what was happening. "Gunter!" she yelled.

As if in slow motion, Catherine could only watch as Gunter's fist connected with Cody's face, sending the defenseless boy reeling into the wall behind him. His head hit with a solid thunk, suspending Cody long enough for Gunter to connect again, this time with Cody's stomach. The battered boy slid in a boneless heap to the floor.

Catherine rushed straight into the fight and stood between the enraged young man and his fallen prey.

Her eyes glaring at Gunter, she didn't see Marcus Saints start in their direction or see Robbie grab him by the shoulder and stop him.

"You son of a bitch!" Gunter growled, trying to move around Catherine.

"Gunter! No!" she shouted when he tried to take another swing. She moved with him, blocking his way. "Enough," she said more calmly. "You will not hit him again."

Gunter turned his anger on her. "You heard! He scared Nora," he growled. "I'm gonna kill him."

"No, you're not," Catherine said firmly, flinching when he tried to shove her out of the way but managing to keep her body between him and Cody.

He grabbed her shoulders, and Catherine lifted her chin. "He made a mistake," she whispered. "Cody would never scare Nora on purpose. He was only playing."

"How can you know that?"

Catherine set her hand on his heaving chest. "Because I trust Cody, Gunter. He just wasn't thinking."

"Then I'll teach the son of a bitch to think!" he snapped, pushing her away, trying to get to Cody.

Catherine stepped between them again, getting a bit angry herself. "How, Gunter?" she hissed, shedding her sweater and pulling up the right sleeve of her shirt, exposing a three-year-old scar. "Is this how you're going to teach him?" She lifted the hem of her shirt enough to expose another scar, this one running from her waist up to just under her breast. "Or maybe like this!" Catherine turned her back on the stunned man and parted her hair at the nape of her neck, exposing yet another scar about two inches long. "Maybe this would teach him to think!"

She turned back to Gunter. "Will giving Cody a beating make Nora feel safe?" she asked through clenched teeth, taking another step forward, causing the suddenly pale boy to back up. "Did spending three weeks in the hospital so my children's father would be sent to prison solve my problems?"

Catherine stopped and blinked through blurry eyes, her anger suddenly deflated. "Don't you see, Gunter?" she whispered. "I've frightened Nora so badly that an innocent game of hide-and-seek scares her."

Gunter stared at her, his chest heaving and his eyes clouded with uncertainty. "How do you know, Catherine? How can you know Cody wasn't being mean?"

"I trust him, Gunter. The same way I trust you."

Catherine reached out and touched his chest again, gently this time, and quietly spoke to the young man she'd come to care so much about. "You acted without thinking, Gunter. You've lived with Cody longer than I have. Would he purposely scare Nora? Is he really that malicious?"

"No."

"You owe him an apology," she said.

Cody, who had either wisely or painfully remained silent until now, suddenly sucked in his breath. "No," he croaked. "I don't need an apology."

Catherine turned and tried to help the battered boy to his feet. Gunter silently moved around her and carefully lifted Cody up, holding him by the shoulder when he started to sway.

Cody ignored Gunter, instead keeping his attention on Catherine, staring at her in silence. "Thank you," he finally said. "I've never really done anything in particular to earn your trust—but thank you," he whispered.

"Don't thank me, Cody. I need to apologize to you. Nora overreacted, and it's my fault. I'll talk with her." Catherine's eyes welled up with tears as she looked at the battered young man. "Will you please let me explain it to her, and— and still be her friend?"

Robbie MacBain watched as Cody tried to comprehend the terrified mother who was apologizing to him for trying to protect her children. He scrubbed his face several times, up and down, hoping to work the blood back into it. He looked over at Marcus and saw that the man was as pale as he was. Never, ever, did he want to witness anything like that again.

He didn't know which had been harder; to see his

defenseless housekeeper standing squarely in front of an enraged young man, to see her anguish at her children's fears, or to see the undisputed testimony of her scars that told him just where those fears were founded. It had taken every ounce of willpower he possessed not to interfere and all of his strength to hold back Marcus Saints.

Never, ever, did he want to see that again.

Breaking into the charged silence, Robbie slapped Marcus on the back. "Come on, warden, I'll buy you a drink in my office."

Saints dazedly nodded and let Robbie lead him out of the kitchen. They walked through the attached shed to the office Robbie had built on the end of the garage two years ago—which was also where he kept his medicinal supply of scotch whisky.

But tonight's dose would probably be the whole bottle before either man would get his emotions back under control.

No . . . never again.

"I want to know where you found her," Marcus demanded half a bottle later.

"Raiding my henhouse," Robbie returned, taking another sip of his scotch.

"What?"

"Just another delinquent for my farm."

"No, really, where did you find her? She got any sisters?"

"Hell, I hope not. One Catherine Daniels is enough."

"She's not from around here."

"Arkansas."

Marcus whistled. "She answer an ad in the paper? How did you word it? 'Position open for adventuresome woman. Pay is two thousand dollars a week. Extensive health plan and a retirement fund after only six months'?"

Robbie scowled at him. "I found her raiding my henhouse six days ago. She and her kids were hiding out in an old cabin up on the mountain."

Robbie could tell Marcus still didn't believe him. He took another sip of his drink and tried again. "She's running away from the bastard who gave her those scars."

Marcus looked at Robbie and then at his empty glass. "Is she divorced?"

"Aye."

"Got custody of the kids?"

"Aye."

"Does he know she's here?"

"Not yet."

"Dammit, give me a break. She told Gunter he went to prison. Is he out?"

"Paroled three months ago."

Marcus closed his eyes. "She'll be safe here."

"Aye, she will."

"Maybe," his friend clarified, glaring at Robbie with slightly drunk eyes. "How the hell could you just stand there and let that happen? How could you know Gunter wasn't going to flatten her against the wall? Dammit! She stood nose-to-chest with the meanest brawler this side of the Canadian border!"

"Let's just call it instinct, Saints." Robbie sighed and looked down at his drink. "At least, that's what I knew at the time. Looking back, I would say I was insane. I honest to God don't know how I just stood there, either." He took a sip of his drink and continued. "But Gunter finally got a good look at violence from a victim's perspective, didn't he? So I guess my instinct was right."

"Do you ever screw up, MacBain?"

"Nay, never. That's why you gave me the boys, isn't it?"

Marcus snorted. "They're here because no one else

wants them. Hell, even the detention center didn't want Gunter."

"It would have only made him harder, and you know it."

Marcus refilled his glass and took another long swallow of the nerve-calming liquor. "Yeah, I know. That's why I moved heaven and earth to get him here."

Robbie chuckled. "You know that fierce little cat you just saw in the kitchen?"

"Yeah?"

"She's been a firecracker waiting to explode all day. She was sure you and Martha would find fault with something and take Cody and Rick and Peter away. I think she would have taken a stick to you both if you had tried."

Marcus snorted. "That's why I was getting suspicious looks all afternoon, when I wasn't getting cookies shoved down my throat." A sudden gleam appeared in his eyes. "You—ah—have room for two more boys, don't you?"

"Nay."

"Oh, come on, MacBain. This house is big."

Robbie set his glass down on the desk, lowered his feet to the floor, and stood up. "I have a logging crew of twelve men—some of which, I might add, have run my rigs off the road when Cat went jogging by in her short shorts. I have four boys who are just starting to get their acts together and now two little children who are afraid of their own shadows. I've got a housekeeper who is scared to death of anything bigger than she is—which is just about *everything*—and now I've taken on the impossible task of trying to court the woman. And you want me to add to that?"

Marcus's jaw, which had gone slack, suddenly snapped shut. "You're going to court her?" he asked, his eyes wide and glazed with drink. "As in marriage?" he croaked, just before he burst into laughter.

"What's so funny about that?"

Marcus snorted. "Robert MacBain, the most eligible bachelor in the north Maine woods," he said, waving his hand at the air. "And a man most determined to stay that way, rumor has it. You want to court Catherine Daniels?" he asked, breaking into another spasm of laughter.

"Aye!"

Marcus finally turned serious and shook his head. "That woman will never become another man's wife."

"Aye, she will. Catherine is going to marry me, and she'll damn well be deliriously happy about it!"

They both refilled their glasses at that arrogant statement. One with determination, one with awe.

Chapter Fourteen

Cody was settled in his bed with an ice bag on his face, a ginger ale for his upset stomach, and the promise of some stew when he felt better. Dinner had been a quiet affair, with Robbie and Marcus conspicuously absent and Nora and Nathan back to their quiet selves. Gunter had decided he needed a walk more than he needed supper, and Rick and Peter were doing the dishes without even being asked.

Catherine was now in the barn, facing her two children as they sat on a bale of hay and stared at her with rounded eyes filled with uncertainty.

"What happened in the kitchen earlier was nothing more than a terrible mistake," Catherine began, sitting on another bale directly in front of them. "Nora, if anything ever scares you, then you are right to come tell me immediately. Gunter is the one who jumped to conclusions without checking the facts first." She leaned forward and touched their knees. "And you saw how misunderstandings can lead to a terrible mess. People can get hurt when you react without finding out the truth first. I still want you both to tell me when something or someone scares you," she said. "But you also have to begin trusting people," she added, pointing to herself. "We all do, including me."

"You told Gunter you trust Cody," Nora whispered.

"I did tell him that," Catherine agreed with a nod. "Because I do. All of the boys have been extra nice to you, haven't they? Do you trust them to look out for you, Nora?"

The little girl nodded.

Catherine pulled her daughter into her arms. Nora was six years old. Not sixteen. Not twenty-six. She was just a little girl who had spent her entire life with a frightened and overly protective mother.

"We are all done running from your daddy," Catherine whispered, leaning forward and putting her hand on Nathan's shoulder, too, smiling at them both. "There's nothing he can do to us, and that's why we aren't going to be afraid of him anymore."

"He could hit you again," Nathan whispered. "He could hurt you bad enough that you go to the hospital like before."

Catherine shook her head. "No, Nathan, he can't," she assured him, relaxing back on her bale of hay. "Just like you guys, I've grown up these last three years, too. Your daddy can't hurt me because I won't let him. I just forgot that truth for a little while and ran away. But it stops here. This is our home now."

She canted her head at them. "Do you know what they call people who live in Maine? Maineiacs. And that's what we are now. We're Maineiacs."

"But that means crazy people," Nathan said.

Catherine nodded. "Then that's what we are. We're so crazy that we aren't afraid of anything or anyone. You both like going to school here, don't you?"

They both nodded.

"And you like the boys?"

"Gunter kind of scares me," Nathan said.

"Gunter learned a very valuable lesson tonight," Catherine assured him. "Remember how I told you to consider all of them guardian angels? Well, wasn't Gunter trying to be a guardian angel to Nora?"

"I guess so," Nathan agreed. "But Mom, you shouldn't have stood in the middle. You could have got hurt by accident."

"Oh, but I have a guardian angel, too, and he wouldn't have let me get clobbered."

"Who?"

"Mr. MacBain. He was standing right there. If he thought I was going to get hurt, he would have saved me."

"How do you know that?" Nora asked.

"Because we have a deal," Catherine told her children. "We watch each other's back. I look out for Mr. MacBain, and he looks out for me."

"Because you work for him?" Nathan asked.

"No. Because of that trust I was telling you about. He trusts me, and I trust him."

"I trust Mr. MacBain," Nora whispered. "And Gunter doesn't scare me at all, 'cause he's my guardian angel," she declared with six full years of authority. "And my bus driver said that the Tooth Fairy lives right here in Maine. Right up on that mountain," she added, pointing at the side of the barn.

Catherine had no idea how their discussion had gone from guardian angels to tooth fairies, but she was grateful.

"How come the bus driver told you that?" Nathan asked, apparently also ready to change the subject.

" 'Cause I showed her my tooth," Nora said, pulling

down her lip, then using her tongue to wiggle one of her bottom teeth. "And the Tooth Fairy will come down the mountain and give me a surprise," she explained. "Just as soon as it falls out and I put it under my pillow." She finally let go of her lip. "But what does she do with all the tooths, Mommy?"

Well, there was a good question if she ever heard one. Catherine mimicked Nora's earlier action, shrugged her shoulders, and held her palms up. "I have no idea," she admitted. She shot her a smile. "But I bet I know who would. Why don't you go ask Cody and Gunter?"

Nathan quickly shook his head, and Nora dropped her eyes to her lap, also shaking her head.

Catherine lifted her daughter's chin. "If you don't make peace with everyone, Nora, the silence will be like a black cloud hanging over the house." She looked at Nathan as well. "I want you both to take a bowl of stew to Cody and ask Gunter to come with you. And take Rick and Peter, too. And then ask all of them what the Tooth Fairy does with all the teeth she collects."

"What if they fight again?" Nora whispered.

"They won't," Catherine promised. "Gunter is very sorry he hit Cody. But now it's up to you to show them that you're all still friends. It's your turn to be their guardian angel."

"But I'm only a little girl. I can't be an angel."

"You certainly can. And so can Nathan. When a group of people live in a house together, they help each other. It doesn't matter how old or young you are."

Catherine pulled her children to their feet. "Remember how you helped me save Mr. MacBain's life up on the mountain? Well, this is your chance to be strong and brave again and chase the black cloud away from the house. Go," she said, urging them toward the door. "And don't forget to take Cody some stew. Have Gunter carry it," she added, thinking of her clean floor.

They slowly headed toward the door at the other end of the barn but stopped when Robbie stepped out of the shadows halfway down the aisle.

"M-Mr. MacBain," Nathan said.

"Nathan, Nora," he returned with a nod.

Catherine watched, her breath suspended, as Nathan squared his little shoulders and looked up at the towering giant. "The hens need grain, sir," he whispered. "And the water bucket leaks because it got all rusty."

Robbie nodded and set his hand on Nathan's shoulder. "Thank you for telling me. I'll pick up some grain and a new bucket tomorrow. I've never much cared for tending the hens myself, and I appreciate your taking over the chore for me."

Even under the weight of that large hand, Catherine could see Nathan's shoulders straighten even more. "I don't mind doing it," her son said. "And the hens have got used to me."

"I'm taking Cody some stew," Nora piped up, not about to be left out. She scrunched up her face at Robbie. "Do you know what the Tooth Fairy does with all them teeth?"

Robbie looked at Nora, clearly nonplussed, and shook his head. "I think you should take your mother's advice and ask the boys," he suggested, releasing Nathan. "They'll likely know."

Nora grabbed Nathan's hand and pulled him out of the barn behind her. Robbie watched them leave, then turned to Catherine.

"How long have you been standing there?" she asked.

He didn't answer but walked down the aisle toward her, and Catherine finally noticed the long, thick stick in his hand. He came within two paces and stopped, tucked his hands and the stick behind his back, and silently faced her.

Catherine took a step back. "You've been drinking," she said, taking another step back.

"Aye, some. But not nearly enough to be drunk, Catherine, so ya needn't look at me that way. I have never, nor will I ever, get drunk, as I don't much care for the feeling of being out of control." He matched her retreat with a step of his own. "And woman," he whispered, "that is exactly how I felt this afternoon in the kitchen."

She had backed all the way up against the end wall of the barn, and still he advanced, until he was so close she could feel the heat of his body. He leaned the stick against the wall beside her, placed his hands on either side of her head, and stared down at her so intensely that Catherine had to lock her knees to keep them from buckling.

"And if I ever again catch you standing in the middle of a fight between anyone bigger than your children, I will not be your guardian angel, Catherine, but your worse nightmare."

He leaned closer, lowering his head so that his face was only inches from hers. "Do you understand what I'm saying, little Cat? You will not put yourself in that position again."

She would have nodded, if her nose wouldn't have bumped into his. "Wh-what's the stick for?" she whispered, turning her head to look past his hand, deciding it was safer than looking into his fiercely disturbing eyes.

He straightened without stepping back, took his hands off the wall, and held them out from his sides, palms toward her. "Ya told me up at the cabin, when I woke up and found myself tied to the bed, that ya didn't care to feel defenseless," he said, his brogue thick with . . . with . . . Catherine couldn't decide if it was anger weighing his words or some other emotion.

"So I've brought ya a stout stick," he said, standing there with his arms open. "And giving ya the choice of how ya wish to end this conversation."

"Wh-what do you mean?"

He spread his hands wider. "You can either walk into my arms, Catherine, with your promise never to do anything like that again, or ya can take that stick and finish bringing me to my knees."

She was finally scared to the point that she started to tremble. "I'm not going to hit you."

"Then walk into my arms. Prove your words to your children that ya trust I'll not hurt ya."

"I-I don't want to do that, either. I just want to walk away."

"Nay," he said, shaking his head. "That's not one of the choices I've given you."

"But why? Why are you doing this?"

"Because I need to hold ya," he whispered. "And feel for myself that you're okay."

"But I am okay. Gunter didn't hurt me."

"Walk into my arms, Catherine," he softly repeated. "Give me the same trust ya gave Gunter."

She dropped her gaze to his shirt. "I can't. It's not the same thing. Hugging leads to . . . it leads to other things."

"Aye. It quite often does."

"I can't do it." She looked up at him, her eyes entreating. "Don't you understand? I can't ever trust my . . . my . . . another man that way."

"Then pick up the stick."

"No!" she snapped, feeling provoked. She crossed her arms under her breasts, refusing to touch that darn stick. "I am walking out of here, Robert MacBain, without hitting *or* hugging you!"

"And just how are you going to do that?" he asked,

crossing his own arms over his chest. "I seem to be standing between you and the door."

She stamped her foot. "This is silly. You can see I'm okay."

"But can't ya see that I'm not?" he whispered, holding out one of his hands.

She glared at him. "That's the liquor making you shake."

"Nay, little Cat. It's you." He spread both hands again. "Walk into my arms, Catherine."

She stared up at him, into his unfathomably deep, pewter gray eyes. What did he want from her? More than trust, she'd wager. But what?

"J-just a hug?"

"Aye. Just for you to allow me to hold you in my arms."

Catherine leaned away from the wall, hesitated, inched closer, took a deep breath, and slowly reached around his waist.

Ever so gently, and somewhat tentatively himself, he closed his arms around her and cupped her head to his chest.

"Ah, Catherine," he whispered with a sigh. "Ya're the bravest person I've ever been privileged to meet."

She stood there, stiff in his arms, and waited for the panic to overwhelm her. But all she felt was his powerful heat and the steady, strong beat of his heart. The taut muscles of his back slowly relaxed as he tenderly engulfed her, one of his hands lightly caressing her spine.

Catherine released her own sigh and melted against him.

His chest rumbled softly. "Aye, Cat, ya feel just fine." He touched his lips to her hair. "And so delicate for one so strong."

A lump rose in her throat, making it impossible to respond other than by digging her fingers into his back. It had been a hundred thousand years since she'd been hugged.

"I can die happy now," he whispered, responding to her touch by tightening his arms.

"It's only a hug," she was finally able to say, although it came out muffled against his chest.

"Aye, but I understand how special it is. Providence is smiling on us both tonight."

"What are you talking about?" she asked, looking up.

He allowed only her head to move, not her body, and smiled down into her eyes. "Do you believe in magic, Catherine?"

"Of course I do," she said, smiling up at his shining eyes. "Magic is what makes the sun rise every morning."

"Nay," he whispered, slowly shaking his head without taking his eyes off hers. "That would be physics. Magic is what brings a woman to my mountain, when she had a million other mountains to choose from, and then lets her pull me back from the brink of death. And magic moves her into my house and then gives her the courage to walk into my arms."

He feathered one large, callused finger over her brow and down her cheek, ending at her chin and lifting her face to his. "It's two people, Catherine," he whispered, his mouth only inches from hers, "discovering a mutual and sacred trust."

He finished his definition with the merest hint of his lips on hers, a kiss so tender and fleeting Catherine felt herself leaning up, yearning for more.

But it was over before she could decide if it had happened at all. She could only gasp when she was suddenly whisked off her feet, carried over to the stack of hay bales in the corner, and set down on the top bale with a light-hearted chuckle.

Robbie hopped up beside her, reached over and took her hand in his open palm, and used his thumb to caress her fingers.

"It never ceases to amaze me how such delicate hands can be so strong," he said. "I've never fully appreciated how a woman's lack of physical strength actually enhances her ability to thrive."

Catherine also stared down at their hands, trying very hard not to let his simple touch make her heart race. "What do you mean?" she whispered.

"When I want something to happen, I have a tendency just to demand results," he explained, using his thumb to draw a lazy circle on her palm. "And when that doesn't work, I rely on my size and strength to get what I want. But you, Catherine," he said, closing his fingers over hers. "You approach a problem quite differently."

"H-how?"

He shifted his shoulders to face her more fully, still keeping her hand gently trapped in his. "Take tonight for instance. I would have taken Gunter by the scruff of his neck and given him a good taste of his own medicine."

"You wouldn't have hit him."

"Nay," he agreed, shaking his head. "But he sure as hell would have walked away with something to think about." He lifted their hands and touched her knuckles to his lips. "Yet you accomplished the same thing without violence. Instead of trying to pound some sense into the boy, you showed Gunter what aggressive behavior looks like from the other side. Same results but much more resounding."

"I was just trying to stop him from hitting Cody again."

"Aye. But where I would have used my strength to stop him, you used shame."

"I don't want to shame anyone," she whispered.

"But is that not a stronger emotion, Catherine? Which

lesson will stay with Gunter? Seeing his action for what it is and being ashamed of himself, or merely being defeated by someone bigger than him? And that, little Cat," he said, using his free hand to tap her nose, "is why women are stronger than men."

Catherine balled her own free hand into a fist and fought the urge to rub her nose. "You're making me out to be something I'm not. I wasn't being brave or smart or trying to teach Gunter a lesson. I just wanted to stop the fight."

He nodded toward the stick leaning against the wall. "You could have found a weapon, a chair even, and stopped it just as quickly."

"If words wouldn't have worked, I probably would have," she said, finally giving in and rubbing her nose.

"Aye," he chuckled. "I don't doubt you would have. Because, just like me, you also find a way to get what you want."

He lifted her trapped hand and opened his, brought her palm to his lips, and kissed it, then closed her fingers over his kiss and let go.

"So, Catherine," he said with a sigh, relaxing back against the wall, canting his head to stare at the far end of the barn. "We've decided that we trust each other; we agree that you are just as strong as I am, only in a different way; and we have six young people in the house who need our combined strengths to see that they become fine adults." He looked at her. "What say we expand our little conspiracy, join your children with my boys, and see what we can do about growing them up?"

"But that's what we are doing."

"Nay. Tonight, when I set my hand on Nathan's shoulder, that was the first time I've touched your son. And other than Nora taking my hand at school, I haven't gone near her."

She dropped her gaze to her lap. "Wh-What are you asking?"

He lifted her chin to look at him. "I'm asking for your permission to be part of their lives. To be an example of what a . . . a father should be. That a man is someone they should look to for shelter and security, not run from."

"Don't you already have enough on your plate with the boys, your family, and your . . . your . . . whatever you're doing up on that mountain?" Catherine asked, waving toward TarStone.

"Nay. You can never overfill a plate when you're sharing it with someone."

"But why would you want to take on my children?"

"Because I want you."

"No."

"I've given you a stout stick."

"I do not hit people!"

"But you will have to, little Cat," he whispered, taking hold of her chin again and leaning close. "Because that's the only way to get rid of me."

"I'll just leave," she said, her words washing against him, only to echo back the regret in her voice.

"You're done running, Catherine. You'll take your stand here, with me, or you might as well dig a hole and crawl inside and pull it closed behind you."

"You're doing it again," she said, scrambling around until she knelt facing him, determined to make him understand. "You're seeing something that's not there. I'm not the brave woman you keep saying I am. I have all I can do to get up every morning and face another uncertain day."

"But ya still get up, lass."

"I don't want you to want me," she whispered. "It will only hurt us both."

"Too late," he murmured, cupping her face. "When you found me on the mountain and chose to save my life rather than run, it was too late for both of us."

Catherine thought about telling him that she hadn't had any choice at all. She thought about going over and getting that stick and finally making him understand. And then she thought about how secure she had felt in his arms when he'd hugged her. How brave. And yeah, how strong.

So strong in fact, Catherine decided as she looked into his compelling gray eyes, that she could finally quit wondering what it would feel like to be kissed by Robbie MacBain and simply kiss him herself.

Mimicking his hold on her, she cupped the sides of his face and pulled his mouth down on hers. And it wasn't a fleeting kiss she gave him, by God, but one that wouldn't leave any doubt that it was happening.

Robbie made a noise—she couldn't decide if he grunted or groaned—folded her into his arms, and leaned back against the wall. He canted his head and deepened the kiss—that she had started—by parting his lips over hers.

He tasted like very fine scotch, a perfect blend of heat and masculine appeal that set her mind spinning. There was nothing tentative about him this time, nothing fleeting or obscure.

Catherine opened her mouth, her growing urgency yearning for more, and melted against him, tasting, teasing his advancing tongue, welcoming the tremors racing through her. She also made a sound but recognized it as her own sense of wonder that she was not frightened but empowered by his response.

The muscles of his shoulders tightened under her hands, the tendons in his neck straining as he moved to taste her. Her breasts felt heavy, her nipples quickening from the blasting heat of his chest against hers.

Catherine rose to meet each new sensation and decided her libido was far from dead. This towering giant of a man, with his maddening choice of a stick or a hug, only mocked her fears with his mouth, his taste, his all-consuming presence.

He broke the kiss, his lips forging a trail of quivering pleasure along her jaw, up her cheek, and across her temple. And then he covered her head with his hand and tucked her under his chin with a sigh so fierce the air rushed from her lungs.

"I'm thinking we should stop now," he whispered. "Before I forget my noble intentions."

Catherine would have sighed herself if his impassioned embrace would have let her. She'd somehow ended up straddling his lap, and the indecent position—and the blatant evidence of his not-so-noble desire pushing intimately against her—finally unnerved her.

She tested those very intentions by trying to wiggle free. He groaned quite loudly, picked her up, and stood her on the floor before she could gasp.

She faced him, clutching the front of her sweater in her fists, her forearms pressed against her sensitized breasts, her face feeling as if it was about to combust.

"No more choices, Cat. Just turn around and walk away."

"I . . . this was . . . that kiss wasn't . . ."

"Go in the house, Catherine."

She spun toward the door.

"And take the stick with you."

Catherine turned back, shaking her head. "I don't want it."

He slid off his perch and walked to the stick, and picked

it up, then came over, put it in her hand, and closed her fist around it. "But I do want ya to have it. Stand it next to the clock in the kitchen, and if another fight ever breaks out and I'm not home, use it."

She tried to shove it back at him. "I won't hit anyone."

He continued to hold her fist closed over the stick. "If a stranger comes to the house and threatens your children, will you waggle your finger at him?"

"Of course not."

"If Rick starts fighting with Peter and won't stop, and there's no one else around, what will you do?"

"I . . . I would . . . I'd . . ."

He gently ran a finger down the side of her face. "It's only a weapon, Cat. An equalizer that can multiply your strength times ten. A stout stick can make the difference between being completely defenseless against someone twice your size or being victorious."

"It's also a weapon that could be turned against me."

"Aye. But tomorrow I'll begin teaching you how to keep that from happening."

"What?"

"Weapons are only as effective as the person using them, Catherine. But with the proper training, you could drop a bear in its tracks with only a stick." He smiled and lightly tapped the end of her nose. "And I'm going to show you how to do that. You can always find something for a weapon, be it a baseball bat, a broom handle, or a tree branch."

She pulled free, clutched the stick to her chest, and rubbed her nose on her sleeve. She opened her mouth, but nothing came out, so she snapped it shut, spun around, and marched toward the end of the barn.

"Sleep well, little Cat," he softly called after her.

Catherine stopped at the door and turned back to him,

still clutching the stick to her chest. "I—I would like for you to set an example for Nathan and Nora," she quietly told him. "And I do want to help with the boys." She lifted her chin. "But I also want you to stop whatever you're doing up on that mountain."

"I'm sorry," he said, shaking his head. "You're going to have to settle for two out of three."

"I could stop you by telling your father."

"Aye, but you won't. It's not adventure that takes me up the mountain, Catherine, but duty. And the one thing you must never do is interfere in my duty."

"Your duty," she repeated, glaring at him. "What kind of duty compels a man to get beat up and nearly killed? That's not duty, that's foolishness." She waved her hand in frustration. "And if you know you're going to get in a fight, why in heck don't you carry something better than that stupid sword you had when I found you?"

He softly chuckled. "That stupid sword is my weapon of choice, just as that stick will be yours once I've instructed you. Go in the house, Catherine. You've dealt with enough for one day. In time, you'll come to understand why I do what I do, but not tonight."

She stared down the long aisle of the softly lit barn; he stood with his feet planted firmly, his arms crossed over his chest, and his piercing gray eyes focused directly on hers.

Catherine turned and quietly walked out of the barn.

Chapter Fifteen

He didn't know why he was surprised that when Catherine Daniels set her mind to something, she approached it with the fierceness of a lion protecting her cubs. But as she again tried to split open his head with her stick, Robbie wondered if he was creating a monster or merely providing an outlet for six married years of abuse.

He robbed Catherine of her target by simply ducking her impressively vicious swing. "You're letting your emotions rule your actions," he pointed out as she turned to face him, her stick raised for another strike.

He held up his hand to stop her. "This is what I was trying to explain earlier, Cat. You started with calculated moves, but now you're just taking wild swings out of sheer frustration. If you become emotionally involved, you've lost the fight."

She stood the stick on the ground and leaned against it as she wiped a shaky hand over her brow. "When someone's trying to knock your teeth out, it *does* get emotional," she said, her face red with exertion.

He walked up and disarmed her, then balanced the stick on one of his fingers. "Nay, it's about control. Your weapon is your lever, you're the fulcrum, and your strength is multiplied when you power your swing through your body."

"My high-school physics is rusty."

"But you still use it every day. You pry the stubborn lid off a jar or displace your weight when you lift a twenty-pound roast out of the oven. Use your body, Cat," he said, positioning her hands, putting one in the middle of the stick and one about eighteen inches off center. He moved to stand behind her and placed his own hands over hers. "Don't swing it like a baseball bat. *Push* the stick away from yourself," he instructed, thrusting her right hand forward.

He followed that move by pushing her left hand in a downward arc and then up, stopping with the shorter end of the stick about level with a man's jaw.

"There," he said. "You smack him on the shoulder first and quickly follow through by using the momentum of his reaction—which will be to push the stick away—and come up and strike him under the chin. Or here," he suggested, jabbing the short end forward again. "You can aim for either his throat or his sternum. One quick, powerful thrust, and he'll be gasping for breath."

"But what if the person I'm fighting knows how to fight?" she asked, stepping out from his embrace and turning to face him. "What if he's someone like you and knows all the tricks?"

Robbie gestured toward the pasture. "Then you revert to your trusty old standby. You run like hell."

"And if I can't run? If I'm cornered?"

He nodded at the stick in her hand. "You'll at least be able to fight your way out of a corner by the time we're done. But Cat, most of the people you encounter won't be trained in hand-to-hand combat."

"And they'll think I don't pose a threat, because of my size and gender," she repeated from his earlier lecture.

"Aye. Surprise is your greatest weapon."

She looked down at the stick, then back up at him, and broke into a brilliant smile. "Thank you. I never thought violence could have a bright side, but being able to defend myself sure beats the heck out of spending three weeks in the hospital."

"Aye. But it's only violence if you allow your emotions to get involved. Properly used, a weapon is nothing more than a tool. You don't want to kill anyone but protect yourself. And you accomplish that by being the one who is in control."

She twirled the stick in her hand like a baton and shot him a smug smile. "I rather like that idea. What other tricks have you got up your sleeve?"

Aye, he was creating a monster, all right. But at least she would be a prepared monster from now on. "How do you feel about knives?" he asked.

Her smile left as quickly as it had come. "You have to get close to someone to use a knife."

He dismissed her concern with a shake of his head and leaned over and pulled his small dagger from his boot. "But it's still better than a stick," he said, holding out the dagger for her to take. "And can be handy for other things as well."

She examined the sharp, tiny knife. "This looks old."

"Aye. It's about the same age as my sword."

She canted her head at him. "Where is your sword, by the way?" she asked, lifting a brow. "And the two plaids I washed and mended and put in your closet?"

"Stashed on the mountain."

She stared at him, obviously weighing her chances of getting him to elaborate. She must have decided he wouldn't, because she dropped her gaze to the two weapons in her hands.

She gave the dagger back to him. "I think I'll learn how to use the stick first," she said, placing her hands where he'd positioned them before. "It's much more scary-looking and will be more intimidating."

Robbie slid the dagger in his boot with a chuckle, then planted his feet and crouched, holding his arms out and waggling his fingers at her. "Come on, then, little Cat. Let's see if you can't take my breath away."

She eyed him, eyed her stick, then looked back up, her fierce expression broken only by her determined smile. But she didn't go for his shoulder first and then his jugular as he had showed her. No, the little monster feigned the expected attack, then aimed her first strike at his knees— just as a green Suburban pulled into the driveway.

Distracted by both the arrival of company and her deception, Robbie misjudged Cat's swing, and the solid maple stick connected with his left knee. He was only able to keep his head from being cracked open as she followed through by speeding up his unexpected journey to the ground.

He heard Cat's gasp at about the same time he hit the dirt. Aye, Dr. Frankenstein had nothing on him when it came to creating monsters.

"Ohmygod! You let me hit you!" She grabbed his shoulder and tried to lift him up. "You're supposed to pay attention!"

He let her roll him over and lay with his eyes closed, hiding his smile as she continued to scold.

"This is why you come home all beat up," she muttered, brushing the dirt off his cheek. "You allow yourself to get distracted."

Robbie heard four truck doors slam, quickly followed by approaching male laughter he would recognize from his grave, and female *tsk-tsk*-ing.

He finally released his smile and opened his eyes. "My papa's about to praise you for your trick and probably give you a hug for bringing me to my knees."

"Th-That's your father?" she groaned, looking toward the driveway, her face turning a lovely shade of red. "Ohmygod," she whispered, glaring at Robbie just before closing her eyes. "He's going to think I'm more crazy in person than on the phone."

Robbie sat up and brought his nose inches from hers. "I'm impressed, little Cat."

"For hitting you?"

"Nay, for deciding I wouldn't retaliate. I saw it," he whispered. "In your eyes, right when you hit me. I saw your horror, and then I saw the moment you realized you had nothing to fear from me."

"All that while planting your face in the dirt?" she asked. She reached over and tapped the end of his nose. "Amazing, considering you couldn't see my swing coming."

Robbie touched his nose and hid his smile by standing up and taking the time to rub his knee.

"Now I'm understanding how ya've been able to keep this one longer than the others," his papa said as he brushed past Robbie and over to Cat. "She's the one terrorizing *you*." He held out his hand. "I'm Michael. We met on the phone yesterday."

"It—it's nice to meet you, Mr. MacBain."

"And I'm his mum," Libby said, taking Cat's hand from his father to hold in hers. "Please, call me Libby. I've been hearing some wonderful things about you. Not from Robbie," she added, turning to frown at him before looking back at Cat. "Rick and Peter stopped by two days ago for a short visit."

"And this is Gram Katie," Robbie added, putting his arm around Libby's mother and bringing her over. "And you've already met Ian."

His poor housekeeper tried to tuck her hair into place, and then she brushed down the front of her grass-stained sweatshirt. "It's very nice to meet you," she told them, giving each a nod as she slowly inched her way toward the house. "I'll just go put on the kettle for tea. I have a pan of blueberry cobbler cooling on the counter."

"We can't stay, I'm afraid," Michael said. "We're on our way to Bangor to shop. We're just dropping off Ian."

Robbie looked at his uncle.

Ian lifted his chin. "I hate to shop. And I feel like a walk in the woods, with you along to protect me from the bears."

"He'll walk with you, Ian," Libby said, staring at Robbie. "Just as soon as I get a hug. You live two miles away, and I haven't seen you in nearly two weeks."

"You've been at Maggie's when I've tried to visit," Robbie said in his defense, reaching out and giving her a hug.

He suspended his breath and waited, but Libby only patted his back, gave him a squeeze, and stepped away with a nod.

"There. I feel better now." She turned to Cat, who had managed to inch her way a good ten feet closer to the front porch. "You'll have Robbie bring you to dinner this Sunday," she told his housekeeper. "And please, bring your children. I'm anxious to meet your family."

Cat looked from Robbie to Libby and nodded. "Thank you. I'd like that. I'll bring dessert."

"I believe you have my lasagna pan," Kate said, taking Cat by the arm and heading toward the house, Libby falling into step on the other side of her mother. Ian muttered something about this taking a while—and something about blueberry cobbler—and tagged along behind them.

Robbie turned to his father, who was eyeing the stick lying on the ground. Michael picked it up, hefted its weight, and looked at Robbie with one eyebrow raised.

"It's a long story," Robbie said, leaning over to rub his knee again.

"I imagine I have time to hear it, considering the women are in the kitchen. They'll likely be there an hour talking about recipes."

Robbie sighed, sat down on the ground, and wrapped his arms around his bent knees. He stared at Pine Lake, waiting until his father was settled beside him.

"She and her children were camping out in that old cabin up on TarStone, on the land I bought from Greylen two years ago." He looked at his father. "She's running from an abusive ex-husband who just got paroled from prison three months ago."

"Aye. I guessed it was something like that from what Peter and Rick said." Michael rolled the heavy maple stick in his hand. "And so you've taken in another stray—three, actually—and you're teaching Catherine how to deal with her ex-husband?"

Robbie shook his head. "Nay. I will take care of Daniels personally, if I'm lucky enough for him to show up here." He gestured toward the stick. "My lessons are only to help Cat feel less like a victim and more like the brave woman she really is."

Michael raised his brow again. "You sound as if you have a vested interest in the woman."

Robbie gazed out over Pine Lake. "I do. If I have any say about it, Cat won't ever be leaving here." He looked back at his father. "She's the one, Papa. I felt it the moment we finally came face-to-face." He turned more fully to Michael. "I want her. But I'm not sure how to handle both my need for Catherine and my calling. You and I have talked about my gift since I was a child, but we never discussed how I would balance it with a wife. She's a modern and won't understand the magic."

"Ya're a modern, too."

"Aye. But I grew up with the magic. Hell, I have conversations with an owl. What do you think Cat's reaction would be if she knew that?"

Michael set his hand on Robbie's arm. "We've all married moderns, son. And some of us have learned the hard way that there's no simple way to explain who we are."

Both men looked toward the house when they heard voices and saw the women standing by the truck. Michael used the stick to lever himself to his feet.

"But if I may suggest?" Michael said quietly. "Have a very firm hold on her heart before ya try to explain anything. For as much as your mother loved me, she wasn't quite ready to hear what I had to tell her." He canted his head. "Mary wasn't even aware of her own gift while she was alive, I don't think, or she would have been able to accept who I was and where I came from." He smiled. "But I think once she felt ya stirring inside her, she understood and tried to come back to me."

It was all Robbie could do not to tell his father that he'd visited with Mary in the storm, as the beautiful woman she'd been when Michael MacBain had loved her.

"Has she not come to you once, Papa?"

"Nay," Michael said, shaking his head. "Not after Libby came into my life. Mary cared enough not to intrude. Not only for my sake but for Libby's as well." He looked up toward TarStone. "She's watching us, though. I can . . . I feel her sometimes." He looked back at Robbie and smiled.

"A whisper or a mere breath on my neck. Or I'll catch a hint of drying herbs in the middle of the tree fields in the dead of winter."

"Aye," Robbie said, slapping his father's back and leaving his hand there as they started toward the truck. "She's always been watching."

Michael stopped and looked him directly in the eye. "If ya're sure Catherine Daniels is the woman ya want to grow old with, then talk to Libby and your Aunt Grace and Sadie and Charlotte. They've gone from moderns to believers in some very interesting ways. Your Aunt Sadie thought she'd actually died, because she couldn't comprehend the magic at first."

"Maybe I should just keep my calling separate from my life with Catherine. Why complicate things?"

Michael snorted and shoved the stick at Robbie's chest. "Aye, you do that, son. And see if ya don't wake up some morning to an empty house. Keeping secrets from each other—even small secrets, much less something as important as your calling—is more abusive than anything Catherine's ex-husband could have done to her. At least physical abuse is openly hostile, but the silence of keeping things from each other is more lethal than a sword slicing through a person's heart."

Robbie dropped his head and sighed. "I'll tell her."

"After you've caught her," Michael reminded him, slapping him on the shoulder and turning them both toward the truck again. "And after you've dealt with Daniels in a way that won't come back to haunt ya."

They reached the truck, and Robbie leaned over and gave first Gram Katie and then his mum a kiss on the cheek. "Are the boys invited to Sunday dinner?" he asked. "That's quite a houseful."

"Of course they are," Libby said, sliding into the front

seat. She looked past him at Cat. "We eat at noon, and then everyone goes for a walk after dinner, so bring boots."

Catherine nodded and said good-bye to Kate as Michael settled the elderly but spry woman in the backseat and handed her the seat belt.

Michael looked over the roof of the Suburban at Robbie. "Something's troubling your uncle. Ian's been restless the last couple of days, and Winter is worried about him. See if ya can find out what's troubling him on your walk home."

"Aye," Robbie agreed, nodding. "We'll have a talk."

"Good," Michael said, ducking into the truck.

Robbie leaned in, gave his mum another kiss on the cheek, and then closed her door and smiled at the red letters printed across it: "Bigelow Christmas Tree Farm, Pine Creek, Maine."

John and Ellen Bigelow had planted their first Christmas tree fifty-six years ago. His father had never changed the name of the farm, though he'd owned it for more than thirty years now. Michael had always cited some excuse about name recognition, but Robbie suspected it was more likely his attachment to the two wonderful people, not a business decision.

Ellen Bigelow had died when Robbie was eight, and John had passed on seven years later. Both were buried on a knoll overlooking their farm, a balsam fir tree planted at the head of their graves.

"Ian's inside eating cobbler, isn't he?" Robbie asked Cat as they both watched their company leave.

"There must be something in the water around here. Everyone has a sweet tooth," she said, walking back to the house.

Robbie fell into step beside her. "How do you feel about your lesson this morning?"

She looked over at him as they climbed the steps. "I'm sorry I hit you."

"I'm not." Robbie handed her the stick. "That's exactly what you're after—do the unexpected. If I get smacked, it's my fault and your credit."

"You didn't just go into the woods and find any old stick," she said, stopping at the door and holding it up between them. "You put some work into this."

He had searched for just the right young maple sapling, stripped off its thin bark, and cut it down to Catherine's size. It was straight as a flagpole, and he'd sanded it smooth and rubbed in a coat of wax to preserve its beauty.

"There's nothing that says a weapon can't look good. You remember the fine craftsmanship of my sword, don't you? It used to belong to my namesake, my great-uncle Robert MacBain. He called it *An Cluaran,* which is Gaelic for *The Thistle.* My father told me Robert always boasted that it was the sting of his sword that men feared."

Cat smiled up at him. "It's a guy thing, isn't it, to name your stuff? Like your truck," she said, nodding toward his Suburban's bug shield.

"Aye. It's called being possessive." He leaned down. "Which is why I've named my housekeeper after a mountain cat."

Her face flushed scarlet, and she spun away and walked into the kitchen. Robbie followed and found Ian sitting at the table, a cup of coffee in one hand, a fork in the other, and more blueberry cobbler on his beard than on his plate.

"If you don't want to be waddling home, Uncle, you'd better push away from the table," Robbie said, watching Cat walk over and set her stick by the grandfather clock.

"I'm coming," Ian muttered, sliding his chair back. He went over to Catherine, started to say something, then suddenly reached out and hugged her so tightly she squeaked.

"Thank ya for . . . well, for everything, lass," he said, stepping back and grinning from his own flushed face. He walked over to retrieve his coat. "I hope ya can keep up with me today, young Robbie," he said, walking out the door. "I don't have time to dawdle."

Robbie looked at his shocked housekeeper, shrugged, and then followed his uncle outside, only to find the old warrior was already halfway up the driveway.

Robbie jogged to catch up, then tucked his hands behind his back and fell into step beside him. "Is this what you've been doing all week?" he asked. "Visiting everyone to say good-bye?"

Ian glanced over at him, then looked back at the path. "I wasn't expecting it to be so hard," he muttered. "How in hell am I supposed to say good-bye if they don't even know I'm leaving?"

"You can't, Uncle." He stopped and turned Ian to face him. "You can still change your mind."

"Nay," Ian growled, squaring his shoulders. "I want to be with my Gwyneth."

Robbie started walking again. "Then you shall. I'll pick you up at Gu Bràth tomorrow afternoon at three. That will give us plenty of time to reach the summit before sunset."

"What can I bring with me?"

"Do you still have your old plaid?"

"Aye. And my dagger." He frowned at Robbie. "We sold my sword to help finance our new life here." He snorted. "Not that I could lift it now."

"Then that's all you can bring. Nothing modern." Robbie stopped him again and touched his uncle's jacket over the chest pocket on his shirt. "You can't even take your reading glasses, I'm afraid. And you must give me your word that you won't use what you've learned in this time to change anything in the past."

Ian started walking again. "There ain't no books to read, anyway," he muttered, waving his hand at the air. "And no malls and cars and millions of crazy people."

"There's no indoor plumbing, either," Robbie reminded him. "Or hot showers or electric lights or central heating."

"But there's my Gwyneth," Ian whispered, his eyes shining as he looked over at Robbie. "And Niall and Caitlin and Megan. That's all I'm needing to be happy. What's our lie going to be?"

"That you and the others were captured by marauding . . . ah . . . Vikings, I think we should say. And held prisoner for ten years. The others died fighting or trying to escape. But when you grew old, they simply sailed back and dropped you off on the beach."

Ian chuckled. "Like anyone will believe that."

"Who's to dispute it? Scotland's been constantly raided throughout history."

Ian stopped and looked up at him with narrowed eyes. "What about my age? I'm thirty-five years older than when I left, not ten."

"You actually have the health of a sixty-year-old man of that time, Uncle. Life was hard on a body back then, and rarely did men reach their eighty-fifth birthdays. Our lie will work."

"And the fact that I speak English?" Ian asked, walking again. "I'm liable to start speaking it without thinking."

"Then we should change Viking to English marauders."

"Aye. That will make more sense," Ian agreed. "And I can say that I walked all the way home from England." He puffed up his chest. "Aye. I could get many a fine tale for the campfires with that one." Ian stopped him again. "You're going to stay with me awhile, aren't ya? Until I get adjusted?"

"Aye, I'll stay as long as it takes."

"What about Daar's book of spells ya're hunting for? Have ya found it yet?"

"Nay. But you might be able to help me with that. We'll see once we get there."

Ian's shoulders straightened, and his eyes sharpened. "I'll help. And I'll—"

They both looked up at the sound of a piercing shrill that came from over their heads. Mary flew past them and landed on a branch hanging across the tote road.

Robbie was stunned. The last he'd seen Mary, she had still been in the old time. How had she managed to return by herself? But then he remembered what she had shown him in the storm. Mary could travel at will just as he could.

"There's yar pet," Ian said, breaking into a wide grin. "I can't believe that old bird is still alive." He looked at Robbie. "Mary has been with you for, what, over twenty years now? How long do snowy owls live, anyway?"

Robbie shrugged. "I have no idea." He presented his arm to the owl. "Come, little one," he said softly.

"She's bleeding," Ian whispered, moving beside Robbie and pointing up at the branch. "There, on the bottom of her belly, just above her left leg. Do ya see it?"

"Aye," Robbie growled. "Come," he told the bird.

Mary spread her wings and glided down and landed on his arm. Robbie stroked her chest and lifted his arm to see her wound.

"You've gone and gotten yourself hurt," he said, using his finger to gently lift her bloodied feathers. "Aye, you've been nicked by an arrow."

"How do ya know that?" Ian asked.

Robbie smiled at his uncle. "She told me as much."

Ian stepped back. "She did? She really does talk to ya?"

"Aye. We've had many conversations over the years." He lifted a brow. "You're surprised? I'm about to take you on an unimaginable journey, and you think it odd that I talk to my pet?"

Ian shook his head. "I quit trying to think years ago," he muttered. "Ya must take her to the veterinarian and have that wound tended."

Robbie looked back at Mary. "Or I can take her to my housekeeper. Cat's father was a veterinarian, and she knows quite a bit about tending wounds."

"Then go," Ian said, waving him away. "It's only a short distance to Gu Bràth. I'll be fine. And I'll see ya tomorrow afternoon." He gave Robbie a wide grin. "I'll hide my plaid under my jacket so no one will suspect anything."

"Uncle," Robbie said when Ian turned to leave. "I wish . . . I'm . . ." He waved him away. "Enjoy your last evening with Grey and Grace and Winter," he said softly. "And know that tomorrow night, you'll be with your Gwyneth."

"Aye. I'll do that," the old warrior said, turning and walking down the tote road, leaning on the stick Robbie had found for him at the beginning of their walk. He waved over his shoulder. "I'll be ready when ya come to fetch me."

Robbie watched after Ian until he disappeared down the last knoll before Gu Bràth, then turned his attention back to Mary.

"I've a good mind to trim your wing feathers!" he snapped, starting toward home. "To stop your recklessness."

Mary let out a deep rattle that sounded more like laughter than owl talk and dug her talons into his jacket sleeve to keep her balance as he lengthened his stride.

Robbie sighed. Scolding his pet had always been an exercise in futility. And Mary was just as determined as he was to keep the Highlanders here. She still loved Michael

MacBain and had no wish to see the warrior's life uprooted again.

"I have someone I want you to meet," he told her, quickening his pace. "Her name is Cat, and she's going to be your daughter-in-law just as soon as I persuade her to trust her heart to me."

Mary blinked at him.

"Aye, I know this is sudden. But if you'd come back with me instead of staying behind and getting arrows slung at you, you could have given me your blessing *before* I realized my intentions toward Catherine. Now you'll just have to accept her."

Robbie stopped and glared at his pet. "Don't even think to give her a hard time. And you needn't test her like you did Libby. Catherine has already survived her trial by fire."

He tucked his arm against his body and cupped the snowy's head to his chest. "Aye, little one," he crooned. "I have every hope she can live with my calling. And that's where you can help. You've been in Catherine's position. You were a modern woman in love with an ancient. You'll know how Cat will feel, and you'll know how I can win her heart. Will you help?" he asked, opening his hand so Mary could look up at him. "Will you join in my courtship of Catherine?"

Mary blinked and nipped at his thumb.

He chuckled and started home again, his step considerably lighter. "Aye. Then you can begin by being a perfect patient and not nipping her fingers when she sews you up with her pink silk thread. And Mary," he added with a laugh, tapping the owl on the tip of her beak, "don't bring her any gifts like you brought Libby. I already have more magic than I can handle right now."

Chapter Sixteen

Catherine couldn't quit smiling all the time she showered and even found herself wondering who owned the face in the mirror as she dried her hair. The woman staring back at her was . . . well, glowing and looking rather pleased with herself.

She also looked as if she knew a secret. Something about feeling alive for the first time in years. Energized. Hopeful. Eager.

But eager for what the day would bring or to be kissed again so thoroughly that her insides still hadn't uncurled?

She hadn't been panicked by their *simple hug* last night in the barn, and that's what must have given her the courage to kiss him. That Robbie had taken over the kiss didn't surprise her, but that he had ended it so nobly did. The guy appeared too good to be true.

She had finally worked up the nerve to tap him on the nose this morning, and been rewarded with a look of such surprise, that Catherine had been tempted to do it again.

And she probably would have, if she hadn't caught sight

of Michael MacBain bearing down on them like a mountain. He'd brushed past his son and right up to her, taken her hand in both of his large paws, and given her a smile that had curled her insides even tighter.

Robbie was the spitting image of his father; though only a few inches shorter than his son, Michael MacBain had the exact same compelling gray eyes, the same cheekbones and jaw, and the same powerful energy that blasted into a person when he looked at them.

Catherine finished brushing out her hair and pulled it into a tail at the nape of her neck. Just two weeks ago, she would have run from Robbie's father as fast as her legs would carry her, she realized, smiling at herself in the mirror.

And that, Catherine decided, was the true definition of magic. In less than two weeks, she'd somehow gone from a mouse to a mountain cat.

She loved that Robbie called her Cat. She loved that she actually felt like one, so much so that she had kissed a towering giant last night without even thinking about where it might lead.

And she had also smacked him with the stick this morning, though she hadn't really meant to. But at least now she understood why Robbie kept getting beat up. Being big and brave and strong were worthless qualities if the guy couldn't even stay focused on what he was doing for more than two minutes. Maybe while he was teaching her to use the stick, she could teach him how to pay attention. Maybe a few more smacks on the knee would sharpen his focus.

"Cat," Robbie called, stomping through the kitchen door. "Cat? I need your help."

Catherine rushed out of the bathroom but came to an abrupt halt at the sight of the large snowy owl perched on Robbie's arm, silently staring at her.

"What have you got there?" she whispered, slowly inching closer so she wouldn't startle the bird. She stopped a few paces away and looked up at Robbie and smiled. "A snowy? Where did she come from?"

He walked over to the rocking chair by the clock and eased the bird onto the back of the chair before turning to her. "She's my pet," he said, shedding his jacket and tossing it on the table. "And she's hurt." He walked to the owl and brushed a finger down her wing. "She's bleeding and needs to be sewn up."

Catherine moved over beside Robbie and peered down at the snowy's belly, seeing the bloodied feathers just above her leg.

"There must be a vet near here," she said. "Somebody with experience handling wildlife."

"Nay. I want you to sew her up, just like you did me."

Catherine frowned at him, then at the bird. "There's a huge difference between sewing up a small cut on your hand and trying to do the same to an animal without anesthesia. We can't explain to her about the pain, and she'll hurt herself even worse by struggling against it." She looked back at Robbie. "She needs a vet who has the proper equipment."

"Nay, she'll lie still for you. I'll hold her," he said, going into the living room and returning with her sewing kit. "Use the pink thread. She'll like that."

Catherine was watching the bird, who was dividing her attention between them by turning her head whenever either of them spoke, as if she were following the conversation.

"I can't just sew her up," she repeated, the snowy looking at her again. "You remember what it felt like to have a needle run through your flesh. Do you think she's going to just lie there and let me poke her?"

"Aye," Robbie said, setting the kit on the table, opening it up, and taking out the pink silk thread, a needle, and her small pointed scissors.

Completely ignoring her argument, he walked over to the cupboard, found a pot, filled it with water, dropped the needle and thread and scissors into it, and set it on the stove to boil.

"She'll understand you're trying to help her," he explained, going over to the owl and holding out his arm.

The snowy stepped from her perch onto his shirt sleeve, folded her wings, and blinked at Catherine as Robbie sat down in a chair at the table. He pulled out another chair to face him and patted it.

"Sit, Cat. Come check out this wound, and tell me if you think it should be stitched."

Catherine eyed the huge, lethal talons curled into Robbie's shirt sleeve. "At least put your jacket back on to protect your arm," she suggested, slowly sitting down beside him, careful not to startle the bird.

But instead of putting on his jacket, Robbie tucked the owl against his chest, cupped her tail feathers with his free hand, and tipped her onto her back, cradling the snowy in the crook of his arm as if she were a baby.

It was Catherine who was blinking now. The owl was lying as still as a statue, looking up at Robbie with complete trust.

"Ah . . . could you hold her feet for me?" Catherine asked.

She waited until he had both sets of sharp talons firmly grasped in his hand, then leaned over and gently used her fingers to lift the blood-stained feathers on the snowy's belly. She leaned closer, using her other hand to part the down just below the small cut. "It's not very deep," she said absently, gently feeling the area around it. "And it's not infected yet. But it would heal better if I set two stitches."

"Aye. Mary will be just fine," he said, running his free hand along the owl's face.

Catherine got up, set a clean towel in the sink, and poured the boiling pot of water over it, letting the towel catch the needle and thread and scissors. She used another towel to pick them up and carried them back to the table. Then she went back to the sink, carefully lifted out the hot towel, waved it a bit to cool it, then wrung it out.

She carried the damp towel back to the table and sat down. "I'm going to clean her up," she explained, positioning Robbie's free hand just below the owl's head. "Try to keep her still."

"She'll not move a muscle," Robbie said in a croon, smiling down at Mary and tucking his index finger just under her beak.

"She'll bite you," Catherine warned. "That beak is as lethal as her talons. Then I'll have two patients to deal with."

"But you love tending me," he whispered, lifting his smile to her.

Catherine rolled her eyes and looked down at the wound, and gently began to clean the blood off Mary's feathers.

"I would prefer to trim the feathers away, but I don't want to leave her with a bald spot." She glanced up. "I don't think you want to cage her, do you?"

"Nay. She wouldn't stand for that."

"How long have you had a snowy for a pet?" she asked, giving her attention back to the wound.

"Since I was eight."

Catherine snapped her gaze up to his, then looked at Mary's face. "Owls don't live that long in the wild. I'm not even sure they live that long in captivity."

Robbie shrugged his free shoulder. "I don't question such things, Cat. I merely accept them for the gifts they are."

She went back to work on the wound, cleaning the blood off the soft, beautiful feathers. Finally, she picked up the thread and scissors, cut a length of the silk, and threaded her needle. She poised her hands over the wound and looked at Mary's face.

The owl's huge yellow eyes were closed.

Catherine nodded to Robbie. "Hold her firmly," she said, leaning over and parting the feathers again.

She very carefully pushed the needle through one side of the wound, darted a glance at the owl's face and saw that her eyes were still closed, and quickly moved the needle across the small tear and through the flesh again, deftly making a snug but not too tight knot. And as fast and as carefully as she could, she repeated the procedure just above the first stitch, using the scissors to snip the thread before she straightened.

She let out a deep sigh, only to realize she'd been holding her breath the entire time. "I can't believe she didn't even twitch," she whispered, running her hand over the smooth feathers of Mary's belly.

The owl's eyes were open again, staring at Catherine. Robbie lifted his arm and set the bird upright on his sleeve.

"There, little Cat. You've just made a new friend," he said, taking Catherine's hand and guiding it down Mary's back. "Everyone should have a pet as special as this lady."

"I can't believe she let me stitch her," Catherine repeated, stroking the calm bird. "She's amazing. And so beautiful. Her feathers look like lace." Catherine smiled up at Robbie. "There really is magic around here. I can't imagine a wild snowy being anyone's pet. They're not usually seen this far south. She's been hanging around for over twenty years?"

"Aye," Robbie said, standing up and taking Mary back to her rocking-chair perch. "We'll put some papers down on the floor so she won't make a mess. What do you have she can eat?" he asked, going over to the fridge before she could reply. "Any raw meat?"

"There's some defrosted hamburger in there," Catherine told him, cleaning up her medical supplies and setting the needle and scissors in the sink with the wet towel.

She went into the laundry room and came back with yesterday's newspaper, slowly walking behind the owl and laying out the paper on the floor.

"Ah, Nathan and Nora will be home soon. What are we going to do about Mary? They might frighten her, and she could hurt herself flying around inside the house."

"Nay," Robbie assured her, spooning out a bit of the meat. "She likes kids." He looked at Catherine. "She's safer than those old hens around children. She won't peck them."

Catherine stepped back and put her hands on her hips, staring at the snowy. "So, we just let her perch there for . . . for how long?" she asked, watching Robbie take some of the meat off the spoon and hand-feed the owl.

"Until she decides she's had enough of us," he said. "She'll walk to the door and stare at you until you open it."

"Have the boys met Mary?"

"Nay. They know about her and that she's special to me, but she hasn't been around here for several months. And she hasn't come inside since they came here." He shook his head. "I have caught her peeking in the window, though, and shaking her head at the mess her house was in."

"Her house?"

"Aye. Haven't I mentioned that my mother's name was Mary?"

"You named an owl after your mother?"

"I was eight," he said, rolling his eyes. "And I wanted a mama in the worse way." He grinned. "But then I found Libby and decided she would make me a good mum."

"You found Libby?"

"Aye. On the Internet." He waved his spoon at the kitchen. "I rented out this house to her. I'd inherited it from my mama, and it was just sitting empty, so I placed an ad on the Internet, and Libby answered."

"When you were eight?"

"Aye." His grin widened. "And being the smart man my papa is, he fell in love with Libby and married her before she could realize what she was getting herself into." He turned fully to face her and waved at the kitchen again. "This house has a history of luring women to marriage," he said, his voice deep and his eyes penetrating. "My Aunt Grace and Mary were sisters, and this is their family home. Grace brought me here when I was only four weeks old, after my mother died from a car accident in Virginia, and she ended up marrying Greylen MacKeage."

He set the spoon on the table and walked over to her, and it was all Catherine could do to stand her ground. He seemed larger than ever and unusually appealing. "So far, it's been two for two for this house," he whispered, running his knuckles down the side of her cheek. "And God willing, little Cat, it will be three for three."

She couldn't respond to save her soul.

He wasn't really implying *marriage*. Good heavens, they had shared one kiss in the barn.

And it looked as if they were about to share another!

He finished his caress by using a finger to lift her chin and then lowered his mouth to hers. The contact was so gentle—and so fleeting—that Catherine was back to wondering if it was happening at all. Darn it, the guy needed lessons on stealing kisses more than he needed lessons on paying attention.

But as soon as Catherine thought that, his arms wrapped around her and he deepened the kiss. Her own arms somehow found their way around his neck, and her tongue also had a mind of its own and eagerly went in search of his.

It didn't even unnerve her this time when he cupped her bottom and pulled her intimately against him, and Catherine felt his intentions poking her belly. She might have even wiggled a bit, because Robbie groaned, tightened his arms, and started her heart racing with his hot, intoxicating mouth.

Their impassioned embrace had her all but lifted off her feet, and Catherine was about to climb up his body and wrap her legs around him when the owl let out a loud, sharp whistle that made her ears ring.

It was followed by the pounding of small feet on the porch.

Catherine scrambled back so fast Robbie had to grab her shoulders to keep her from falling. She tugged down the hem of her sweater—how had it gotten that high?—and scrubbed her swollen, tingling lips with her sleeve.

Robbie spun on his heel, snatched her sewing kit off the table, and strode into the living room. She noticed his walk was a bit stiff, and saw him give a quick tug on his pant leg.

She slapped her hand over her mouth to check her laughter, just as the kitchen door slammed open and Nathan and Nora came running inside. They dropped their backpacks on the floor, tossed their jackets toward the pegs—missing them completely—and kicked off their boots in four different directions.

"Did you ask him, Mom?" Nathan asked, padding up to her in his sock feet. "Can I have it?"

"Oh, honey, I haven't asked him yet," she told him, rushing over to catch Nora before she got the lid off the cookie jar. "Wash your hands first, young lady," she said, pointing her toward the bathroom.

But Catherine changed her mind and guided Nora over to Nathan, squatted between them, wrapped her arms around both children, and turned them toward the rocking chair.

"Calm down, you two, and see who's come for a visit."

Both children gasped, and Catherine hugged them tightly when they tried to rush forward. "Her name is Mary. She's a snowy owl and Mr. MacBain's pet. And see the pink thread on the bottom of her belly? She hurt herself, and she's staying with us so she can get well. I don't want you to touch her," she continued. "Wounded animals are dangerous, and jumping and yelling will scare Mary, and she could hurt herself even more. And see her feet? Those are her talons, and she uses them to hunt for mice and rabbits and to defend herself. And her beak is strong, and she could peck you quite badly if you scare her."

"She's the prettiest bird I ever seen," Nora whispered.

"She's got really big eyes," Nathan added, also whispering.

"And Mr. MacBain told me she likes children. But that doesn't mean she wants you to touch her. Only go near Mary if Mr. MacBain is holding her and lets you come up and pat her. Understand?" she asked, giving them both a squeeze.

They both nodded, and Catherine stood up and pointed them toward the bathroom. "Go wash your hands, and I'll give you a snack."

Robbie came back into the kitchen and sat down at the table. "I want a snack, too. And what did Nathan want you to ask me?"

Catherine walked to the fridge, resisting the urge to lick her lips. She could still taste him.

Still feel his heat surrounding her.

"He wants your permission to move into the spare bedroom upstairs," she said, grabbing the bowl of gelatin and taking it to the counter. She shot him a grin over her shoulder. "Our bed is a bit crowded, and Nathan complained that Nora is all elbows and knees. But I think it's more that he wants to be one of the guys and move upstairs with them."

"There are two twin beds in that room," he said. "Does Nora want to move up, too?"

Catherine took down three bowls and started spooning out the gelatin. "She's not ready to cut the apron strings."

"We could set up a cot in your room, then, and at least get her out of your bed," he suggested.

Catherine took him his bowl of dessert, set it down in front of him, and stuck a spoon in it. "That's a good first step. Nathan is right, my daughter is all elbows and knees when she sleeps."

The children came out of the bathroom, wiping their hands on their clothes, and sat at the table facing Mary. Catherine gave them their dessert.

"You got a really cool pet," Nathan told Robbie. "Can she still fly, even though she's hurt?"

"Aye. And as soon as you're done eating, I'll hold her so you can pet her. And after that, I'll help you get settled in your new bedroom upstairs."

"Oh, great!" Nathan said. "It's right next to Cody's room, isn't it? He's going to show me how to shoot the potato gun this weekend." Nathan thought for a minute, then added, "We're going to shoot it at that big rock up in the pasture, so you don't got to worry we'll hit anything important."

"Aye. Rocks make good targets. And I think I'll join you.

It's been a few years since I've shot a rock. Nora, would you like to move upstairs with your brother?" Robbie asked, giving the girl his attention.

Nora filled her mouth with gelatin and shook her head.

Catherine turned back to the counter to hide her smile. That was the longest conversation Nathan had had with a man in over three years. Well, heck, were they all settling in here or what?

She looked over at Mary and caught the bird staring at her. Then the owl lazily blinked one eye and emitted a low, humming chatter.

Chapter Seventeen

It was Friday afternoon, Mary was perched on the front porch railing watching Robbie give Catherine her lesson in stick fighting, and Catherine was trying to knock her sweet-kissing boss's head off again.

But Robbie wasn't letting himself get distracted today, and Catherine was only beating herself up. She'd lost her grip on the stick twice already, and once it had hit the ground and bounced back up and smacked her in the thigh. Then, not five minutes later, she'd tripped over her own feet and ended up with a mouthful of dead grass.

Not even trying to stifle his laughter, Robbie had picked her up and given her another lecture on physics.

But for the last twenty minutes, Catherine had noticed him checking his watch, and she even managed to catch the edge of his foot with her stick because he had glanced toward TarStone.

Darn it. He was going back up there! And he would come limping home tomorrow morning all beat up again.

"That's enough for me," she said, leaning against her

stick and brushing her hair out of her face. "I feel as if I've run a marathon."

Robbie straightened from his crouched position. "But it was just starting to get fun," he said, breaking into a wide grin. "It's not every day I get to watch someone beat themselves up."

"Which is why we're stopping," she said, walking toward the house. "I'm not providing entertainment for you and your bird."

Robbie fell into step beside her. "Mary wasn't laughing at you. She was cheering you on."

Catherine glanced at the bird. She had hopped down off the rail and was standing at the kitchen door, waiting for them to open it for her. Robbie held the door, and Catherine followed the owl inside. She went over and leaned her stick next to the clock as Mary flew up to her rocking-chair perch.

Catherine turned to Robbie. "Do you want me to pack you some food?"

"What for?"

"To take with you. You're going back up the mountain this afternoon, aren't you?"

He crossed his arms over his chest and faced her. "You're very perceptive."

"No, I'm angry. You'll come dragging in here tomorrow morning, looking like hell, and expect me to patch you up again."

"Aye," he said, walking to her. "And you'll do it, won't you?" he whispered. "Because, like me, you have no choice." He ran a finger down the side of her face. "We each do what's required of us, little Cat. I must go up the mountain, and you must let me. And tomorrow morning, if I do come dragging in, you'll take care of me, not ask any questions, and not tell my family. That's how trust works. I trust you to be here when I come back, and you trust that I will come back."

"Maybe," she hissed, stepping away from him. "*Maybe* you'll come back, and *maybe* I'll be here."

He lowered his hand and crossed his arms over his chest, saying nothing, just staring at her with his dark, penetrating eyes.

Catherine turned, walked into her bedroom, and softly shut the door. She leaned against it and closed her eyes with a disheartened sigh.

Why did she care so much? What should it matter to her that Robbie MacBain was a stubborn idiot? If the man wanted to go get himself beat up, she had no right to stop him.

But what in heck was he doing up on that mountain?

Catherine pushed away from the door, went to her closet, and found her backpack. She stuffed it with a heavy sweater, an extra pair of socks, her hat and mittens, a flashlight, and the small utility knife she'd carried from Arkansas.

People do what is required of them, he had told her. Well, by God, she was required to watch Robbie's back, since he didn't seem capable of doing it himself.

Because that's how trust works, darn it.

Catherine set her loaded pack by the door, then went over to the bureau and started brushing out her hair as she thought about how she was going to follow him up the mountain.

The boys could watch Nathan and Nora, she decided. They could take them to the ice cream shop tonight, just as they'd planned, and babysit them for the evening. Yeah. The six of them would be perfectly fine, and she'd be back before they woke up tomorrow morning.

Catherine waited another ten minutes, until she heard

the porch door bang shut. She opened her bedroom door, peeked in the kitchen, then walked over to the sink window just in time to see Robbie go into the barn.

Mary was sitting on one of the paddock fence rails.

Catherine looked at the clock. It was almost two; Nora and Nathan's bus would be here soon, and the boys should be home at about the same time.

Catherine kept herself busy, adding some herbs to the stew she had cooking in the huge crockpot and finishing a salad to put in the fridge, all the time watching out the window.

Robbie finally came out of the barn, leading his horse, and stopped and looked toward the house. Catherine started for the door but stopped and stood at the window until he finally mounted up. But again, he waited another minute, staring toward the house, before turning his horse toward the pasture.

Catherine ran out the door and down the porch stairs. "Robbie!"

He stopped, and she ran up and touched his knee. "You . . . you be careful," she whispered.

He dropped the reins, leaned down, grabbed her under the arms, and lifted her onto his lap before she could gasp.

He held her in a fierce embrace. "Aye, little Cat," he whispered, kissing her hair. "I will. And I'll try very hard to make this my last trip." He tipped her face up to his. "Thank you for not letting me leave with anger between us. That's a bad habit to get into."

"So is sewing you back up."

He ran his hand over her hair until he came to the cloth-covered band she used to tie it back. He worked it off, freeing her hair to fall down to her shoulders.

"It's tradition that a knight going into battle carries a token from his lady," he told her, tucking the band inside his jacket, in his shirt pocket. "Will you give me a kiss as well, if I promise to be back just after sunrise?"

"I'd prefer to give you a gun," she said, reaching her arms around his neck. "So you won't have to get close enough to need stitches again."

"Aye. But where's the sport in that?" he whispered, leaning down to capture her mouth as she reached up to kiss him.

Their meeting was gentle, more sweet than needy. Catherine savored the soft, warm taste of his lips, only to realize that kissing Robbie MacBain was becoming as much of a habit as sewing him up was.

But oh, what a pleasant habit.

The man felt like granite covered with flannel, as solid as a mountain cloaked in sensuous heat. She tightened her arms around his neck, canting her head to get more of his taste, pressing her breasts against him until she could feel the strong beat of his heart.

It was happening again, the magic of his touch wooing her into wanting more. It had been years since she'd truly thought to want a man, to feel her fingers dig into hard, warm flesh and make him respond. Catherine's insides clenched as images danced through her mind of them naked, in bed, exploring each other's body.

He broke the kiss and tucked her head under his chin, holding her tightly as he took a shuddering breath. "Aye," he whispered. "This is much better than leaving with anger between us." He kissed the top of her head. "But as I'm tempted to stay and see just how brave you've become, little Cat, I have to go now."

He lifted her chin and gave her another quick, chaste kiss, then slowly pulled her arms from around his neck, lifted her off his lap, and stood her back on the ground.

"If you have any problems with the boys or anything

else you can't handle, call my father," he told her. "And if it should happen that I'm not back by noon tomorrow, tell him to go find the priest."

He leaned down and covered her mouth with his finger before she could speak. "Don't worry, Catherine. I *will* be back." He straightened, gave her a sassy wink, and spurred his horse toward the pasture. "Sleep well, little Cat," he called over his shoulder with a wave.

Mary lifted off the fence rail and followed.

Catherine stood staring after them, her finger covering her lips where his had been, the breeze blowing her loose hair across her face.

How foolishly romantic that he wanted to take a token from her into battle. How . . . how crazy. The guy spoke of duty and calling and ancient traditions, and owned a sword and dressed in a Scottish plaid. Either Robbie MacBain was weird, or she was, because she was beginning to accept his strange behavior as almost normal.

It certainly didn't stop her from wanting to kiss him.

But that didn't mean her trust was blind. Robbie finally rode out of sight, and Catherine ran into the barn and down the length of the aisle, looking in each of the stalls.

One stall door had a note pinned to it, for Davis, the man who came every morning and evening to tend the horses, that said the horse in this stall, named Boots, had a loose shoe.

Catherine moved on to the next stall and found the horse Gunter had been riding the night she'd been rescued off the mountain. The plate on the door said his name was Sprocket.

She hooked Sprocket in the cross-ties, went into the tack room, chose one of the saddles, pulled Sprocket's bridle off the peg, and headed back down the aisle.

In ten minutes, Catherine had him saddled up. She ran

to the house, got her backpack, brought it out and tied it to the saddle. She was doing a final check of her equipment when she heard the boys arrive home.

She ran out to greet them just as the school bus stopped at the end of the driveway.

"Gunter," she called as the four boys started down the driveway to meet Nathan and Nora.

Gunter walked back to her while the others continued on.

"Can you watch Nathan and Nora for me tonight?" she asked when he stopped in front of her. "I'm going out for the evening and wondered if you could babysit."

"Out?" he asked, clearly surprised. "Where?"

"Ah . . . I'm going up to the old cabin where you found us," she told him, waving toward TarStone.

That surprised him even more. "What for?"

"For a night off," she said, realizing she hadn't completely thought out her excuse. "I . . . ah . . . I asked Robbie if I could use the cabin. I'm bringing a book to read as a little vacation from cooking and cleaning."

Gunter frowned. "But why the cabin? It's a drafty old place, and you shouldn't be up there alone." He suddenly stiffened and got the strangest look in his eye, turning toward Robbie's Suburban and then looking back at her. "Where's the boss man?"

"Ah . . . he's gone out for the night. That's why I need you to watch the kids. They can get themselves ready for bed, if I'm not back in time. And you can still take them out for ice cream tonight. I left some money on the table."

That strange look turned into a gleam, and Gunter canted his head at her. "O-kay," he said slowly, breaking into a smile. "We'll watch Nathan and Nora. You just go on up to the cabin, and don't worry about anything here. We'll take good care of the squirts."

"And you'll all stay out of trouble," Catherine added,

fighting the blush she felt rising up her neck. Lord, Gunter thought she was going to meet Robbie!

"Don't worry about a thing," Gunter assured her, walking with her to meet her children.

"Mommy, Cody told me Gunter's going to teach him how to defend himself," Nathan said, leaving Cody behind to run up to her. "Can I learn, too?"

Catherine looked at Gunter, only to have the young man shrug in response and tuck his hands in his pockets. She looked back at her son. "Gunter's going to wait until Mr. MacBain gives his approval first, Nathan," she said, ruffling his hair.

"When are we going for ice cream, Mommy?" Nora asked. "Now?"

"No, sweetie. After supper," Catherine told her, squatting down to her level. "And Gunter and the boys are going to babysit you guys tonight," she added. She looked over to include Nathan. "So I want you to be good for them and do what they tell you."

"But where are you going?" Nathan asked.

"Up to the cabin we stayed at. I probably won't be back by the time you go to bed, but I'll be right here in the morning when you wake up."

Nora clutched Catherine's hand. "I want to go with you."

"No, sweetie. I'll just be sitting around and reading the whole time. It wouldn't be any fun for you. Certainly not as much fun as going for ice cream and hanging out with the boys for the evening."

Nathan tugged on Nora's sleeve to get her attention. "Come on, sis. It'll be fun," he told her, obviously eager to be rid of his mother and be one of the boys. "Remember when Rita used to babysit us? We made popcorn and always got to stay up late."

Gunter reached down and swept Nora into his arms.

"We'll rent a movie," he offered. "Ever see *The Little Mermaid?*"

Peter's groan quickly turned into a smile when Gunter glared at him over Nora's shoulder. "I love *The Little Mermaid,*" Peter gritted through clenched teeth.

Catherine straightened and started to the house. "Supper's in the crockpot, and there's salad in the fridge. Nora, you can sleep in Nathan's room tonight, if you don't want to go to bed alone in our room."

"Yeah, squirt," Rick interjected, holding the door open as Gunter carried Nora inside. "I'll make the popcorn."

Nora was suddenly done with her worry. "I like it with lots of melted butter," she told Rick over Gunter's shoulder, smiling now. She looked at her mom. "I'm gonna sleep upstairs with the big kids," she proclaimed.

And that was that, Catherine realized. These four *hoodlums,* as everyone kept wrongly calling them, were more than mere guardian angels—they were miracle workers. Her babies were turning into happy children right before her eyes.

Catherine slipped into her jacket, went to the clock and grabbed her stick, and headed toward the door. "I'll be here to cook breakfast," she told them, stopping and then walking back to Gunter. She leaned up and kissed Nora on the cheek. "You be a good girl," she whispered before going over to Nathan. She gave her son a kiss on the cheek, despite his obvious embarrassment at being kissed in front of the boys. "You be good, too," she told him, heading for the door.

Gunter set Nora down and followed Catherine out to the barn. "You're riding up?" he asked.

Catherine slid her stick into the rifle sheath on the saddle, unhooked Sprocket, and led him out of the barn. "I'm certainly not walking," she told him.

"Are you an experienced rider?"

Catherine mounted up and smiled down at him. "Careful, Gunter. You're beginning to sound like an old mother hen. I've been riding since I could walk. I grew up on a ranch in Idaho."

Gunter chuckled. "When you see the boss, tell him he needs to come to school tomorrow and sign a progress report for my work-study class, would you?"

"You'll probably see him before I will."

"Yeah, right. I forgot," he chuckled, turning toward the house and waving over his shoulder. "You're going up to the cabin to *read*. See you tomorrow."

Catherine opened her mouth to say something but sighed instead and urged her horse toward the pasture. Some things just weren't worth arguing over. She spurred Sprocket into a trot, following the fence line, and finally entered the woods, keeping her eyes on the tracks in the muddy trail.

But not far into the woods, the tracks veered to the right, up a tote road that led across the mountain instead of toward the summit.

Robbie was headed to the ski resort?

Once on the tote road, Catherine moved Sprocket into a slow canter, trying to make up for the time she'd lost. She rode for about ten minutes but pulled to a stop at the sound of voices.

Darn it, he was heading back toward her. And he had someone with him.

Catherine scrambled off the tote road and into the thick forest, urging Sprocket down a steep knoll to hide behind a large boulder. She waited, breath suspended, as Robbie came riding by with a man mounted up behind him, and she immediately recognized Ian MacKeage's voice.

"Will Daar be at the summit?" Ian asked.

"Aye," Robbie said. "But he'll be of little help. Have you noticed how smooth his cane has become lately?"

"I did notice that," Ian agreed. "When he came to supper last night. Grey noticed, too, and seemed pleased. What if Grey hears the storm? He'll know, won't he? It's a sound none of us can ever forget."

"Aye. But there will be nothing he can do by the time he realizes what's happening. And tomorrow I'll call a meeting of both clans and explain that . . ."

Darn. They had moved too far away for Catherine to hear what Robbie was going to explain to the clans. What clans? Was he talking about the MacKeages and his father's family?

Why was he taking Ian up the mountain, especially if whatever he did up there was so dangerous?

Catherine waited another minute or so, then slowly inched Sprocket out of their hiding place, thankful the horse hadn't nickered to its stable mate when Robbie rode past. Returning to the tote road, Catherine kept her pace to a walk, stopping whenever she came to a straight section so they wouldn't see her if either of them happened to look back.

What storm had Ian been talking about? She had heard a loud crack of thunder the morning she'd found Robbie, and the night before, just around sunset, she'd heard the same sound. But there hadn't been any clouds or rain. Could it have been a gunshot? It had sounded more like a cannon, though, loud and powerful enough to shake the mountain.

Catherine tried to shrug off the nagging voice in her head that kept saying curiosity had killed the cat. She was just worried about Robbie, is all. She wasn't being curious, she decided, but watching his back.

She and Sprocket slowly rose in elevation, following the

winding path up through the dense forest, and Catherine had to keep reining in her horse, who kept trying to catch up to his stable mate.

The trees became shorter and more gnarled the closer they got to the summit, until Catherine had to stop for fear of being seen. She took off Sprocket's bridle and tied him to one of the trees by his halter, leaving the rope long enough for him to graze. She slid her stick out of the rifle sheath and continued after Robbie and Ian on foot, keeping hidden behind the short trees and large boulders, until they finally stopped.

She continued up and to the side, making her way to a ledge just above them, and lay down on her stomach and watched. They'd dismounted, and Ian was taking off his jacket and unwrapping a length of cloth from around his waist.

It was the same pattern as one of Robbie's plaids.

Daar came trudging up to them from the opposite direction. "Ya better have given yar word to Robbie," the priest said, waggling his finger as he approached Ian. "Ya mess things up, and there'll be hell to pay."

"I won't mess anything up, old man," Ian muttered, turning his back on the priest and unbuttoning his shirt. "I've given Robbie my word."

Both Ian and Robbie were taking off their clothes!

Robbie suddenly stopped and looked up. Catherine flattened herself to the ground and held her breath, not daring to move again until she heard Robbie speak.

"We only have a few minutes to sunset," he said. "Do you still want to do this, Uncle?" he asked, his voice more tender than questioning.

Catherine lifted her head and peered down, thoroughly confused. *Sunset . . . sunset,* she repeated to herself, looking off to the southwest. The bottom of the sun was nearly touching the horizon. She looked back at the men and saw Ian, completely naked now, wrapping the plaid around himself with sure, deft movements, as if he'd done it a thousand times.

Robbie was also totally, beautifully naked and was wrapping a plaid around himself that was the same color as the one Ian was wearing. Both men secured the cloths with wide leather belts, and Catherine saw Ian tuck a small dagger—similar to the one Robbie had shown her—into a sheath on his belt.

Robbie reached down to one of his discarded boots, pulled his own dagger out, and tucked it in his belt, then picked up his sword and the second, different-colored plaid she'd washed and mended over a week ago.

What in heck were they doing? Was this some sort of ritual that Scotsmen did at sunset in the spring? Was it something for Ian, maybe, relating to his age?

What in heck was going on?

Father Daar looked at the sun, which was already halfway hidden behind the horizon now, and turned and pointed his cane at Robbie and Ian. "Ya must go," he said.

Catherine inched forward to the edge of the cliff just as Robbie settled his sheathed sword over his shoulders. He then wrapped his arms around Ian and curtly nod to the priest.

Father Daar held his cane up, and the wood appeared to glow as the last rays of sunlight touched it. A harsh wind suddenly rose with a howling scream, and dark, boiling clouds swept down from the summit.

"Lend me yar own power, MacBain!" Daar shouted, lowering his cane to point at Robbie and Ian. "Godspeed to the two of ya!"

Catherine used one hand to protect her face from the wind and blinding light, leaning further over the ledge to see a storm of crackling, sparking clouds tighten around Robbie and Ian.

A loud, piercing shriek came from above her, and Catherine rolled over, holding up her stick to ward off Mary's sharp talons. The owl dove toward her, snatching at Catherine's coat sleeve just as Robbie shouted.

No, not shouted. The man roared!

Catherine twisted and clawed at the moss-covered ledge, but the wind and Mary and her momentum made it impossible for her to hold on. She suddenly felt nothing but air beneath her, then hit the ground so hard, it knocked the breath—and a startled scream right out of her.

Hard, powerful hands picked her up, and Robbie again roared over the howl of the roiling tempest. "Dammit, Cat!" he shouted, pulling her tightly against his chest, squishing her against Ian, and wrapping his arms around them both. "Hold on to my belt!"

She struggled against him, only wanting to get away from the violently raging storm and these crazy men as fast as she could. The air sizzled and popped and crackled around them, and the ground pitched and rolled with rumbling shudders.

Robbie's arms tightened until it felt as if her bones were being crushed. "Too late!" he growled next to her ear, covering her head as the fierce wind sucked the air from her lungs. "You're coming with us!"

Chapter Eighteen

Robbie couldn't remember ever being so scared. He held Ian and Catherine to his chest, straining against the sizzling light crackling through the roiling clouds. Mary dug her talons into his plaid and spread her wings over the three of them, adding her own guardian powers to help him fight their way through the chaos.

If he lost his grip, Catherine and Ian could end up anywhere—or in any time, for that matter.

Robbie felt the energy he was disturbing pull at Catherine's modern clothes, and her scream of terror pierced his soul. She clung to him, trembling, her screams buried in his chest as the violent storm raged on.

Ian shouted the MacKeage war cry and slapped at the forking tendrils with the courage of a warrior determined to get home.

Time churned and twisted with the roar of a wounded beast, until finally the maelstrom stopped with the suddenness of a train slamming into a mountain. The ground they fell upon rumbled in protest as the vortex exploded in one final, brilliant flash before disappearing.

The silence was more deafening than the storm had been, and Robbie sat hunched over his charges, every muscle in his body quivering with exhaustion and his heart pounding so hard he feared it might explode.

Neither Catherine nor Ian stirred, and Robbie forced himself to release them. Catherine took a deep, shuddering breath, opened her eyes, and screamed at the top of her lungs. She scurried away from him, her face washed with terror, only to scream again at the realization that she was naked.

She scrambled to her feet and bolted into the forest.

Robbie lowered Ian to the ground and ran after her. "Cat, no!" he yelled, ducking through the trees. "You mustn't run. I need to explain what happened. Catherine!"

He heard her shout of surprise, and Robbie came to a halt just in time to see her tumble down a steep bank. He scrambled after her and took hold of her shoulders.

She came up swinging. He pulled her against his chest and wrapped his arms around hers to capture her wild, panic-driven punches.

"Ssshhh," he crooned as she dug her nails into him and pushed to break free. "Easy, little Cat. You're okay. Nothing and no one is going to hurt you. Easy, Catherine."

But she continued to struggle mindlessly, her terror-filled whimpers piercing his heart like a rusted dagger.

"We have to go back to Ian," he said, thinking to refocus her fear. "He could die. Please, help me with Ian."

She suddenly stilled and tried to cover her naked breasts.

"I have the other plaid for you to put on," he whispered, slowly easing his grip. "Come back with me to Ian."

"Wh-what happened?" she asked so softly he barely heard her. "Wh-where are my clothes?"

"I'll explain everything as soon as we see to Ian," he

promised, taking hold of her wrist to pull her up the steep hill.

She twisted her arm, trying to break free. "I-I'll come. Let me go."

"Nay. I'll never catch you if you run. And Ian needs us."

She fell silent and moved with him, but Robbie could feel the tension humming through her. It was dusk, and the forest was growing dark with looming shadows. They walked back to where Ian lay and found Mary standing next to him. Robbie picked up the MacBain plaid and held it out to Cat without looking at her, his attention on his uncle.

He cupped Ian's face, using his thumb to feel for a pulse on his neck. "He's alive but weak from fighting the storm."

"Wh-where are we?" Cat whispered, moving to the other side of Ian. "Th-this isn't TarStone Mountain."

Robbie looked up and nearly smiled. She had the MacBain plaid wrapped around her a dozen times, like a sari. "Nay, it's not. We're in Scotland."

"Scotland? That's impossible."

Robbie slid his arm under his uncle's shoulders and gently lifted him into a sitting position. "You think so?" he asked, running a hand over Ian's brow and head, feeling for bumps. He looked at Cat. "Then it's also impossible we're in thirteenth-century Scotland, I guess."

She gasped, clutching her plaid, her eyes wide with horror around her stark white face. "Thir-thirteen . . ."

Ian groaned. Cat set aside her fright long enough to cup Ian's face and turn him toward her. "Ian," she said firmly. "Wake up now. Open your eyes." His eyelids fluttered, he groaned again, and tried to roll away. "Ian!" she snapped. "Wake up!"

Robbie leaned near his ear and whispered to him in Gaelic, adding Gwyneth's name to his petition.

"What did you say to him? What language was that?"

"Gaelic," Robbie said, prodding Ian's shoulder. "Come on, Uncle," he repeated in Gaelic again, louder this time. "The men are lined up at Gwyneth's door, wanting to court her."

Ian opened his eyes and struck out with his fist. Robbie caught it before it could connect with anything other than air and smiled at his scowling uncle.

"Who's Gwyneth?" Cat asked, looking from Ian to Robbie.

"She's my wife," Ian growled in English.

"Your wife? You have a wife? But I thought . . . Cody said something about you and . . . and Kate," she ended on a whisper, looking back at Robbie.

"Gwyneth is my wife," Ian repeated, reclaiming his fist so he could scrub his face. He finally looked at Robbie, his beard twisting into a grin. "I survived, MacBain." He pounded Robbie's shoulder, though his attention was turned to the landscape around them, his grin widening even more. "I survived," he repeated. "I'm home!" He looked back at Robbie. "Ya brought me home." He suddenly stiffened and looked at Catherine, then back at Robbie. "Ya brung yar housekeeper?"

"Not by choice," Robbie said, glaring at Mary, who had sidled over to perch on a rock. He looked at Catherine, lifting one brow. "It seems she has a curious streak."

Her pale cheeks darkened with two flags of red. "I was just following you to . . . I wanted to . . . I only . . . darn it, I didn't want you to get beat up again!"

"Aye. So you nearly got us blown to oblivion instead," he muttered, standing up and lifting Ian to his feet, not letting him go until he was sure his uncle wouldn't fall. Robbie looked around the small clearing. "I think we should camp here for the night and go to the village in the morning."

"Aye," Ian agreed, rolling his shoulders to shed the last kinks from his journey. "I've a wish to clean up before I see my Gwyneth."

"And we have to come up with a new story." Robbie nodded toward Catherine. "We're going to have to explain her."

Ian snorted. "And why she's wearing the MacBain plaid."

"What village?" Cat asked, inching away and looking down at herself. She fingered the cloth tucked around her breasts. "Why do you have to explain this plaid?"

"You're wearing MacBain colors," Ian said. "And they're our enemy."

"Robbie's your enemy?" she whispered, taking another step back. "But he's your nephew."

Ian sighed. "It's a long story, Catherine, but I suppose it's one ya should hear before we go to the village."

"Don't run," Robbie said when she took another step back. "There's no place to go."

She lifted her chin. "I'm going home. This is crazy. You're all crazy. We can't be standing on a mountain in Maine one minute and in Scotland the next. And certainly not in the thirteenth century."

"Aye, but we are," Ian said. "The storm brung us here, with the priest's help."

"Th-the priest?"

Robbie pounced the moment her attention turned to Ian and captured Cat before she could bolt. She lashed out with a yelp of surprise, pummeling him with her tiny fists as she twisted to get free. He used his weight to drop them both to the ground and stilled her legs by throwing his thigh over hers, grabbing her fists and pinning her hands beside her head.

"I'm sorry," he said. "But I can't let you run. Give me

your promise to stay with us, or I'll be forced to hobble you."

"I just want to go home," she whispered, her face as pale as new-fallen snow. "Please, just let me go home," she ended in a sob, her eyes tearing and her chin quivering.

Robbie leaned down and kissed her forehead. "Nay, little Cat, I can't. Not for several days yet."

"Days!" she cried, twisting beneath him again. "No! I have to get back to Nathan and Nora. I can't be gone for days!"

"You won't," he assured her, lowering his weight to stop her struggles. "Catherine," he softly entreated. "You'll be back by sunrise, I promise."

She stilled and stared up at him. "But you said . . . you said days."

"Aye. The last time I left, I was here a week, but when I came back, I'd only been gone from sunset to sunrise. That's how it works." He let go of her wrists, waited to see if she lashed out again, then brushed the hair off her pale cheek. "Even if we stay here a month, you'd be back before Nathan and Nora woke up."

She used her freed hands to swipe at her eyes. "H-How's that possible? People can't travel through time."

"Aye, we can," Ian said, crouching beside her and touching her shoulder. "Thirty-five years ago, the priest caused a storm exactly like the one we just went through and brought ten of us warriors, including Robbie's father," he added, nodding toward Robbie, "forward to your time."

Catherine snapped her gaze to Robbie. "Your father comes from here, too?"

"Aye. And Winter's father, Greylen MacKeage. And my uncles Morgan and Callum. They were all born in twelfth-century Scotland."

"That's not possible," she repeated. "It isn't!"

"Nevertheless, it happened. The priest is really a *drùidh*. A wizard," Robbie clarified. "He has the power to manipulate time." He cupped his hand over her cheek, using his thumb to still her trembling chin. "Catherine, you won't believe any of this until you see it for yourself. Tomorrow morning, we'll take you to the MacKeage village, and you'll finally understand."

She tried to get up, but Robbie wouldn't let her. "Your promise first," he said. "That you won't run."

"I—I won't run," she whispered.

He hesitated, then slowly lifted off her, standing up and reaching out his hand for her to take.

She stared at him, then put her hand in his and stood up. "Wh-what happened to my clothes?" she asked, tucking her plaid back into place. "Why did they disappear and yours didn't?"

"Your clothes were made from modern materials," Robbie explained, guiding her over to beside Mary and urging her to sit down. "Nothing that wasn't invented by the thirteenth century could come back with us." He smiled down at her. "Which includes spandex and elastic and nylon. Uncle," he said, turning to Ian, "do you think you can build us a fire?"

"Is that wise?" Ian asked, looking around them. "I'm guessing we're on Crag Mountain, and that's not far from the MacBain border."

"We're safe here," Robbie said, reaching down and picking up Catherine's stick that had come through the storm. He handed it to her but was unable to read her expression now that night had finally settled over the forest. "Here, this should make you feel a bit safer."

She clutched the stick to her chest and tugged the hem of her plaid down over her bare knees. Ian headed out of their tiny clearing in search of firewood, and Robbie took off his sword, set it on the ground beside Cat, and looked at Mary.

"We could use something for breakfast," he told the owl. "A plump rabbit would be nice."

Mary silently opened her wings and lifted off her rock toward the night sky.

"Y-you talk to Mary?" Cat asked. "And she understands?"

"Aye. She even talks back, though not out loud," he said, sitting down beside her. "Remember the magic I spoke of? And my duty?" She nodded, and Robbie shifted to face her more fully. "I truly am a guardian, Catherine, charged with the duty of watching over my family. And I, too, have powers that allow me to manipulate not only time but other things as well."

"You mean that wasn't only an expression? You don't just consider yourself a guardian angel and only *feel* that you need to take care of everyone?"

"Nay. It's my calling, ordained by providence."

"Robbie," she said, leaning toward him and placing her hand on his arm. "Magic isn't real," she whispered, as if trying to break the news to him gently. "It's what we tell children when we can't explain something, like how Santa Claus can go to every house in one night and how tooth fairies can take a tooth from under their pillow without waking them up."

Robbie decided he would give up his sword to have Libby or Aunt Grace here with him now. How in hell was he supposed to explain to Catherine what he was just beginning to understand himself?

"Cat," he said, covering her hand on his arm. "It's as real as the sunrise. The magic is everywhere and in everything; it's the miracle of life itself, the air we breathe, the blood that pumps through our veins. It's been with us since the beginning of time, and it's only been in the last few centuries that man has thought to explain it with science." He reached up and gently ran his knuckles over her cheek. "But magic is the foundation of that science, Cat. That some of us can manipulate it only proves how real it is."

"Are you a . . . are you saying you're a wizard or something?"

"Nay. I'm only a man who's been given the duty of protecting my loved ones."

"Protecting them from what?"

"From the magic itself, should it be used improperly. And from those who would change destiny to suit themselves. From *drùidhs* like Father Daar, who have the power to bend the laws of nature."

"Father Daar is bad, then?"

"Nay. He's merely an ancient who can't see beyond his own wants. He brought Greylen MacKeage to our time thirty-five years ago to sire his heir. That my own father and Ian and the others got sucked into the storm with Grey is proof that Daar needs watching over. He's selfish and often manipulative, but his intentions are not evil."

"But why do you keep coming back here? Did Ian come with you each time?"

"Nay. My father and the others don't know anything about my journeys here, and that's why I couldn't tell them. They can't know because they would want to help me, and that would only upset their wives and families."

"Help you what?"

Robbie sighed and pulled Catherine into his lap, pleased that she didn't shrink away but leaned into him instead. "The spell that brought the Highlanders to modern time will reverse itself on this summer's solstice, and they'll be sent back to their original time. I'm here to make sure that doesn't happen. And to do that, I have to find a tree of spells for Daar, so that he can stop it."

"You mean that on the summer solstice, your father and uncles will just disappear?"

"Aye. Their lives will be uprooted again." He lifted her chin to look up at him, wishing he could read her expression. "Are you starting to believe me now, little Cat?"

"No."

"No? Then how do you explain what's just happened?"

"I'm dreaming. Just like Dorothy in *The Wizard of Oz*, I was hit on the head during the storm and knocked unconscious, and I'm dreaming."

Robbie gave her a firm kiss on the mouth. "Ah, Catherine," he said, tucking her against his chest. "Now I'm understanding why you're being so calm." He leaned down and tried to see into her eyes, using his thumb to lift her chin. "But what if it's not a dream? What if all of this is really happening?"

"It's not," she said, reaching up and feathering her fingers over his smile. "Because it's impossible."

"Okay," he conceded. "So will you allow me to be your guide through this dream? Will you promise to listen to me when I tell you to do something?"

"It's my dream," she said, turning rigid in his embrace. "You can't boss me around."

"Catherine, you're dreaming that we're in the thirteenth century, when women had little or no say in their lives. If you wish to survive here, you'll have to defer to me. Especially in front of others," he added.

"No. I promised *myself* never to be in that position again."

Robbie pulled her back against him with a weary sigh. How in hell was he going to protect her if she wouldn't cooperate? How could he make her understand?

Ian came back and dropped his load of firewood, then sat down beside them with an even wearier sigh of his own. "I'm old," he muttered. "And my eyesight is gone. I can't tell what I was picking up for wood. Hell," he said, waving at the pile of sticks. "There could be a snake in there for all I know."

Robbie set Catherine back beside him and used a piece of the wood to scrape out a fire pit. He then started arranging the damp sticks in the middle of it.

"Matches weren't invented in the thirteenth century," she said, wrapping her arms around her knees and leaning closer to watch him. "How are you going to start the fire?"

"With magic."

Ian sucked in his breath and leaned away. "Ya can do that? Just like the priest?" he whispered, sidling farther away.

"Aye, Uncle. I've recently discovered I can do a lot of neat tricks."

"Like what?" Ian asked, moving a few more inches away.

"Like this," he said, reaching his hand into the center of the pile and coaxing the wood to release its stored energy. He leaned over and softly blew on the smoking sticks until they burst into flames.

Ian stood up and moved a good distance away. Robbie chuckled and also stood up. "It's okay, Uncle. I'm still the nephew you used to carry on your shoulders. That I've finally realized the full extent of my calling is to your benefit," he said, reaching out and laying a hand on Ian's shoulder. "It's how you got here," he softly reminded him.

The flames from the now dancing fire reflected in Ian's hazel eyes as the old man stared back at him. "I . . . I'm just surprised, is all," he whispered, suddenly wrapping Robbie in a fierce embrace. "Aye. Ya're still my young pup," he said gruffly, pounding Robbie's back before stepping away and swiping at his eyes. "I hate being old," he muttered, walking to the edge of the clearing. "It's a terrible affliction. The air is always making my eyes water. I'm going to look for more wood."

Robbie watched him disappear into the night forest and turned back to the fire, only to find Catherine staring at him, her jaw slack.

"You're dreaming, remember?" he said, sitting down beside her again. "Now, how about I show you how to wear a plaid properly?" He kissed the tip of her nose. "As cute as you look, you're going to be laughed out of the village tomorrow if you walk in dressed like that."

"Ian's not coming back to modern time with us, is he?" she whispered. "You . . . you brought him back here to die."

"Nay, Catherine. I brought him here because he asked me to, and because he wants to be with his wife and children and grandbabies. He's got many good years in him yet and should spend them in the bosom of his family."

"Do the others know he's here? Your father and Greylen?"

"I'll tell them once I get back."

"He . . . he didn't even say good-bye to them?"

"He did. They just didn't know it. They'll be happy for Ian, once they think about it."

"Do they want to come back, too?"

"Nay. Their wives and children and grandbabies are in Pine Creek, and they've lived with the fear of being torn from them for the last thirty-five years. That's why it's so important I bring back the spells for Daar to stop it."

"Why can't Daar get his own spells, if he's a wizard?"

Robbie shook his head. "There's another *drùidh* here, named Cùram de Gairn, who doesn't want that to happen. He's younger and more powerful than Daar. That's why the priest sent me."

Her eyes clouded with worry in the dancing firelight. "Is he more powerful than you?" she whispered, leaning closer and clutching the front of his plaid in her fists. "Is he the one who keeps beating you up?"

Robbie laughed and pulled her hands up to his mouth and kissed them. "Nay, little Cat. Cùram is keeping himself and his tree of spells hidden from me."

"A tree? I thought spells came from a book or something?"

"Tradition thinks of it as a book, I guess, but it's really a tree of wisdom. All *drùidhs* have one that they guard and nurture. I'm looking for Cùram's tree, so that I can steal a piece of its tap root."

She pulled away, wrapped her arms around her knees again, and silently stared into the fire for several minutes, obviously trying to understand what he was telling her. She looked at him again. "So, if you get this piece of root, you won't have to keep coming back here?"

"Aye. Daar will use it to grow his own tree of wisdom and cast a new spell to keep the Highlanders in modern time."

She stood up, her fists clenched at her sides as if she were expecting a fight. "Then I'll help you. We'll find this Cùram de . . . this wizard guy and his tree and steal the root so you won't ever have to come back."

Robbie also stood, the tips of his bare toes touching hers.

She didn't back away but only smiled up at him.

"You can't help me, Cat. This isn't a treasure hunt but a dangerous quest. Cùram is dangerous." He waved at the landscape around them. "Hell, this whole world is dangerous for a woman."

She snorted, lifting her chin. "It's apparently dangerous for guardians, too." She crossed her arms under her breasts, leaned back on her hips, and angled her head at him. "Do your magical powers make you infallible?"

"What? Nay, of course not. I'm a mortal man."

"Then who watches your back?"

Robbie rubbed a hand over his face. "Haven't we had this conversation before? I don't need anyone watching my back. *I'm* the guardian here," he growled, thumping his chest.

"It's my dream," she growled right back, thumping her own chest. "And I can give myself whatever powers I want. And I think I'll be *your* guardian angel." She gave him a lopsided smile. "Lord knows you need one."

Robbie couldn't decide if he wanted to kiss that sassy smile off her face or shake some sense into her.

"I'm thinking we should say Catherine helped me escape from the English," Ian said, walking back with an armful of sticks. He dropped them by the fire and turned to Robbie, his eyes shining with excitement. "And I brung her home to reward her. She can stay with Gwyneth and me until ya have to go back. That way, I can keep an eye on her while ya do your business."

"That sounds like a good plan, Uncle."

"Aye," Ian said, puffing out his chest. "I was thinking it would also explain why she can't speak Gaelic." He looked at her and shook his head. "But the plaid's got to go.

"Nay, wait!" he said before Robbie could speak. "I have a good tale. We can say she was stolen by a MacBain who was wanting a wife and that I stole her back. And I took his plaid as a prize and sent him home bare-assed." He nodded, his chest puffed even more. "Aye. What do ya think of that tale?"

From the way Catherine was glaring at Ian, Robbie guessed she didn't think much of it. "It's perfect, Uncle," he said, patting Ian's shoulder. "And it'll ease my mind to know you're watching out for Cat. She'll be safe from any other warriors looking for wives."

Cat sat back down on the rock, and Robbie looked over just in time to see her cover a yawn. Come to think of it, he was quite tired himself. And Ian looked as if his plaid was holding him up rather than his weary old legs.

"I think we should call it a night," Robbie said, crouching to feed more wood to the fire. "We'll bed down on that moss over there," he added, using a stick to point to the other side of the fire. "Cat, you can sleep between us to stay warm. Ian, you take the side near the fire."

It looked as if his housekeeper didn't care for that plan, either. But she picked up her stick, walked around the fire, and stood staring at the moss. She looked over at Robbie. "Can't you conjure up a feather bed or something?" she asked, lifting her chin and daring him to try.

"It's your dream. You do it."

She looked back down at the moss, gave a sigh that finished in another yawn, sat down, laid her stick on the ground on the side where Robbie would be, and tried to readjust her plaid to cover her shoulders.

"I can show ya how to fix that," Ian said, crouching beside her. "It's long enough to wrap over yar arms like a shawl and around your legs. Here," he said, grabbing one end of the cloth and taking three wraps from around her, which still left her well covered. "That's how ya do it," Ian instructed. "My Gwyneth showed me how women cover themselves differently than men. Tomorrow we'll get ya a MacKeage plaid and a blouse to wear with it."

"What about shoes?" she asked, concentrating on what Ian was doing. "What do women wear on their feet?"

"Leathers," he said. "Tall leggings with double-soled bottoms so ya don't get stung by sharp rocks. And wool socks to keep ya warm."

She looked up at him and smiled. "I've never had a dream that involved a history lesson."

"A dream?" Ian asked, his face screwing into a frown. He looked at Robbie. "She thinks she's dreaming all this?"

Robbie shrugged, picked up his sword, and walked over behind Catherine and sat down just as she yawned again. Ian settled himself between her and the fire so that the two of them made a warm and protective sandwich around Catherine.

Catherine lay back rather stiffly, looked at Robbie, then at Ian, and turned on her side toward the older man, tucking her hands under her head and snuggling into her MacBain plaid.

Robbie reached his arm around her, pulled her back against his chest, and sighed when she went as rigid as a board. "Relax, little Cat," he whispered, tucking her head under his chin and pulling some of his own plaid over her. "You're only dreaming that I'm holding you."

Chapter Nineteen

Catherine woke up expecting that she was home in her bed, that the breath she felt on her neck . . . and the weight across her legs . . . and the hand tucked inside her pajamas between her breasts . . . all belonged to Nora.

But she opened her eyes and discovered she was still locked in her fantastical dream, that Robbie MacBain was the one taking such intimate liberties with her body, and that Ian MacKeage had nearly rolled into the dying fire and was snoring loudly enough to wake the dead.

So, what would Dorothy do upon finding herself still in Oz—not with a tin man and a lion and a scarecrow but with an owl, an aging warrior, and a handsome knight who wanted her to believe they had traveled through time?

"Are you second-guessing your promise not to run?" Robbie whispered in her ear.

She turned her head to look at him. "I keep my promises."

He kissed her cheek and pulled her more firmly

against him. "How's the dream working out for you this morning?"

"Pretty well, actually," she said, covering his hand between her breasts, pressing it closer instead of pulling it away. "Because if this were real and I found myself waking up with you wrapped around me, I'd likely have a panic attack."

His eyes sparkled in the rising sunlight, and he moved his thumb just a bit, just enough to brush the inside of her left breast. "So you're saying that since it's only a dream, I could make love to you and you wouldn't be afraid?"

Catherine had to think about that.

What an intriguing idea.

She turned in his arms, leaned in, and boldly kissed him on the lips, then smiled up at him. "They didn't have condoms in the thirteenth century."

"But pregnancy is of no consequence in a dream," he said, his own smile making his eyes crinkle at the corners. "Or are you worried we might truly be making love, even though you're dreaming? Like sleepwalking?"

That got rid of her smile. "Thanks," she said with a snort, pulling his hand out of her plaid and sitting up. "You just ruined your best chance to score, MacBain."

He sat up beside her. "Aye. I realized my mistake the moment I spoke." He stood up, picked up his sword, and settled it over his back, then reached out his hand to her. "There's a stream running down the mountain about a hundred yards through those trees," he said, facing her toward the woods once she stood up. "Why don't you go do whatever women do to start their day, and I'll wake Ian and cook breakfast? Mary will go with you," he added, gesturing at a pine tree.

The owl was sitting on a branch, staring at them.

"Did she get a rabbit?" Catherine asked, looking around.

"Aye. Two," he said, pointing at the rock by the fire.

Catherine put her hands on her hips and canted her head. "I thought cleaning game and cooking was woman's work in medieval times."

He lifted a brow. "You volunteering?"

"No," she said, heading toward the stream. "Just checking to see how authentic my dream is."

"Well, then, little Cat, I'd say you're about to get the history lesson of a lifetime," he said with a chuckle.

The moment she stepped into the forest, Catherine pressed her hands against her still throbbing breasts. Whew! If she were dreaming, she hoped she never woke up. It had felt so wonderful to wake up in the arms of a man, so sensually exciting it had been all she could do not to attack him.

Dismissing the idea that they could make love because this was only a dream had been prudent, but it also might have been rather foolish. This could be her chance to *feel* again, actually to make love without risk.

Catherine decided she could control Robbie's actions even if she couldn't exactly predict them. That was the funny thing about dreams; they didn't follow the usual laws of nature. In them, people could fly, be animals, run without going anywhere, and not really feel pain. Even time didn't exist.

Then again, dreams could suddenly spin out of control and turn into nightmares in the blink of an eye. It had happened more than once to Catherine, and she was not willing to risk it happening again.

Especially not with Robbie MacBain. He was her dream guy. The perfect male, handsome and rugged, protective and possessive without being a caveman, patient and good-natured, and sexy as all get-out. Even when she was wide awake, the guy could woo her into forgetting herself.

Heck, but for his *noble intentions,* she might not have needed this dream at all. His kisses in the barn and the kitchen could have led to a rather salacious conclusion with only the slightest urging from her.

"What are you staring at?" Catherine asked, smiling at Mary, who had glided down to perch on a rock in the middle of the tiny stream. "Yes," she said, going to her knees and dipping her hands in the cold water. "If Robbie can talk to you, then I might as well, too."

But Mary said nothing, not even a rattle.

"He's blaming you for my being here," Catherine said, continuing the one-sided conversation. "You made me fall off that ledge and bump my head. That's the thanks I get for sewing you up."

Catherine tucked her tangled hair behind her ears, splashed water on her face, scrubbed her cheeks with her hands, then leaned down and drank directly out of the stream. She used the corner of her plaid to wipe her face, stood up, and looked down at Mary—specifically at the pink threads on her belly.

"You . . . ah . . . didn't get hurt while helping Robbie hunt for that wizard's tree, did you?"

Mary spread her wings, stretched to her full height, and bobbed her head.

Catherine stepped back in surprise. "What did you say?" she whispered, finally knowing for sure that she was dreaming. She could swear she had heard a voice, a woman's voice, say that it was time to get back to camp, that there was danger in the woods.

She twisted the knot of her plaid. "H-How do you know that?" she asked, scanning the dense forest as she took another step back. "What MacKeages?" she breathed, staring at the owl, shaking her head to clear it. "What warriors?"

Catherine decided she didn't care *who* was talking, she

was getting back to Robbie. She spun on her heel and ran smack into a solid chest. Large arms wrapped around her so tightly her scream of surprise came out as a squeak. She was lifted off her feet, only to find herself nose-to-beard with a wild-haired, dirty-faced, green-eyed giant.

And if that wasn't enough, the stinky brute was grinning. Or he was until the blade of a sword silently slid between them, right along the man's neck, actually slicing off some of his beard.

The giant stilled, his eyes rounded in surprise.

Catherine didn't dare breathe.

Robbie, his voice guttural and soft, said something, in what Catherine guessed was Gaelic, that sounded rather threatening.

Her captor opened his arms without warning. Catherine tumbled to the ground, scurried backward like a frightened crab, and stood, not once taking her eyes off Robbie, who was holding his sword under the man's chin and glaring at him so hard it was a wonder the guy didn't fall over.

"Go back to camp, Catherine," Robbie said, keeping his eyes on the man.

The giant glanced toward Robbie without moving his head and very hoarsely and very quickly started speaking.

Catherine didn't wait around to see what he had to say and scurried past them and ran toward the clearing, where she found three more giants dressed in the same plaid as Robbie and Ian. They were sitting beside the blazing fire, and Ian was sitting in the middle of them, clutching the hands of one of the men and quietly sobbing.

Two of the men stood as soon as she broke into the clearing, their hands going to the hilts of their swords. Ian and his companion were a bit slower getting to their feet, with the younger man putting a protective arm around Ian.

Okay, she wanted to wake up now.

"Catherine," Ian said, rushing to her, tears streaming down his face into his beard and his smile so big it must hurt. "This is my son, Niall," he said, pulling her by the arm over to the large man. "He's Laird Niall now," he added excitedly. "That means my son is their leader," he explained, puffing his chest even further.

Ian then said something in Gaelic to Niall, who was staring at her as if she'd just crawled out from under a rock.

"I've been telling him the story we decided on last night," Ian told her, giving her arm a pat. "Don't let his glare scare ya, lass. He's not caring to see ya in that MacBain plaid, is all."

Niall said something to one of the other men, and the guy frowned at him, then at her, and started undressing. Catherine squeaked and turned away, only to come nose-to-chest with Robbie.

"What is it with you Scots?" she muttered, looking up at him. "You're always undressing."

"Better us than you," he said, reaching around her and taking the man's plaid. "Here, why don't you step into the woods and put this on? Then we can go to the village."

Catherine leaned to the side to peek around him. "Ah . . . where's the other guy?" she whispered, taking the plaid—which smelled like a dead horse—and holding it away from herself.

"He decided he wanted to walk home," Robbie said, nudging her toward the woods.

Without looking back, for fear of seeing the naked Scot, she marched to the trees, still holding the plaid away from herself.

She didn't realize Robbie was following her until she

turned to duck behind a dense bush. "What are you doing? I can change without your help."

He started unwrapping his own plaid. "I prefer you wear mine."

Catherine spun away with a groan of frustration. "So, that's Ian's son?" she asked, willing her cheeks to cool while she listened to Robbie undress. "And he's really their leader?"

"Aye. And he's called a laird," he said, setting his much nicer-smelling plaid over her shoulder and taking the stinky one out of her hand. "They heard the storm last night and were scouting the area to make sure a fire hadn't started from a lightning strike. Poor Niall looked as if he was seeing a ghost once he recognized Ian."

"They believed Ian's story, that he's been in England for . . . for . . ." She glanced over her shoulder, only to find herself staring at Robbie's wonderfully masculine body as he wrapped the smelly plaid around himself. Darn it! What was her question?

Oh, yeah. "How long has Ian been gone? Thirty-five years?"

"Nay. We've come back only ten years after Ian left."

"But he's eighty-five years old."

"He has the health of a sixty-year old of this time."

Catherine forced herself to tear her gaze away and step behind the thick bush. "Gwyneth will know the difference," she said, undoing her MacBain plaid and tossing it over a branch.

"You think so?"

"But maybe she'll be so glad to have him back she won't care," Catherine speculated. "Why did that guy grab me? Because I was wearing the wrong colors?"

"Nay. He didn't see your plaid, only a young, beautiful, unprotected woman."

Catherine paled to the roots of her tangled hair. "He would have . . . he wanted to . . ."

"Nay. He wouldn't have harmed you. He was only thinking he'd found himself a wife."

"A wife!"

"I warned you that women have little say here. And an unprotected lass is fair game. Hell," he said, waving his hand with his back to her. "Stealing wives, especially from other clans, is more of a sport than warring is."

Catherine stopped trying to figure out how to wrap the plaid as Ian had shown her and stared at Robbie. "You're kidding, right? Men don't actually *steal* their wives."

"Ian stole Gwyneth from the Macleries."

"And the Macleries didn't come after her?"

"Now, why would they want to do that? It's a matter of pride when a daughter is chosen by a MacKeage warrior. The MacKeages are a powerful clan."

"Does anyone *ask* the woman if she wants to get married?" Catherine muttered, trying again to adjust the plaid. "Darn it, I can't get this right."

Robbie stepped around the bush and took the end of the cloth from her, unwrapped it two wraps, settled it over her shoulders, and tucked it into her cleavage. He smiled when she gasped and took her in his arms and kissed her firmly on the mouth.

Catherine clung to him. She might not be ready to make love to the man, but kissing him back was definitely okay—since this was only a dream. So she surrendered to the need she'd bottled up inside her for so long, canted her head, and grabbed his hair, deepening the contact.

He lifted her off her feet with a satisfied groan and swept his tongue inside her mouth. She had a wonderful time exploring his taste while reveling in the feel of his powerful arms wrapped around her. His hand on her backside felt quite pleasant, too. And his noble intentions pushing into her belly compelled her to lift her knees and wrap her legs around his waist until she was nestled intimately against him.

He broke the kiss the moment she did that and looked down at her so fiercely that Catherine stopped breathing.

"You come alive at the most inopportune times," he growled, letting her slide down his body until she was standing again. He shoved her head against his chest with a shuddering sigh and squeezed her tightly. "One of these times, I'm not going to care who's around or what's happening," he continued over her head, his guttural voice rumbling under her cheek. "My noble intentions be damned."

Catherine smiled into his chest. "I love it when a man talks romantic."

He tilted her head back so she could look up at his scowl. "Every man has his limits, little Cat. And we're about reaching mine."

Her smile broadened. "Women have limits, too," she said, reaching up and tapping the tip of his nose.

His arms tightened. "I'm having a hell of a time reading you, woman. One minute you're a wary mouse, and the next minute you're all but exploding in my arms."

She stuck out her lower lip. "Then maybe you should quit kissing me."

"Like that's going to happen," he muttered, lowering his head and capturing her mouth. "Catherine," he said, once he was done kissing her again. "While we're here, you only have to remember three things. That you carry your stick with you at all times and that you never go anywhere alone."

"And the other thing?" she asked, kneading her fingers into his strong shoulders.

He kissed her once more, his mouth lingering posses-
sively. "That you're mine," he whispered fiercely, setting
her away and taking her hand to lead her back to camp.

Catherine was beginning to doubt her dream theory,
wondering how she could know so much about medieval
Scotland that she could picture it in such detail: such as
the saddle she was sitting in for their ride down the mountain, with its crude buckles and uncomfortable wooden
seat, and the swords and daggers and ancient gear of the
warriors.

Come to think of it, she couldn't remember ever having
a dream that involved so many senses. The rabbit she'd
eaten before they'd left camp had been delicious, roasted
on a spit over a crackling fire. And the smell of the campfire had permeated her plaid. And the men! The three
MacKeage warriors and the one who had accosted her in
the woods smelled of pine and spruce and male sweat and
horses.

Catherine couldn't remember if she usually dreamed
in black and white, but she was certainly seeing techni-
color now—the bright red hair of some of the warriors,
Robbie's rich gray eyes, the warm purples and grays and
greens in their plaids, and the sharp, vibrant blue of the
sky slamming into the peak of the dark granite mountain.

Even sounds were vivid and eerily real, such as the
rhythm of the horses' hooves sliding over rock or muffled
by moss and the low, guttural conversations among the
men as they rode single file down the winding path.

Catherine found she liked the cadence of Gaelic speech.
It sounded as if they were singing one minute but had a
hairball caught in their throats the next. The rhythm was
strong, rather musical in tempo, with forced and then
whispered syllables punctuating each sentence.

They finally reached level ground, and Catherine stretched in her saddle to see Ian riding behind his son, one hand waving excitedly through the air as he talked nonstop. She turned and looked behind her to see Robbie riding one of the other warriors' horses. The man who had stripped naked to give her his plaid had apparently decided to walk home with the man who'd grabbed her by the stream.

She pushed her stick back over her shoulder as she smiled at Robbie. He'd fashioned her a sling from a length of rawhide, so that she could carry it without smacking herself silly.

Robbie pointed over her head, and Catherine turned forward to look, only to gasp. She could see the towers of a tall, imposing castle through the trees, looming like a dark specter that was anything but fairy-tale pretty.

"That's the MacKeage keep," he told her. "We're almost to the village. Listen, you can hear it."

What she heard was the sound of children shouting and laughing, and it made her suddenly homesick for Nathan and Nora. Robbie had said she'd be back before they woke up, but to her, she'd already been gone almost a day. As interesting as this dream was, she didn't know how much longer she could stand being away from her babies.

The path opened up at the edge of the village, and Catherine couldn't even begin to take it all in. There were huts, maybe a hundred of them, dotting the hillside, reaching all the way to the castle. No, to the *keep*, Robbie had called it.

There were people and children and chickens and goats and dogs everywhere. Smoke rose in lazy clouds from several of the huts, forming a blanket of haze over the village. Several children rushed toward them, and Robbie moved his horse up alongside hers.

"Stay right beside me," he said. "And try not to look so overwhelmed," he added with a chuckle. "We'll be going to Gwyneth's cabin first."

Within minutes, they had a parade of curious people following them. The women were quite pretty, with long hair in varying shades of auburn pulled back in braids and loose tails. They wore colorful blouses, dark skirts that looked to be woven wool, and shawls of the MacKeage plaid.

Catherine sidled her horse closer to Robbie when she noticed some of the women pointing and the men crowding toward them. Several of the men were half naked, their plaids rolled down around their waists, exposing broad chests and beefy arms.

Their impromptu procession wound through narrow village lanes, scattering animals and people who quickly closed back in behind them. They finally came to a stop in front of a cabin that sat in the shadow of the keep, and Niall tossed his leg over his horse's neck, slid to the ground, then turned and helped Ian down.

Catherine was close enough that she could see the old man was trembling, swiping at his eyes several times, and not knowing what to do with his hands, until he finally clasped them together at his waist.

The murmur of the crowd hushed, and Catherine saw a tiny woman, nearly as old as Ian, step out of the cabin with a baby in her arms and a child of about three clutching her skirt. Niall took the baby and handed it to the younger woman who had stepped out of the cabin behind Gwyneth. He took his mother's hand and guided her to a stool by the door as he whispered something to her. Niall gently lowered her down onto the stool when the older woman gasped and her knees buckled, her wide, shocked eyes staring at Ian.

Ian wasn't moving a muscle now, except for his hands, that he kept wringing and twisting at his waist.

Robbie reached over and took Catherine's hand, and held it on his thigh as they sat on their horses, his thumb rubbing her knuckles in soothing circles.

Ian took a hesitant step forward, then stopped and stood trembling. He suddenly fell to his knees with a loud cry, wrapped his arms around his wife, and buried his face in her chest.

Gwyneth MacKeage dug her fingers into her husband's back, buried her own face in his hair, and quietly sobbed.

Catherine used her free hand to wipe the tears streaming down her cheeks, and Robbie leaned close. "This is what I'm about, Catherine," he whispered thickly, his warm breath caressing her ear. "This is when my duty becomes my calling."

It was also when Catherine's infatuation with Robbie MacBain became love. She looked over at him, at his own shining eyes as Robbie watched Ian hugging his one true love, and her heart swelled, and thumped, and started racing. This man—this incredible, fascinating, towering giant—was more than a dream guy. He was *her* dream. *Her* true love. *Her* calling.

And by God, he was her duty now, too.

That was the wonderful thing about dreams; they were a person's subconscious attempt to expose a fear until it became nothing more than a mere worry. Until Dorothy had visited Oz, the young girl had thought she had a world of problems too big to overcome. But there was nothing like an incredible journey to put things in perspective.

Catherine certainly had perspective now. The last ten years of her life shriveled to nothing and changed from being a nightmare to being the gift that had given her Nathan and

Nora and the determination to fight for the life she wanted.

And the courage to love Robbie MacBain.

"My God, woman, if you don't quit looking at me like that," Robbie growled, "I'm going to scandalize this entire village."

Catherine smiled up at him and gently cupped his beautiful face in her hand. "Was that a threat or a promise?"

His eyes narrowed, his nostrils flared, and his jaw clenched so tightly she could feel his teeth grind together. "You're killing me, little Cat."

She patted his cheek, smiled with the confidence of a woman in love, and straightened back on her horse and looked at Ian and Gwyneth.

They were standing now, but Ian still wasn't done hugging his wife. The tiny woman barely came up to the old warrior's chin, but her frail arms were wrapped so tightly around his waist that her knuckles were white. The young woman with the baby was sobbing uncontrollably, using the child's blanket to wipe her eyes. Niall finally took the baby from her and nudged her toward Ian.

"That's Caitlin, Ian's youngest daughter," Robbie whispered. "He has another daughter named Megan, but she married a Maclerie and lives about twenty miles away." He dismounted and helped Catherine down from her horse. "News will travel fast, and I expect Megan will be here in a few days."

Finding herself in a sea of people, Catherine clung to Robbie as he led her to the cabin, and stood quietly as everyone spoke at once, in Gaelic, about only God knew what. Ian's hands flew wildly, punctuating his speech, as everyone listened with wide eyes and occasional gasps.

Ian suddenly pulled Catherine into the center of his gaping family. He spoke rapidly, his words spitting on her several times, his hand waving about her head.

Robbie finally rescued her and whispered in her ear. "Ian is telling them how you helped him escape from the English," he said. "He's making you into quite a hero."

It was Catherine's turn to gasp. "But I don't want to be a hero. *You're* the one who brought Ian back to his family, not me. You should get the credit. Tell them," she said, stepping closer when someone reached out and touched her hair. "Tell them it was you, not me."

"Nay, Cat. It's better if I remain anonymous here."

"But I want to be anonymous, too," she squeaked, scooting to the other side of him when somebody touched her arm.

Robbie pulled her into the cabin, and Catherine blinked at the sudden darkness as he led her to a stool. She lifted her stick off her back, laid it on the floor, and sat down with a sigh of relief. "What happens now?" she asked, looking at his silhouette against the doorway.

"Now you stay here with Ian and Gwyneth, and I go look for Cùram's tree."

She jumped up from the stool. "But I want to go with you."

"Nay, Catherine, it's too dangerous." He took hold of her shoulders. "If you want me to stop coming here, you'll have to let me finish this. Just as soon as I get the root, we'll leave."

"But I can help."

"How?"

"By . . . I can . . . oh, I don't know," she said, stepping back to cross her arms under her breasts. "I can at least make sure you don't get beat up or killed."

He stepped forward and took hold of her shoulders again. "You can't even speak the language. And I need you to keep an eye on Ian. It's going to take him time to readjust."

She grabbed the front of his plaid. "Do you even know what you're looking for? Or where?"

"Mary thinks she's found Cùram's lair. And I'm guessing his tree will be nearby. I'll head out first thing in the morning." His hands on her shoulders tightened. "And you will wait here."

Ian walked into the hut with his arm wrapped around Gwyneth and Caitlin's arm wrapped around him. Niall followed, carrying the baby and towing the little girl by the hand. Catherine moved away from Robbie, picked up her stool, carried it to the corner, and sat down out of the way. Not that it did her any good. Caitlin and Gwyneth rushed over, took her by the hands, and led her behind a blanket hanging from the ceiling that was hiding a tiny cot.

Catherine didn't have a clue what they were saying to her, but before she knew what was happening, they had her stripped naked and started redressing her in beautiful, colorful clothes that Gwyneth pulled from a trunk at the foot of the bed.

From that point on, she had no time to dwell on Robbie's dictate or what she intended to do about it or even what in heck she was eating. The entire village came by in groups of two to ten people at a time to welcome Ian home. Everyone brought food, and Catherine was urged to try some of this and some of that. By nightfall, she was stifling yawns and starting to feel sick to her stomach.

Again, her guardian angel rescued her by taking her for a walk through the village and up past the keep in the bright spring moonlight. But instead of bringing her back to Ian once her stomach settled down, he took her inside the huge granite castle through a door big enough to fit the Jolly Green Giant.

"Niall lives here now," he told her as he led her into a massive, high-ceilinged, sparsely furnished great room, past several gawking people, and up a narrow staircase. "He's offered us a room for as long as we need it."

Catherine stopped walking. "Us?"

Robbie pulled her forward again, down the narrow hall. "You're dreaming all this, remember?"

He opened a small wooden door and led her into a dark, chilly room, let go of her wrist, walked to a huge hearth, and crouched down and started a fire. Catherine didn't watch to see *how* he started it but stood in the middle of the room, her arms wrapped around herself, looking around in the stingy firelight.

She spotted a bed against one wall, that was quite small by modern standards but quite big compared with the one in Caitlin's home. There was a trunk at the end of it and woven cloths and a tapestry hanging from the walls. She could see a narrow window at one end, with what looked like a sheepskin hanging over it, swagged to the side.

"It'll warm up soon," Robbie said, walking back to her, taking her hand, and leading her to the bed. "And there's plenty of blankets," he continued. "Although you might want to shake out the bedbugs and sleep by the fire."

He sat down on the bed and pulled her between his knees, locking his hands behind her back and looking her level in the eyes. "Caitlin's home is full," he told her. "And you'll be safe here in the keep for tonight. Tomorrow, Ian and Gwyneth will move back to their old hut, and you can stay with them once they get settled." He unlocked his hands and spanned them around her waist. "Are you brave enough to stay here alone tonight, Cat?"

"Wh-Where will you be?"

He shook his head. "I can't stay with you. We'd find

ourselves standing in front of a priest tomorrow morning if I did, with the entire village witnessing our wedding."

"What?"

"It's 1210, Catherine. Men and women who share beds had better be married or willing to face the consequences. Remember the warrior who found you by the stream? He wouldn't have touched you until after you'd stood before a priest. A woman's reputation is all she has to bring to her husband." His smiled slashed white in the firelight. "That and maybe a good dowry of a horse and some sheep and, if a guy's lucky, a milk cow as well."

"You're not answering my question. Where will you be?"

He took her stick from her back and tossed it down on the bed, shrugged off his sword, laid it beside her stick, then took her back in his arms. "There's a chamber pot behind that screen and fresh drinking water in the pitcher on that table," he continued, nodding at the far wall. "And someone will be up shortly after daybreak to take you back to Ian."

"Robbie."

He kissed the tip of her nose. "I'm leaving tonight," he said softly, covering her mouth with his before she could protest, his lips warm and sweet and coaxing.

Catherine refused to respond.

He pulled back and cupped the sides of her face to look directly into her eyes. "You have my word, little Cat, that I'll return safe and sound. Mary will be guarding my back, and I'll get in and out before Cùram even knows I'm around."

"I—I think I love you."

He went utterly still for a good ten beats of her racing heart, then broke into a smile. "You think you love me?"

"I don't know for sure. This is a dream, remember?"

"Aye. And you're safe in your dream, are you not, to say what's in your heart? And when you wake up, will you still think you love me?"

"I don't know. That's the funny thing about dreams."

"Aye. But when we're home, standing in our modern kitchen, and I remind you of your words here tonight, will that not prove that you said them to me? How else could I know what you're dreaming, if I'm not here with you?"

Catherine thought about that, and while she was thinking, he apparently decided he might as well kiss her again.

And this time, she responded. She backed up her words with actions, opening her mouth to his, leaning into him as she wrapped her arms around his neck and kissed him back.

Only this time, it was different. *She* was different. Catherine felt as if a hundred and eighty weight had finally been lifted off her shoulders. But what most amazed her was that she'd replaced it with a two-hundred-pound giant, and she wasn't at all scared.

Lord, she loved the freedom of dreams.

Catherine used her own insubstantial weight to push Robbie back until he was lying on the bed and she was lying on top of him. He was very cooperative. Helpful, even. He slid his hands down her spine to her backside and squeezed, groaning into her mouth as he positioned her hips directly over his. And there were those noble intentions again, solid and hot against her most intimate place. Catherine couldn't stop herself from wiggling just a little bit, just enough to slide along him, and she smiled against his mouth when he growled and grabbed her hips to stop her.

He was wearing his own plaid again, the one that

smelled like him, and Catherine ran her hands under it, slid it down his shoulder, and traced her fingers over his broad chest. She wiggled backward until she could follow the path of her fingers with her mouth, kissing the soft, silky hair on his chest until she found one of his nipples.

His entire body turned to stone the moment her lips closed over the firm bud, and his hands moved from her hips to her shoulders, lifting her face back to his. He claimed her mouth with fierce urgency, pressing her hips with one hand on her backside and crushing their chests together with the other.

Sensations exploded inside her. Shivers of pleasure wracked her body as his heat blasted through their clothes to scorch her skin. Catherine refused to give in to her need to breathe, using her mouth instead to savor his sweet, masculine taste that held just a hint of the scotch he'd had earlier. It was so simple, she decided as she lay sprawled across him, to give herself over to the passion.

His hand began exploring ways to get under the colorful blouse Gwyneth had given her. But after several frustrated, unsuccessful attempts, Robbie rolled them over until Catherine was on her back and he was looming above her, glaring at her clothes.

"I'm not in the habit of undressing medieval women," he growled, his voice guttural with desire as he impatiently tugged at her belt.

His plaid was hanging down to his waist, his broad upper torso completely naked and heavily muscled, blocking out the light from the fire. He looked powerful and imposing and . . .

Old fears rose unbidden as she lay beneath him, his solid weight pushing her into the bed, making her unable to move. The terror of being trapped and vulnerable and utterly helpless suddenly rushed through her, pricking her skin and quickening her breathing, urging Catherine either to fight or run.

She tried to do both and suddenly cried out and bucked beneath him, slapping at his hands as he tugged the hem of her blouse up over her breasts.

Chapter Twenty

Robbie reared back in surprise. "What the—Cat!" he growled, capturing her flailing hands, pinning them beside her head, and tightening his knees around her thighs.

She whimpered and frantically bucked beneath him, twisting to throw him off, kicking at his back, and turning her head to bite his arm.

"Catherine, no!" he shouted, using his weight to pin her down. "Easy," he said more softly.

She was panting uncontrollably now, her desperation to get free closing her mind to all but her struggles. Robbie realized she couldn't hear him, couldn't even see him anymore. She was completely consumed by the terror, her mindless panic dictating her actions. He immediately rolled off her and stood by the bed. She scrambled away in the opposite direction, grabbing her stick as she did, until she was standing with the bed between them, her weapon poised to strike.

He stepped toward her, his hands up in supplication, and she whimpered and scurried back until she was pressed up against the wall. Robbie stopped, tucked his hands behind his back, and went utterly still. "It's okay, little Cat," he whispered. "No one is going to hurt you. *I'm* not going to hurt you, Catherine."

He fell silent after that, realizing there was nothing else he could say, and waited for his words to reach her. He watched her eyes, wide with terror in the firelight, and saw the moment she came back inside herself.

She blinked at him, standing there so small and vulnerable and scared, and started to tremble. Robbie stayed where he was, keeping his hands behind his back, and put every ounce of warmth he could muster into his smile.

It was a difficult task, considering the rage inside him right now—rage that warred between his desire to kill Ronald Daniels and his need to pull Catherine into his arms and never let her go.

But he stood his ground, not moving closer, not backing away, and continued to wait. It took her a good three minutes, though, before her shoulders stooped and her head dropped to stare at the floor. She suddenly threw down the stick, covered her face with her hands, and started to sob.

And still he didn't move.

"Oh, my God," she whispered. "What have I done?"

"I can't say for sure," he whispered back, "but I'm guessing that was the panic attack you mentioned this morning."

Her shuddering sobs wracked her body as she stood there, her face buried in her hands.

"Catherine," he said, gently but firmly. "Look at me."

It took her another full minute to do as he asked, before she slowly lifted her head and blinked through her tears at him.

Robbie untucked his hands, settled his plaid back over his right shoulder so that most of his chest was covered, and then held his hands out from his sides, palms forward. "Come here, Catherine," he softly entreated. "Walk into my arms."

She swiped at the tears streaming down her cheeks, then balled her fists and shook her head as she looked at the floor again. "No," she whispered. "I want you to leave. Please. Just go find your wizard's tree."

"Nay, Catherine. A dozen warhorses couldn't drag me out of this room. Not until you walk into my arms."

"I—I can't!" she cried, looking up. "Don't you get it?" She angrily waved at the bed between them. "I can't even make love to a man in my dreams without panicking!"

"But you can handle a hug," he whispered. "Especially from someone you think you might love."

"That was a mistake. I was just overwhelmed by what you did for Ian."

"I can't come to you, Catherine," he said, widening his arms. "You must come to me."

It took her an interminable measure of time to realize that he wasn't leaving until she did. With her hands fisted and her tear-soaked eyes glaring at him, she finally marched over until her toes were nearly touching his.

"Hug me," he whispered, having a moment's hope that she might hit him instead.

She made a noise that sounded much like a kitten's growl, reached her arms around his waist and hugged him fiercely and quickly. Then she tried to step back.

Robbie wrapped his arms around her and held her in place, using his chin to tuck her head against his chest. "Aye," he said, sighing with relief. "You might not know if there's love between us, Catherine, but you can't deny there's trust."

She slowly relaxed against him. "I'm sorry," she whispered. She leaned her head back and looked up, her eyes swimming with turmoil. "I was doing okay until you . . . until I felt your weight pinning me . . ." She buried her face in his chest.

"Daniels didn't just beat you, did he?"

She said nothing, only shook her head against his plaid.

Robbie closed his eyes and clenched his teeth on his raging desire to kill Daniels. Now was not the time for anger. But the day would come when he would take the bastard by the throat and squeeze the life out of his soulless body. Robbie vowed to be smiling while he did.

He gently kissed the top of Catherine's head, leaving his mouth to linger as he brushed her hair with his hand. He could feel her heart racing as she clutched the back of his plaid and her tears dampened the front of it. "Hush, little one, it's going to be okay," he promised. "You've fallen in love with a very patient man."

Catherine muttered something Robbie couldn't make out and sagged against him. He swept a hand under her knees and carried her to a chair by the fire, and sat down with her in his lap, then lifted her chin so she could see his smile. He brushed a tear from her cheek with his thumb. "You must not dwell on what just happened, Cat. It's of no consequence to us."

"Of no . . . you're saying that . . . I had a panic attack," she finally said. "I was kissing you one minute and hitting you the next."

"Aye, I noticed that." He caressed her cheek with his thumb again. "I also noticed that you survived and walked right back into my arms when it was over."

She leaned her head on his shoulder with a lingering sob. "I want to do it," she whispered, staring into the darkness. "But I can't." She tilted her head just enough to look at him. "I might never be able to have a normal relationship with a man."

He tapped her upturned nose. "Aye, you will. With this man," he said, lifting her hand and holding it over his heart. "When you're done thinking you might love me and are knowing it instead, your only thoughts will be of me."

"Th-That's an arrogant statement."

"But a true one." He cupped her face, gently kissed her gaping mouth, then smiled at her. "We have the rest of our lives, Catherine. We'll eventually figure it out."

She looked down at her hand on his chest, still covered with his. "Maybe that's why I'm having this dream, to figure out that I shouldn't want you." She looked up at him, her eyes filling with tears again. "When you kissed me in the barn and in the kitchen, I thought . . . I hoped that I . . . I thought I was okay. But tonight," she said, pulling her hand away and gesturing toward the bed. "I finally realized that I'm not. This dream is trying to show me that I can't hope to get involved with you. That I can't want you."

"You think dreams are our way of working things out?"

"Yes. They're how we deal with our problems."

"And you consider me a problem?"

"No. I'm my problem," she said, touching her own chest. "I'm too scared to let go of my fear."

He nodded. "So, because you fear men, you intend simply to avoid them."

"That's a perfectly good solution." She lifted her chin. "A woman doesn't need a man to have a full life."

"Aye," he agreed, standing up and setting her on her feet, then tilting her chin to face him. "But what happens if she falls in love, only her fear keeps her from following her heart? Can her life still be full?"

"Of course not."

He kissed the tip of her upturned nose. "Then that's

what your dream is telling you, Cat. When you wake up in modern time, you'll have learned to let your heart rule instead of your fears. And the rest will take care of itself."

"Just like that," she said, crossing her arms under her breasts and glaring at him.

"Aye, Catherine. If you want something—*anything*—badly enough, there is no power on earth that can keep you from it. And that," he said, leaning down and smiling, "is the true definition of magic."

Catherine leaned in even closer, either to kiss him or to give him a scathing reply, but Mary suddenly glided through the window with a piercing shrill. She landed on the bed, wrapped her talons around the hilt of Robbie's sword, and let out an angry chatter of rattles.

Catherine stepped away from him with a gasp, her hand flying to her chest as she looked first at Mary, then at him.

Robbie studied Catherine and considered her reaction to Mary's arrival. It had to be the owl's loud and sudden appearance upsetting her and not what Mary was saying—because Robbie knew he was the only one his pet spoke to.

He walked over to the bed and brushed Mary off his sword so he could pick it up and settle it over his back. He turned to Catherine, who was still clutching her throat and still gaping at Mary. She slowly raised her worried eyes to his, then suddenly ran to the door and stood in front of it, her hands spread to stop him from opening it.

"You're not leaving," she said. "I don't care if they make us get married in the morning, you are not leaving this room."

He walked over, took hold of her shoulders, pulled her against him, and kissed her firmly on the mouth. "Aye, how I wish I could stay for our wedding," he whispered once he was done. "But I have to go, Catherine. Mary has new information."

She balled the front of his plaid in her fists. "Then take me with you. I can run fast—you know I can. I won't be in your way. I can help, because Cùram won't think I'm a threat."

"I didn't mention Cùram," he said. "Why do you?"

"Because that's where you're going, isn't it? After Cùram and his tree?" Her grip on his plaid tightened, and she tried to shake him into complying. "Take me with you!"

"Nay, Cat," he said, leaning down and kissing her again, lifting her off her feet and turning so that she was away from the door before he set her back down. He broke the kiss, opened the door, and stepped out, then quickly closed it and threw the bolt, locking her in.

"No!" she shouted, banging her fist on the door. "Dammit, don't you dare lock me in here!"

He leaned his forehead on the wood and smiled. "Aye, Cat," he said loudly enough that she could hear him. "I can handle your anger. I'll be back soon enough, and you can spend the rest of your dream giving me hell." He lifted his hand and laid it on the door, right where she pounded on the opposite side. "Sleep well, little Cat," he whispered when she suddenly went silent, only to wince when he heard Mary squawk and flap a hasty retreat out the window.

He turned and quietly walked away, his smile broadening when something hit the door with enough force to rattle its hinges. Aye. He much preferred Cat's anger to her tears.

Robbie would have been really pleased with her the next morning, because Catherine was so angry she was seeing red—although that might have something to do with the fact that she hadn't slept all night, and her eyes were swollen and bloodshot from crying.

As clear as Caitlin was talking to her—in Gaelic—while they walked to Ian and Gwyneth's home, Catherine had heard Mary speaking last night.

Cùram was up to something, the owl had told Robbie. She'd seen the *drùidh* on Snow Mountain, standing inside a ring of eerily glowing boulders as he spoke to the moon, his staff sizzling with sparks of energy as he raised it to the sky.

Caitlin suddenly pulled Catherine out of the way when at least twenty mounted warriors rode by, looking angry and tired and dirty. Catherine recognized Niall bringing up the end of the fierce-looking parade. He stopped when he spotted them and spoke to Caitlin. Again, Catherine didn't have a clue what they were saying, only that it wasn't pleasant by the looks on their faces. Caitlin took hold of Catherine's arm again when Niall rode toward the keep and pulled her back into the lane, her steps rushed.

As soon as they reached Ian and Gwyneth's home, Caitlin spoke to her parents at length, and Ian started shaking his head and wringing his hands.

Catherine pulled him outside the moment the conversation stopped. "What's going on?" she asked. "Is it news of Robbie?"

"Nay," Ian said. "Niall has just come back from a farm over near Crag Mountain. The MacBains burned it down and stole all the animals last night."

"Was anyone hurt?"

"The family is unharmed. But Niall is upset because it was a bold move for the MacBains. The farm is only three miles from our village. And the farmer said he was given a message for his laird, that if we don't tear down the dam that stops the Snow River from flowing onto MacBain land, they'll bring every warrior they have and do it themselves."

"Niall built a dam that cut off their water?"

"Nay. Nature built it about a month ago. There was a landslide off Snow Mountain that blocked up the river." He shrugged. "Niall is willing to remove the debris to let the water flow again." He screwed his face into a fierce scowl. "He just doesn't care to have the MacBains telling him to do it."

"But why are you all so worried? You only have to take down the dam, and everyone will be happy."

"The reason my son hadn't touched the landslide before now is because no one dares go near it," Ian explained. "It was an unnatural occurrence. The sky lit with a terrible storm that night, Gwyneth told me, and the thunder was so loud that even the huts in the village shook, and several stones fell from the keep."

Catherine clutched Ian's arm. "Robbie went to Snow Mountain last night."

"He did? Why?"

"Because he thinks Cùram's tree of wisdom is there."

Ian stared off into the distance, toward the tall range of mountains looming above them. "Aye," he said, looking back at her. "That would make sense."

"We have to go after him. We have to warn him that he's going to be in the middle of a war."

"Nay. The boy must accomplish his task without our interference." Ian set his hand on her shoulder. "His papa trained Robbie well, Catherine, so that he can fulfill his calling. A woman and an old man would only get in his way, no matter how good our intentions. Come," he said, urging her inside. "If he's not back by tomorrow noon, then we'll start worrying."

That was easier said than done for Catherine, as she

spent the rest of the day helping Gwyneth put her house in order. Not that she was much help, compared with all the women who came over with rags and soap and crude brooms and the men who came with hammers and material to stop the old roof from leaking.

Catherine kept getting in their way, until she finally decided she could best help by watching all the children they brought with them. Language wasn't much of a barrier when it came to kids. Catherine drew pictures in the dirt with a stick, and the children would tell her the Gaelic names.

The sun took forever to move across the sky, and playing with the children made Catherine homesick for Nathan and Nora and the boys. She ate more indescribable food for lunch, and after an even scarier supper, she went for a walk with Ian to settle her stomach. He led her up to a cemetery surrounded by a white, weathered fence and stopped in front of a headstone.

"This is my son's grave," he said softly. "James. He was my fourth child, after Maura and Niall and Megan. He died six years ago, Gwyneth told me, in a hunting accident. His horse fell while he was chasing a stag, and James broke his neck."

Catherine squeezed his hand. "I'm sorry," she whispered. "You have another daughter named Maura? Will I meet her?"

"Nay," he said, pointing beyond the fence. "She died when she was only seventeen." He looked at Catherine and suddenly broke into a smile. "This Sunday after church, we're going to extend the fence around her grave and bless the ground she rests in."

"But why wasn't she buried in here?"

"Because it was thought she killed herself," he whispered fiercely, shaking his head. "And we were forbidden to lay her in hallowed ground. But I've since learned it was an accident," he added, squaring his shoulders. "She was running away to marry Robbie's father when she fell through the rotten ice of the *loch*. It was a tragedy, not a sin."

"She was going to marry Michael MacBain?"

"Aye." He continued their walk, heading out of the cemetery and back onto the path. "It's a long story, Catherine. Let's just say it's the reason the MacBains and the MacKeages are at war. But I can right our wrong now and restore the peace."

"You can do that without exposing where you've been for the last thirty-five years?"

"Aye. I've come up with a good story. I'll tell them that when we were captured—*ten* years ago—I had a chance to talk to Michael and learn the truth."

She squeezed his arm as they walked down the path toward his hut. "I'm glad Robbie brought you home."

He patted her hand in the crook of his elbow. "Aye," he said with a sigh. "But not nearly as glad as I am, lass."

She was just about to say something else when three young men barely out of their teens stepped into their path and all started talking at once. Ian immediately pushed Catherine behind his back and spoke to them in rapid, spitting, and angry-sounding Gaelic.

"Run to Gwyneth," Ian suddenly said, pushing her away.

Catherine didn't bother to ask what the boys wanted but turned and ran down the lane when two of them sprang toward her. She darted between huts, scattering chickens and avoiding laundry lines and playing children.

She finally started to pull away from them when one of her pursuers suddenly shouted in surprise. Two minutes later, the other one grunted, tripped, and smacked into the wall of a hut.

Catherine kept running, unsure where the third boy was. She would have made it to Gwyneth's house if a dog hadn't started chasing her. She tripped and almost fell flat on her face, but for the strong arms that caught her and swept her off her feet with a laugh.

"You're safe," Robbie said, crushing her against his chest and continuing down the lane at a more sedate pace. His mouth was turned in a frown, but his eyes were smiling. "You were about to get your second, third, and fourth marriage proposals."

"What?"

"You're a prize, Cat. You saved Ian from the English, and there isn't an unmarried warrior around who doesn't want you to be the mother of his children."

"Oh, for the love of—Phew! What's that smell?" she said, wrinkling her nose. "Good heavens, it's you! Have you been rolling in manure?" Then she remembered she was mad at him. "Put me down," she snapped, wiggling to get free.

He set her on her feet with a laugh and tucked her hand through his arm, holding it firmly. "I may have to marry you just to keep the warriors away." He stopped so that she would look up at him. "Unless you're expecting to wake up anytime soon, Cat, it's the only way to keep you safe here."

"Did you find the tree?"

"Nay. But I did find where Cùram's been staying. And I felt the energy of the tree, but I couldn't seem to pin down its exact location."

"You could *feel* it?"

He started walking again, keeping her hand tucked in his. "Aye. There was enough energy humming through the air to power an entire city."

"Was it near Snow Mountain? Did you see the landslide that dammed up the river?"

"Aye, and I've already spoken with Niall about last night's raid." He stopped them again. "It was about a month ago that the landslide happened. And Daar thinks that's when Cùram hid his tree, once he realized Daar was looking for it."

"How did Cùram know he wanted it?"

Robbie started them walking again, waving his free hand at nothing. "Who knows? He's supposed to be a young, cunning, powerful *drùidh*."

"And Mary wasn't any help?"

"She showed me where he's been living. Anyone else would have missed it. He's disguised it well."

"But you didn't see Cùram?"

"Nay," he said, stopping them outside of Gwyneth and Ian's hut. "I'm not joking about the wedding, Cat. It will still take me several days to find that tree, and the attempts to steal you for a wife won't stop until you're caught."

"But don't I have to say 'I do' or something?" she asked, wrinkling her nose and stepping away from his smell. "Doesn't the marriage have to be consensual?"

"Not really. If your reputation is compromised, Niall can simply force you to marry."

She took another step back, not from his smell this time but from the gleam in his eye, and shook her finger at him. "I'm not getting married," she said with a curt nod, just to show she meant it. "Not even in my dreams."

"Not even to someone you think you love?" he asked, matching her retreat with a step of his own.

"I told you that was a mistake," she said, eyeing the lane and judging her chances of escaping.

But to where? That was the problem; she had no place to go. Her only hope was to wake up now. But when that didn't happen and when Robbie read her intent and lunged toward her, Catherine turned with a squeak and took off down the lane.

Darn it, this was *her* dream, not his. She was not marrying Robbie MacBain just to fulfill his silly fantasy.

"Come here, you little cat!" he shouted as he ran after her, his voice sounding more amused than mad.

Within minutes, she left the village behind and was powering up the mountain path they'd traveled down just yesterday. Was it only yesterday? It felt like a month ago!

The sun had finally set, and the trail was deeply shadowed by the stingy light of dusk. She could hear Robbie behind her, growing less amused and more angry every time he called her name. She kept looking for another path that turned toward the village, so that she could backtrack to Ian's hut and be waiting for Robbie when he finally gave up the chase. It would serve him right for her to best him again, after locking her in her room last night.

Catherine nearly missed the narrow trail to her left. She grabbed a tree and spun around it, then darted up the even steeper path, only to slam straight into a huge horse that was more startled than she was. She fell backward with a yelp of surprise when the horse reared up, but large, bruising hands grabbed her before she could hit the ground and lifted her up, away from the flying hooves.

Her back was slammed against a hard, smelly chest, and she got dizzy when the horse she was sitting astride spun and started galloping up the path. Catherine slapped at her captor, but he simply tightened his beefy arm and squeezed the air out of her scream.

She heard shouts behind her and the sound of metal striking metal, and Catherine gasped at the realization that there was a swordfight going on back down the trail and that Robbie was right in the middle of it.

She dug her fingers into the arm holding her, then twisted and reached up to claw the guy's face. But she went utterly still when she saw that the man wasn't another MacKeage idiot trying to steal a wife—he was wearing a MacBain plaid. And Robbie was back there, fighting MacBains.

Oh, how foolish she'd been to run away. Ian had warned her that the MacBains were getting bold, and now Robbie was paying the price.

The sound of pounding hooves came galloping toward them. Catherine twisted to look around her captor and cried out in relief. There was just enough light for her to see Robbie break from the woods into the clearing behind them.

The MacBain warrior stopped and turned his horse to face the charge, and Robbie pulled his stolen horse to a stop. He held his sword in his left hand, its tip pointed at them, and looked angry enough to chew nails.

"Catherine," he growled. "I want ya to fall forward and bury your face in the horse's neck when I say so, and don't move an inch, no matter what happens. Nod if ya understand, lass."

She was trembling too hard to nod. Holy mother of God, she was caught in the middle of a swordfight.

Robbie advanced his horse when the MacBain warrior backed them away. "Do it now!"

She threw herself against the horse's neck, closing her eyes and wrapping her arms around it, squeezing so tightly she could actually feel the horse choke as the brute tightened his arm around her waist and charged. She was nearly dragged to the ground when her captor suddenly lost his seat with a shout, tumbled backward off the rump of his horse, and hit the ground with a heavy thud.

Another arm snaked around her waist, and Catherine tightened her hold on her horse's neck. "It's me," Robbie said with barely controlled anger. "Let go."

Catherine opened her arms but kept her eyes closed as she sailed through the air and landed against Robbie's familiar chest. She turned in his arms and clung to him as they galloped into the woods.

She waited for him to give her hell for running away, but he said nothing as they raced down the dark forest path that only he—and, she hoped, the horse—could see. Catherine could feel each bellowing breath Robbie took, his heart pounding against her cheek and his taut muscles flexing as he balanced them both with the skill of a man born in a saddle. Even a thirteenth-century saddle, apparently.

He stopped at Ian's hut but didn't dismount or loosen his grip on her. He said something in Gaelic when Ian came outside and then turned the horse and continued on to the keep.

Since he didn't appear to have anything to say to her, Catherine decided she wasn't going to apologize for running away or for getting stolen or even for nearly getting them killed.

He stopped outside the keep, dismounted, pulled her down to the ground, then took hold of her wrist in an unbreakable grip and towed her through the huge door. He led her to the blazing hearth and set her down on a stool beside it, giving her a pointed glare that said she had better stay put. He turned to the group of staring warriors, women, older children, and a dozen dogs and spoke in Gaelic.

Several of the women suddenly cheered, and quite a few

of the men groaned loudly. Niall got up from the table he'd been sitting at with several warriors and came over and pounded Robbie's back with a smile.

Not ten minutes later, Catherine found herself standing beside Robbie MacBain, both of them facing a priest, with Ian beside Robbie and Gwyneth beside her and at least fifty people she didn't know in attendance.

The ceremony was succinct, more spit than spoken, and Catherine never did get a chance to say "I do," or even "I don't," for that matter.

The priest suddenly shut up and looked at Robbie. Mary silently flew down from the tall rafters of the great hall, as if appearing out of nowhere, and landed on Robbie's shoulder. He held out his hand, and the snowy opened her beak and dropped two rings into his palm.

With the owl still on his shoulder, he turned to Catherine, took hold of her left hand, and slid one of the heavy gold bands onto her finger. She waited for him to pass her the other ring so she could throw it at his chest, but he simply slid it onto his own finger, took her left hand back between his, and smiled.

"It's done, little Cat," he whispered, pressing her hand between his palms, touching their rings together. "You're mine."

The wide band on her finger warmed until it felt as if it would burn her, and Catherine dropped her gaze with a gasp. Robbie's ring appeared to glow with an energy of its own, and her hand sandwiched between his gently tingled as light shone through his fingers.

She tried to pull away, but he leaned down until his mouth was only inches from hers, causing Mary to flap away with a high-pitched whistle, back into the darkness of the rafters.

"Welcome to your new calling, wife," he whispered, claiming her gaping mouth with a kiss that was far more possessive than gentle. "And to the rest of our lives, Catherine MacBain," he added, sweeping her into his embrace, kissing her until her toes curled with excitement and her heart pounded with dread.

Chapter Twenty-one

Robbie only half listened to the grudgingly given well-wishes of the warriors he was standing with, his attention tuned in to Catherine sitting on the stool by the large hearth. His poor wife was looking small and fragile and rather bewildered as she inconspicuously tried to work her wedding band off her finger.

He nodded to the warriors and walked through the crowd of celebrating villagers, crouched down beside her, and lifted her left hand to his mouth and kissed her fingers.

"It won't come off, Catherine."

"It wasn't that tight when you put it on," she muttered, pulling free and tugging on the ring again.

He stilled her actions by taking both her hands in his as he brushed his lips across her cheek, ending his moist caress in her hair. "Aye, but it's a special ring that is as much a part of you as I am now," he whispered. "It's the ring my mama would have worn, had she lived long enough to marry Michael MacBain."

He lifted his left hand for her to see his own wedding band. "And this is the ring Mary would have given my papa. See," he said, tugging on his own ring. "As long as we breathe, Catherine, neither ring will leave our fingers. Our bond has been blessed by providence."

She stared at him, her huge brown eyes unblinking, and he couldn't decide if she was even more confused by what he'd just told her or horrified.

He stood up and pulled her off the stool, and a hush fell over the great room as he led his wife to the narrow staircase on the far side of the hall. He stopped at the foot of the stairs, gave her trembling hand a gentle squeeze, swept her into his arms, and carried her up the stairs to the clapping and cheers and raucous encouragement of the villagers.

She was a bundle of shivers by the time they reached their room, and Robbie walked to the chair by the hearth, sat down, and settled her comfortably in his lap.

"Be easy, Cat," he softly told her, tucking his finger under her chin to lift her pale face to his. "Nothing is going to happen tonight unless you wish it."

"I don't want to be married," she whispered. She touched her hand to his chest. "Don't take it personally, Robbie. It has nothing to do with you. It's me. I just don't want to be . . . to feel like I'm . . . to be . . ."

"Trapped?" he finished, pressing her hand over his heart. "Catherine, our union is not a trap for either of us but a sacred trust between two people who love each other."

"Y-you love me?"

He couldn't help but smile at her obvious surprise. "Aye, since the moment I woke up and found myself tied to your bed."

"But you didn't even know me then."

"I knew you, Catherine. And I also knew that you felt it,

too. Enough that you placed yourself and your children's welfare in my hands and took over my household with the determination of a mountain cat."

"I was scared to death."

"Aye. But that didn't stop you, did it?" He leaned over and kissed the tip of her nose. "One day, you'll realize you're brave enough to take me on. But until then," he said, standing up and carrying her to the bed, "we'll play by your rules."

He laid her down, kissed her pale white cheek, pulled one of the blankets over her, and straightened.

She shot up into a sitting position, threw back the blanket, and tried to swing her legs over the edge of the bed. "Are you leaving again?"

He gently laid her back down. "Nay," he said, covering her back up and then quickly climbing on top of the blanket. "Husbands do not abandon their wives on their wedding night."

He threw his arm over her waist and pulled her backside into the crook of his body. "We've both had a long day, and we need to get some sleep." He gave her a squeeze. "Tomorrow, you and Ian are coming with me to Snow Mountain, to help me hunt for Cùram's tree."

She turned her head in surprise. "We can go with you?"

"Aye, but only so that Ian can tell me about the lay of the land before the valley was flooded. Then the two of you are coming straight back here."

She relaxed and faced the window, actually snuggling her backside against him. "I think we should take Niall and a hundred warriors with us," she said. "For protection from the MacBains."

"Nay, no one must know what I'm doing," he told her, quickly bunching the blanket between them so he couldn't feel her sweet feminine heat. "I've already spoken with Ian, and he'll meet us out front at daybreak." Robbie tightened his arm to stop her wiggling. "Go to sleep, Cat," he said through gritted teeth. "Tomorrow's going to be another long day."

But it was the night that was long for Robbie, as he lay beside his soft, warm, delicious-smelling wife, unable to claim her as his.

"My God, the destruction was great," Ian said, staring out over the waters of the newly formed lake. "A good deal of Snow Mountain slid into the valley."

Catherine resettled her stick on her shoulders when her horse sidestepped impatiently and let her gaze follow the densely forested shoreline until it came to the massive earthen dam of boulders, whole trees, and muddy debris wedged between a towering mountain and a smaller hill. Looking up, beyond the dam, she could see a gaping hole in the side of Snow Mountain, making an ugly scar of exposed granite running from its summit down to the lake.

Robbie turned to Ian. "How deep was the valley here?"

"There's still as much mountain under the water as you see above it," Ian said, looking at Robbie and frowning. "Do ya think Cùram's tree was in the valley?"

"Aye, and I believe it still is."

"But the *loch* would have drowned it."

"Nay. Not if Cùram found a way to protect it." Robbie turned his horse to face Ian and Catherine. "And what better place to hide something than under the water? Who thinks of anything but fish being in a lake?"

"But how did he protect it?" Ian asked. "A tree needs air to live."

"Do you know of any caves on Snow Mountain, Uncle?"

Ian scratched his beard, staring at the ruined mountain and frowning. His eyebrows suddenly rose. "Aye! When I was a lad, we used to hide from our mamas by playing up here. I remember there were caves." He suddenly frowned again. "But the landslide most likely destroyed them."

"Maybe not," Robbie said. "Exactly where did you play?"

"There," Ian said, pointing to the other side of the dam. "I remember there was a cave about a hundred yards up from Snow River, that ran deep into the mountain and came up over there," he added, his hand moving across the scar until he was pointing at an island in the middle of the lake. "Only that wasn't an island then but a steep hill. The cave narrowed up until ya had to brace your feet and your back against it and climb out like it was a chimney."

Robbie started his horse through the trees along the shore of the lake, heading toward the dam. "Come on," he said. "We'll look for the lower entrance first. If it's covered by debris, I'll swim to the island and see if I can find the other entrance."

Catherine eyed the tiny island as she urged her horse after the two men. It appeared to be a good mile from shore, and the water looked cold. But trying to keep her promise to Robbie this morning, that she would not interfere in his work, Catherine said nothing and followed in silence.

They guided their mounts down through the forest into the deep valley, the earthen dam of boulders and mud and splintered trees rising above them on their right. They finally reached level ground, rode across the dry riverbed that had once been the obviously large Snow River, and started up the other side.

Ian moved into the lead, scanning the forest around them. "There," he said, stopping his horse and pointing. "It's been years, Robbie, but I think the entrance to the cave is up there."

Robbie dismounted and handed the reins of his horse to Catherine. He looked first at the earthen dam, then back at her. "If I find the entrance, I'll come back and tell you before I go inside. The dam doesn't look stable to me, so I want you and Ian to wait on higher ground."

"You won't go inside without telling us?"

He set his hand on her thigh. "I promise I won't if you promise not to follow me."

"You've been asking for a lot of promises this morning."

His grin slashed across his face. "Aye, and I've noticed you've been keeping them quite well."

She snorted and urged her horse forward, pulling Robbie's horse with her. She moved past Ian and picked an easy route up the hill. But when she turned back to look, to remind Robbie to be careful, he had already disappeared into the woods.

"I'm relieved the boy has found himself a good wife," Ian said, pulling up beside her. "None of us wanted to see him so dedicated to his calling that he neglected his own happiness. His papa especially was starting to worry." He grinned at her. "But now he has you. And I wish to tell ya, lass, that I'm proud of how you're taking all this. Most women would be nothing but a ball of tears for finding themselves on this journey."

Catherine had no idea how to respond to his relief or his compliment, other than to smile and whisper a thank you. She didn't have the heart to tell Ian that it was easy for her to be brave in a dream and that once she woke up, she would no longer be married to his nephew.

They dismounted and tied their horses to some bushes, and Catherine sat down beside Ian and accepted the snack he handed her. It was a dry oat cake of some sort and looked as if it had been pounded flat with a hammer and probably tasted like sawdust. But, again, she didn't have the heart to refuse his gift and took a bite, then quickly washed it down with even nastier-tasting ale. Dreams of living in the thirteenth century were a great way to lose weight, Catherine decided. She'd only been here three days, and she'd dropped another five pounds.

She stood up, surprised when Robbie suddenly appeared after being gone only twenty minutes.

"I found it," he said, coming over and helping Ian to his feet. "And Cùram's tree must be in there. I could feel how strong the energy was the moment I stepped inside." He took hold of Catherine's shoulders and made her face him. "I want you and Ian to go back to the village."

"No. We'll wait until you come back with the root."

"Nay. I might be a while. The cave forks off in several directions just inside the entrance. Go back to the village, and I'll return as soon as I can." He leaned down, gave her a quick kiss on the mouth, and straightened and smiled. "And then you and I will go home," he whispered. "I miss our kids as much as you do."

"Please let us wait here?" she asked, grabbing the front of his plaid. "We'll keep an eye out for the MacBains. What if they come to take down the dam while you're inside? The caves could flood." She tightened her grip. "And Cùram. What if he suddenly shows up?"

"And just what do you plan to do if he does? Fight the *drùidh* with your stick?"

"It's about as useful as your sword!" she snapped, stepping away. Catherine sigh and canted her head at him. "Do you remember what you said to me right after you put the ring on my finger?"

"I said welcome to the rest of our lives."

"No, first you said, 'Welcome to your new calling, wife.' And you were right. If I'm going to be a guardian's wife, then it's my duty to guard the guardian."

"Dammit, Cat. That's not what I meant."

"But you can't deny that husbands and wives have certain responsibilities to each other. Just as you feel it's your duty to protect me, do I not have the same privilege? Or is this one of those 'I'm the brave warrior, and you're the helpless little woman' marriages?" she asked, dropping her voice to sound like her dictatorial husband.

She smiled when his jaw clenched and stifled a chuckle when Ian snorted and said, "She's got ya there, MacBain. Even guardians need help sometimes, and who better than your wife?"

"It's too dangerous," Robbie said, glaring first at her and then at Ian. "And I did not bring you home, old man, to get you killed in three days."

"Aye, but everyone needs to be needed, Robbie," Ian said softly. "Including wives."

"No! This is not open to discussion."

"Then let me put it to you this way," Catherine said, continuing the discussion anyway. "If something happens to you, then I'm stuck here. I'm never going to see my children again." He gave her such a confounded look that Catherine decided to press her advantage. "And I'll be widowed and remarried to the first warrior fast enough to catch me."

The noise started deep in his chest, rumbling with lethal warning, and erupted in a full-blown growl. Catherine simply smiled and tapped the end of his nose. She spun away before he could react, and sat back down on the mossy ledge and picked up her sawdust pancake.

"Go find your root," she said, waving him away. "Ian and I will be right here when you get back."

Ian, rubbing his hands together, moved to sit beside her, his chin lifted defiantly and his smile ruining his glare.

Robbie pulled his sword from the sheath on his back,

and Catherine had a moment's worry that he intended to send them home at sword-point. But Ian quietly reached over and squeezed her hand, then popped a piece of his cake into his mouth and chewed.

Robbie turned on his heel and started back toward the cave, then stopped and pointed his sword at them. "You'll leave an hour before sunset if I'm not back by then," he growled. "And if something happens to me, Mary can get you home."

"Unless Mary dies trying to save you."

He growled again, his face hard and his eyes glaring.

"Where is your pet?" Ian asked, looking up at the trees. "I haven't seen her since we left this morning."

"She went to check on the MacBains," Robbie said, still glaring at Catherine. He finally looked at Ian. "Have my wife home by sunset, Uncle," he softly commanded as he turned and disappeared into the woods.

Ian looked at Catherine and smiled. "It's going to take him time to adjust to being married," he told her, patting her arm. "But see, you've already won your first battle. We get to wait here, and you get to do yar worrying up close."

And worry she did, for three long hours. She ate several more sawdust pancakes and drank nasty ale until her stomach protested by throwing up. She paced a rut in the forest floor and watched Ian doze on and off, until the old man suddenly suggested they move themselves to the entrance of the cave.

Ian used her stick as a cane for the walk through the woods, and Catherine led their horses. She was surprised that Ian even found the cave and was even more surprised when she discovered the entrance was nothing more than a crack.

Warm air softly whistled from the crack, and Catherine settled Ian directly in front of it so he could soak up some of its warmth. Then she started wearing a new path in the dirt, pacing from their horses to Ian and back. But after another agonizing hour of worrying, wondering if Robbie was lost or stuck or had run into Cùram, she stopped when she heard a shrill whistle coming up the valley.

Mary landed on a branch in a tall pine tree and told Catherine her news. Catherine ran over to Ian and gently shook him awake.

"The MacBains are coming up the dry riverbed," she said.

Ian came awake completely alert, canted his head, and listened. His eyes suddenly widened. "I'm guessing they've brought a legion of warriors," he whispered, using the granite at his back to lever himself up. "Quick, we must hide ourselves and the horses."

"What do you want me to do?"

"Run down to where we were earlier and brush away our tracks leading up here. I'll unsaddle our horses and send them away, and we'll stash our gear and hide in the cave."

Catherine ran to do as he told her, breaking off a spruce branch to brush the ground with. She even swept their path up from the riverbank and had just made it back to the cave when they heard the warriors stop at the base of the dam.

"Can you get inside, Ian?" she whispered, using her hand to protect his head when he tried to duck through the crack. "Do you fit?"

"Aye," he said with a grunt, expelling his breath to squeeze through the narrow entrance. "It opens up once ya get inside," he whispered, reaching out his hand. "Come quick, Catherine."

She squeezed in after him, blinking to adjust to the low light, and gasped in surprise to see that the walls of the cave appeared to be glowing. She crawled further in and touched them, and found that they were unnaturally warm.

"What does this mean?" she whispered, crawling back to Ian. "How can they glow like that?"

"It's the magic, lass," he said as he watched through the crack and listened. "Aye, they've stopped, all right. I'm thinking they're making good on their threat to tear down the dam themselves. But don't worry, lass. Niall will be here shortly."

"Niall?"

"Aye," he said, looking back at her and smiling. "My son was elected laird because of his cunning. He likely had someone guarding the dam."

"But wouldn't Niall's scout have stopped us?"

Ian shrugged. "We're just three villagers out enjoying the countryside, upsetting no one." He grinned and patted her hand. "And we're wearing the right color plaids. Nay, the scout will see the MacBains and go get my son."

Catherine gasped and looked down. "Oh, my God, that's water," she hissed, getting up on her hands and knees as the floor became soaked and water started to trickle toward the crack. "Robbie!" she cried, trying to move deeper into the cave.

Ian grabbed her ankle. "Nay, lass. Ya cannot go after him. He'll be back soon."

The water quickly rose to about three inches deep, quietly babbling at first and then gushing into a small river that ran out the crack. Loud splashing came from deep in the cave, along with a roaring sound that shook the ground, and Catherine turned and saw Robbie hunched over, holding his chest as he ran toward them, a wall of water behind him.

"Get out!" he shouted when he spotted them. "Now!"

The frothing water beat them to the crack, washing them up in its path and spewing them from the cave in a churning deluge of chaos. A strong hand clamped around Catherine's wrist, anchoring her against the current. She thought she was going to drown before she was suddenly pulled free of the water's grip and slapped onto damp earth next to Robbie.

Ian shouted as he tumbled into the woods. Robbie pulled something from his chest, shoved it into her lap, and took off after the old warrior. Catherine sat up and blinked at the squirming, hissing bundle in her hands. A tiny mouth with miniature fangs spit at her as the black kitten twisted to get free.

But it was the thick piece of curling wood clutched in its sharp little claws that made Catherine smile. Robbie had found Cùram's tree! She hugged the kitten to her chest, ignoring its spitting attempts to bite her.

"Shhh," she crooned, rubbing its neck. "You're safe now. Robbie wouldn't leave you to drown."

The wet little bundle trembled in her arms and finally settled down. She tried to pull the root from its claws, but it growled and hugged the wood tighter.

"Okay, you can hold on to it for now," she whispered, using her thumb to stroke its shivering body.

She looked up when Robbie came striding through the water with Ian. He set him down on the ground beside her and cupped Ian's sputtering face in his hands.

"You're okay, Uncle. Just get rid of what you swallowed."

Ian leaned over and coughed up a stomach full of water. He wiped his mouth, looked up at Robbie, and grinned. "I thank ya, MacBain." But his smile disappeared when he looked over at Catherine. "What in hell is that?" he asked, pointing at her chest.

"That," Robbie said, taking the once again spitting kitten from her and holding it against his own chest, "is a piece of the tap root from Cùram's tree," he said, pulling the wood from the kitten's claws and holding it up. "I found it," he said, clutching his prize in his fist. He looked over his shoulder at the stream gushing from the crack beside them, then turned back. "But I've killed the old tree of wisdom," he whispered, shaking his head. "It was in a deep crevice on the island, just its top branches exposed. When I dug at its base to get this root, I opened the floodgates."

"But what in hell is that?" Ian asked again, pointing at the kitten.

Robbie held the growling black ball up to face him. "A panther cub, I'm guessing," he said, smiling when the kitten took a swat at him.

Ian snorted. "We don't have panthers in Scotland."

Robbie handed the cub back to Catherine and shrugged. "It was all alone in a tiny den not far from the entrance and was still there when I came running out. I couldn't leave it to drown."

Catherine held out her hand to Robbie as the cub squirmed and growled in her arms. "It wants the root. It's his security blanket."

Robbie hesitated, obviously reluctant to give his prize away, but then handed it over. The cub dug its tiny claws into the wood, clamping its teeth over the root before finally settling against Catherine's chest.

She pulled open the front of her shawl and tucked the kitten and root inside, tightened the knot securely, and patted it as she smiled at Robbie. "I promise not to let either of them out of my sight," she said. "Ah . . . we chased the horses off so the MacBains wouldn't find us. How are we going to get back to the village?"

No sooner had she asked that than at least four dozen MacBain warriors emerged from the woods, swords drawn and pointed at them, each looking fierce enough to stop Catherine's heart.

Robbie stood up and pulled his own sword from its sheath, which caused several of the warriors to step forward.

"Nay," Ian said, scrambling to his feet. "Angus, ya old bastard, it's me, Ian MacKeage."

"You would have better luck in Gaelic, Uncle," Robbie whispered, not taking his eyes off the wall of warriors.

"Aw, hell," Ian muttered. He started speaking in Gaelic and walked toward them. Catherine watched as one of the warriors, a man nearly as old as Ian, took a step back, his face paling and his eyes widening in shock.

"What's happening?" she asked, getting to her feet to stand beside Robbie, clutching the kitten and tree root to her chest.

"That's Angus MacBain he's talking to," Robbie told her, still not taking his eyes off the threat. "He's my grandfather. And he can't believe he's seeing Ian, as his son, Michael, was lost with Ian ten years ago."

"But what is Ian saying?"

"That he was with Michael when they were captured by the English. He's telling Angus how his son died and of Michael's great love for his own daughter, Maura. That they were going to run away and get married when she died."

"Angus didn't know about Maura?"

"He knew Michael was hellbent on going to war over a MacKeage woman, but Angus didn't know Maura had been pregnant with his grandchild at the time of her death."

Robbie darted a look at her, then back at the two older men. "Angus heard that Greylen and Ian and the others had disappeared with his son in a great storm, but he really thought the MacKeages had killed Michael and the five other MacBain warriors. There, Ian just told him that Michael died a hero by saving his life."

Angus scowled at Ian and pointed at Robbie and Catherine.

"Ian is telling him . . . aw, hell," Robbie growled, wiping his face with his free hand. "Ian just told him I'm a powerful *drùidh* named Cùram de Gairn and that if they don't go home peacefully, I'm going to drown them all." Ian pointed at the water spewing from the crack in the mountain, and Robbie groaned. "Now he's telling them I can reroute the Snow River and that if they want it to flow through MacBain land again, they should bow to my benevolence instead of daring to point their swords at me and my wife."

"So I'm a wizard's wife?" Catherine squeaked.

Robbie snorted. "Ian does love to spin tales," he said, shaking his head. He resheathed his sword and took a deep breath. "Well, I might as well give them a show, so my uncle won't be a liar and they can go home and tell their own tales around the campfire."

"What?"

He took hold of her hand and led her straight toward the wall of warriors. He stopped in front of Angus MacBain and said something to him in rapid, spitting Gaelic.

Catherine leaned toward Ian.

"He's telling Angus that he knew his son and that Michael MacBain was a great warrior that any papa would be proud of," Ian translated for her.

Robbie pulled his dagger out of his belt and handed it to Angus. The old MacBain warrior clutched the dagger in his fist until blood ran through his fingers and snapped his gaze back to Robbie.

"That's Michael's dagger," Ian said in a whisper. "And

now Robbie is turning so that Angus can see the hilt of his sword, that used to belong to Robert MacBain, Angus's brother."

Angus was Robbie's grandfather? Robbie certainly hadn't inherited his height from him. Angus MacBain was only an inch taller than she was. "Is he going to give up his sword?" Catherine asked in a hushed voice, leaning closer to Ian even though Robbie still held her hand.

"Nay," Ian said. "Angus asked for it, but Robbie told him that Robert wanted him to have it, to remind him of his duties to the MacBains. They should know they have a powerful guardian looking out for their welfare and that he's going to breach the dam so their livestock can drink from the Snow River again."

"C-Can he do that?" Catherine whispered.

Ian shrugged. "The boy's not one to give empty boasts."

Robbie then led Catherine right past the gaping warriors, speaking in Gaelic as they strode past, and Ian and Angus fell into step behind them. But instead of also following, the warriors suddenly scrambled down the hill toward the riverbed.

"I've told them to move their horses to dry ground," Robbie explained as he helped Catherine over a fallen log. "How's your passenger doing?"

"Fine," she said, patting the lump on her chest. "I think he might even be sleeping. Can you really break the dam?"

"Aye. It's unstable and should only take a small effort."

The clamor of pounding hoofbeats rose from the other side of the lake. Catherine, Robbie, Ian, and Angus stepped out of the woods and onto the edge of the dam just in time to see Niall and an army of at least two hundred warriors come to a halt on the opposite shore.

Robbie shouted to Niall and pointed to Ian and Angus, then spoke rapidly in Gaelic to the young laird for several minutes, until Niall finally dismounted and strode across the dam toward them.

"It's time for you to go home now, Uncle," Robbie said in English, turning to him.

He pulled Ian into a fierce embrace, holding him in his arms for several heartbeats before he kissed his cheek and used his thumb to wipe a tear from the old man's cheek. He whispered something to him, clapped his shoulders rather soundly, smiled, and whispered something else.

"Give Ian a hug good-bye, Cat," Robbie said, pulling her over to them. "You won't be seeing him again."

His words hit Catherine like a sharp blow to her heart. She hadn't thought about never seeing Ian again. She'd never again hear his beautiful lilt, get one of his bear hugs, or gaze into his eyes that wrinkled at the corners.

"Ah, Catherine," Ian said with a sigh, pulling her into a bear hug. "Ya remember what I told ya about husbands needing time to adjust," he whispered in her ear. "Just love my nephew and try to laugh more than ya scold, lass. And thank ya for sharing my journey home."

She was crying so hard she couldn't see anything when Robbie dragged her away from Ian and tucked her back against his side. The kitten finally settled down again, now that it wasn't getting squished by Ian's hug, and Catherine had to use the edge of Robbie's plaid to dry her own face.

Niall walked up to Ian, stopped long enough to glare at Angus MacBain, and then put his arm around his father and started walking him back across the dam. He stopped, stared at Robbie for several seconds, then nodded and turned to help Ian onto his horse.

Robbie led Catherine off the end of the dam and lifted her up onto a huge, flat boulder. "Stay put," he said, his smile softening his command. "I'm just going to free the Snow River, and then I'll be right back to get you."

He spoke briefly to Angus, then spun around and scrambled down through the woods, toward the base of the dam. Angus jumped up on the boulder beside her, standing not too close, giving her a grin that was more feral than friendly.

That is, until her chest started wiggling. The old MacBain warrior stepped back, looking as if he thought she might explode. Her passenger popped its head out of her shawl and hissed at Angus. Angus took another step back and pulled the dagger Robbie had given him out of his belt. He held it down by his side in a guarded but unthreatening position.

Catherine caught sight of Robbie just then, scrambling over the large boulders at the base of the dam, examining each one he came to and then scanning the mud and trees above it.

Darn it, what was he doing? If the dam was broke, he would be washed away.

He stopped suddenly, turned to face the dam, and set his hands on two large tree trunks sticking out of the wall of dirt. A collective murmur rose from across the lake, and Catherine looked up to see the MacKeage warriors, Niall with Ian mounted behind him, back their horse up a safe distance away. Angus also backed up with a gasp, taking hold of Catherine's arm and pulling her with him.

Catherine looked at Robbie and couldn't stifle her own gasp. The trees were starting to glow like burning embers, whiffs of smoke puffing into the air around them. Robbie suddenly straightened, brushed his hands together, looked up at her, and smiled.

"Get out of there!" she shouted. "You're going to drown!"

He jumped from boulder to boulder and disappeared into the forest, only to emerge suddenly on the rock beside her. Angus scrambled away, his wide hazel eyes filled with awe and a healthy dose of horror. Robbie spoke to him in Gaelic, and the old man gaped, then slowly nodded and ran into the forest.

"What did you say to him?"

Robbie turned and took her in his arms, locking his hands around her back and leaning his chest away so he wouldn't squish her passenger. "I told Angus that if he doesn't quit warring against the MacKeages, I'm going to come back and melt every MacBain sword into a rake or shovel."

He leaned over the kitten and kissed Catherine's nose, then straightened and grinned. "Are you ready to wake up from your dream now?"

She blinked at him, then looked across the lake at the army of MacKeages. She let her gaze travel to the MacBain warriors sitting on their horses on a distant ledge overlooking the dry Snow River, then down at the flaming logs in the dam, and then up at the scarred side of Snow Mountain.

She stiffened and pointed toward the summit. "Wh-Who is that?" she whispered.

Robbie looked where she was pointing, and Catherine felt him stiffen as well as they stared up at the silhouette of a tall man standing on a point of ledge high above them, a sword in one hand and his long, dark hair blowing in the breeze.

"Cùram."

"The wizard? What's he going to do?"

"Nothing," Robbie said softly, looking down at her. "There's nothing he can do. His tree of spells is destroyed."

"He's lost his power, then?"

"Nay, only his ability to plague us," he said, taking one last look at Cùram before bringing his gaze back to her and smiling. "Are you ready to go home?"

The boulder they stood on suddenly started to vibrate, and the earth began to rumble with gentle vibrations. A tiny trickle of water started near the logs, sputtering the flames into steam, until geysers suddenly spewed in a dozen different directions, shooting the logs free, breaching the dam with an ever widening wall of water.

Catherine nodded. "Yes. I'm ready to go home."

Robbie gathered her in his fierce embrace, leaving only enough room between them for the kitten and tree root. "Then hold on tight, wife!" he shouted above the wind howling down the mountain, covering her head as the air sizzled around them. "And finally decide that you love me!"

Chapter Twenty-two

The only thing Robbie had to decide during their violent journey home was how he was going to explain to his wife that it didn't matter if they had stood in front of a priest in modern or medieval times, they were still married in the eyes of God.

The ever tightening vortex exploded with a deafening boom, the winds quieted to a gentle breeze, and the storm disappeared as suddenly as it had arrived. Robbie sat up and loosened his grip on Catherine enough to brush the hair from her face so she could look around.

Her eyes swimming with confusion, she stared at his plaid-covered chest, dropped her gaze down to her own clothes, and then lifted her trembling left hand and stared at the ring on her finger. "We're back on TarStone, but I didn't wake up," she whispered.

"But you are awake, Catherine," he assured her. "See, the sun's just risen, and that's the trail of a jetliner making that streak in the sky. And there's Pine Creek. See the lights in the homes? You're back in modern time, but you didn't dream all that's happened, because you lived it."

"But . . . it's not . . . I can't . . ."

He covered her lips with his finger. "It's okay, Catherine. You don't need to understand how the magic works, only accept it. Embrace the journey we shared, and know that you helped reunite an old man with his family and saved my father and uncles from a great tragedy."

She couldn't quit staring at her hand.

"It won't come off, wife," he told her. "Not while there's still breath in my lungs."

She snapped her troubled eyes to his, her face as pale as the snow-covered summit of TarStone Mountain. "But I don't want to be married."

"You've decided you no longer think you love me?"

"That's not what I'm saying." She took a shuddering breath and looked down. "I just don't . . . I can't . . . can we discuss this later?"

"Aye," he agreed, lifting her chin. "Until you're ready to accept our marriage, we will continue as we were before." He reached out and tugged on the knot of her shawl. "I wonder if our stowaway is ready to give up his security blanket?"

She gasped and looked down at her chest, undoing the knot and pulling out the shivering kitten. "Oh, it's scared to death."

Robbie took the cub from her and held it against his own chest, ignoring its attempts to bite him as he worked the tap root from its tiny claws. "Our fierce little friend left its teeth marks in the wood."

"Should we have brought it back with us? Was that wise?"

Robbie shrugged and handed the kitten back to her, keeping the root. "Why not? Its mother likely drowned." He canted his head and smiled. "We'll give it to Winter.

She'll be thrilled to have another spitting hellcat to keep her company."

"Oh, yes," Catherine said, scrambling to her feet. "That's perfect." She suddenly looked worried again. "But what about Mary? She didn't come back with us."

Robbie stood up and tucked the root in his belt. "She'll be along when she's ready. She probably stayed behind to see if Angus keeps his promise to stop warring." He looked around them. "We're not far from where our clothes should be," he said, taking her hand and leading her up the ridge toward the summit.

"Can I keep these beautiful clothes?" she asked, looking down at herself, only to gasp suddenly. "My stick! It didn't come back with us."

"I'll make you a new one." He smiled at her crestfallen face. "Unless you'd like a sword instead. I have a small one my father made for me when I was four."

"No. No more swords. But I would like a new stick."

She let go of his hand because she needed both of hers to control the kitten. "We should probably let Winter name it," she said, laughing as it gnawed on her finger.

Robbie snatched it from her, held it up, then gave it back with a smile. "It's a him," he said.

"Winter could call him Snowball, since he came from Snow Mou—ow!" she yelped, sucking her thumb. "He bit me!"

Robbie chuckled. "I don't think he cares for that name. And he's not white, he's coal black."

"But that's only his baby fur," she said, tucking him safely inside her shawl, then taking Robbie's hand as he helped her down a steep incline. "There's Father Daar."

Robbie looked where she was pointing and saw the old priest striding toward them, his weathered staff looking more frail than he did.

"God's teeth, I've been worried," Daar said, stopping and glaring at Catherine. "Ya should have left her there!" he snapped. "She nearly got us all killed."

"Be thankful she was with me, priest," Robbie said softly. "Or you wouldn't be having a tree to grow." He took the root from his belt and held it up. "I couldn't have found this without Catherine's help."

"Now who's telling wild tales?" she whispered out the side of her mouth. "You're worse than Ian."

Daar's entire countenance changed, and his glare turned into a huge smile as he rushed up to Robbie and grabbed the root. "Ya got it!" he cried, examining the root. "Aye, it's a strong piece," he whispered, closing his fist around it as he looked at Robbie with shining eyes. "I knew ya could do it, MacBain. I knew it. God's teeth, what's that?" he shouted, stepping back and pointing at Cat's chest. "Holy Mother, ya brought back a demon."

"He's just a kitten," Cat said, lifting her shawl to cover Snowball's spitting face.

Daar pointed at her but glared at Robbie. "Ya drown that accursed thing," he hissed. "It's a panther cub, and if ya found it in Scotland, it only means trouble."

Catherine turned away, as if to protect her charge from the priest's anger. "Nobody is drowning him! He's a present for Winter."

Daar suddenly gasped again. "What's that on her hand? And yours!" he cried, looking at Robbie's left hand. He lifted his startled gaze. "Ya're married?" he whispered.

"N-Not really," Catherine said, drawing his attention. "Not in this time, anyway."

Daar raised one eyebrow. "Did ya stand in front of a priest?"

"Well, yes, we did, but I didn't say . . ."

She snapped her mouth shut when Daar waggled his

finger at her. "It don't matter *when* ya got married, girl," he said. "As long as ya both live, the vows are binding."

"But I didn't vow anything. I couldn't even understand what the priest was saying."

Daar shook his head, his glare turning to a look of sympathy as his gaze moved from Catherine to Robbie, then back to Catherine. Only Robbie didn't know who the priest felt sorry for, him or his poor, protesting wife.

"Catherine," Daar said, stepping toward her. "Ya stood before a priest and accepted Robbie MacBain's ring. That's all the vows ya have to take."

Robbie took her hand and led her toward his horse. "You worry about growing your tree, old man, and I'll worry about my wife."

Daar fell into step behind them. "Did ya see Cùram? Did ya have to fight him for the root?"

Robbie stopped and glared at the old *drùidh*. "Our paths never crossed. But be mindful you plant that root where it will be safe. I had to destroy Cùram's tree to get it, and once he discovers what's happened, he'll likely be looking for revenge."

Daar gasped, stepping back and clutching the root to his chest, his eyes wide with horror. "Ya killed a tree of wisdom?"

Robbie gestured at Daar's chest. "Not completely. There's still the root."

"But to destroy all those years of knowledge, MacBain. All that energy. The energy had to go somewhere. Where did it go?"

Robbie shrugged. "I have no idea, priest, and I don't care. I did my duty to protect my family, and now you will do yours and reverse your original spell."

"Aye, aye, I'll start right now," he said, nodding and stepping back, his eyes still wide with both awe and a good bit of fear. "And I'll hide it well," he added, turning and beating a hasty retreat down the mountain.

Robbie looked over at Catherine, only to find her staring up a him with her own look of horror. "What?" he asked.

"He . . . he couldn't decide if all that energy went *into* you, or if it *cursed* you," she whispered.

He leaned over, kissed her worried lips, and pulled back just enough for her to see his smile. "I can promise you I'm not cursed, wife," he said, and kissed her again when she gasped.

He did a thorough job of it, too, and then took hold of her hand and led her over to their clothes. "If we hurry, you can still make it home before the school bus comes," he said, stripping off his plaid and slipping into his modern clothes.

"Today's Saturday," she told him, rolling the kitten up in her shawl and setting him on the ground. "Everyone's probably still sleeping," she added, gesturing for Robbie to turn his back so she could change her own clothes with a bit more modesty. "And you said *I* can make it home in time. Aren't you coming with me?"

Robbie finished tying his sword and MacKeage plaid to his saddle and reached down and plucked the kitten from Catherine's shawl. "I have to go to Gu Bràth first," he told her, mounting up and tucking the cub inside his own plaid. "And I'll give Winter her new little friend, explain to Greylen where Ian has gone, and ask him to call a clan meeting for this evening." He held out his hand to her, moving his foot from his stirrup so she could mount up behind him. "And I would like you to schedule your day so you can come with me this evening."

"To your clan meeting? But why?"

He patted her hand around his waist and started his

horse down the mountain. "Because you were there. You can help assure them that Ian is happy."

"But they'll believe you. I don't want to go."

"But I want you to," he said, stopping when he came to her horse. He reached around, lifted her off his saddle, and plunked her down on her own. He untied her horse's halter and handed her the rope. "You needn't bother with the bridle. Hell," he said with a chuckle. "You could sleep for the ride home if you want. Sprocket's only concern this morning is a bucket of grain and a nap in his stall."

Catherine nudged Sprocket forward and started down the mountain. Robbie followed, wondering how to bring up his next concern. It wasn't fair to ask anything else of his poor wife right now, considering all she'd been through, but dammit, until this one final matter was resolved, she would never be able to accept their marriage.

"I've been thinking, Catherine, that it's probably time you invite Daniels to come visit his children."

"What?" she cried, turning in her saddle to look at him. "Invite Ron to—are you crazy?"

He shook his head. "You and Nathan and Nora need to face your demon," he softly told her. "Because until you do, the three of you will never be free."

"So, you're suggesting I just call Ron up and invite him to come see us."

"Aye. Think about it, Catherine," he said, moving his horse beside hers when the path widened. "To you and your children, Daniels is still the terrifying monster he was three years ago. But all of you have grown quite a bit in those three years, and maybe now you can see him for the pathetic creature he is."

"There is nothing pathetic about Ron. He *is* a monster. And you want me to expose my children to him? My God, I nearly got killed trying to get us away from him."

"That won't happen again," Robbie softly promised. "Because instead of having two well-meaning friends watching your back, this time you have me."

"No."

"And you have the boys." He leaned over and touched her shoulder. "I'm just asking you to think about it, Cat. For your children as much as for yourself. Let Nathan and Nora see their father again and finally realize they have nothing to fear from him. Give them the gift of courage, Catherine."

"You make it sound as if it's all in my head."

"Nay. Only a fool would be unafraid of something or someone trying to destroy them. But Catherine," he whispered, grabbing Sprocket's rope and stopping them both. "You have five guardian angels this time. Face your demon with us standing behind you, and show Daniels that he no longer holds any power over you or Nathan and Nora." He reached up and caressed her cheek with his knuckles. "Your children can't be free until they do. And neither can you."

"I—I'll think about it," she whispered, urging Sprocket along the path ahead of him.

Robbie looked down and scratched his passenger's chin. "What do you think, my little friend? Did I just blow it?"

The cub clamped his sharp little teeth over Robbie's thumb and growled.

"Aye," he whispered. "She's mine."

The first thing Catherine did when she got home was run into the living room and hug and kiss her children. And then she hugged and kissed them some more, until Nathan finally wiggled free, told her he was too big for that kind of stuff, and went back to watching cartoons. Nora just wrinkled her nose at Catherine and told her she smelled funny.

Neither child mentioned missing her last evening or this morning, apparently quite content to have the boys babysit them. Nora did mention that she ate too much ice cream but that Gunter had stopped the truck on the side of the road so she could throw up, that Rick had held her shoulders, and that Cody had washed her face with water from a brook. Nathan piped up, apparently listening to them as much as the cartoons, and said it had been ditch water, not brook water.

Gunter came tiptoeing downstairs just then, stopped on the bottom step, and smiled at Catherine. "Did you have a good vacation?" he asked. "What book did you read?"

"*A Connecticut Yankee in King Arthur's Court*," she said, standing up and heading into the kitchen. "You should read it sometime," she continued over her shoulder as he followed her. "It's quite an adventure."

"Why don't you go take a shower?" he suggested, waving her away from the coffee maker. "I'll cook breakfast this morning."

Catherine headed to her bedroom but stopped at the door and looked back at him. "Be careful, Gunter," she whispered. "You just might turn into one of the good guys."

"Where's the boss man this morning?"

"He'll be along shortly. He had to go to Gu Bràth first."

The moment the words were out of her mouth, Catherine wanted to smack herself. Gunter's dark eyes suddenly lit with the knowledge that he'd been right yesterday afternoon.

Catherine sighed and walked into her bedroom, deciding it wasn't worth arguing over. She stripped off her dirty clothes, which were still damp from having spent the night lying on the summit of TarStone, and turned on the shower, stepped under the hot spray, and moaned at the joy of hot indoor plumbing.

She thought about her fantastical journey and how

impossible it was. She lifted her left hand, blinked through the spray of water at her wedding ring, rubbed her finger with soap, and tried to take it off.

It still wouldn't budge.

She'd been gone for less than sixteen hours but had spent three days in thirteenth-century Scotland. She'd eaten some indescribable food, been nearly stolen five times, and caught in the middle of a war. She'd stood before a priest and gotten herself married to Robbie, she'd watched her new husband start fires at will, and her right thumb still had teeth marks from a panther cub bite.

So, if it hadn't been a dream, what had it been?

Magic, Robbie had told her.

Okay, maybe it was magic, but what did that really mean?

It meant that Robbie could not only kiss her socks off, but he really could talk to owls, travel through time whenever he wanted, and start fires without matches. It meant . . . it meant that she was in really big trouble.

She was in love with Robbie MacBain, either despite the magic or because of it, and how it had happened or why it had happened didn't matter—it was as real as the ring on her finger.

But face Ron Daniels? Now, that was a nightmare. Why would Robbie think she'd want to ruin the peace she'd found here with him by leading her ex-husband straight to them?

Because as long as she feared Ron Daniels, she could never be Robbie MacBain's wife.

Darn it, she hated it when guardian angels were right.

Gu Bràth really was a castle, though only the outside bore any resemblance to the MacKeage keep from eight hundred years ago. Inside, the craftsmanship and attention to detail not only were stunning and opulent but somehow still managed to be cozy. And this modern version had indoor plumbing, bulbs blazing in every nook and cranny, and central heating.

Catherine sat in the corner of the huge dinning room, her hands clasped on her lap, feeling like an interloper among the four Scotsmen, their wives, and Winter MacKeage sitting at the table—that is, until Robbie pulled her to stand beside him at the head of the table and introduced her as Catherine MacBain.

Greylen MacKeage, the rather imposing man sitting at the foot of the table, was the only one who stood up and welcomed her to the family.

Everyone else just gaped in shock.

Michael MacBain slowly stood and stared at his son.

"Catherine came with me when I took Ian home," Robbie told him, wrapping his arm around her trembling shoulders. "And now she knows everything."

Michael moved his gaze to Catherine, still not saying anything, still not smiling or frowning or showing any emotion that she could see.

"And she accepts it. And me," Robbie added, squeezing her shoulders, apparently expecting her to dispute his bold claim.

But Catherine couldn't have spoken if she wanted to. Not with Robbie's father staring at her.

He was Angus MacBain's son? There wasn't an ounce of resemblance between them. Angus hadn't been over five-foot-eight, compared with Michael's six-foot-three or -four frame. And the old warrior's eyes had been hazel green, not gray like Michael's. And Angus's hair had been bright red, not deep auburn. Heck, they even carried themselves differently. Michael had a quiet but lethal awareness about him—just like his son.

And just like Greylen MacKeage, come to think of it.

"It's done, Papa," Robbie whispered, drawing his father's attention.

Michael finally spoke, but he spoke in Gaelic.

Catherine stiffened, but Robbie only squeezed her shoulders again and answered his father in English.

"Daniels will be dealt with," he said. "When my wife is ready to do it herself."

His *wife* wanted to crawl into a crack. Why was he bringing up her ex-husband in front of all these people?

Libby MacBain stood up, gave her husband a pointed glare, walked to the head of the table, and pulled Catherine out of Robbie's embrace and into her own arms. "Welcome to the family, daughter," she whispered. "Michael and I are both overjoyed that Robbie has found such a special woman to love."

Catherine was suddenly pulled from Libby's arms and all but smothered in a fierce but surprisingly gentle embrace. "Aye, my son chose well," Michael told her, kissing the top of her head. "I'm thinking you'll be able to handle him. I welcome ya to my family, Catherine."

And with that resounding endorsement, Catherine found herself being passed from hug to hug, getting well-wishes and welcomes from Morgan and Sadie MacKeage, Callum and Charlotte MacKeage, Greylen and Grace, and finally Winter, who seemed to be the only one of Robbie's cousins at the meeting.

"Robbie told me you suggested I call him Snowball," Winter said, peeling back the front of her vest to expose her passenger. "But he doesn't seem to like it. I'm going to get to know him better before I name him. Thank you for bringing him to me."

Catherine scratched the cub under his chin. "It was just a thought, because he came from Snow Mountain."

"Aye," Winter said as she tucked him away, her eyes suddenly turning sad. "I wish I could have gone with you." She looked up at Robbie with accusing, tear-filled eyes. "Or at least known, so I could have said good-bye to Ian."

"But Ian did say good-bye," Robbie told her as he turned to face the others. "He visited with all of you this past week, did he not? But he couldn't say anything because I swore him to silence."

"But why?" Callum asked.

That was when the conversation moved from Catherine to Ian and then on to Daar. Relieved, Catherine returned to her chair in the corner and listened while Robbie explained why he had traveled back in time and why he hadn't told them he was doing so and why it was important for the old priest to have his powers restored.

But it was when she heard Robbie promise that as long as he lived they would all be safe from the magic, no matter how strong the *drùidh* became, that Catherine finally realized what she'd gotten herself into.

She truly had fallen in love—not with a guardian angel but with a true *Guardian* ordained by providence. And from what she was hearing, she was going to be so busy watching his back she wouldn't have time to worry about looking over her own shoulder.

Yes, it was time to face Ron Daniels.

Chapter Twenty-three

𝒯he *only problem* with inviting Ron to come for a visit was that nobody knew where he was. Catherine had called the parole officer assigned to him, several of his old acquaintances, and even his old precinct sergeant, only to run into dead ends.

She had finally told Robbie about her decision but that she couldn't find Ron, and after he'd kissed her until her toes had curled, he explained that he had his own connections and quickly put out the word that Daniels's ex-wife wanted to see him.

That had been four weeks ago, and there was still no ex-husband darkening her doorstep.

As for being Catherine MacBain, Catherine had told Robbie she couldn't just say they were married and expect Nathan and Nora to understand. So she'd spent the last four weeks sleeping in her bedroom downstairs and planning a wedding where she would not only know what she was vowing but would get to say "I do" sometime during the ceremony.

The only problem was the date. Even though Robbie was willing to get married again to satisfy everyone in modern time, he refused to set a date until they could have a true wedding night. And they couldn't have that, he insisted, until Daniels was completely out of her life.

Catherine was getting sorely tired of Robbie's noble intentions—especially when he pulled her into his arms, kissed her senseless, and whispered heated, heart-thumping promises of what he wanted to do on their honeymoon. Her own noble intentions were about ready to explode, and when she wasn't looking out the window expecting to see Ron standing there, Catherine was trying to figure out how to get Robbie alone long enough to curl his own toes.

The solution to her problem came from a most unlikely source one bright spring day, when Catherine heard a noise on the porch. She opened the door, and Mary walked into the kitchen, flew onto the back of her rocking chair, folded her wings, and started talking to Catherine.

Their amazing conversation lasted over an hour.

The wise snowy owl convinced Catherine that it was time she took matters into her own hands and put an end to Robbie's noble intentions by staging a seduction a saint couldn't resist.

And so, armed with Mary's surprisingly simple and insightful opinion on courage and fear, and with her blessing, Catherine set a wedding date for that Friday. Mud season had shut down the logging operation, and the boys were only too eager to help put an end to Robbie's bachelorhood—although Catherine suspected they really saw the marriage as a guarantee that they'd be keeping their housekeeper.

For three days after school, the boys rode up to the cabin where Catherine had first come face-to-face with

Robbie. They cleaned it from top to bottom, stacked fire-wood, made some minor repairs, and even tied a mattress to poor Sprocket's back and lugged it up the mountain.

With Winter's help, Catherine called Robbie's extended family and told them where and when the wedding was and asked them please to keep it a surprise. She also promised they'd have a nice reception the next day at the farm.

Even Kate got into the spirit of things, though she was still wrestling with losing Ian—torn between missing him and being happy for him, knowing he was where he belonged. Kate had a doctor's appointment in Bangor that Friday and asked Robbie to drive her to it. If Robbie thought her request was strange, he never said anything. He'd only kissed Catherine good-bye that morning and left to go pick up Kate.

It was now four-thirty on Friday afternoon, the summit of TarStone was littered with three generations of MacKeages and MacBains, Catherine had twisted her bouquet of forget-me-nots into a tangle of weeds, and Robbie was late.

"Maybe he didn't get yar note," Michael said, standing beside her, his hands tucked behind his back as he watched the path coming up the mountain.

"He couldn't miss it. I set it on the table, right on top of an apple pie."

"Aye, that would catch his attention," he agreed with a chuckle. "Catherine," he said, turning to face her. "Have ya not heard from Daniels?"

She looked down at her mangled bouquet. "No, nothing," she whispered. "Maybe he's dead."

Michael lifted her chin to look at him. "Pray he isn't, lass," he said softly. "Because I agree with my son. Facing your past is important."

She gave him a brilliant smile. "But I no longer need to

see Ron." She widened her smile. "Heck, after what I went through four weeks ago, Ron Daniels isn't even a worry anymore, much less a fear."

Her almost-father-in-law lifted one brow. "Just like that?" he asked. "You've simply erased several years of yar life?"

"Every day of it," she confirmed. "Except for Nathan and Nora's birthdays. I've decided that sometimes, to find something wonderful, you have to go through a great trial." She stepped closer and touched his arm. "After all you've gone through in your life, was it not ultimately worth it to have Libby and your children and grandchildren? Would you wish it all away in order to avoid the trials you endured to get here?"

Michael stared down at her, not smiling, not frowning, not one readable expression on his face that she could see. When he finally did respond, the last thing she expected was amusement. "Aye, I can see my son is in for an interesting future," he whispered, wrapping her in a fierce embrace and shaking her with silent laughter. "I couldn't have wished for a better daughter-in-law, Catherine."

"She's not your daughter-in-law yet," Robbie said from right beside them.

Catherine gasped and tried to step back, but Michael wasn't through hugging her yet. "Nay?" he chuckled, looking at Robbie and grinning. "Then maybe she should slip off her ring and give it back to ya."

Robbie pulled her from Michael's arms and led her away from the staring crowd. "What's going on here?" he asked, turning them so that his body blocked her from the gathering.

"We're getting married in five minutes."

Looking very much like his father, Robbie lifted one brow. "With or without me?"

Catherine shrugged. "You apparently didn't need my

consent eight hundred years ago, so I guess I don't need yours today." She stepped closer and lowered her voice. "But whether you say your vows or not, I'm sleeping in your bed tonight, husband." She gave him a challenging smirk. "So if you don't care what sort of example we'll be setting for our children, go home and eat your pie. I'll be down as soon as the ceremony is over."

"You need a marriage license in this time."

"Already done and filed at the county courthouse. Martha Bailey helped me." She canted her head. "Not everyone has their marriage license notarized by a judge."

"And just when did I sign this license?"

"You didn't. Cody did. He's really good at forging your signature. You might want to check with his teachers and see what other papers you've signed."

"You let a judge notarize a forged signature?"

Catherine sighed, stepped around him, walked over and stood in front of Father Daar, and waited for Robbie to join her.

She hadn't wanted the old priest to marry them, considering all the trouble he kept causing, but Michael and Greylen had asked her to, for their sakes and for Robbie's.

Catherine smiled at Nora standing beside her and then over at Nathan, who was crowded beside Gunter and Rick and Cody and Peter, all waiting to stand as witnesses for Robbie. Finally, after what seemed like forever, a dark shadow blocked the setting sun, and Father Daar lifted his book and started speaking.

"No, stop," Catherine said, setting her hand over the pages. "In English," she demanded, removing her hand and reaching over and lacing her fingers through Robbie's.

Her new husband whispered his vows, and Catherine was tempted to shout hers, but in the end she repeated the words softly and clearly.

Since they were already wearing their rings, Robbie took her left hand in both of his and pressed their bands together. Catherine was expecting the magic this time, and when her ring warmed and her hand tingled, she simply smiled.

Their nuptial kiss, however, couldn't have been more modest.

But Robbie's kiss to Nora, when he scooped the beaming little girl up in his arms and gave her a loud, laughing smooch on the cheek, was heartwarming. And his handshake with Nathan was most manly.

Winter came forward leading Robbie's horse, its mane and tail braided with long, flowing ribbons in the MacBain colors, its rump covered with an ancient-looking MacBain plaid. Catherine also noticed that Robbie's sword—and the new stick he'd made her—were strapped to the saddle.

Her husband lifted her by the waist onto his horse and climbed up behind her amid a shower of birdseed and the cheers of those gathered on the summit.

"Where to, wife?" he whispered.

"To your cabin on West Shoulder Ridge," she said as she waved and threw kisses to Nathan and Nora. "We'll be back by noon tomorrow," she told them. "You be good for the boys."

She leaned back against Robbie's chest with a sigh, looked up at him, and smiled. "How are your twelve toes feeling, Mr. MacBain?"

"They feel fine," he said, looking confused.

Her smile widened. "Well, they won't be in about an hour."

"They won't?"

"No, because I'm about to curl them, husband."

Chapter Twenty-four

Robbie barely recognized the place. And from the look on his wife's face as he carried her through the door, Catherine was just as surprised as he was.

The old cabin was spotless. All the broken furniture, the years of accumulated junk, and every last spider web and squirrel nest were gone. All that remained was a recently painted wrought-iron bed, a table and two chairs, a rocking chair, and the newly reblackened woodstove. The counter and cupboards had been painted red, there were new curtains in the windows, and even the floor was freshly painted.

And dozens of candles, just waiting to be lit, sat on every available surface.

Robbie looked down at his wife in his arms and found her looking around the cabin in shock. "I had no idea they were doing all this," she whispered, looking up at him. "I just asked them to clean it up a bit."

Robbie lowered Catherine to her feet and picked up the envelope leaning against the large three-wick candle sitting in the middle of the table. "I'm almost afraid to open this," he said, holding it between them. "The last note I got was an invitation to my own wedding."

She took the envelope from him, slit it open, and pulled out the card. "It's the boys' wedding present to us," she told him, handing the card back. "They said every married couple with a houseful of hoodlums needs someplace to escape to."

Robbie quickly read the card and tossed it down on the table, picked up his wife and set her on the counter, slipped between her knees, and locked his hands behind her back.

"I thought our deal was that our marriage didn't start until you faced Daniels."

She covered his lips with her fingers. "Sshhhh. Don't even say his name. He no longer exists."

"Aye, but he does, Catherine. I'll not spend our wedding night with his ghost in our bed."

"Even his ghost is gone," she whispered, smiling into his eyes as she started unbuttoning his shirt.

Robbie covered her hands with both of his, shocked by her eagerness.

Shocked but not really surprised.

He'd been living with a stranger for the last three days, a woman who appeared confident and determined and now, obviously, quite brave.

"What happened this week?" he growled, holding her hands safely in his.

"I had a talk with a wise and rather insightful owl," she said, pulling free and working the buttons open again.

"You talked with Mary?" he whispered, stopping her and holding on tighter this time. "She *spoke* to you?"

Catherine nodded. "We had a wonderful conversation.

Mary explained how I was letting you do my thinking for me and that our marriage was never going to work as long as I allowed it to continue, that I had to start thinking for myself."

"I was doing your thinking?" he repeated, feeling heat creep up the back of his neck. "What in hell are you talking about?"

She tried to wiggle free, but once she realized he wasn't letting her have her hands back, she sighed and shook her head. "Mary explained that it's a guy thing, this need you and your father have for me to confront my ex-husband. Men choose the most direct approach to a problem, and it usually involves fighting. Your solution is for me to barge in with my stick raised, hellbent on purging my memories by beating them away. Am I right?"

"I didn't mean for you actually to fight Daniels. I was thinking more of you facing him with me standing beside you."

"And exactly what would that accomplish, other than for me to feel safe only as long as you're around?"

"You'd also see that Daniels is nothing more than a bully."

"But I already know that." She shook her head again. "Mary is right, it is a guy thing. But Robbie, women think differently. We don't need a huge confrontation or some defining moment to tell us we're over our problem. We only have to let it go in our own minds."

"Then why didn't you do that three years ago, when you divorced him?"

"Because I was still thinking like a victim. And when I came here and met you, and even after visiting Scotland, it was easier just to go along with your idea to confront Ron because I knew you would protect me." She looked down at their clasped hands. "That's the problem with falling in love with guardian angels," she whispered. "It becomes too easy to let them take over."

Still holding her hands in his, he lifted her chin with his knuckles and smiled. "It's even easier for us guardians to take charge, because that's how we think." He leaned over and gently kissed her sweet lips, then pulled away only slightly. "I'm sorry, little Cat, for nearly taking away your power instead of helping you find it. That was the last thing I wanted to do."

The moment he freed her hands, she wrapped them around his waist and hugged him. "So, now we're married in all times," she said, her lips caressing his chest where she'd unbuttoned his shirt. "Does that mean we can finally start the honeymoon?"

"Aye," he growled, lifting her off the counter and carrying her to the bed.

She jumped up the moment he set her down. "We have to light the candles," she said, racing to the table and picking up the box of matches. She stopped, looked from the matches to him, and tossed them back on the table. "You light them, husband, with your magic."

He walked over, took her hand in his, and held it to the candle on the table. "All you have to do is wish for the energy to show itself," he told her, touching their fingers to one of the wicks, then pulling it away once the flame appeared.

She gasped and looked up at him.

He moved their hands to the next wick and repeated the magic, then moved to the third, releasing her fingers. "Just ask, Catherine," he whispered. "See the flame in your mind first, and expect it to appear, and it will."

"But I can't do magic," she said, despite holding her finger to the last wick.

"But you *are* the magic, little Cat," he whispered, smiling as she tried to all but glare the wick into lighting. He took hold of her shoulders and added his own will, catching her when the wick suddenly burst into flame.

"You did that!" she said with a laugh, turning and wrapping her arms around him.

He kissed her deeply and quite thoroughly, then lifted her off her feet and carried her back to the bed. He set her on the quilt and stared down at her.

Again she got up but knelt on the mattress, pulled his shirt from his pants, and pushed it off his shoulders.

He unknotted the shawl she'd brought from Scotland.

She unbuckled his belt.

His wife had him half undressed before he could even get her blouse unbuttoned.

She pushed his hands away and stepped off the bed, facing him as she slowly undid her own buttons, looking up with the smile of a woman who knew exactly what she wanted.

And damn if Robbie didn't feel his toes start to curl as she slid her blouse off her shoulders and let it fall to the floor, revealing a lace bra that lovingly cupped her plump breasts, her two beautiful pink nipples straining against the satin material.

Completely forgetting his own need to get undressed, Robbie reached out and ran a trembling finger across the top of the thin lace, marveling at the contrast of his large, dark hand against her pale skin.

She was so delicate. So utterly feminine. So . . . his.

The candle on the windowsill above the bed burst into flame, reflecting in Catherine's shining eyes as she unfastened her skirt and let it slide to the floor, revealing matching panties that were more lace than material. She stood in the pool of her clothes, her eyes dancing with blossoming excitement. Robbie tucked his hands behind his back and balled his fists in an attempt to control his own volatile energy.

A second candle on the windowsill flared to life.

"You have the most beautiful body," she whispered, sliding down the zipper of his pants with maddening slowness.

Another candle—this one clear across the room on the counter—flared to life.

"You've done nothing but tease me with your body since I met you," she continued, her voice husky as his pants fell to his own feet. She looked up at him, her womanly smile widening. "And now you're all mine," she whispered, walking her delicate fingers up his stomach, sending ripples of desire quivering through him.

She covered his chest with both hands, lightly feathering her fingers through his chest hair, and leaned forward and kissed one of his nipples.

The candle on the bedside table flared like a blow torch before settling into a gentle flame.

"Touch me, husband," she whispered, pulling his mouth down to hers as she pressed against him. "Set me on fire."

As difficult as it was, since his toes were curled so tightly, Robbie finally scuffed off his shoes, wrapped his arms around her, and stepped out of his pants. He lifted Catherine out of her own discarded wardrobe and carried her to the bed, setting her on the quilt and quickly lying beside her before she could jump up again.

Not that she tried. She rolled toward him, entwined her arms around his neck, and kissed him with the eagerness of a bride about to share her greatest gift with her husband.

Robbie kissed her with the eagerness of a bridegroom about to explode.

One by one, the candles scattered around the cabin

began to flicker to life as their wedding bed heated with an energy unlike anything Robbie had ever experienced.

She was so tiny and delicate yet so trusting and suddenly bold. Her hands were all over him, caressing, exploring, exciting him until he could barely stand it.

He didn't know how it happened, being so busy reeling with sensation after sensation, but his bride was suddenly sitting astraddle his hips, her fingers kneading his chest and her moist, puffed lips curved into a smile.

"Am I going too fast?" she asked, looking not the least bit worried that she might be.

He took hold of her hips, stilling her movement. "Aye, I'm thinking ya are, lass. If we don't slow down, this whole place will go up in flames."

She blinked in confusion, looked around the cabin, then shot him a glorious smile. "Did you do that?"

"Nay, little Cat, you did."

Her lovely chest puffed up until her breasts all but spilled from her bra. Robbie reached up and covered them with his hands, feeling her nipples pushing into his palms through the lace. She reached behind her back, undid the clasp of her bra, and slid the straps off her shoulders until only his hands were holding it in place. He let the bra drop down to his own chest and quickly returned his hands to her naked breasts. She threw her head back with a moan of pleasure, placed her hands over his, and moved her hips along the length of his shaft.

Robbie could no longer stand the sweet torture. He rolled until she lay beside him and spanned one hand across her chest to keep her in place while he propped his head on his other hand so he could stare down at her.

Satisfied that she'd stay put, though unable to still her restless movements, Robbie leaned over to kiss her—but shouted instead when she wrapped her strong, delicate fingers around his shaft. "Nay," he growled, quickly trapping both her hands over her head. "You've had weeks to explore my body, little Cat. Now it's my turn to become acquainted with yours."

"But I haven't explored *all* of you," she countered, sticking out her lower lip.

"Aye," he said with a chuckle, kissing her pout and then letting his mouth trail down her chin to her neck. "But ya needn't worry," he whispered at the base of her throat. "We won't leave this bed until ya have."

"Is that a promise or a thre—oh!" She gasped, arching her back as he covered one firm, budding nipple with his mouth.

It seemed he had found a most interesting way to subdue her. Robbie spent several minutes keeping Catherine so busy moaning and writhing in pleasure that she forgot all about driving him crazy with her own explorations. He made delicious love to her breasts, then continued his mouth's journey down over her stomach to the top of her panties.

He slid his fingers under the elastic and slowly lowered the thin lace, exposing more and more of her, drinking in the dew of her heated body. Her freed hands dug into his shoulders before grabbing his hair and guiding him on a savory journey from one sensitive spot to another. He slipped her panties down her long, beautiful legs and then off completely, and came back and kissed her belly button. He moved lower, opening her thighs and covering her feminine bud with his mouth, sliding his hand under her backside when she arched into him.

He could feel her tightening, straining toward her orgasm, and Robbie continued to pleasure her, reveling in the feel of her blossoming fire. He moved quickly, settling himself between her thighs, keeping his arms rigid so he wouldn't crush her.

"Open yar eyes, Cat."

His voice seemed to startle her, and her eyes flared with recognition as she came back to her senses. She reached up, grasped his shoulders, and smiled. "Yes. I certainly wouldn't want to miss anything," she whispered, lifting her hips and wiggling until his shaft touched her entrance. "I've been told this is the best part."

Despite his urgency and overwhelming need to claim her, Robbie couldn't stop the laugh that broke from his chest. He lowered his forehead to hers, closing his eyes with a frustrated groan. "Dammit, Cat. This is serious business."

She flexed her fingers into his shoulders and licked his lips with her tongue.

Robbie reared back and glared down into her sparkling eyes.

"Aye, husband," she murmured in a guttural mimic of his brogue, lifting her hips just enough that he started to enter her. "Being in love is a most serious business."

He kept his gaze locked on hers and slowly eased inside her, then retreated just enough to return even deeper with another careful thrust.

Her smile disappeared, replaced with a moan of pleasure, and her eyes widened as her fingers bit into the straining muscles of his shoulders. "Yes," she gasped on an indrawn breath. "It truly is magic."

"Aye," he whispered when he became fully embedded inside her. He leaned down and kissed her smile, then started moving in a primordial rhythm that sent bolts of energy rushing through him.

And again, he felt Catherine tightening, straining

toward fulfillment as she met his thrusts with eager and rather loud cries of encouragement.

He couldn't stop looking at her. She was so freely and boldly giving herself to him, so unabashedly enjoying their pleasure, so vividly open with her response that Robbie lost the last of his control. He quit being careful and began feeling instead—every flex of her muscles sheathing him as he unleashed the full force of his urgency.

The cabin filled with blinding light, the flames on every candle flaring with simmering heat as the air charged with the pulsing glow of a magic so powerful that time stopped for the merest of heartbeats, only to start again with the explosion of their mutual fulfillment.

Catherine cried out, and Robbie actually shouted as the crashing waves of chaos took them over the edge of reality and into the realm of their consummated union—into that magical, wondrous world where two hearts start beating as one.

The pleasure lasted for what seemed like forever, and Robbie refused to move, instead holding himself rigid, deeply inside her as her lingering pulses continued to tighten around him.

Apparently, Catherine had more presence of mind than he did, for she reached up and trailed one finger down the side of his face, ending at his chin and gently pushing his mouth shut. She smiled—a warm, smug, I've-got-you-now smile.

"That really was the best part," she whispered, lifting her hips slightly. "And definitely better than anything I could ever dream up." She looked around the cabin flickering with candlelight, then brought her shimmering gaze back to his. "If I didn't love you so much, I might be a little freaked out. Is this going to happen every time we make love?" She cupped his chin in her palms. "Because it's going to cost us a fortune in candles."

Realizing he was about to collapse, Robbie rolled off her, bringing her with him and tucking her against his side as he stared up at the shadows dancing over the ceiling. "I truly hope not, little Cat, or I'll be dead before my next birthday."

She threw an arm and a leg across him, kissing his nipple before settling her head in the crook of his arm. He could feel her smile against his chest as she let out a satisfied sigh.

Then she suddenly lifted her head, looked at the table beside the bed, and started laughing. Robbie turned to see what was so funny and started them both shaking with his own laughter. There on the bedside table, leaning against a gently burning candle, were three packets of glow-in-the-dark condoms.

"I'm guessing it's Cody," Catherine said, settling back against him and drumming her fingers on his chest. "No, it's Rick." She tilted her head to look up at him and frowned. "I think there's really a prankster lurking behind that quiet demeanor of his."

Robbie captured her drumming fingers and kissed her upturned nose. "Do we need the condoms, Catherine? We really haven't discussed adding to our family."

She pulled herself up until she was straddling him again and slowly shook her head. "No. We don't need anything between us," she whispered. "I could never have too big a family. You want a boy or a girl, Mr. MacBain?"

Robbie thought about that, looking up into his wife's beautiful, glowing face as he tried to picture her pregnant. "Maybe six of each," he finally said.

Which made her laugh.

Which made his toes start to curl again.

"I love you, wife."

She gave him a smile that outshone the candles. "And I love you, husband." One of her eyebrows rose inquisitively, and those maddening fingers of hers started walking up his stomach again. "Have you gotten your strength back yet?"

Every candle in the cabin suddenly flared again.

Chapter Twenty-five

Catherine would say one thing about Scots: it didn't seem to matter if it was eight hundred years ago or today, they certainly knew how to celebrate a wedding.

There was enough food laid out on several tables in the yard to feed a small nation. And the people! There were dozens and dozens of MacKeages and MacBains. Cousins had come from all over the country, towing husbands and wives and babies with them, to add their blessing to their marriage. Catherine was a bit overwhelmed to find herself in the middle of such a large family, considering she'd been an only child and orphaned at nineteen. Even Nathan and Nora were in a daze, inundated by hordes of children wanting to play and suddenly calling them cousin. Then there were the townspeople who kept coming up, welcoming Catherine to Pine Creek and wishing her well, almost to a person telling her that Robbie was the catch of three counties.

"That was a very big mistake you made, asking me to notarize a forged signature," Martha Bailey said over her cup of punch just before she took a sip.

"You knew it wasn't Robbie's signature?" Catherine asked.

Martha nodded.

"Then why did you notarize it?"

"Blackmail," the judge said with a smile. "Marcus Saints told me there's room for two more boys here."

"We're going to fill those beds with babies," Robbie said as he walked up and wrapped an arm around Catherine's shoulder.

"You can build more bedrooms," Martha said, waving that away. "And besides, everyone knows kids are cheaper by the dozen." She batted her eyelashes at Robbie. "I have two boys in juvenile right now who are due to be released in July. You should be able to have the addition finished by then."

"I'll be in your office Monday morning to sign a new license," Robbie told her. "And when Gunter gets an apartment, we'll continue this discussion," he finished with a nod, leading Catherine away.

Marcus Saints stepped into their path, rolling down his shirt sleeves and buttoning his cuffs. He spotted his dirty hands and wiped them on his pants with a laugh. "I'll be a millionaire," he told them. "Cody and I are going into business manufacturing potato guns to sell on the Internet."

Nathan came running over, his own shirt covered with potato pulp. "Did you see me, Mom? I splattered the rock three times." He looked up at Marcus. "I heard what you said to Cody. Can I be in your business? I can test each gun before you sell it."

Marcus ruffled Nathan's hair, realized he had only smeared potato pulp through it, and tried to wipe it down with his sleeve. "Sure, Nathan. You can be our quality control manager."

"In ten years," Robbie clarified, again dragging Catherine away with a wave to Marcus.

Father Daar rushed over, a can of soda in one hand, a bowl of dip in the other, and several carrots and celery stalks sticking out of his chest pocket. "I'm wanting a word with you, Robbie," he said, just before he lifted the bowl and licked dip off the edge.

"Tomorrow," Robbie told him, turning Catherine away again.

She was starting to feel like a horse being dragged around by the cart. She planted her feet and pulled her husband to a stop. "What's your problem, Father?" she asked.

Daar shook his head. "It ain't exactly a problem I got," he said. "It's more like a mystery."

Robbie sighed and pinched the bridge of his nose. "And what would that be?" he whispered.

"It's the root," Daar whispered, looking around and taking a step closer. "It's not what I was expecting."

Robbie glared at the priest. "What do you mean, not what you expected? It's from Cùram's tree. I know it is."

"Aye, aye," Daar said, bobbing his head. "And it's growing just fine, but it's not an oak. The tree is a white pine sapling."

Robbie shook his head. "Nay. That root came from an oak."

Daar took a sip of his soda and then canted his head. "Are ya sure? Could ya have taken a root from a nearby pine by mistake? Was there one growing near Cùram's oak?"

"Nay. It stood alone in the cave. Are you saying the root is worthless? That you won't be able to reverse your spell?"

"Nay," Daar said. "It has the energy of a tree of wisdom. I can feel it. I just don't know what it means, is all, that ya brought me an oak root and it grows into a pine tree." The old priest suddenly gasped, spilling dip on his hand. "Cùram!" he whispered. "That blackheart is up to something."

"He can be up to whatever he wants," Robbie growled, "as long as you can still reverse the spell."

Daar absently nodded. "Aye. That's not a problem, MacBain. Yar papa and the others will be staying here." He looked at Robbie for several seconds, then turned and walked away, shaking his head and muttering to himself.

"Do you believe your father and uncles are safe?" Catherine asked, looking up at her scowling husband.

"Aye. Daar knows better than to lie to me." Robbie forcibly shook off his black mood and suddenly smiled. "Come to the hayloft, wife. My toes are wanting to be curled again."

"We can't just sneak off. There's too many people here."

As if on cue, they spotted Libby and Michael approaching. Michael was holding his granddaughter, smiling with the pride of a grandfather who thought he'd had something to do with her creation.

"Go wait for me in the hayloft," Robbie whispered, placing his hand on Catherine's backside and giving her a push. "I'll meet you there in ten minutes."

Catherine pretended she didn't see her new in-laws and quickly ran toward the barn.

She stopped just inside the door to let her eyes adjust to the dimness and then walked down to Sprocket's stall and pulled a carrot out of her pocket. "Here, big boy," she said, letting him bite off a large piece. "I stole this for you before it made it to the platter."

"Whose wedding are you celebrating, Cathy?"

Catherine spun around with a gasp and found herself facing Ron, who was standing in the doorway of the tack room. "What are you doing here?"

"Word on the street is you invited me here," he said, stepping into the aisle, placing himself between her and the barn door. "But I don't think it's because you missed me. If you did, you would have been waiting at home when I got out."

Catherine tucked her hands behind her back and touched her thumb to her wedding band. "The celebration outside is for me. I was married yesterday."

Ron's face darkened, and his fists clenched at his sides as he took a step forward. "Then why did you put the word out you wanted to see me?"

She untucked her hands and crossed her arms under her breasts, inconspicuously looking around the barn for a rake or shovel or anything else that would work as a weapon. "I thought you might like to see your children," she said, walking to the center of the aisle while keeping her distance from him. "One last time before getting out of our lives for good."

He matched her move with one of his own. "How kind of you," he sneered, stepping between her and the shovel leaning against the wall. "Do you have any idea what prison is like for a cop?" he asked, his voice pitched low in a tone Catherine recognized as the first stage of the coming tantrum. "I had to fight for my life."

Unable to stop herself, she smiled at him. "Welcome to my world, Ron. I spent six years fighting for my life."

Catherine watched his rage kick up another notch, and her smile widened. She relaxed her arms at her sides. "Do you want to see your kids or not? Because I need to get back to my husband."

He lunged probably before he even realized he was

going to. But Catherine was ready and feinted to the right, toward freedom, but then darted to the left and grabbed the shovel. By the time Ron had twisted toward her, she had her grip balanced and the shovel handle moving toward his shoulder.

She pushed her right hand forward with all her might, using her body as a pivot point. Ron reacted just as Robbie had said he would, and Catherine used the momentum of his defensive block to follow through with an upper cut to his jaw.

Ron dropped like a stone, his wide, surprised eyes turning glassy, then dazed, and then closing completely as his body hit the concrete floor with such a painful-sounding thud that Catherine couldn't stop herself from wincing.

Her sympathy, however, lasted less than a second.

Laughing chatter came from the rafters of the barn, and Catherine looked up and saw Mary.

"Don't you dare laugh!" she snapped. "Violence is not supposed to feel good."

Mary glided down and landed on Ron's chest. She gave him a nasty peck on his cheek, drawing blood, and then hopped off and walked down the aisle toward the barn door.

Catherine threw down the shovel and rubbed her forehead. "Okay," she muttered to the retreating bird. "Maybe Robbie's plan did have some merit. But only because Ron's a guy, and violence is the only thing he'd understand. Go on," she said, waving Mary away. "Go get my husband. We'll let him clean up this mess, since this whole thing was his idea."

"But you know what?" she said softly, stopping Mary. "It was almost anticlimactic, for all the worrying I did. I thought there would at least be some sort of emotion, but I don't feel anything. Not anger or relief or even pity. Just . . . nothing," she finished with a shrug.

Mary blinked, then turned and flew out the door.

Catherine sat down on a bale of hay and studied Ron while she waited, only to find herself surprised by how small he was. Three years ago—heck, three months ago—Ron had seemed twenty feet tall. But after living with, loving, and making toe-curling love to a true giant, Catherine decided that five-foot-eleven was rather tiny. Insignificant. And yeah, downright wimpy.

Ron had gained weight, she noticed, to the point that he looked slovenly. He had a paunch, his cheeks were puffed, and the peck Mary had given him—oh, that bad bird—would likely leave a scar on his sallow face.

Catherine was just covering her mouth to stifle a giggle when her husband burst through the barn door, came sliding to a halt on the other side of Ron, and stared at her.

"Mary said you had something to tell me," he whispered.

He was looking calm, but Catherine could read worry and fear and anger on every inch of his towering body.

"Well, I guess I have several things to tell you," she said with a sigh. "I, ah, I should probably start by thanking you for the fighting lessons." She smiled. "I can see where they might come in handy from time to time."

"And?" he whispered ever so softly.

"And I suppose your idea of facing my demons might have had some merit." She smiled again. "It felt kind of good to be the one in control for a change."

"And?" he asked even more softly, the muscles in his neck and shoulders slowly relaxing.

"And I need a little help with a problem I have."

"What problem?"

She gestured toward Ron. "Now that he's here, I don't know what to do with him."

Robbie looked down, then back up at her. "Do you want me to offer a suggestion or simply take care of the problem for you?"

Catherine set her elbows on her knees, cupped her chin in her palms, and stared at Ron. "I don't know. I think this might be one of those times when a husband can be quite handy." Her chin still in her hands, she looked up and smiled. "And it might satisfy your own manly need to be protective, if I let you dispose of him."

He crossed his arms over his chest and lifted one brow. "You're going to have to give me an instruction manual, so I know when to be your husband, guardian, or minion."

Catherine stood up, walked around Ron, stopped in front of Robbie, and smiled up at him. "I think we've done okay without the manual so far," she whispered, wrapping her arms around him and leaning into his chest. "How are your toes doing?"

"Don't tempt me, woman," he growled, hugging her fiercely. "I told you my guardian work comes first."

She nuzzled his chest, soaking in his scent and closing her eyes with a sigh. "Then I guess you'd better dump him off at the edge of town before he wakes up."

Robbie gave her one last squeeze, set her away, and stepped over to Ron.

"But take the boys with you," she said.

He straightened from picking up her trash. "What? Why?"

"And Nathan. I want you to take Nathan with you."

"What?"

"He was old enough to remember Ron as a monster. Let him see there is nothing to be afraid of. And that way, I know you won't . . ." She gestured toward Ron. "You won't add to mine and Mary's fine work," she finished, brushing her hands together and walking toward the door.

She stopped and looked back. "I'll be waiting up at the cabin," she added, giving him a brilliant smile. "So don't take too long, husband. I'm bringing fresh candles."

Pocket Books
Proudly Presents

THE DANGEROUS PROTECTOR

Janet Chapman

Available in Paperback
May 2005

Turn the page for a preview of
The Dangerous Protector . . .

Duncan Ross leaned against the candy-red SUV in the dimly lit parking lot, his arms folded over his chest and his feet crossed at the ankles, in a pose that might appear almost languid to anyone who didn't know him.

He was soon rewarded by the sight of Willow Foster climbing out of the restroom window of his pub; one shapely, jean-clad leg appearing first, followed by a deliciously firm little butt, followed by another leg, until she was hanging suspended over the sill. Her sweater caught on a protruding nail as her waving feet searched for a toehold, and she suddenly tumbled down over the stack of firewood with a curse loud enough to be heard all the way across the parking lot.

Despite his dark mood, Duncan couldn't stifle a smile. It was a wonder she could even walk after putting first one foot in her mouth earlier that evening in the pub by spilling her sister Rachel's secret, then cramming in her other foot when she'd blurted out that she wouldn't be home until late tomorrow morning. Rachel's having confided in Duncan that she'd heard Willow on the phone with an old high-school boyfriend earlier, also didn't bode well for the sassy-mouthed little tyrant.

He was one second away from dragging Willow home—kicking and screaming if that's what it took— and tying her to his bed and not letting her go until she agreed to marry him.

Duncan's smile widened at the image of her tied to his bed. He watched Willow creep toward freedom while looking over her shoulder at the front corner of the building. A cool ocean breeze was blowing her long, blunt-cut hair across her face, the hem of her heavy wool sweater was hiked up over one shapely breast, and there was a smudge of white paint on her left knee. She was also fishing in her pocket for her keys, obviously forgetting that she had the same bad habit as most of the citizens of Puffin Harbor, and had left them on the floor of her truck.

Those keys were now tucked safely in Duncan's pocket.

Apparently satisfied that she had made her escape relatively unscathed, Willow started sprinting toward her truck, only to finally spot him, swallow a gasp, and skid to a halt just four paces away.

Duncan continued to watch in fascination as her chin came up, her shoulders squared, and her large hazel eyes glittered with challenge. Still he didn't move from his negligent pose, but simply stared back, not saying a word, and waited to see how inventive her lie would be.

Lord, he enjoyed her games.

She made a major production of looking at her watch, holding her wrist toward the dim light of the street lamp. "I'm going to be late, Dunky," she said with a hint of impatience, lifting one brow as her shimmering gaze returned to his. "Was there something you wanted?"

"Aye. You."

She smoothed her sweater back down into place, settled her hands on her hips, and shook her head. "We both know that's never going to happen."

"Never say never, counselor. It's a word that always comes back ta haunt ya. Where are ya going tonight, Willow?"

"If it's any of your business, I'm going to visit an old friend I haven't seen since high school."

"All night?"

Her chin rose the slightest bit higher, and her hands on her hips balled into fists. "We'll probably have a few drinks, so I won't be able to drive home. And if I know his wife, she'll cook a breakfast so big, I won't be able to walk away from the table, either."

"Ray and Patty Cobb separated three months ago."

Willow's hands fell from her hips. "They're separated?"

Her surprise wasn't fake, Duncan realized. She truly hadn't known. "Aye," he said quietly. "So tell me, did you call Cobb or did he call you?"

Though he hadn't moved so much as an inch, she took a cautious step back. "How do you know I'm going to see Ray Cobb?" Her eyes narrowed. "And who told you he and Patty are separated?"

"Your sister just told me, while you were hiding in the restroom," he said with a negligent shrug. "As payback, I suppose, for so eloquently telling Kee she's pregnant."

Duncan saw her wince. "Rachel's not even sure yet," she muttered. She took another step, this one sideways instead of back, obviously hoping to work her way toward her truck door.

Duncan was on her before she could react. He caught her around the waist and lifted her up as he turned, dropped her down on the front fender of her truck, and settled himself between her knees so quickly that she had to grab his shoulders to steady herself.

He threaded his fingers through her hair and cupped the sides of her face firmly enough to warn her against struggling. She went perfectly still, her eyes widening in alarm.

Or was it awareness?

"Come home with me tonight."

"I can't, Duncan. And you know why." There was anger in her whispered response. And also regret.

"Then stay and help me finish my bottle of scotch."

She slowly shook her head inside his hands. "I'll just find myself waking up in your bed again."

"Eighteen months is a long time to be celibate."

Her face under his hands flushed with heat, and her eyes shimmered defiantly. "What makes you think I've been celibate? I'll have you know I've had lots of dates in the last year and a half. Probably hundreds," she said, waving an angry hand over his shoulder.

"But not one of those dates ended in bed."

"How do—dammit!" She squirmed to break free and pushed at his shoulders. "Get out of my way. I have to go kill my sister!"

He ignored her struggles and covered her mouth in a kiss that was long overdue, holding her firmly as he tasted peat-dried barley malt mingled with her own sweet flavor.

She stiffened on an indrawn breath, her hands on his shoulders digging into his leather jacket. Duncan dropped his own hand to her backside and slid Willow forward, pulling her pelvis firmly into his. He groaned into her mouth, and with an aggression born of need, deepened the kiss—not backing down until he felt her shudder in response.

"Sweet heaven," he growled, forcing himself to come up for air. "Dammit, Willow, don't do this to us. You want it as much as I do."

She set trembling, delicate hands on either side of his face, and smiled sadly through passion-bright eyes. "You blew any chance for us eighteen months ago, Duncan, when you took me home, made incredible love to me all night, and then turned into a chest-beating caveman the next morning."

"It's troglodyte," he whispered, flexing his fingers on her hips. "I'm a troglodyte."

"Yes, you are," she whispered back, her own hands tightening on his face. "You're possessive, protective, and wonderfully physical, and you haven't evolved into this century. If I ever let down my guard with you, for even a minute, I'd find myself in more trouble than I could handle."

Duncan took her hands from his face and held them securely against his pounding heart. "But that's the very thing we have going for us, lass. Your own strength matches mine in a way that promises us a lifetime of passion."

"I'm not capable of making that kind of commitment, Duncan. Can't you understand that?"

"Aye," he said on a sigh, leaning forward and giving

her mouth a gentle kiss. He pulled back slightly. "I've understood that from the beginning. Cancel your date with Cobb."

"I can't." She also released a shuddering sigh. "It's not even a date, really. I'm meeting Ray tonight because he has something to show me."

Duncan just bet Cobb had something to show her. "Then let me come with you."

She shook her head. "I can't. This is business."

"Attorney general business?" He canted his head. "Your sister said Cobb is a lobsterman. What's he got that concerns your office?" Duncan tightened his grip on her hands. "And why did you have to come here to meet him, and at night? *All* night, for that matter."

She wiggled free, and Duncan allowed her to shove him away and slide down off the fender of her truck. She turned with a snort and finally opened the driver's door. "This is exactly why we can't be together. I can't even have a simple meeting without you getting all possessive and protective. I've been doing my job for over two years now, and I've been doing it damn well without your help. Go tend your bar."

"I have a staff for that. I'm taking tonight off."

"You can't come with—" She stopped in mid-sentence and reached inside her truck, picked up the bottle he'd set on the seat while waiting for her, and turned back with one brow raised in question. "Pretty damn sure of yourself, aren't you?" She returned her gaze to the bottle, lifting it toward the street light to read the label. "Rosach Distillery," she read out loud, looking back up at him. "It's the same name as your bar—The Rosach Pub."

He took the bottle from her. "They're my silent partner."

"But I thought you bought and remodeled the bar with your share of the reward you and Kee and the others got when you recovered Thaddeus Lakeman's stolen art?"

"Aye, I did. But I also went into partnership with the Rosach Distillery."

After giving him an odd look, Willow reached into the truck again and reemerged with the small leather box that had been sitting next to the bottle. "What's this?" she asked, running a finger over the faded gold letters embossed into the top of it. "Who's Galen Ross?" she asked, opening the box.

Willow shot him a quick look of surprise, then lifted the tulip-shaped glass from the velvet and held it up to see the etching. "This is the glass I just used inside," she said, looking back at him. "It has the same crest as the label on the bottle. Who's Galen Ross?" she repeated.

"My father."

"You have a father?" she blurted, only to shake her head and smile. "I mean, I know you didn't really crawl out of a cave, but I never thought of you as having a family. You never talk about them.

He tucked the bottle under his arm and took the box and glass from her, set the glass back in the velvet, and carefully closed the lid. "My father and I were supposed ta share this scotch when it came of age, but he died six years ago."

"I'm sorry, Duncan," she said softly.

He tucked the bottle and box under his arm. "Life happens," was all he could think to say.

"So that's why you know so much about whiskey,"

she continued brightly. "Your father worked for the Rosach Distillery. Was he one of those . . . what do you call them? A noser?"

"Aye, Galen Ross had a legendary nose for blending whiskey."

"And that's his nosing glass," she said, stepping forward and lifting up on her toes as she pulled on the sleeve of his jacket. "Thank you for sharing your special scotch with me, Duncan," she whispered. "And for letting me drink from your father's glass."

She gave him a quick kiss on the cheek and then turned and climbed into her truck. Duncan watched her grope around on the floor for her keys, then bend over with a muttered curse and continue her search in front of the passenger's seat.

Duncan took her keys out of his pocket but said nothing, deciding to let the woman's frustration build—even though he knew it wouldn't even come close to his own.

He smiled when she suddenly stilled, his grin widening when she bolted upright, glared at him, and held out her hand.

He dangled the keys just out of her reach. "Take me with you and I promise ta be as quiet as a church mouse and not interfere in your work."

She climbed back out of the truck, stood directly in front of him, and stared up with a fierceness that would have worried the devil himself. "Do you trust me, Duncan?"

He relaxed back on his hips and folded the hand holding the keys under his arm holding the scotch. "I trust ya not ta lie to me about the important things," he said softly. "And I trust that ya know what you're doing when it comes ta your work. But I don't trust an old boyfriend not ta have an agenda."

"Ray and I only dated for three months," she snapped, clearly at the end of her patience—and seemingly not at all impressed that he trusted her. "I am not interested in Ray Cobb that way."

"Then ya shouldn't have any problem with my tagging along."

She shoved her hand out again. "You are not coming with me."

He held his own hand over hers, the keys locked in his fist. "Then agree to have dinner with me tomorrow night."

She actually stamped her foot, and Duncan realized she'd just barely restrained herself from kicking him. "I will not be seen on a date with you. It would only feed the rumors about us."

"Then we'll eat in. At my house."

She looked down at his leg, specifically at his shin, her mutinous eyes obviously judging her aim.

But she looked back up at the sound of her jangling keys as Duncan made them disappear behind the zipper of his jacket, to an inside pocket over his chest. And then her eyes widened when his hand returned not with her keys but with a pen. He stepped forward, the bottle and box tucked firmly under his arm, and took her still extended hand in his and started writing on her palm.

Just as he'd known it would, Willow's curiosity held her still as she tried to read what he was spelling out in small, bold blue letters.

"What does it say?" she demanded, pulling free the moment he finished. She held her hand flat, facing the light, and squinted down at it. *"Potes currere . . ."* She looked up and scowled at him. "Either you can't spell worth a damn, Dunky, or this isn't English." She looked back down and tried reading it phonetically. *"Potes currere, sed te occulere non potes."*

Duncan winced. "Ya're slaughtering it, lass."

"What language is it? French? Latin? *Stone Age* gibberish? And what does it mean?"

He placed the pen back in his pocket. "You're an educated woman, counselor. Do what I did when you wrote *troglodyte* on my palm two years ago. Look it up."

Her eyes glittering in the streetlight, Willow balled her hand into a fist and spun back to her truck with a muttered curse. She climbed in, slammed the door shut behind her, and tripped the electric locks. Then she reached up, pulled down the visor, and took out a hidden key—shooting him a triumphant smile as she crammed the key into the ignition and started the engine.

Duncan stepped back with a long-suffering sigh, and turned to avoid the parking-lot dust and debris shooting from her screeching tires as Willow exited the parking lot with all the poise of a spoiled brat.

He was going to have to do something about her recklessness, Duncan decided as he loped to his car. He climbed into the right-hand seat, tucked the scotch and leather box safely under the left-hand seat, fished his own keys out of his pocket, and started the fifteen-year-old Jaguar.

The engine rumbled to life with the distinct purr of a

jungle beast, and Duncan slowly pulled out of the parking lot. But the moment he turned onto the road, he pushed the powerful engine through the gears, only easing back on the throttle when he caught sight of Willow's taillights.

Aye, he thought with another sigh. The game continued.

Visit
❖ Pocket Books ❖
online at

---

www.SimonSays.com

Keep up on the latest new
releases from your favorite
authors, as well as author
appearances, news, chats,
special offers and more.

SIMON & SCHUSTER
A VIACOM COMPANY
www.SimonSays.com

Pocket
Books